MIDNIGHT
CURSE

By Melissa F. Olson

Boundary Magic series

Boundary Crossed
Boundary Lines
Boundary Born

Scarlett Bernard novels

Dead Spots
Trail of Dead
Hunter's Trail

Short Fiction

Sell-By Date: An Old World Short Story
Bloodsick: An Old World Tale
Malediction: An Old World Story

Also by Melissa

The Big Keep: A Lena Dane Mystery
Nightshades

MIDNIGHT
CURSE

MELISSA F. OLSON

47N⬢RTH

Text copyright © 2017 by Melissa F. Olson
All rights reserved.

Published by 47North, Seattle

www.apub.com

Amazon, the Amazon logo, and 47North are trademarks of Amazon.com, Inc., or its affiliates.

ISBN-13: 9781503942820
ISBN-10: 1503942821

Cover design by Mike Heath | Magnus Creative

Cover photography by Gene Mollica

Printed in the United States of America

But first, on earth as Vampire sent
Thy corse shall from its tomb be rent:
Then ghastly haunt thy native place,
And suck the blood of all thy race;
There from thy daughter, sister, wife,
At midnight drain the stream of life;

—*Lord Byron, "The Giaour"*

Prologue

It had helped that she knew exactly how the whores would react.

The setting had changed, but the setup hadn't: A large "visiting" room where the girls had to parade around in whatever passed for sexy at the time. A gaudy, ornate staircase leading to a long hallway of doors upstairs. Every door led to a small room that contained only a bed and a chair. Unlike most brothels, there were no security guards here, no bouncers. It wasn't necessary. Abuse of the girls was not only expected, but welcome, and no one knew that better than the girls themselves. It didn't matter where they came from, what cultures or languages or backgrounds. They first thing they were taught in their new lives was *never fight back*. And they didn't. They couldn't. The magic didn't let them. She had been an anomaly that way.

She arrived in the most expensive outfit she owned: a scarlet-red pantsuit with nothing underneath, so that the suit jacket gaped almost to her navel. It was sexy, and made her look like she had money and power, which she did. Female clients may have been rare at the brothel, but it was common enough that her presence didn't even raise an eyebrow, just welcoming smiles. The female manager began to lead her into the visiting room, and for a moment she felt a sharp slash of panic. She could see the girls posed around the room, holding watery drinks and making small talk with listless smiles and empty eyes. Many young women in their position took something to numb the senses, but no drugs in the world would work on *these* girls.

She felt the familiar urge to fight, to snap the manager's neck and run out of there, but she reminded herself that she was no longer property. She gave the aging woman her name and explained that she was not here for a date, but to see the owner. They were old friends. The manager paused and eyed her with renewed speculation. Then she simply shrugged and walked over to a black telephone.

Within moments she was being led into his office.

He looked the same, of course. Why wouldn't he? True, the cut of his suit was different, and his hair was brushed straight back instead of parted in the middle. But he had the same powerful movements and calculating eyes that were always judging the value of goods. Those eyes took in her suit and her heels and her warm, apologetic smile, and concluded that she was exactly who she'd claimed to be: an old friend, looking to make amends. He was arrogant enough to believe it.

Vampires did not hug, but she came around the desk and moved to kiss him on each cheek, in accordance with European fashion. He had always loved that continental bullshit. He smiled genially and reached for her. As she'd expected, he turned his head to kiss her on the mouth, testing her compliance. She forced herself to melt against him, her arms winding around his neck.

While his slimy tongue probed her mouth, her fingers worked the makeshift clasp of the "bracelet." She was proud of the garrote, which she'd fashioned herself out of titanium cord and oak. The sharpened wire was strong enough to cut through even vampire bone. She had practiced on a tree stump. When he pulled back to leer at her, she smiled as sweetly as she could, flipping one end of the weapon around his neck with supernatural speed. She had drawn it tight and begun to pull before confusion even registered in his eyes. Fast as he was, by the time he got his fingers up to claw at the garrote string, it was too late. She pulled with every bit of her considerable strength, and the garrote snapped the bone of his spine. His head was turning to dust before it hit the tacky shag carpet.

Later, some of her accusers would argue that her actions were a treacherous betrayal of her own kind. They insisted that she should have challenged him to an honorable fight. But she didn't care about being honorable. She cared about him being dead.

Chapter 1

"What *is* that thing?" came a disgusted voice from across the table.

I smoothed the sweat-dampened hair off my forehead so I could lift my gaze to the speaker. It was nearly dinnertime, but the heat from the day seemed to linger in the air, making our table at the Downtown LA Art Walk almost unbearable. If that weren't uncomfortable enough, a ray of sunlight had managed to find a crack between skyscrapers and was rapidly intruding across my table like a three-foot melanoma laser. I knew from experience that in a few minutes it was gonna hit me right in the eyes.

Despite the heat, the woman standing in front of me was immaculate, a heroin-thin fortyish blonde with a Prada bag in the crook of her elbow. Her perfectly made-up eyes were fixed on Shadow, who was curled up on the sidewalk, her chin resting on my foot. I *think* the woman's features were trying to convey revulsion, but they were having a hard time fighting through all the Botox. Shadow, for her part, cracked open one eyelid, glanced at the woman, and went back to sleep. I was suddenly very jealous.

"This is my dog," I said, trying to keep my voice pleasant. Well, okay, I tried a little. Shadow had started life as a dog, it was true, but a hundred-fifty-pound dog that was part hairless Peruvian, part wolf, and God knew what else. And that was *before* she was spelled to be ink-black and have superpowers.

"Well, that is the *ugliest* dog I have ever seen," the woman sniffed, tossing her perfectly blown-out hair.

I hear this line at least once a day, and it's astounding how many ways there are to deliver it. Some people are shocked, and some are even sort of admiring. I don't really mind that because, well, Shadow's ugliness is so thorough that it really is impressive.

But this particular woman was using a tone that suggested I should really consider putting Shadow down to liberate the world from the blight of her hideousness. I put down the binder of notes I'd been studying. "That's so funny," I said to the Prada woman. "I was just going to say the same thing about you."

She gave me a blank look. "But I don't have a dog."

I sighed. She was literally too stupid to insult. "Are you going to buy a sculpture?" I demanded, waving a hand at the beautiful hand-made carvings spread across the table in front of me.

She turned her nose up. "No."

"Then go away, or I shall taunt you a second time," I said in my best French accent.

The woman gave me a bewildered look but had the sense to back away. "Your customer service is appalling," she snapped as a parting shot.

"So are your shoes," I called back. There. That was hitting her where she lived. The woman made a "humph" noise and flounced away on her Chanel espadrilles. Not for the first time, I wished Shadow and I could high-five.

I felt the buzz of a werewolf behind me a moment before I heard Eli's amused voice say, "Making friends again, I see."

Shadow lifted her head, and was halfway through a growl before she saw who it was. She settled back down, resigned to being near Eli again. As a null, I negate supernatural powers and abilities within a small area around myself. This works out nicely for my werewolf boyfriend, especially when it comes to getting along with my "dog," who has been magically altered to hunt and kill werewolves. Yes, I know how all that sounds, but I wasn't the one who turned Shadow into a bargest. I was just the one tasked with keeping her from murdering anyone. Well, anyone who didn't deserve it.

Eli deposited a lemonade in front of me and sat down in the empty chair, taking a sip from a clear plastic cup of iced tea. "She's not wrong about the customer service, you know," he said mildly.

"Hey, I asked her if she was going to buy something *before* I insulted her shoes," I protested. "That's tremendous customer service."

Eli grinned at me and shook his head. "I told you you'd be bored. This just isn't your thing, Scarlett. I get that."

I chewed on my lip, squinted against the sunshine, and said nothing. Eli created beautiful sculptures out of driftwood he found on the beach. Plenty of people sold carvings at these art events, but Eli's were stunning: he had a gift for using the wood's natural shape and grain to make it look like the subject—a mermaid, a sea star, a humpback whale—had formed organically out of the wood, or maybe vice versa. At my urging, he kept raising the prices, but he still sold at least three-quarters of what he brought to each event.

Between carving the sculptures, his bartending job, and his position in the werewolf pack, we were reaching a point where if I didn't hang out at either the art walks or the bar I never saw him. And hanging out at a werewolf bar came with its own complications.

Still, if I scared the customers away, he was eventually going to stop inviting me to come along. "I'll be good," I promised him.

He leaned over and planted a kiss on my cheek. "Nah. You were right. Those shoes were totally last season."

"Right?" I said happily. Neither of us knew anything about fashion.

He nodded at the unlabeled binder in front of me. "You studying for tomorrow night?" He'd made an effort to sound casual, but I knew him too well to miss the edge of anxiety in his voice. In his own way, Eli was as nervous as I was.

"Yeah."

Eli squeezed my hand. "I'll be right there in the audience, for every minute. And you're gonna do great, babe. You know that, right?"

An older couple covered in wrinkly tattoos came up to exclaim over Eli's sculptures, which saved me from having to answer. Beginning the following night, the Los Angeles Old World would be staging the dramatically named Vampire Trials, which was sort of our answer to *The People's Court.* It's supposed to happen every three years, but it had been more than six since the last one, for the simple reason that there hadn't been very many interspecies disputes.

Overall, of course, this was a good thing, proving that our odd way of doing things in the Los Angeles supernatural community was more or less working. Eventually, though, enough minor problems had stacked up that the powers that be in LA—Dashiell, the cardinal vampire, Kirsten, leader of the witches, and Eli's alpha Will, plus myself—had decided to put on the Trials, if for no other reason than to clear the air.

The name makes it sound huge and ominous, but the event itself is fairly straightforward. The three heads of the supernatural communities listen to complaints and make judgments on various conflicts; it's more "holding court" than "legal court."

But the pressure on us was still huge. Los Angeles is the only city in America where all three supernatural powers share power and live more or less in peace. If we fucked that up, there would be a lot of repercussions, which could include anything from snide "I told you so"s to violent attempts to take over our city.

I'd attended the last Vampire Trials, but two huge things had changed in the last six years. First, back then my psychotic ex-mentor Olivia had been the null on the scene, and I had attended as more of an unpaid intern than anything else. Now I would be the one sitting at the "defendant" table, making sure the vampire, werewolf, or witch sitting with me didn't try anything.

Second, three years earlier I'd fought for and earned my own place among the little group that made decisions for the supernatural world in my city. I'd gone from janitor to partner, and this would be my first Trial carrying the weight of that responsibility. I was nervous as hell, which was why I had been reading the binders of handwritten notes from all the previous Trials.

When the couple wandered off with a wrapped sculpture in tow, Eli turned back to me. "Hey, I forgot to mention, I'm taking the pups out for brunch tomorrow morning, kind of a chill-before-the-Trials thing," he said, looking hopeful. "Do you want to come?"

"Uh, maybe," I said. The "pups" were the three newest members of the LA pack: Lizzy, Troy, and Yola. Part of Eli's job as the pack beta was to look after them and make sure they were acclimating. "Did they ask for me to come?" I asked.

"Yes," he said, avoiding my eyes.

"Eli . . ."

"What?" he said stubbornly.

I raised an eyebrow, but didn't bother responding. Eli knew damn well that my relationship with the werewolf pack was complicated. Whenever they got close to me, werewolves became human again, which meant that they were free of the uncomfortable, relentless magic that was always scratching at the back of their brains, urging them to do wolfish things. A few of them really did hate me, because they were proud of what they were and didn't want it taken from them. A few of them were indifferent, and plenty of them, including the pups, adored being near me. To them, proximity to me was like being on a truly spectacular painkiller. And I hated it.

Being a null didn't exhaust me or hurt or anything—that wasn't the problem. Whenever I got close to those werewolves, though, it was like being the most popular girl in high school, suddenly forced to sit at the loser table. They would alternately kiss my ass, go into stunned silence, or jostle to bring me small treats or do little favors, like fetch me extra napkins or pick up Shadow's poop. Seriously. They competed for who got to pick up bargest poop.

Some people might enjoy the attention and solicitation, but I didn't love being around people—Eli excepted—at the best of times. Unfortunately for me, wolves are extremely social creatures, and Eli needed to be with them. He also didn't really understand why I would dislike people being nice to me.

It was, as I said, complicated.

"I don't want to have to deal with Shadow scaring the pups," I said finally. Shadow heard her name—or perhaps picked up on the tension—and lifted her head to look between the two of us. If she got more than fifteen feet away from me, Shadow's instincts about werewolves returned, and although she wouldn't *kill* anyone without a command from me, she became fairly terrifying. This was one of the reasons she went everywhere I did. It had taken nearly two years before she could remain alone with Eli long enough for me to go to the bathroom.

"So we'll leave her at the house," Eli persisted.

"You know I don't like doing that." We had a special room—okay, it was a cell—for Shadow when she absolutely needed to stay at home, like on some of my messier jobs. She hated it, though, and every time she was put in there she found a way to punish me later—pee on the carpet, shredded furniture, that kind of thing.

"Scarlett . . ." he sighed. "They'd really like to be your friends. Give them a chance."

"I don't need any more friends," I muttered.

Eli raised his eyebrows, but didn't comment on the fact that *he* was my only real friend. In my defense, regular friendships are tough in the Old World, where supernatural politics or danger tend to ruin things. I'd lost one friend, a werewolf named Caroline, because she'd been poisoned and the alpha werewolf had needed to put her down before she could kill any humans. Then my former roommate, a vampire named Molly, had evicted me because I'd repeatedly brought danger home with me. We'd initially promised to keep in touch, but it was awkward and uncomfortable, and I hadn't spoken to her in years. I'd also sort of been friends with a human cop named Jesse Cruz, but he'd wanted more and I had chosen Eli.

Eli knew all of that, but he was too kind to bring it up. Lucky for me, an older hippie couple wandered up to the booth, holding hands, and Eli got sucked into another conversation. I sipped my lemonade and held my tongue.

A few hours later the sun had dipped all the way behind the downtown skyscrapers, and we began packing up the few remaining sculptures. The art walk ran until ten, but Eli was bartending tonight, so we would throw in the towel early. I added up the day's figures while Eli dismantled the booth. "Nice haul," I said appreciatively. We were only boxing up three pieces, having sold nearly a dozen.

Box in hand, I walked back to my van, the White Whale, with Shadow, while Eli lagged a dozen feet behind, making a great show of heaving the folded table and chairs. He was far enough behind me to have his werewolf strength back, but it was important not to look too powerful in front of the humans. He was maybe having a good time with the farce.

As Eli loaded the table into the back of my van—we had driven separately so he could go straight to work—I let Shadow into the van's passenger seat, rolling the windows down so she could sniff the air and eyeball the passing strangers who stared at her. I found myself staring right back and realized my antisocial tendencies were threatening to surface. I wasn't sure how much longer I could hold up the Supportive Girlfriend exterior without snapping at someone.

Well, someone *else*, if you counted the Botox lady. I sure didn't.

Eli had just loaded the gear when a gay couple he'd waited on earlier approached him and began to chat. They seemed like they were settling in to a long discussion of art, and after hours of dealing with people, I didn't have it in me to join them. There was just too much of a risk that I might have to smile at someone. I reached forward to turn the ignition, planning to wave at Eli as I backed up, but then I realized the van's rear doors were still open. So I sighed and waited.

I was mentally reviewing my DVR list, trying to decide what to binge on while Eli was at work, when I noticed a young woman moving down the street toward me. She had a strange, mechanical walk: arms jammed against her sides, head locked in the "forward" position, not bothering to account for anything in her peripheral vision. Next to me, Shadow tensed, her eyes fixed on the girl.

I leaned forward, reaching under my seat for my handheld Taser. Don't leave home without it, that was my motto, although the girl didn't exactly look like a threat: she was younger than me, dressed in a Cal State Long Beach T-shirt and jeans that had been artistically shredded at the knees. As she approached me I could see that her expression was unnaturally blank, her eyes empty and unfocused. And that one of her hands was clenched in a fist.

With a little effort I extended my normal radius, the sphere of nonmagical space that emits from me, an extra ten feet so it would encompass the girl. I could feel Eli and Shadow, but the girl wasn't registering any kind of signal, which meant she was human. Shadow must have smelled this at the same time, because her body seemed to relax, her clubbed tail giving me a reassuring thump.

Human or not, I did feel the tiniest little zing, like when a witch tries to use a spell against me. Witch spells usually flare out in my radius, sort of like a June bug hitting one of those bug zappers. This felt more like a mosquito. I'd known enough vampires to recognize the sensation: this girl had had her mind pressed, which was our term for when a vampire compels someone magically. And I'd just undone it.

The girl's vacant expression cleared, and she looked around with confusion. Her forward momentum propelled her the rest of the way to my van door.

"What was I . . ." she mumbled, her brows furrowing.

I needed to help this along. "What do you have there?" I asked, pointing to her hand.

The young woman followed my gaze and raised the hand with the fist, looking at it curiously. She uncurled her fingers and revealed a folded scrap of paper. Shadow let out a sudden growl, trying to climb into my lap to protect me. It confused me for a second, until I registered that the folded paper was splotched with red, as though paint had been sponged on it. Or as though a bloodstained hand had written the note.

"Shadow, sit," I ordered, pointing at the passenger seat. She didn't like it, but she lowered her haunches until they *almost* touched the car's seat. "You must have brushed against that painting back there," I told the wide-eyed girl, nodding over her shoulder at an imaginary artist. "I thought it looked like it might still be wet."

It was flimsy as hell, but the girl's shoulders relaxed a little. Human brains just love having "rational" explanations to cling to, even if they border on ridiculous. Without turning away from her I leaned my body to dig into the small packet of baby wipes I keep between the seats of my van.

She read the name on the outside of the folded note. "Scarlett Bernard." She looked up at me, her face a mask of bewilderment. "Are you Scarlett Bernard?"

"I hope so; I'm wearing her underwear," I replied. The girl's expression didn't change. Tough crowd. "That's me," I confirmed. She held out the note, and I held out a wipe. "For your hands."

We traded, and I unfolded the note quickly, knowing she was about to ask a lot of questions. There was an address scrawled at the top, 2310 Scarff. In block letters below it, the writer had added, DON'T TELL ANYONE. EVEN ELI.

I had already opened my mouth to ask where the note came from when I saw the extra scribble at the very bottom of the paper, done in desperate, hurried cursive: *please Scar*. I snapped my mouth shut. I knew that handwriting.

Molly.

Chapter 2

Once upon a time, I sort of had a fake best friend.

Okay, that's not fair. Years ago, when I needed a new place to live, I moved in with a very young-looking vampire named Molly. It was a mutually beneficial thing: I needed a break on rent, and Molly wanted to be near me so she could age. She'd become a vampire back in the nineteenth century, when seventeen was more or less an adult, but her options were extremely limited in modern society. I could help her with that—hanging around a null would let her body age like it was supposed to, at least when she was close to me.

Molly and I had become friends, although I often thought she wasn't letting me see much of the real her. She liked to pretend the two of us lived in a fun, *Sex and the City*–type world where we gossiped and hung out and did girlie things together, and I played along, because . . . well, it was surprisingly comforting. I knew that Molly was also reporting some of my activities to Dashiell, the cardinal vampire of the city, but because she was open about it, this was weirdly okay too.

But that had been three years ago. I hadn't heard from Molly since shortly after she'd asked me to move out, when things had gotten awkward. Until I opened the note I hadn't even known for sure she was still in Los Angeles. It wasn't like Dashiell and I spent a lot of time chatting about our mutual acquaintances.

I crumpled the note, my stomach roiling with sudden nerves. Molly had gone to a lot of trouble to make sure there was no record of her contacting me. And there was only one possible reason for doing that: she didn't want Dashiell to know.

This scared me more than the blood, more than the prospect of dealing with the confused twenty-year-old in front of me. As long as I'd known her, Molly had been a compliant little vampire. She had always followed all of Dashiell's rules, and lived very quietly, especially compared to some of the other vampires in this town. Hell, her desire to stay on the fringes of supernatural society, keeping her head down, was most of why she'd kicked me out. And now she wanted to hide something from *Dashiell?*

Relieved of the paper, and the only discernible reason for being here, the girl in front of me began to panic. "What . . . where am I?" she said, her head swiveling around.

"You're at the downtown art walk, remember?" I said helpfully.

Her eyes met mine again. "But how did I get here? I was just . . . I was going to a party . . ." Her tone was almost a whine, but I couldn't really blame her. Losing patches of memory is a college female's worst nightmare.

"Check your pockets," I suggested.

Her hand emerged with a few twenties and a receipt. "It's a cab company," she said wonderingly. "But I never take cabs."

Luckily Eli chose that moment to come around the side of the van. "Sorry, I kind of got stuck there . . . who's this?" He looked at the girl, eyebrows raised pleasantly.

I looked pointedly at the girl. "I'm Britt?" she said hesitantly, as if afraid her recent blackout may have included a name change.

"Eli," he said, reaching out to shake her hand. He studied her confused expression for a moment and then turned to me. "Um, can you give me a quick hand in the back?"

Britt automatically stepped back so I could get out of the van. I left Shadow inside and followed Eli toward the rear doors—and held up a finger for him to wait. I was watching Britt. Now that I'd moved away, she just stood there with her eyebrows knit together, not moving. Which was unusual.

Vampires usually press humans for two reasons: to make them forget something—like a feeding—or to get them to do a single task. "Get this message to Scarlett Bernard," for example. But every pressed human I'd encountered had recovered better and faster than Britt. Once the . . . okay, we'll call them "victims"—had completed their task, they went smoothly back to whatever they had been doing. The human brain is complex and interesting—capable of filling any logical gaps with its own little assumptions. I'd never seen a human victim so untethered after being pressed, and it wasn't because I'd zapped out the vampire's influence. If anything, that should have made her recover *faster*.

It was like whoever pressed her mind had done it with very little control. A brand-new vampire wouldn't have had enough power and precision to manipulate a human mind. It must have been someone old enough to press hard, but upset enough not to do it well.

This was very bad.

"You seeing this?" I asked in a low voice.

"Yeah. Who pressed her?"

"One of the vampires," I said. It was obvious, but I didn't want to lie to him more than I had to. I held up the blood-smudged note, not letting him see what was written on it. "It's a job, probably just a blood spill or something. But I should go take care of it. Good thing we drove separate."

I was trying to sound casual, but his frown didn't budge. Eli had served as my assistant for a few months, and he still tagged along on the occasional job just to hang out with me. The unfortunate part of dating a guy who knows about what I do is that he also knows how it's supposed to work: usually, I just get a call on my cell from the person with the problem—or possibly one of the Old World leaders, if it's a really bad crime scene. This cloak-and-dagger thing was uncharted territory.

"How did they know you were here? Why didn't they just call?" he asked, not unreasonably.

I shrugged. "Anyone who knows we're together could Google art fairs and figure it out. As far as the phone . . . I don't know, maybe they had a dead battery or something. I'll be sure to ask, though," I promised, fighting not to squirm.

Eli studied my eyes for a moment. "I want to go with you," he said.

"You can't." I gestured at Britt, who was still standing next to the driver's door, staring at the side of the van. "I need you to get her home. And then you have to get to work."

"I don't like you walking into some weird situation by yourself," he said. He was planting his feet, obviously gearing up for a fight.

"Hey, that's my job. I do that all the time," I replied, trying to keep my voice light.

It was the wrong thing to say. Eli glowered at me. "And I dislike it *all the time*," he said, mimicking my tone. "You know how I feel about your safety."

I sighed. This again. "My safety is fine. I can take care of myself."

He started to argue, and I pointed a finger at him. "Stop. This is the part where you say, 'I can't help it, Scarlett, my wolf instincts want to protect you.' And then I say, 'Bullshit, Eli, you don't have wolf instincts this close to me,' and around we go. But right now, I have a job, and that girl needs your help."

We both glanced at Britt, who was still standing there staring into empty space. She didn't even seem to notice the enormous bargest panting a few inches from her face.

Eli turned back to me. "You have blades on you?" he asked. He was wavering.

"Of course," I said, resisting the urge to add "duh."

I loved my handheld Taser, but I could only use it a few times before the battery ran out. I needed a weapon that could hurt someone who might be out of arm's reach, and I really wasn't comfortable with guns. Lucky for me, there was a werewolf in Will's pack who knew everything there was to know about throwing knives.

I'm the first to admit that "training with knives" sounds cheesy, like a crappy action movie, but working with Marko had proved anything but hokey. I now carried at least two knives—one silver-plated, one not—on my person at all times, usually in my boot sheath. Partly this was to appease my overprotective boyfriend, and partly it was out of fear of Marko—if I ran into him somewhere without a knife on me, he would make me do burpees until I puked. Seriously. It had happened.

"I still don't like you charging into—" Eli began, but I stepped forward and planted a kiss on his lips, silencing him.

"Look," I said when I pulled back, "I'll stop by the bar when I'm done, and we can finish this argument then. I don't know about you, but I remember all my lines."

Eli's lips wobbled as he struggled not to smile. He lost the battle. "You are so frickin' stubborn," he said, but there was fondness in his voice.

Rising to my tiptoes, I brushed another, lighter kiss on his cheek. "Strong-willed. I prefer the term 'strong-willed.'"

Then I dashed toward the van door before he could think to ask me for the address.

A few minutes later, I was driving the White Whale south on a long stretch of Figueroa, fighting the traffic toward USC. Shadow was accustomed to the concept of "bumper-to-bumper," so she'd gone back to lie on her bed. I tried calling the last number I had for Molly, but it was out of service. Typical vampire. For a moment I considered trying to find a newer number for her, but who would I ask? Dashiell? That would kind of eliminate the whole point of keeping this from him and Eli.

Suddenly I felt like a moron. I was keeping a secret from my live-in boyfriend *and* my boss, for a person who had dropped me from her friend list years ago. "What are you doing, Scarlett?" I said out loud. By not telling Eli, I was risking my relationship with him, and by not telling Dashiell, I could conceivably be risking my job. I picked up my cell phone, willing myself to call Dashiell and explain the whole situation. But I hesitated.

For the past few years, whenever I faced these moral dilemmas I would hear a little voice in the back of my head. *What would Jesse want you to do?* Jesse Cruz, the ex-LAPD detective who used to be my friend, was one of the few humans in LA who was allowed to know about the Old World, despite not really being connected to it. He also had serious ethics, and I knew damn well that in this situation he would want me to help my friend. Not because she was worth more or less than my other relationships, but because she needed me. The way this was done—pressing Britt, sending the note—it was desperate. Hell, contacting me after three years of radio silence was desperate in itself. Whatever had happened between us, Molly needed me bad.

I tossed the cell phone back onto the passenger seat, half-certain I would regret this later.

Even the last bits of cloud-reflected sunlight had been swallowed into the ocean by the time I reached campus, although the streets weren't exactly dark, thanks to the new-looking streetlights. The buildings on the streets around USC tend to fall into two categories: Some of them are still shitty hovels that have been slapped with *just* enough paint and landscaping to prevent rich parents from constantly calling the university to complain about safety. The rest, on the other hand, *used* to be crappy houses until investors dumped piles of money into renovating them into subdivided apartments that would suit the expensive tastes of Mommy and Daddy's little princes and princesses. The finished products were astonishingly swanky, considering the inhabitants were eighteen years old and didn't know how to do their own laundry. Nearly all of the buildings on Scarff fell into the latter category.

There was no parking right in front of number 2310, but I stopped the van there for a moment anyway, leaning over the passenger seat so I could see the property. It was beautiful, actually, nearly as pretty as the little bungalow house Molly and I had once shared. There was a small, extremely tidy front lawn, enclosed by a wrought iron fence with tall gates. They opened onto a pretty cobblestone path leading to a porch that had been painted with contrasting shades of green and yellow. The building itself was an emerald-green Queen Anne–style Victorian that had been converted into two large units, one on each floor. I had to respect the designer, who'd pulled together a look that felt both secure and classy. The lights downstairs were on, but the upper floor was dark.

I drove past and parked in the closest street spot I could find, a few hundred feet away. I threw on a denim jacket, pocketed my Taser, and looked at Shadow, who was giving me the same expectant, hopeful look that normal dogs pull out when there are Snausages nearby. I weighed the pros and cons for a moment. Shadow could be a very useful weapon, but I'd gotten the bloody note from Molly forty minutes ago; whatever danger there had been had passed by now. We were in a highly civilian area, and if I was being honest, I had a really bad feeling that I was going to find something horrifying in there. I wasn't sure how the bargest would handle it. "Sorry, girl," I said. "You have to stay here."

Shadow made a whining noise, not liking that, but we both liked it a lot better than leaving her at home. Besides, if she sensed I really was in danger, she would break through the van's window to get to me. It had happened before.

Outside, I was relieved to see the sidewalk was deserted. There was a small security box next to the gate, but no one answered when I rang the buzzer. I pushed lightly on the gate, and it swung open easily. Looking closer, I saw that the locking mechanism, a small but solid chunk of metal, had been bent out of shape. There were no scratches or tool marks, which suggested a vampire. Or, I amended, a werewolf. The last time I'd seen Molly, the werewolves hadn't been very fond of her. Part of me was hoping this was a retribution thing, and I was going to find Molly in there next to a dead werewolf. I hated myself for the thought, but it was looking more and more like the best possible scenario.

Just in case, I leaned down to the top of my knee-high boot and pulled out a small, balanced knife tipped in silver. Silver makes vampires itch just a little, but it would drop a werewolf pretty much instantly. I put my hands in my jacket pockets so I had the knife in my right and the Taser in my left. Then I made my way up the cobblestones.

There were two doors on the front of the building. One of them had clearly been retrofitted fairly recently, and was secured with several padlocks. The other door, which looked like the original wood, was closed but not quite latched. I gave it a light push, and the door swung inward.

There wasn't actually an ominous creak, but it was definitely implied.

I peered into the entryway. "Molly?" I called, keeping my voice soft. There was no reaction. I took a breath to try again, louder—and the smell hit my nose.

Nulls don't have heightened senses, but even I could recognize the odor of blood and evacuated bowels when it was that overpowering. "Oh, shit," I muttered. I pulled my hands from my pockets and closed my eyes, beginning to extend my radius. Then I thought better of it. I had a feeling no one in this building was going to appreciate having humanity foisted on them. I fumbled at the wall until my fingers found a switch.

Light flooded my eyes, forcing me to blink as my eyes adjusted. I was in a small, empty foyer, flanked by open doorways on either side. Straight in front of me was a new-looking wall decorated with framed photos. Before the building was renovated into upper and lower apartments, the wall had probably been the entrance to a staircase. I took a quick glance at the pictures. They showed young women in groups of four or five, striking friendly poses in front of the house, on campus, and in a living room. As far as I could tell, Molly was in every nighttime shot.

It was so disconcerting that I couldn't help but stare for a moment. The last time I'd seen her, she'd had a blonde bob and a casual, pricey wardrobe. Now her hair was long, black with bright streaks of blue, and she sported a nose ring and a miniskirt—not quite Goth, but maybe one of Goth's descendants. Punk-adjacent.

I automatically stepped closer so I could see the largest photo, an eight-by-ten forming a centerpiece in the display. All of the girls—thirteen total—were in the center of campus, grouped right in front of the Tommy Trojan statue. They were trying to do a cheerleader-style pyramid on the bricks, but it wasn't going well, and they were laughing. In the center, a pixie brunette with square glasses was holding up a crooked sign reading "the Ladies of 2310." Molly was at the bottom right, cracking up as the girl on top of her started to fall off. It struck me how happy she looked.

I stepped back, forcing my eyes away from the smiling young woman. So all thirteen of them lived in this building, in the various bedrooms, like a sort of unofficial sorority. That was kind of shocking. Given the popularity of recording devices in modern society, plus the vampires' sensitivity to sunlight, it was rare for a vampire to try to "pass" in a human community anymore. They usually lived alone and sought out the company of other vampires when they wanted more than casual contact. How the hell had Molly pulled this off? And why take the risk?

My eyes caught movement in the doorway on my right, low to the ground. I tensed, expecting maybe a mouse, but it was moving liquid: a slow, thick ooze of blood on the hardwood floor. More than a trickle, not quite a river.

Molly, what did you do?

Chapter 3

I stepped toward that doorway, skirting the channel of red. My hand automatically reached for the light switch on the wall, my eyes still glued to the blood trail. Then the light burst into the room and I followed the blood to its source. My stomach, lungs, and throat all contracted at once. One hand flew to my mouth as though it was magnetized.

They were everywhere.

It was a large living room, obviously the social center for the apartments' residents. Or it had been, before they were all killed. The bodies—all female, probably the other women from the photos—lay crumpled on the sofa, draped across the coffee table, abandoned on the floor. Bloody handprints covered the walls, the hardwood floor, the girls' clothes, and everything from the lampshades to the magazines that had probably once sat on the coffee table. There must have been an indentation in the floor—thanks, earthquakes—because blood had trickled from each corpse into a large pool at one end of the room. From there, it had made its way into the front hall.

I'd seen a lot of terrible things since I'd begun this job—there had been a nighttime forest massacre that was particularly memorable—but never so many bodies. For just a second the room seemed to lurch sideways, and I felt nearly dizzy with shock. It just didn't seem *real*. Then I saw that one of bodies was stretched on the floor near a window, one arm reaching toward the latch. Trying to run. And she was wearing the same Lucky Brand T-shirt that I had in my closet at home. The irony of the brand name felt like a blow, and I had to force my eyes away from her.

I registered a small sting in my palm, and I realized I'd automatically reached for the knife in my pocket, slicing a shallow cut in my skin. The pain actually helped me to focus.

Something was wrong here.

Vampires don't kill for sport—if they bleed a victim, it's for food. But no vampire could drink this many people at once. A whole bunch of vampires? No, that didn't make sense either. In that scenario, there wouldn't be any blood left, much less an enormous puddle in the middle of the room.

I stepped up to the edge of the pool and crouched down, sniffing the air just above it. Above the reek of blood, urine, and fecal matter, I could make out a familiar sickly smell. Stomach acid. Then I got it. There had been just one vampire and she had gorged herself on blood. When her stomach couldn't hold anymore, she had vomited it back up. Judging by the size of the puddle, she'd done this a few times. Maybe a lot of times.

Molly.

It was suddenly all I could do not to puke up the lemonade in my own stomach. I swallowed hard and dug a pair of surgical gloves out of my pocket with my uninjured hand. I snapped them on right over the damn cut, ignoring the sting. Avoiding the blood pool, I moved toward the nearest body, the one draped across the coffee table. I had to push aside the blood-matted mass of blonde hair so I could check for a pulse on her neck. Nothing. But I needed to be certain, so I stepped my way around the room, checking wrists and necks, one by one.

They were all dead.

When I was sure there was nothing I could do for them, I moved toward the opposite doorway, intending to check the rest of the house. I felt a vampire hit my radius before I even hit the light switch.

It was a compact, eat-in kitchen, but I didn't bother taking in the details. My gaze followed the blood smears to the small figure huddled on the floor behind the kitchen table, out of sight of the doorway I'd come in through. Molly.

Brightly colored makeup had ridden a wave of tears down her face and into her blouse. It hadn't done much to wash away the red stains at her mouth, as though she'd tried to use blood as shaving cream. Her pale arms and bare legs were stained with so much blood they looked red with patches of white, rather than the other way around. She was hugging her arms around her knees, rocking back and forth, mumbling something in a quiet singsong, like a nursery rhyme. Her eyes were fixed on the floor three feet in front of her.

"Molly?" I whispered again.

Her head jerked up, her blue eyes wide. "Didn't do it did it did do it," she blurted, in the same singsongy tone. I took a step toward her, but she shrank away, making herself even smaller. I held still.

"Did you kill them?" I said gently. "By yourself?"

She nodded, her lips still moving, though I could no longer make out any words.

Panic rose up in my throat like a chunk of ice I couldn't swallow. I had never seen Molly freak out like this. I'd never seen *any* vampire freak out like this, and now I had no idea what to do. Hell, it had been years since I'd had *one* dead body, let alone a dozen—

Stop it, Scarlett, I scolded myself. I didn't have time for self-pity. I had to figure out how the hell we were going to cover this up.

On the rare occasions when I had to get rid of an intact human body, I usually hid it in a refrigerated compartment of my van and then drove to an industrial furnace in the Valley. Dashiell had pressed (and paid) the right people to ensure I could use the facilities freely. But if I went that route, I would have to take these girls in a whole bunch of trips. The risk of getting caught was just too great.

Unless I could make it look like something else?

"*How* did you do it?" I asked Molly. There had been too much blood for me to really examine the wounds.

She blinked, and her rocking finally ceased. She reached up one reddened finger and pointed at her mouth. I sighed. She'd pressed them to hold still, and killed them one by one with her teeth. Great. If she'd used a blade or a gun, I could have spun it as a human crime, but no one was going to buy bite marks as the cause of mundane human violence. Which was why vampires rarely used their teeth to draw blood these days.

As I weighed my options, Molly's rocking picked up again, and I realized that I needed her to snap out of it before I could do anything else. I went over and crouched right in front of her so our eyes were on the same level, like you do with frightened children. "Molly, we need to go," I said. "We have to get out of here before someone shows up."

Her eyes widened in sudden fear. She whispered, "If Dashiell finds out . . . "

"I know." Vampires, especially very new vampires, occasionally make a feeding mistake that kills someone. It's terrible and unfortunate, but there's really no punishment—the first time. Maybe even a second time, depending on the circumstances. But mass murder was a huge no-no. It drew too much attention to the Old World, and moreover, it just wasn't in line with vampires' very nature. They were efficient, careful predators, taking what they needed to live without attracting the attention of the prey. Vampires who blood-gorged were put down. It was one of the unwritten laws that we lived by, and every new vampire knew the drill. At best, Dashiell *might* be gracious enough to grant her a trial the next night, but it would look pretty open-and-shut.

Too open-and-shut, actually. Someone had gone to a lot of trouble to make sure Molly would be sentenced to death. I needed to think about how the hell I was going to help her, but that was a problem for Future Scarlett. Right now, the important thing was to cover up the evidence and get Molly out of here. That was, after all, my actual job.

"Molly!" I said, firmly enough to get her attention. "Where's your car?" She'd driven a late-model Mini Cooper as long as I'd known her.

"I have a spot in the off-campus garage," she said numbly. "No, wait. It's at the dealership for an oil change. Bridget was going to pick it up for me tomorrow." Her eyes flicked in the direction of the living room. Toward Bridget, I assumed.

"Okay. We need to go," I said again. "Right now."

She looked down at herself. "Good point," I said as though she'd delivered an argument. She couldn't go out on the street like that. "Is there a shower?" I asked. She nodded. "Go. I'll get started here."

She stood up and tottered toward a doorway on the other side of the kitchen, which must have led toward a bedroom. The blood on her had dried too much to leave any drips or marks on the tile where she walked, which was a small mercy. But I was never going to be able to clean up that blood pool in the other room.

As soon as she was gone, I went around and made sure all the doors and windows were locked and the curtains closed. Then I went into the first bedroom I could find and grabbed clean clothes for Molly from the closet: a belted dress, a wireless bra, underwear. I left them on the floor in front of the bathroom door.

I did that much just on instinct and experience, but then I paused in the living room doorway, feeling like my brain was bouncing around inside a hamster wheel. How the hell could I make this look like an accident? Or at least a human-on-human massacre?

My phone buzzed in my pants pocket, making me jump. When I pulled it out, I saw a text from Eli. *You on your way?* I stared at it, puzzled, until remembering I'd promised to stop by the bar after my "simple" job. Right. It seemed so ludicrous that I had to stifle a laugh. I was afraid if I started, I wouldn't be able to stop.

After a moment of thought, I texted: *All good, I think I'm just gonna head home. Battery is low. Love you.*

I didn't *really* think Eli would use the computer in Will's office to check my location, but it wouldn't exactly shock me if he did. There was GPS or LoJack or whatever on my van, but it could only be accessed through Dashiell's security people, and as long as no one raised an alarm there would be no reason for the cardinal vampire to hunt me down. Assuming I could take care of this mess.

I glanced at the heap of bodies in front of me, feeling guilty. I shouldn't have called them a mess.

"I need pot," I said to myself. "Lots and lots of pot."

When I heard the water in the bathroom stop, I went back to find Molly. She had opened the bathroom door, but was now just standing in the middle of the bathroom wrapped in a towel, staring dubiously at what remained of her bloody outfit. When I got close enough to make her human, she began to shiver, water dripping from her black-and-blue hair.

I picked up the pile of clothes I'd grabbed and held it out to her. She took it obediently, her gaze still fixed on the blood-soaked fabric on the floor.

"Molly, do you know where we can get some marijuana?"

She finally lifted her eyes, looking at me in confusion. "What?"

I repeated my request. She seemed no less bewildered, but at least she answered me. "A few of the girls keep it in their rooms, I think. I've smelled it."

"Good. I need you to get dressed and get me everything you can find, including bongs, papers, whatever." I didn't smoke; my understanding of pot accouterments and slang was limited to what I saw on television. "And some nail polish and nail polish remover, if you've got it. As fast as possible."

She opened her mouth to ask questions, but then she visibly shook herself, sending sprinkles of water across the tiles, and began to dress in slow, careful movements, like she had to remind herself how it worked.

The dress was a little baggy and long for her, but it looked okay when she tightened the belt.

"Hurry, Molls."

She moved past me toward the living room, and there was a burst of air as she got outside my radius and hit vampire speed.

While she searched, I went back to the entryway for my duffel bag, digging out several dead AA batteries, an almost-new bottle of nail polish remover, and a baseball cap. I tucked my hair up into the cap and went to back to the smoke detectors in the kitchen and living room, replacing the batteries with my dead ones.

A few seconds later, Molly came back with a pile of baggies, bongs, matches, nail polish, and a bottle of nail polish remover. "What are you going to do with them?" she asked.

"I'm going to make a story."

I instructed Molly to dump a few of the polish bottles out on the wood floor and scatter the marijuana and the bongs around the room. When she was finished, I handed her my duffel bag and said, "Get your jacket and anything that could ID you. We're not coming back here." She looked like she wanted to protest, but after a moment's hesitation she nodded. "Then wait for me in the foyer," I added. "Keep an eye on the door."

After Molly had retreated, I splashed acetone on each body, taking the time to make sure I got all of the bite marks. Then I backed out of the room, leaving a little trail of flammable liquid. Molly had already returned to the foyer with a bright pink backpack, and was taking down the last of the photos that showed her face. "I can't find my phone," she said over her shoulder. "It's not where I left it."

I frowned. "Are you sure?"

"Yes."

We didn't have time to search the house, not with a room full of dead girls. We were just going to have to hope the phone was destroyed, if it was still here. I crouched where she'd left my duffel and got out a book of matches. I lit three at once and dropped them onto the trail of acetone, watching the flame spread along the floor toward the closest girls.

I had seen and done a lot in this line of work, but even I didn't have the stomach to watch the girls burn. I turned my back on the doorway, snapped off my gloves, and stuffed them in my pocket. Then I gripped my duffel bag strap in one hand and Molly's hand in the other. Cradling the framed photos with one arm, she allowed me to tug her through the door and down the cobblestones.

Chapter 4

There were a couple of people out walking dogs, but they were too far away to get a good look at us as we hurried down the sidewalk toward the White Whale. When the van doors closed behind us, I slumped in my seat, nearly sick with relief. Shadow was already at my shoulder, snuffling me for injuries. I gave her a distracted pat, then leaned forward to start the van, holding my breath until we had made it down the street and around the corner. Any second someone was going to notice the smoking building.

"No one's going to buy your story," Molly said from the passenger seat. She'd been so quiet since my arrival at the house that I almost jumped. "Twelve girls pass out at the same time and nobody wakes up when the fire starts?"

"No, they're definitely not going to buy it," I agreed. "Especially if the bodies don't burn all the way and the coroner doesn't find any smoke damage in their lungs. But my job isn't to conceal crimes, necessarily; it's to conceal any Old World connections to crimes. Meanwhile, the evidence we added will confuse things, slow down the police."

She nodded, hugging the small backpack in her lap. Shadow gave her a quick sniff. The bargest had only met Molly once or twice, but it seemed like she instinctively understood that Molly was a friend. When it was clear no one was going to pet her or ask her to kill something, she yawned and went back to the dog bed.

I wasn't sure where we were going, so I cruised aimlessly down Adams Boulevard, watching my speed. Adams forms one of the borders of campus, and will take you halfway to the ocean if you let it. I drove west for a few miles, past all the campus activity, until I was sure we were too far to be spotted by the fire department or campus police. Then I pulled into the parking lot of a twenty-four-hour 7-Eleven. I looked at Molly, not sure what to say.

I had so many questions—about the murders, of course, but also about how Molly had gone from living the life of a West Hollywood heiress to a punk college student. I searched for a place to start, and when nothing elegant came to mind, I blurted, "Did you sell the house?"

"Rented it out. I had been there too long," she reported, looking a little sad. I understood. Vampires can only stay in one place for a decade or so before someone starts asking why they never age. But Molly had loved her Hollywood bungalow. If she'd rented instead of selling, she probably intended to go back in twenty years or so and pose as her own daughter. It was a pretty common way for vampires to hang on to property. I felt oddly relieved—I kind of loved that house.

"And USC?" I asked.

She shrugged. "I've always wanted to try college. I was taking film classes at night."

Molly had loved movies as long as I'd known her. "Why didn't you get your own place?"

"I *had* my own place," she insisted, a little defensive. "There's a little one-bedroom apartment in the basement. I told the girls I had EPP. Most college students are half-nocturnal anyway."

Erythropoietic protoporphyria is a very rare immune system disorder that made you basically allergic to sunlight. The few vamps who still tried to pass in human society often claimed to have EPP. For the longest time I'd actually thought the whole disorder was invented by vampires, but one day I saw a photo in the newspaper of a little girl with EPP smiling from beneath a beach umbrella.

Photos. I thought about all the framed pictures in the foyer of Molly's place. She wasn't telling me something. "Dashiell knew about this plan?"

A pause. "Dashiell knew most of it," she said at last. "I told him about the night classes."

"But not how close you were to those girls, I'm guessing."

Molly's shoulders hunched. "No."

I winced. Mass murder aside, Molly had obviously gone native—gotten so involved in leading a human-style life that she'd let herself get in too deep. As mistakes go, this was not small, especially for a fairly seasoned vampire like Molly. Once you hit a hundred years or so, you're expected to follow the rules. And as long as I'd known her, Molly had kept her head down and followed the rules.

I wanted to ask her why she'd suddenly let herself fall down the rabbit hole, but it seemed too much like an accusation, and this wasn't the right moment for it. Besides, who was I to accuse her of screwing up? It wasn't like I'd never messed up myself.

But I couldn't think of anything else to say, and the van filled with pregnant silence. Fidgeting, I tossed the baseball cap into the back and pulled my hair back into a loose bun with the hair tie on my wrist. "I didn't mean to," she said at last, her voice trembling. She was talking about the murders now. Her eyes were glued to the dashboard in front of her. "It's like . . . it wasn't me. I mean, it was me, I was doing it, but I didn't . . . want to. I didn't have control."

"Of course you didn't," I said stoutly. "I never actually thought you meant to kill those girls."

She lifted her head to look at me in surprise. "Really?"

"Molly, remember when you came along with me to clean up that body that was left on Will's doorstep? She'd been mauled by a werewolf. And you . . . *mourned* for her. For the cavalier loss of life." I gave a little headshake. "I've seen you be a little callous about pressing humans or even hurting someone, but I know you, Molls. That wasn't you."

"Thank you," she whispered, her voice breaking. Brushing the tears from her eyes, she cleared her throat. "But Dashiell's not going to see it that way."

"I know." Willingly or not, Molly had committed a very splashy mass murder, no pun intended. It would be all over the news in a few hours, and Dashiell knew where Molly had been living. He would immediately make the connection, and then buy the simplest explanation: that Molly had lost control and killed her roommates. Even if Dashiell did believe someone had forced her, he was the leader of the supernatural community in an enormous city; his priorities were containment and politics, not justice.

Then I remembered the Trials. They were supposed to start in less than twenty-four hours, and the whole Old World would be watching to see how our weirdly peaceful city handled this mass murder. Dashiell would have to lay down a death sentence . . . unless Molly could prove what had really happened.

But even if there was a way to do that, there was no time.

"It's not a coincidence, is it?" I said, thinking aloud. "This happening the night before the Trials?" Whoever had forced Molly to kill her friends wanted her to get caught, go on trial, and be executed before she had a chance to prove her innocence. It wasn't a bad plan, if you wanted Molly dead and didn't think you could do it yourself. Oh, and if you didn't object to the brutal deaths of twelve human kids. A lot of vampires wouldn't mind that at all. They didn't kill for sport, but they didn't spend a lot of time mourning the loss of human life, which was fleeting by definition.

"No. It's not," Molly agreed.

"Do you have *any* idea who did this to you?" I asked, my voice coming out desperate. "Who hates you this much?"

She shook her head. "I can only think of one person, and he's been dead for years."

"Are you sure?"

Her face darkened, and though she was human next to me, I could still see the predator lurking in her eyes, reflected in the neon lights of the store. It shouldn't have been creepy, but it very much was. "Believe me," she said. "I'm absolutely positive."

Shit. "So what do you want to do?"

"I have to run," she said bitterly. "I don't know where I can even go at this point, but if I want to live, I have to run again."

Her voice broke, and her shoulders hunched. I reached over and laid a hand on her arm. She was right, of course: there was no way we were going to find out what had forced her to kill those girls before Dashiell heard about it.

I'd had to restart my life once, and at the time, it was the hardest thing I'd ever done. I couldn't fathom how vampires went through it over and over, especially considering how complicated it was for them to travel.

"You should just let me out here," Molly added, her voice still trembling. "You haven't crossed a line yet."

She was right, I realized. Aside from lying to Eli about where I'd gone, I hadn't technically done anything wrong . . . as long as I took Molly straight to Dashiell now. Or, at the very least, called him to report her transgression. I could say she'd left before I arrived at the house, and no one would question it—after all, capturing wayward vampires wasn't part of my job. Cleaning up after them was.

Moreover, not one person in the Old World would judge me harshly for breaking my ties to Molly right now. Especially considering how she'd asked me to move out after I'd gotten into my own dangerous misadventures. I couldn't exactly blame her, even then, but I didn't owe her anything now.

But I could still hear Jesse's voice in my head, as clearly as if he were in the back seat. *She's your friend. You have to help her.*

"What do you need?" I asked.

Molly's lip trembled for a moment, but she just nodded at me, too overwhelmed to speak for a moment. Her eyes darted to the clock on the dashboard. It wasn't even eight o'clock yet, although it seemed hours later. She cleared her throat. "Can you give me a ride to Thousand Oaks?" I frowned, trying to review my mental list of Los Angeles neighborhoods. "North on the 101," Molly added, seeing my confusion.

I swallowed. Right. Thousand Oaks was just outside the county line, which I was absolutely not supposed to cross with Shadow. The bargest was with me as a sort of . . . mmm . . . exchange student from a group of evil, werewolf-hunting European witches. They had agreed to stay out of North America as long as Shadow never left LA County. If anyone inside their organization had connections to the Old World, it could theoretically get back to them that I'd broken the rule.

But helping Molly was already breaking the rules. Would it really matter that I was bringing Shadow too?

"Are you sure?" I asked her.

She nodded. "My friend Frederic works at a twenty-four-hour storage facility. I have reserves there."

Vampires kept cash and IDs stashed here and there in case they had to flee town. Either it was Molly's closest stash, or any other supplies she had were too close to Dashiell's home base.

I nodded and restarted the van, but before I shifted into Drive, I did something I never do: I turned off my phone. Technically, this made me unavailable for other crime scenes, which was breaking my contract with the Old World leaders. But "business" had been slow for over a year, thanks to the relative peace. Besides, I'd never done it before, and I was betting I could get away with it once by claiming a dead phone battery.

I was betting a lot.

Chapter 5

The first part of the drive was very quiet. Molly stared out the window, her face empty. I couldn't imagine what she must be feeling. Forced or not, she'd killed her friends, and now she was going to have to burn down the life she'd spent years building. Every now and then, when I glanced over, I saw fresh tears running down her cheeks.

The pile of framed pictures was still on her lap, and after a while she began lifting each one, carefully removing the photo, and dropping the frame on the floor by her feet. When she was finished, she tucked the small stack of photos into a pocket of her backpack.

"I can't believe they're really gone," she said softly. "Harper and I were supposed to study for our final tonight. I can't stop thinking of how they—" Her voice broke into a sob, and she sniffed hard, turning to face me. "Can we, like, talk about something else? Tell me how you've been."

This was dancing very close to the subject of how our friendship had fallen apart, but of all people, I understood the value of distraction. "Work's been pretty good," I offered. "Corry went off to college in the fall—Berkeley—but I've had fewer crime scenes, so I've been able to handle things on my own." Corry was the only other null on this side of the Mississippi, and sort of my protégé, although that word felt weird. "I've also been working more with Will on security for the bar, and with the Haynes."

Dashiell's security was overseen by a single family that had served him for hundreds of years. Until I was a partner, I hadn't realized that Theodore Hayne, the head of security, wasn't the only Hayne currently on Dashiell's payroll. Theo's brother, a CPA, handled some of Dashiell's finances, and his sister, Abigail, took care of all of Dashiell's electronic security—cell phones, computers, etc. She was the person you called if a vampire's picture appeared on Facebook, or the werewolves were caught changing on a public security camera. And for a human, she was pretty scary.

Molly's face broke out into a smile. "You're working with *Abby*? How's that going?"

"Uh . . . you know." I waved it away. Abigail hated me, but I didn't want to discuss it.

"What about your brother? How's Jack doing?" Molly said hurriedly, before a really decent silence could get going.

"Jack is good. He's doing his internship at the hospital now. He actually got married last weekend."

Molly brightened. "He did? That's fantastic!"

I smiled a little. "Her name is Juliet, she's a guidance counselor at an elementary school, and she's got two kids. I don't see them that much, but they're pathologically adorable."

"Were you a bridesmaid?"

Of *course* that would be Molly's first question. "Yes," I grumbled. "Eli was an usher. We managed to survive the formalwear, but it was a close thing."

"That's right, you're still with Eli." For a second I was startled, but then I remembered she would have figured that out in order to find me at the art walk. Was I crazy, or was there a sort of skepticism in her voice? Like she was surprised.

"Yeah, why wouldn't I be?" My voice came out a little defensive. Before she could answer, a half-dozen insecurities flashed through my mind. *Because you two have nothing in common. Because he likes being around people and you don't. Because he's dependent on you to keep him human.* And so on.

But Molly just shrugged. "No ring on your finger. I always figured Eli for the settling-down type."

I went quiet, but despite the years we'd spent apart, Molly knew me too well not to pick up on it. "He asked you, didn't he?" she guessed.

"No! Well, not in so many words. He just sort of brought it up. At Jack's reception. As a . . . possibility."

I couldn't really blame him—there we were, all dressed up, the shiniest possible versions of ourselves, surrounded by evidence of love and commitment. Of course it had crossed his mind. I shouldn't have been surprised . . . but the thing is, I was. I had never really expected us to get married . . . no, that wasn't right. I hadn't even considered marriage as a viable option in my life. I was happy with the way things were—living with Eli and Shadow, working my job and my side projects, taking a few college classes on things that interested me. In fact, I'd spent the last three years living in the here and now, trying not to think too much about where I would be in five years, ten years. The marriage conversation had been a rude awakening.

Molly spread her hands wide, impatient for me to continue. "And?"

I shifted uncomfortably in my seat. "I told him I wasn't sure." I was nearly twenty-seven, plenty old enough for marriage, and Eli and I loved each other. We lived together, we shared expenses, and we were even kind of raising an abominable dog-monster together.

The trouble was, even if you set aside Eli's maddening overprotectiveness, there were a dozen small reasons not to marry him. Part of it was that Eli wanted kids, and for reasons no one can really explain, nulls can't have them. We could adopt, of course, but I wasn't sure that I could be a mom, or sure that I even wanted to anymore. Back when I'd thought I was just a regular human being, I'd always figured that I'd have children eventually. But now . . . just thinking about it terrified me, and I didn't really know why.

There was also the problem of Eli's loyalty to the pack. In a life-and-death situation, I knew he'd choose me first, but in a hundred small ways, he had to take them into account. They were a constant drain on his time and attention, for one thing, and everything Eli did had to be run past Will, which meant I had to be very careful about what I told him. If I didn't want Will to know something, I couldn't tell my boyfriend about it without putting him in a terrible position. Most of the time there was no reason why Will couldn't know what I was doing, of course, but having to report to someone, even by proxy, chafed me.

And then there was the quiet tension that always simmered beneath Eli and me because being close to me gave him humanity. He was, in a way, dependent on me. And that was sort of my own fault. Years ago I had managed to cure him of his werewolf magic, but it had landed me in a lot of trouble, since nulls weren't supposed to be able to do that. To keep me safe, Eli had accepted a second werewolf curse. Which wouldn't have happened if I hadn't put him in the position of needing to do so to save my life . . .

It was complicated.

Molly was studying me. "How did you leave it?" she asked quietly. "After Jack's reception, I mean."

I chewed on my lip for a moment. "We decided to put a pin in it," I said finally. "Since then, I've . . ."

"Been on your best behavior?" she suggested.

I wrinkled my nose at the wording, but she was right. I nodded.

"I'm sorry that I asked you to lie to him tonight," she said earnestly. "I thought he might need to say something to Will."

"I know." I didn't need to say, "He probably would have." We both already knew.

I'd seen plenty of LA storage facilities from the freeway, but they were always dingy beige buildings with lights missing in the signs. The

Hollywood Storage Center was something else. It was an attractive stucco building with beautiful landscaping and a surprisingly tasteful sign, surrounded by blooming flowers. Through the glass windows we could see a big open reception area with one wall taken up by security camera monitors. The floors were a beautiful glowing hardwood, setting off the lifelike statue of Marilyn Monroe off to one side. The place was classier than a storage center had any right to be.

"Nice digs," I said, turning off the van. Shadow's enormous upper body was thrust between the seats again, her tail wagging a little with curiosity.

"Lots of vampires keep containers here," Molly said, her voice subdued. "I have a large one with some things from the house, but I also keep a safety deposit box."

"Do you guys own it?" I asked, meaning the vampires.

"No, but we keep careful tabs on the family that does. They're small and local, which makes it easy to press them when we need to. And of course, we've got someone on the inside."

Molly started to open the door, but I grabbed her arm. "Molls, you can't say anything about . . . tonight."

"I know."

"And you can't let Frederic know that anything's wrong."

She blinked a few times, nodding to herself. "Right. I can do that."

Without another word, she got out and marched determinedly toward the entrance. I sighed and looked at Shadow, who was now watching my face intently. "You have to stay, girl," I told her. I avoided her betrayed expression and followed Molly.

A disproportionate percentage of LA residents are good-looking, but the Asian man behind the counter was next-level handsome. He was around thirty, with a low ponytail and a tight black T-shirt that outlined muscles I could probably have counted, given a bright light and a couple of beers. I figured him for night security, but as we entered through the glass doors I extended my radius wide enough to reach him.

His face went stricken, and I felt the familiar sensation of another vampire in my radius. He doubled over just a bit, reaching for something underneath the counter.

"He's turning off the cameras," Molly murmured to me.

"*That's* Frederic?" I whispered.

She flashed me a smile. "Not what you were picturing?"

"Is it racist if I say he doesn't look like a Frederic?"

"Not really," Frederic called, in a voice that suggested he'd heard this a lot. I blushed. Vampires couldn't use super-hearing around me, so this was a good old-fashioned case of me talking too loud. "My father was German; Mom was Japanese," he added, still looking me over with great curiosity.

To cover my embarrassment, I stuck out my hand, over the counter. "Scarlett Bernard."

He raised an eyebrow, his eyes flashing between Molly and me, but he accepted the handshake cautiously, as if tasting a foreign food. His expression was openly uncomfortable. A lot of vampires got that way around me. They were used to easily containing whatever emotions they felt, and forgot how to keep their thoughts off their faces. Frederic seemed more unsettled about it than most, though.

He dropped my hand quickly and looked toward Molly. "What brings you here?" His head tilted slightly toward me, and the unspoken words were obvious: *with her*. Oh yeah, being a null was fun.

"Just need a couple of things from the safety deposit box," she said with a brittle smile.

My attention was caught by the security monitors behind Frederic. There were more than a dozen, showing empty hallways and corridors in black and white. Three of the screens had gone dark; those had to be connected to the cameras covering the lobby. But there was another monitor in the bottom right, and this one was in color. It was showing a commercial for laundry detergent. "Can I get the second key?" Molly asked.

Frederic blinked hard but didn't move. "That's your reserve, right? Are you running from something?" he blurted, then looked shocked, like he hadn't intended to say that.

The first red flag popped up in my head, and I took an instinctive step backward, looking around. There was no movement, no other cars pulling in. Frederic's hands were resting on the counter, nonthreatening. Why did I suddenly feel watched? Automatically, I let my radius flare out, checking for other people. Nothing registered. I allowed it to resume its normal size.

"Nah, Scarlett just needs to borrow some cash," Molly said, more or less calmly. She held out a key on a small leather thong. Her hand was trembling a little. "Can I get the other key? Or do you want to walk us back there?"

On the bottom monitor, the laundry detergent ad was over, and a woman from the local news appeared at her desk. The tiny screen over her shoulder was filled by a USC logo. "Molly—" I began.

But it was too late. I felt the new vampire hit my radius, like a cool stone dropping into an aquarium of water. Only this one was *powerful*. So powerful that I recognized who it was before I could finish turning around.

A tallish, elegantly dressed man in a dark overcoat stepped through the door we had just entered. With every step he took into my radius, his face clouded over with a little more fury.

I swallowed, trying to work up enough saliva to speak. "Hi, Dashiell."

Chapter 6

Ignoring me, the cardinal vampire of LA County strode forward with gritted teeth. He seized Molly around her upper arm, hard enough for the fabric of her dress to sink into deep wrinkles. Molly winced. Dashiell may have been human in my radius, but he was still a strong, relatively large man. And she was currently a small woman of about twenty.

"How did you find us?" I blurted, but he cut me off with a wave.

"Do not speak," he snarled, throwing me a glare. "You, I will deal with later." A chill tingled up my back.

"Dashiell," Molly began in a desperate voice, but he was so angry that he *shook* her, jostling her into silence. I winced, and one hand automatically drifted toward my knife pocket. Dashiell didn't notice, but Molly did. Her eyes widened and she shook her head slightly. I froze, watching helplessly as Dashiell began dragging her toward the front door.

Stupidly, I turned to look at Frederic, but he'd vanished into the hallway behind the monitors. What a coward. Behind me, I felt Dashiell and Molly pop out of my radius. I spun around again.

"She didn't do it, Dashiell!" I yelled just before he pushed open the glass door.

He paused, and when he turned, I could see how much he wanted to scream at me. He stalked back over, Molly's arm still trapped in his punishing grip. When he reached me, he was technically human, but his eyes were cold as dry ice. "She *didn't* blood-gorge in my territory?" he said sarcastically. "She *didn't* kill a bunch of rich white girls in the middle of the city's most high-profile university?" Molly flinched away from him, equal parts ashamed and defiant.

I could have made a case for UCLA being more high-profile, but occasionally even I can make a smart decision. "Someone forced her," I insisted, my voice sounding weak even to me.

He blanched for a moment, then shook his head. "Impossible."

"How do you know?"

He gave me an irritated look. "There are two vampires who could force her to do something. The one who made her was beheaded twenty years ago, by *her*." He didn't actually say "you idiot," but the implication was there. "Then there's the vampire who holds her troth," he continued, "and that is me. Are you suggesting I am responsible for this?" His eyes flashed dangerously.

Troth was an oath of service, made to a cardinal vampire. It was almost impossible to break. "No, but—"

He pulled his trump card. I should have expected him to have one. "And did you know that one of those girls was a Friend of the Witches?"

Whatever I was about to yell died before it reached my lips. Molly's face was as shocked as I felt. Witches are the only Old World species who are allowed to talk a little bit about what they are. Friends of the Witches are human families who have helped the witch community at some point and earned a sort of protected status. They're like an endangered species in a game park.

"I didn't know," Molly wailed. "She never wore an anti-vampire charm!"

"Maybe she didn't think she had to," Dashiell said coldly. "And now, if I don't come down hard on Molly, Kirsten will be irate, as she should be. That family was supposed to have protection." He rounded on me, his hand never leaving Molly's arm. "And you are never supposed to take the bargest out of LA County. Do you have any idea how much trouble you'd be in if the Luparii found out what you've done tonight?"

Before I could answer, Molly swung her body around to face him. "Please," she begged, tears running down her cheeks. "Please, let me say goodbye. I'll go without a fight. Just let me give her a hug." Her voice broke, and something about her actually made Dashiell pause for a moment. He wasn't used to human emotions, which meant he wasn't entirely immune to a crying young girl.

Molly saw his hesitation and took advantage, taking one careful step to close the gap between us. Dashiell let her slip her arm out of his grasp, but hovered a foot away.

Molly threw her arms around my waist, her head turned so her mouth was near my ear. "I love you," she said simply. Tears stung my eyes, but in my peripheral vision I could still see Dashiell relax just a bit, allowing this. "You gotta be understanding to Eli," Molly added, in a voice so quiet that I wasn't sure he would hear her. Then I felt her shove something small into my back pocket. "And one of these days, you should really dig Jesse out of that hole you left him in."

I flinched. "That's enough," Dashiell snapped. He grabbed Molly's upper arm again.

"I made Scarlett help me," she blurted, startling all three of us. Dashiell and I both stared at her. "I threatened her protégé. Corry," Molly said, her voice gaining strength. "I said I'd kill the girl if Scarlett didn't drive me here."

Dashiell raised a skeptical eyebrow and turned to me. "Is this true?"

I stood there with my mouth open, completely trapped. I didn't want to dig Molly's grave any deeper, nor did I want to expose her for lying. "What are you going to do to her?" I asked, desperate to change the subject.

"Put her on trial," he said over his shoulder as he dragged Molly off into the night, tugging her out of my radius. His voice floated back through the door as it swung closed. "You're lucky I don't do the same to you."

I darted forward, but by the time I made it through the door there was no sign of them. Vampire speed. I looked over my shoulder for Frederic, but he'd completely disappeared. Typical.

I knew better than to check my pocket immediately. Instead, I walked back out to the van as calmly as I could, noting that there were still no other vehicles in the lot. Had Dashiell parked around back? A few blocks away? Or had he simply *run* here from Pasadena? It seemed far-fetched, but then again, I didn't know that much about actual vampire powers. Dashiell kept me in the dark on purpose, although I tried not to take it personally. I was fairly certain that vampires had invented the concept of "need to know basis" long before the military had gotten a hold of it.

Back in my van, I had to spend a few minutes reassuring the freaked-out bargest, who had seen my exchange with Dashiell from the window. Shadow was extraordinarily protective of me, and there were fresh scratches on the dashboard and the armrests, which meant she'd come close to bursting through the window again. I sighed at the damage, but it was really the least of my concerns.

Eventually Shadow settled down in the passenger seat, and I leaned back for a moment, thinking. It was oddly reassuring that Dashiell planned to go ahead with a trial. When he'd first walked through the door and hit my radius, I had been sure he was going to kill her on the spot for trying to skip town. Still, that only gave me about twenty hours to figure out who had set Molly up and how.

It seemed impossible.

I felt something small and poky in my back pocket and remembered Molly's hug. Shifting, I reached into the pocket and pulled out the small safety deposit box key that Molly had been about to use. I frowned at it. Was she telling me I should take her stash and leave town? Or was there something in there that would point toward the bad guy? I looked back up at the building, but the front desk stood empty. Frederic probably had a second monitoring system, and was hiding until I drove away with my dog-monster. Smart man. Just to cover my bases, I got out of the van and went up to the door, rattling it in the frame. The electronic lock had been engaged.

That seemed excessive, and for the first time I wondered if Frederic was the one who'd called Dashiell and warned him Molly and I were going to the storage facility. No, wait. How would he have known? *I* hadn't even known we were coming until we were on our way. My van could be GPS-tracked, but it wasn't like Dashiell or anyone on his team to sit staring at a little blipping screen every night, watching my movements. They had better things to do, and even Dashiell trusted me more than that.

But somehow he had been informed that I was doing something off-book. How?

When I figured it out, I slammed my head backward against the headrest, causing Shadow to rise in alarm. Molly had gotten there before me. "Be understanding to Eli," I said out loud. Of course. My own boyfriend had called Will, who would have immediately called Dashiell. Dashiell would have taken one look at our progress on the freeway and figured out where we were going.

I automatically reached for my phone so I could yell at Eli, but I stopped myself. He had been worried about his girlfriend's safety, so he'd done what any wolf would do: checked with the alpha. I couldn't be mad at him for that. Well, I could, but privately, at least for now.

What was the other thing Molly had said to me? I looked down at the key in my hand, then up at the empty reception area. And I groaned.

"Dammit, Molls," I said out loud.

Chapter 7

Jesse leaned heavily on the grocery store cart, tapping out a rhythm on the handle with impatient fingers. The grocery store was surprisingly busy for 9:45 p.m., and of course there were only three checkout aisles open. As the twenty-something girl in front of him loaded bottle after bottle of diet soda on to the conveyer belt, talking on her cell phone the whole time, he was tempted to ram his cart into a display and stomp out of there. To make it even worse, she kept tossing her hair and giving him coquettish eyes over her shoulder. He was too annoyed to admire her multitasking.

Finally, the girl made enough progress down the line for Jesse to start setting out his own groceries. And that's when he caught sight of the hardcover book at the top of the stand next to the clerk. His own face stared back at him from the book's cover.

"Shit," Jesse said under his breath.

The young woman ahead of him glanced over her shoulder again, this time with obvious curiosity, but Jesse just pulled his Dodgers cap lower over his forehead, not meeting her gaze.

Hopefully the short beard he'd acquired in the last month would provide enough camouflage—the Jesse Cruz on the book cover was clean-cut and well-dressed, leaning against a brick wall with crime scene tape strewn all over it, eyes hooded in a look the photographer had called "broody." At the photo shoot Jesse had complained that cops would never put crime scene tape on a wall, but no one had listened to him.

Jesse finished unloading his meager groceries and waited, trying to keep his eyes off the row of books. He couldn't help but steal quick glances, like a scab that you can't stop yourself from picking at. There was the cringe-inducing title, *Wunderkind: The Rookie Detective Who Caught Two of LA's Most Notorious Killers*, followed by his own name embossed in embarrassingly large letters. Beneath it, in a small, easy-to-overlook font, sat the name of the ghostwriter who'd done basically all of the work: A. P. Cox. Jesse flinched and looked away.

The young woman was finally done, and Jesse stepped forward, not looking at the clerk, a young Hispanic woman who was a foot shorter and fifty pounds heavier than Jesse. She was giving him the eyeball, but he couldn't tell if it was because of the book cover, the scruffy look, or his pathetic groceries: Hungry-Man meals and beer. Wait, could it be the smell? Had he showered that morning? The night before? He couldn't remember. Two days ago, his brother Noah had dragged him out of the apartment to the gym. Surely he'd showered after that . . . right?

His phone buzzed, startling him. Lately the only people who called were agents and editors, who stuck to business hours, or his family. But it was a little late for his parents, who went to bed early, and Noah had said he had a date tonight. Jesse mumbled an apology and dug the phone out of his pocket. The lawyer's name was on the screen, so he sighed and answered, ignoring the young woman's irritated look. "Working late, Esteban?"

"I wasn't planning on it," said the lawyer. His tone was just this side of annoyed. "But she has a couple of last-minute requests before we finalize the paperwork."

The clerk in front of him pointed at the register, where the total glowed in front of him. Jesse nodded and pulled out cash. He'd learned the hard way that it was hard to stay anonymous if you used a credit card with your name on it. "I told you, Esteban, give her whatever she wants. I don't care."

"This is serious money, Jesse," the lawyer insisted, but without any heat. This was an old argument, and he knew he wouldn't win.

"And Ava earned it," Jesse replied, holding out his free hand for the change. "I told you, fifty-fifty, plus she gets the car and the condo. Is she asking for more than that?"

"Jesse, some of that furniture is worth—"

"I don't give a shit about the furniture," Jesse snarled, and in front of him, the clerk shrunk back. He winced and mouthed an apology, but she shook her head, her eyes darting to the rent-a-cop at the store entrance. Jesse sighed and picked up his bags, shifting so he was holding the phone in place with his shoulder. "This conversation is over," he said into the phone.

"Yeah, I can tell," Esteban said shortly. He hung up.

Jesse stuffed the phone back in his pocket, his teeth clenched together in frustration. He turned back to apologize to the clerk, but now she was standing there with the book in her hands, giving Jesse a look that was right on the brink of "a-ha!" He hurried out the door instead.

Great. Another Vons he had to avoid now.

It was only a few blocks back to Jesse's bunker-like apartment. The place was tiny and utilitarian, but it came with a parking spot and he liked the location: close to Echo Park, an easy drive away from his parents' place. Jesse had leased the place for almost six years now, even paying rent on it throughout the whole thirteen months of his marriage. In retrospect, maybe some part of him had known his relationship with Ava wasn't going to last. Why else would he have left himself a bolt-hole?

Maybe it would have lasted if you hadn't *left yourself a bolt-hole*, said the voice in the back of his head, for the hundredth time. Jesse got the bags out of his trunk and sighed, suddenly too tired to take the stairs. He rode the ancient elevator up to his floor and began trudging down the shabby hallway on autopilot. As he turned the corner, his thoughts were already sinking back into the swirling tar pit of the last two months. Jesse fumbled all the bags into one hand so he could dig the keys out of his jeans pocket—

He smacked full-on into the small woman in front of him, her forehead nearly knocking into his nose. There was a growl from the floor, and in the confusion Jesse was halfway through an apology before he realized who he'd run into. "Scarlett?" he said incredulously. "What are you doing here?"

"Hey," she said, rubbing her head and backing away from him. "Ow. Sorry. I was looking for you, but I couldn't wait . . . I . . ." she trailed off, looking him over. The bargest was standing just beside her, wearing one of those service dog capes. Shadow's tail swished when she saw Jesse, but she stayed where she was.

For a long moment, Jesse couldn't make his mouth work. For the first time, he realized that he hadn't actually thought he'd ever see Scarlett again. It had been too long, and so much had happened. But here she was. There was a suspicious-looking stain on her denim jacket, and her hair was slipping out of a loose bun at the back of her neck. A faint smell of smoke—possibly from pot—clung to her hair, though he'd never known her to smoke anything. Her bright-green eyes looked exhausted, and her expression was haunted—or maybe hunted. Even so, there was something new about her, something different. She held herself with confidence, and her shoulders were squared like she was ready for a fight. Not necessarily with him, just in general.

She was lovely.

For just a second, the old emotions resurrected themselves in Jesse's numbed brain. He felt like he'd been knocked down, though he was still standing there with the bags, frozen like an idiot. Shadow whined, looking back and forth between them. Scarlett murmured something to her, and the bargest bounded forward to greet Jesse, her clubbed-off tail waving frantically.

He finally snapped out of the trance and bent down, dropping some of the bags so he could scratch at her fur. "Hey, Shadow," he said, letting her give his face one quick swipe with her tongue. "I missed you too." Jesse had been with Scarlett when she'd rescued the bargest, but he hadn't seen either of them in years. He was pleased that Shadow remembered him.

The bargest darted back to her mistress's side, but her tail still wagged for Jesse. "Listen, can we talk?" Scarlett asked, gesturing toward his apartment door.

"Um, yeah, I guess." He winced, remembering the state of his place. "It's kind of a mess."

She shrugged. "I won't tell Martha Stewart if you won't."

He unlocked the door, leading them both into the cramped living room. Shadow immediately darted past him, trotting off to check the apartment for threats.

"Wow." Scarlett paused in the doorway for a moment, taking in the empty pizza boxes, beer bottles, and dirty clothes. "Just *fully* embracing the divorced guy cliché, aren't you?"

He was so surprised that he laughed out loud. His family had been tiptoeing around that kind of comment for weeks, even Noah. Trust Scarlett to just come right out with it. "Something like that, I guess," he replied. "I need to put this stuff away."

She trailed him into the kitchenette, where he stacked the frozen dinners in the freezer. Out of the corner of his eye, Jesse could see Scarlett looking at the copies of his book stacked on the small table, not to mention all the mail and random junk. Shadow returned from her inspection and curled up under the table, giving Jesse a disappointed look. He wasn't sure if it was the mess or the lack of enemies to kill, but he grabbed a couple of leftover hamburgers out of his fridge and tossed them to the bargest. Her tail wagged as she wolfed them down. All was forgiven.

Scarlett was toying with the cover of the top copy. "I hate this picture," she commented.

"Me too."

"Why the hell would they put crime scene tape on a long brick wall?"

He smiled briefly, but he didn't like the way she was looking at the book. "Did you read it?" he asked. She hesitated, which pretty much answered the question. "You read it."

"Dashiell asked me to make sure you stuck with the official story. He got me a copy before it went to print."

Jesse nodded, the small candle of warmth and hospitality in his chest flickering out. He should have expected that. He hadn't heard anything from Scarlett, or anyone else from the Old World, so the book must have been acceptable. "Don't tell me what you thought," he said tiredly. "I don't want to know."

She hesitated again, looking exactly as though he'd demanded to know her opinion and she was trying to dredge up a compliment. He didn't want to hear whatever she scraped up, so he changed the subject. "Why are you here?" he asked, motioning to the only kitchen chair that wasn't covered in stacks of junk or boxes. He was still moving things back here from the condo.

Scarlett sat down, tucking her feet close to the chair so she wouldn't kick Shadow. "Have you seen the news tonight?"

He gestured to the state of the apartment. "Does it look like I'm keeping up with the news?" His voice came out sharper than he'd intended, and Shadow lifted her head from her front paws to eye him.

"Jesse . . ." Scarlett looked pained. "Maybe this was a bad idea." She stood up again. "I'm sorry, I didn't realize things were . . ." She gestured helplessly around the apartment, and he let her flail. He found that he was now perversely interested in how she'd sugarcoat it. "It seems like you're having a tough time," she said eventually. "I didn't mean to add to it."

"My hard time has nothing to do with you," he said, annoyed now. Did she think he was still pining over her? That had been a long time ago. "It's been three years. You have no idea what's going on in my life."

That got her attention. "Of course I do," she replied, a little heat in her voice. "You quit the consultant business because you couldn't stand trading on your reputation as a cop. But you ran out of money, and then a publisher offered you a truckload of cash for a book. You figured, hey, tons of books are published every day, you'd take the advance and the book would pretty much vanish. Am I close?"

He didn't answer her, but he dropped into the chair she'd vacated, suddenly too tired to stand. But Scarlett wasn't done. "Then you fell for your ghostwriter and did the whole quickie Vegas marriage. And I bet you were more surprised than anyone when the book was a huge hit," she continued. "I don't know why you're getting divorced, that's true, but you can't say I haven't paid attention."

"Because your boss made you," he countered.

"Jesse." It was her turn to sound tired. "Do you know how many humans in this county know about the Old World, but aren't a part of it in some way? There are like six of you. Of course we have to keep tabs."

We. She had never talked like that before, as though she were on the side of the Old World authorities. The cop part of his brain wanted to ask what exactly "keep tabs" meant. Surveillance? Bugs?

Really, though, did it matter? He sat around in gym shorts watching television. What would they find? "Why are you here, Scarlett?" he asked again. An embarrassing new thought occurred to him. "Did my family call you to do an intervention? Because I'm gonna—"

"No, nothing like that," she interrupted. "I came to ask for your help."

He laughed, a full-throated sound that came out more broken than jovial. "Of course you did. You've got some nasty case you can't solve, and you thought you'd crook your finger and poor stupid Jesse would come running in to throw himself in front of it. *Am I close?*"

She just glared at him, turning on her heel to stalk toward the front door. Shadow was suddenly next to her, though Jesse hadn't heard the bargest move from under the table. Jesse thought about calling them back, but before he could open his mouth, Scarlett paused with her back to him. She muttered something under her breath and then turned around again.

"It sucks that you think I'd treat you like that," she said matter-of-factly.

"So this is like a pity thing, then?" Jesse countered, suddenly wondering again if Noah· had contacted Scarlett. "Throw me a bone?"

"Why would I pity you," she snapped, "when you've so obviously got that covered?"

He started to argue, but she lifted a hand. "Just . . . stop. I'm not here for me, or for the Old World leaders, and I'm definitely not here to fight. It's Molly."

His brow furrowed. "Molly the vampire? Your old roommate?" He'd met her a few times, and actually kind of liked her. He didn't know many vampires, but Molly had struck him as . . . good. She had an edge of intensity, sure, but she'd always seemed kind and interested, and she'd clearly loved Scarlett. Jesse had been there when Molly asked her to move out, and he'd seen how it had hurt both of them. "What happened?"

"She's being set up. I've got about"—she checked her watch—"nineteen hours to figure out what happened, and then they're going to kill her."

He stared, but she didn't laugh, or take it back. "I guess we'd better sit down," Jesse said at last.

Chapter 8

Jesse managed to pull together a pot of coffee from the ruins of his kitchen, and I started relating the events of the evening. It took me the better part of an hour to explain everything: the Trials, the bloody note, Molly, the murders. Jesse was as surprised as I had been about Molly's living situation before the murders, though he had a theory about why she'd arranged her life that way.

"She missed you," he said, in a tone that suggested it was completely obvious. "She had to kick you out so she could feel safe, but she missed the camaraderie. So she set herself up with twelve little replacement Scarletts."

My jaw dropped open.

"Think about it," he went on. "College kids have tons of spare time, weird schedules, and they love to sit around drinking coffee and analyzing movies. Who does that remind you of?"

"Me," I admitted.

"How old were you when you moved in with Molly?"

"Twenty, twenty-one."

He nodded. "Same as those girls, I bet. But their lives are—were—simpler than yours. I can see Molly feeling at home with them."

I didn't know what to say to that, so I picked up the story again. I kept my description of the crime scene straightforward, but it was hard to make it sound anything but grisly. Jesse was taken aback, but he'd seen worse things when he was a cop.

To my surprise, he readily agreed that Molly wouldn't have killed those girls. I had thought I would need to talk him into it.

"If you told me she'd killed some guy who tried to attack her, I would believe it," he said. "But she wouldn't hurt those girls any more than she'd hurt you."

I felt a weight lift from my chest. Someone else believed Molly. I wasn't alone anymore.

He tilted his head, considering. "But just to play devil's advocate, what if she slipped and killed one of them, maybe by overfeeding, and then had to kill the rest because they'd witnessed it?"

"She'd just press them to forget, Jesse." I said. "Besides, there were too many of them. That scenario relies on the girls stumbling in at intervals to witness the crime scene and then get murdered. This isn't a British farce."

He bobbed his head, conceding the point. "Besides," I went on, "if Molly absolutely had to kill them, she would have done it fast and painlessly. Probably snapped their necks." I swallowed hard, thinking of the girl wearing the same T-shirt I owned. "Those girls suffered. Vampires don't do that."

He raised his eyebrows again. "You're saying there are no evil psychopath vampires?"

I sighed. "Of course, it's theoretically possible, just as with humans. But that's why all vampires go through a twenty-year apprenticeship after they're turned. If Molly were a serial killer, her master would have terminated her a hundred years ago."

He rubbed his face with both hands. "It's a good argument, Scarlett. Wouldn't Dashiell realize all of this too?"

"Yes, but the Trials are tomorrow night. Dashiell isn't concerned about justice. He's concerned about squashing it quickly. And there's Molly, literally caught red-handed."

Jesse pointed a finger at me. "That's another thing I don't get. I think I remember you mentioning the Trials once, but what exactly happens?"

"It's a little like a cross between a human court trial and a business convention," I explained. "They do trials for about eight hours, and then they party until sunrise."

"Who goes on trial?"

"Anyone. If you have a grievance with someone else in the Old World, you can ask to be put on the agenda. Usually, it's minor skirmishes between two different races. Both parties get to speak, and then they each get a sort of rebuttal. Then Dashiell and the others decide. It's actually pretty simple."

"Do you get a vote, now that you're a partner?"

I watched him suspiciously. Had there been the slightest note of bitterness when he'd said "partner?" *Not the time, Scarlett.* "No. We talked about it, but four voting members would wreck the numbers. I do have the opportunity to put in my two cents before they vote, though."

He nodded. "Give me an example of a typical case."

"Okay, um . . ." I tried to remember some of the cases I'd read about that afternoon. "At the last Trials, a vampire named Gregory accused one of the witches of bad-mouthing him to his favorite human. Not only did she tell the human that Gregory was a douche, she also made the human a witch bag to protect her from being pressed."

"I remember Gregory," he said, making a face. I'd forgotten that Jesse and I had questioned him during our first case. "What happened?"

"The witch explained that Gregory was stealing money from this woman and forcing her to run his daytime errands, which was hurting her job." I smiled. "Besides, Gregory *is* a douche. Dashiell and the others basically agreed that the witch was justified. She got a verbal reprimand for handling it herself instead of going through the proper channels, but that was it."

He blinked a few times. "That seems . . . pretty fair. I'm kind of surprised."

"It's not a medieval inquisition, Jesse; the three of them are fairly reasonable people. Even Dashiell." I suddenly remembered the look on his face as he dragged Molly away, and I winced. "Well, most of the time."

"What are the punishments like?"

"For all the minor stuff, it's usually monetary. Pay damages, restitution, or whatever. It's often kindergarten stuff: you broke his toy, buy him a new one. But in *very* rare cases, usually involving vampires, they might serve time."

Now it was Jesse's turn to stare in surprise. "You guys have a prison?"

I shrugged. "Dashiell has a couple of cells in his basement. They're almost never used, though. A vampire would have to do something bad enough that it can't be fixed financially, but not so bad that they deserve a death sentence. Not a lot of crimes fall into that category." A new thought occurred to me. "That's where Dashiell will be keeping Molly now, I bet."

Jesse started pacing the small kitchenette as he considered this. The pacing reminded me of Eli, and I felt a jolt of guilt. My phone was still off, and I doubted Dashiell had bothered to fill him or Will in on what had happened. But I was also still angry.

Jesse turned to face me again, and I pushed the thought aside.

"You said it's usually between two species, but not always," he reminded me. "What are the exceptions?"

"There are two." I held up one finger. "If the disagreement is with Will, Dashiell, or Kirsten. For example, Kirsten sells spell materials to one of the witches, and the witch feels she's been overcharged. Those kinds of trials are really rare, especially because no one wants to be the idiot who accuses Dashiell of something. It happens once in a while, though, and then I do get a vote, instead of whoever's been accused."

"What's the second exception?"

I held up another finger. "Crimes against the Old World itself. People who did something that could have exposed us. Some of my cleanup jobs end up on trial, like if someone did something risky or exceptionally stupid. Last time, one of the werewolves went on trial for filming himself changing." I shook my head. "He said it was for his personal curiosity, but Will was pissed."

"So that's how Molly will be tried?"

"Yes."

"And you're sure she'll be sentenced to death?"

"For killing twelve girls with her teeth? Hell, yes." A terrible new thought hit me, and if I hadn't been sitting down, I would have dropped. "Oh, my God."

"What?"

I met his eyes. "I'll have to be there. Like, next to her. When she dies." Killing a vampire was difficult and messy, and it left a body that decayed back to the condition it would have been in if magic had never touched it. It was much simpler and cleaner to kill a human being, so the null at the trial would need to stick close to the accused. "I had forgotten," I said softly.

Jesse shot me a sympathetic look, and for the first time since I'd arrived, he looked like his old self. "One thing I don't get," he said. "So Molly commits this huge crime—"

"Blood-gorging," I supplied.

He nodded. "And you were there when she was caught. So why didn't Dashiell just kill her right away?"

"Because killing a member of the LA Old World is a big deal," I answered. "This is the only major city on the continent where all three groups share power and live in peace. The only way that works is if we agree that all our lives have value. If Dashiell had just chopped off Molly's head without a trial, or at least consulting the others, he would be contradicting that."

"Everyone was ready to kill the nova wolf," Jesse pointed out.

"Because Remus was never part of Will's pack. It was also very likely that the only way to stop Remus was to kill him—it's very hard to take a werewolf alive, unless I'm right there. But even in that case, Will consulted Dashiell and Kirsten before deciding."

Jesse nodded, acquiescing. He rubbed the stubble on one side of his face, considering the situation. "The timing is still weird. What would have happened if the Trials weren't coming up? If this thing with Molly had just happened on some random Thursday?"

It was a good question. No vampire had blood-gorged in LA as long as I'd been the only crime scene cleaner, but it had happened once under Olivia. "In that case, I think they would have held a sort of miniature version of the Trials, with just Dashiell, Kirsten, and Will."

"Hmm."

"What?"

"Say I'm the one who set her up," Jesse began. "What do I gain by doing it tonight instead of two months from now? If the trial happens either way . . ."

Another good question, and one I should have considered earlier. "Publicity," I said finally, thinking it through. "By the end of the night every vampire in LA is going to know what Molly did, and it'll start trickling into the other communities, if it hasn't already. There's no way this can be hushed up or glossed over. And that means Dashiell is going to have to make an example of Molly, especially since one of those girls was a Friend of the Witches. Since it's the Trials, he'll have to do it publicly." I wasn't sure if whoever had orchestrated the massacre had known one of the girls was a Friend of the Witches, but it seemed likely. That particular element made the whole thing political—and potentially explosive.

"Plus, now you have no time to figure out who the real bad guy is," Jesse pointed out. "You're right; even if I'd never met Molly, I would think the timing was sketchy. Especially since the blood-gorging thing doesn't happen very often?" He'd made it into a question, his eyebrows raised.

"Definitely not," I said. "I've never even heard of a vampire drinking down that many people in one . . . sitting. With the vomiting and all. There's just no point to it."

Jesse nodded, but mostly to himself. I could see the wheels turning in his head. "Does this mean you'll help me figure out who did this?" I asked, unable to keep the hope out of my voice. "I've only got a day, and Molly's life is on the line."

Jesse hesitated, his eyes darting around the room for a moment. "I can't, Scar," he said finally. "I can help you brainstorm over the phone, maybe, but I just can't be a part of this again."

A knot of disappointment and sadness tightened in my chest. It wasn't so long ago that Jesse had promised me he'd be my partner. How had so much changed between us? "Why not?" I whispered.

"I'm not going to be any help, for one thing." His face shifted into something . . . broken. "I don't think I have anything left, Scarlett. I'm pretty much just a void at this point."

"Sounds like a sitcom," I offered. "Null and Void: crime solvers who need therapy."

He didn't laugh, so I tried again. "Jesse, you've already helped, just by talking through it with me." *And I'm scared, and this is really big, and I need someone I can trust.* Once, I might have said that out loud, but not anymore.

He gestured around the room. "There's also the thing where every time I get involved in one of your cases, my life goes to shit."

Whoa. "Excuse me? I didn't make you get married, or divorced, or write that book."

"Yeah, but all those things happened because I quit the LAPD."

Anger built in my chest. "I didn't make you do that, either!"

"Didn't you?" he countered, his voice icy-quiet. It unnerved me. Jesse and I had gone toe-to-toe plenty of times, but I'd never seen him so resigned. Like nothing I said would pull him out of his own personal black hole, so why did this fight matter?

Molly's voice rang in my head. *The hole you left him in.*

"No," I said firmly, both to her and to Jesse. I wasn't taking this on too. "You made your own choices, Cruz, just like everyone else. It's not my fault you can't live with them."

Shadow, who was on her feet watching this exchange, now moved to stand solidly between us, her teeth pointed toward Jesse. He gave her a hurt look. To me, he just said, "I think it's time for you to go."

"I couldn't agree more," I said through my teeth.

As I walked—okay, stomped—into the elevator with Shadow, the conversation ran on a loop in my head. Despite what I'd said, I couldn't help but feel a little bit responsible for Jesse's situation. Three years ago, I had pushed him into breaking his moral code, which had kicked off this whole downward spiral.

Or maybe I just felt guilty that I hadn't tried to stop his descent. During the years I'd been happy with Eli, I hadn't bothered to do anything about this other person I'd affected deeply. I had known Jesse was flailing, but I'd told myself that calling would only make things worse for him. I'd been a coward.

And now Molly would pay the price. He wasn't going to help me, and I'd just wasted a very precious hour and a half learning that.

I slammed open the building's front door, which ended up being very dissatisfying because it was on those air-compressed hinges that refuse to slam. Shadow had to trot by my side as I stormed down the street toward my van. What the hell was I going to do now? I needed to get back to that storage unit, but I had to wait for daylight, when

Frederic wouldn't be there. That left me with hours to kill—and no idea how I could use them to help Molly.

I was so busy fuming, my eyes fixed on the sidewalk in front of me, that I never saw the SUV creeping up the street behind me. I didn't even register it until it was nearly alongside me, and even then I didn't bother glancing over. If I had, I probably would have seen the window go down and the rifle barrel appear. But I didn't notice the car.

Not until the first shot hit me.

Chapter 9

As Scarlett stomped down the hall, Jesse was practically tingling with indignation. He wasn't happy about Molly's predicament, of course, but his first instinct about Scarlett had basically been correct: she'd thought he would come running again the second she batted her eyes.

Not this time, he thought, feeling self-righteous.

Jesse went over to his couch and dropped down. His eyes landed on the ground in front of the apartment entrance, and he noticed a folded piece of paper just inside the doorway. He frowned. A note from one of the neighbors?

Sighing, he heaved himself to his feet and went to retrieve it. It was a flyer for guitar lessons, complete with the little tear-off tabs on the bottom. On the back side, however, he recognized Scarlett's scribbled handwriting. She'd written it when she'd thought he wasn't home. He hadn't spotted it when they walked in.

Jesse—I don't have your current cell phone number, but I'm taking a chance that you still keep this place. I need your help, as quick as possible. Please call me. She'd underlined "please" several times. *I know a lot has happened between us, and most of it's my fault. But I find myself in need of a partner again, and you're the only one I trust. I'll think about how sad that is later. —Scarlett*

Jesse found himself smiling faintly. He had resented Scarlett and the Old World for manipulating him into those cases, and he'd hated himself for getting sucked into the excitement and the danger. He still had nightmares about destroying the bodies of Henry Remus's victims, denying their families the closure that came with burying the dead. Jesse had violated so many laws that it had felt like too much of a betrayal to put on his badge again. And yes, he did sort of blame Scarlett for that. How could he not? She had broken his heart in so many ways.

He moved his finger, and saw a small postscript near the bottom of the sheet, just above the tabs. *P.S.: I understand if you don't want to get sucked back in. You're free now. But why did we go through all that if not to do some good?*

Jesse looked up, around the pathetic living room, and experienced a strange sense of vertigo—followed by an epiphany.

She was so right.

A million years ago, he had become a cop so he could help people. Then Dashiell and the others had taken his feelings for Scarlett and his desire to minimize collateral damage to the public, and they'd twisted him into breaking laws. But he wasn't a cop anymore. And he wasn't in love with Scarlett. There was nothing left for them to manipulate him with, no career left to compromise. He *was* free. And what was the point of all that turmoil if he wasn't going to do anything with his freedom? Scarlett was offering him a chance to save a life again, and she wasn't threatening or extorting him to do it. So why not *choose* to help her save Molly?

What the hell else was he doing?

He felt like he'd just woken up from a restless sleep. Jesse dropped the paper and started running.

He went straight for the stairs, which were generally a lot faster than taking the old elevator, and bounded through the exterior door only a few seconds after Scarlett. She was up the street, her head down, the bargest glued to her side.

Then he saw the SUV. Jesse's guts twisted with fear as the back window slowly lowered. "Scarlett!" he shouted.

She turned, looking surprised, and the first bullet exploded the sleeve of her jacket, causing her to cry out.

By then Shadow was on her, moving so fast that Jesse couldn't see what was happening. He thought Shadow had knocked her to the ground, but a metal trash can was blocking his line of vision. In nearly the same moment, there were two more rifle shots, and Jesse bolted forward, his hand on his hip—and then he remembered he wasn't carrying. His personal weapon was locked in a safe in his bedroom, probably gathering dust.

To his surprise, the SUV driver began to back up quickly, and Jesse realized too late that they were coming for him too. He dropped down as a round whistled over his head. It impacted the glass door and kept going, embedding itself into the wall of mailboxes in the lobby. A second shot ricocheted off the steps above him, and Jesse felt a sudden sting on his face as a tiny piece of shrapnel embedded in his cheek.

He heard tires squeal as the SUV tore down the street. Jesse stumbled to his feet and raced the twenty yards to Scarlett, who was lying on the sidewalk with blood on one side, groaning quietly. The bargest was lying beside her, panting shallowly.

He dropped to his knees next to Scarlett. "How bad? How bad?" he blurted, his hands running over her, searching for the source of the bleeding. "Scarlett?" He touched her cheek, drawing her head toward him. Her eyes were unfocused. "Scar, where are you hit?"

"Arm," she mumbled. She tried to roll herself over, but hissed with pain. "Just my arm. Bonked my head though. Shadow . . ."

"She's alive. I have to roll you, okay?"

She nodded, her jaw clenched, and he carefully eased her body over. Despite that, she gasped, her face going another shade whiter. When he had her settled on her back, Jesse flipped back the side of her jacket, exposing her chest. There was a second, faint bloodstain right above her heart. He bit down on a curse, not wanting to scare her. He needed to get the jacket off, but it didn't give when he pulled at it. "I need to cut this off. Do you have something in the van?" It was only fifteen feet away.

"Jacket pocket," she said through clenched teeth. He thought she meant her keys, but when he reached into the pocket he found a sharp knife, nearly six inches long. It was balanced for throwing. That surprised him, but it wasn't the right moment to ask. He pulled it out and cut back the tight denim.

Jesse sighed with relief. The second wound was just a thin cut from a shard of her phone. "I think the bullet grazed your phone as you were turning, which slowed it down some," he reported. Carefully, he ran the knife down the sleeve of the jacket, causing her to groan again. "Sorry . . . okay. This isn't too bad. It's bleeding a lot, though. You need some stitches." He expected her to protest, but she nodded, her face still dazed. "Do you have a concussion?"

"Don't think so. Check Shadow."

He ignored this, first cutting a slice of the denim to cinch around her arm. She screamed when he pulled it tight, involuntary tears running down her grit-smeared cheeks. "Shadow," she insisted, panting.

Jesse finally turned toward the bargest, noticing that there was absolutely no blood near her. She was lying on her side, her enormous chest heaving. He began to touch her, but stopped as he saw the two small bald patches to the right of her spine, where her fur had been blown off. "Oh, wow," he said softly.

"How is she?"

"I think her ribs are cracked," he said in an awed voice. Getting shot at such close range should have turned her into meat rain. He had known in theory that she was tough, but seeing it in action was surreal.

"She'll—" Scarlett began, but she was interrupted by the first scream of sirens, still a distance away. One of the neighbors must have called the police. Scarlett started to struggle to her feet. "We've got to go."

"No!" he rested his hands on her shoulders, and that light contact alone was enough to force her back down. "You need an ambulance. That arm needs stitches."

"Jesse, we'll lose *hours*—"

"I mean it," he said firmly. "You want my help, you've got it. But that's my condition."

She met his eyes for an endless second before nodding. "Fine." She propped herself on her good elbow, looking around like she was mentally calculating the evidence dispersal. "You've got to get Shadow out of here, though. They can't find her."

"What will you tell the police?"

"That I came to see you, but you weren't home. Someone tried to shoot me as I left."

The sirens were getting close now. "They might check your van. Are they gonna find anything incriminating?"

She had to be in a lot of pain, but she gave him a skeptical look. "Not without a blowtorch. Shadow, come!"

Hearing her mistress's voice, the bargest struggled to her feet. "Go with Jesse," Scarlett instructed. "He'll bring you to me in just a little while."

The bargest gave her a mournful look, but began to trot gingerly toward Jesse. Already she was shaking off the effects of the gunshot.

"Take the key out of my back pocket," Scarlett said to Jesse. "I don't want anything to happen to it." She leaned onto one side, wincing, and Jesse awkwardly dipped in her pocket for the little safety deposit key.

"I'll find you at the hospital," he promised, climbing to his feet. She just nodded weakly, then let her head rest on the ground.

At the corner, Jesse herded Shadow next to the building, peeking around to keep an eye on Scarlett until the ambulance came. When she was loaded into the back and the doors closed behind her, Jesse finally relaxed and turned toward the bargest, who sat watching him expectantly. "She's going to be fine," he promised. Jesse didn't really know how much of human language Shadow understood, but it was definitely more than the average dog. "They'll bandage her arm," he added, touching his own sleeve, "and then we'll meet up with her. Okay?"

Shadow thumped her clubbed tail, and Jesse nodded to himself. "Okay. Good."

He led Shadow back up to the apartment so he could retrieve his personal handgun, his cell phone, and his jacket. He found an old leash in the back of a closet, left over from walking his parents' dog, Max. Shadow accepted the leash graciously, though she didn't look thrilled about it. Now that they were away from Scarlett's radius, Shadow's healing had sped up, and even the bald patches in her fur filled in.

Then they were in Jesse's car, pulling out into traffic—and Jesse realized he had no idea where to go. He needed to get away from the apartment in case the police stopped by, but he probably had at least a couple of hours to kill before Scarlett was released from the hospital. He didn't know what he could do that might help prove Molly's innocence.

Or did he? Jesse had one impartial contact in the Old World. And she happened to owe him a favor.

Jesse pulled over at a 7-Eleven and checked the dashboard clock. It was well after midnight in Colorado now, but he was betting she'd still be up. Allison Luther hadn't seemed like the kind of person who slept much, anyway. Jesse had known a lot of ex-soldiers like that.

Lex, as she preferred to be called, was an Army veteran who had lost her sister Sam to a serial killer—or at least, that was the official story. Although Lex and her family were originally from Boulder, Sam had been killed in Los Angeles, by the nova wolf, Henry Remus. Jesse had been assigned to the case, and met Lex when she came to look for Sam's killer. It was only later that Lex learned that she had witchblood, and her family line came with a particular specialty: power over the boundary between life and death. Lex was powerful, and Jesse knew she could contact her dead sister, among other abilities. Jesse had heard rumors, but it was time to confirm them.

Sure enough, she picked up on the second ring. "Cruz?" she said warily. "What happened?"

"Hello to you too," he said, a little amused. "But you're right, I've got a problem. Well, a question."

There was just the slightest pause, and then she said, "I haven't forgotten what you did when I had my own 'problem.' How can I help?"

"Scarlett told me once that boundary witches can press vampires," he began. "Is it true?"

"Yes," she said matter-of-factly.

"Could you press them into killing someone else? A human?"

Another hesitation. "What's going on, Cruz?"

"I'll tell you, but please answer the question first."

"Okay . . . well, you've probably heard that vampires can't press people to do anything too far outside their comfort zone," she said. "A vampire could press someone to make out with a stranger, but they couldn't make you, say, fall permanently in love, or ax-murder your parents or anything like that. But that's because those things are outside of your basic nature."

"And killing humans is part of a vampire's nature?"

"Well, yeah. At least some of them. So in theory, I think a boundary witch could get a vampire to kill a human."

"Even someone they cared about?"

Lex blew out a breath. "Yeah, probably. If the witch was strong enough."

"Is it something you could do?"

There was a pause. When she replied her voice was stiff. "Are you accusing me of something, Cruz?"

"No, no," he hurried to say. "But there's a vampire here who claims she was forced to kill a bunch of women. She says she didn't want to, she actually liked these girls, but she was sort of . . . compelled to do it. Is that possible?"

"Hmm." Jesse gave her a moment to think it over, idly reaching so he could scratch Shadow beneath her collar. The bargest licked his hand appreciatively. "Obviously I've never done that," Lex said at last. "But yeah, I think I could. I'm stronger than most, though."

"Okay. Thanks, Lex."

"Wait! If there's a rogue boundary witch running around LA, I should probably know about it. Can you keep me updated?"

He promised to call her back when he knew more, and hung up the phone feeling a familiar rush of internal satisfaction. He'd fit a piece into the puzzle. He could now explain to Scarlett and Molly how it was possible that Molly had been forced.

Then his elation faded. A rogue boundary witch running around LA. That couldn't be good. But what would she have against Molly?

Chapter 10

As expected, the emergency room trip took frickin' forever.

The paramedics got the bleeding under control, thanks to Jesse's tourniquet, and the ER doc gave me a local and some stitches. He offered me a prescription for oxycodone, but I declined. I needed to be sharp when I got out of there. The whole time he was working on me the nurses kept asking me who they could call, but I just shook my head, claiming I didn't have any phone numbers memorized and I would be fine. Luckily, we weren't at the hospital where my brother worked. If I'd bumped into him, I *never* would have gotten out of there.

The moment after the last stitch went in, two uniformed police officers shouldered their way past the doctor to ask me questions. I kept it very simple: I had stopped by to check on my friend, who was having a hard time since his divorce. He wasn't home, but while I was walking back to my van someone rolled down a window and shot me. I told the police I didn't have any enemies and that it was probably just a random thing.

Under other circumstances, they might have let it go at that, but they were suspicious about the tourniquet on my arm. I considered saying that I'd done it myself, but realized that whichever neighbor had called the police may have seen Jesse with me. So I said it was some Good Samaritan out with his dog, and I couldn't remember what he looked like.

The hardest part of the conversation was maintaining the right amount of shock and fear: I wanted to look as upset as a victim of random gun violence should, but not so upset that I seemed like I was overdoing it. I also wanted the cops to drop the whole investigation, so I had to imply that it was probably just random kids shooting guns—without seeming like I was implying it. Trying to walk that fine line after blood loss proved to be exhausting, and in the end I didn't need to work very hard to look shocked or confused.

The cops still insisted on going through a bunch of background on me: my job, my boyfriend, my regular activities. They were clearly hoping I'd reveal secret connections to the mob or a gang, but the joke was on them. My cover story was airtight. Dashiell had made sure of that. On paper, I was a freelance housecleaner who lived with her bartender boyfriend in San Marino. I had a perfect tax history, thanks to Hayne's CPA brother, plus health insurance, good credit, and my own vehicle. Anyone who dug into my records would get the image of a twenty-something with all her shit together.

That was a little hilarious to me, all things considered, but it worked. After more than two hours of me repeating the same story consistently, the police finally gave up. I'd like to think that I wore them down with my personality.

When Jesse finally walked in, I was in the middle of bartering with a nurse named Rochelle, who wanted me to sign a form absolving the hospital of responsibility when I walked out. "I'll sign the AMA," I insisted, "as soon as you give me some scrubs to wear out of here."

"Nuh-uh. Those are hospital property," she countered.

"But the people *at* the hospital are the ones who shredded my other clothes!"

"Here," Jesse interrupted, tossing me a plastic bag with a logo I didn't recognize. "I got you these while I was waiting."

"Yes!" I did a fist pump with my uninjured arm. "How's my dog?"

"She's fine."

Rochelle "hmph'ed" and turned to Jesse, shaking a finger in my general direction. "She still needs to sign the paperwork before she walks out of here!"

"Ma'am," he said, busting out his thousand-watt smile, "I'm sure Scarlett would be happy to do that right away. If you can go get the papers, I promise I won't let her leave without signing."

Even when he's scruffy and bedraggled, few females can resist Jesse's powers of hotness. I almost felt sorry for Rochelle. "All right then," she mumbled. "Be right back." She blushed her way out of the room.

I made a face at her back and reached for the bag. "Where did you find clothes at this hour?"

He shrugged. "My mom knows the woman who owns one of those shops on Melrose. They're open till eleven, anyway, so she didn't mind hanging out a little longer."

I dumped the shopping bag out on my lap. Inside were a pair of black ponte pants, a simple blue T-shirt, and a sports bra. At the bottom of the pile there was also an olive-green canvas jacket with pockets. Lots of pockets. It looked a lot like a jacket I used to own years ago, one of my all-time favorite clothing items. I'd had to burn it after a werewolf fight. "Oooh, Jesse!"

"I wasn't sure about your exact size, so I went for mediums."

I touched the material. It looked like leather, but was actually waxed cotton, which made it waterproof. If—okay, when—I got blood on it, I could just hose it off. "It's awesome." I flipped over the price tag and dropped the jacket like it had bitten me. "Ack! Okay, I can't afford this, but I'll pay you back for the shirt and pants." Regretfully, I began rolling the jacket back into the bag.

Jesse put a hand on mine, then lifted it away quickly. "Keep it. Consider them belated birthday presents."

I raised my eyes to meet his. "Jesse . . ."

"Scarlett," he said back, mimicking me. "Trust me, I can afford it."

Oh. Right. The book. "Thank you!" I said, resisting the strong urge to hug the jacket.

"I almost forgot." He dug in the pocket of his leather jacket and handed me a much smaller bag with a Target logo. "New phone."

"Nice!"

I dumped it out too. A pretty basic model, but it would have everything I needed. The packaging was open—Jesse had been charging it in the car. I could get Abigail Hayne to transfer all my information over to the new phone. It wasn't the first time—I was hard on what little technology I bothered to use.

"How's your arm?" Jesse asked.

"Sore, but I can move it."

"Do you want me to get Rochelle to help you get dressed?"

"You mean the president of my fan club? No thank you." I twirled my finger in the air, and Jesse took the cue to turn around. I pulled on the pants first, which made my arm ache a little but was otherwise fine.

"I think I figured out how the bad guy—or bad guys—made Molly kill her friends," he said, facing the wall.

"How?" I dropped the hospital gown—they'd let me keep my underwear, thank goodness—and stuck the sports bra over my head.

"A boundary witch could have pressed her."

Oh my God, I was a moron. I jerked the sports bra down too quickly, letting out an involuntary whimper as the material scraped against my stitches.

"Scarlett?" Jesse said, concerned.

"I'm fine." But my voice came out as more of a squeak. "Just give me a second."

"Sure."

My arm hurt, but I also wanted to smack my head against the wall. Of *course* Molly had been pressed by a boundary witch. How had I not thought of that? I mean, I'd never actually seen Jesse's friend Lex do her thing, but I'd heard somewhere that boundary witches could press vampires. I was an idiot.

This mental berating went on for a while. I was also very focused on getting the T-shirt over my stitches, so I didn't realize Jesse had turned on the ancient mounted television until I heard a crisp, news-anchor voice say, "Thankfully, the fire was contained before it reached the buildings on either side."

I whirled around with my arms still in the air, the shirt stuck on my elbows. The news team camera was fixed on the smoking ruins of the building I'd been in only a few hours earlier.

The fire department had managed to get the flames out before the whole place was cremated, but all that was left were some waist-high walls that ended in charred tips. "Fire department investigators have recovered the bodies of eight young women who were likely residents of the house," the reporter announced.

Jesse and I looked at each other. I'd completely forgotten that my arm and one elbow were stuck in a shirt that was partially over my face. "Did she just say eight?" I demanded. "There were twelve. I *counted*." My voice came out more defensive than I'd intended.

"Maybe they haven't recovered the others yet," Jesse suggested.

But the reporter went on. "There is no word yet about the other five women who were residents of this building, but Los Angeles Fire Department investigators have found accelerants which suggest those remains were completely incinerated."

Like hell. Molly was one of the missing, but what the hell had happened to the other four?

Chapter 11

The news anchor droned on, but I didn't hear her. My brain was whir-
ring. "We gotta go," I told Jesse.

He strode over to me, placed one hand very lightly over my wound
to protect the stitches, and yanked the T-shirt down over my head.

"Thanks." My boots were fine—the cops had even let me keep my
knives, which were just small enough to be legal. I pulled on the boots,
stuck a knife in each holster, and followed Jesse out the door. I didn't
even think about the long-suffering nurse until we had left the building. Poor Rochelle.

The second we were in the parking garage, I started dialing numbers
in the disposable phone. "Who are you calling?" Jesse asked.

"Remember when the nova wolf was running around, and a couple
of the werewolves betrayed the pack?" I asked, not waiting for him to
answer. "We set up a couple of protocols after that. I'm activating one
now."

Before I could explain further, a female voice answered the phone.
"This is Kirsten," she said, her voice guarded. Right, she wouldn't recognize my number.

"It's me," I replied. "I was wondering if you're free for a drink at
our usual place."

There was a long pause, and then: "Really?"

"Yes. Thirty minutes?"

"See you there."

We reached Jesse's sedan, and a very excited bargest spent several minutes licking me and sniffing the stitches on my arm. I checked her ribs, but she seemed completely fine now, probably thanks to our hours-long separation. The bargest spell that had been performed on Shadow—a spell that required a *goddamned human sacrifice*, like something out of a fairy tale—was complex and layered. Being a null meant I affected the parts of it that required active magic: Shadow's intense drive to hunt (and eventually kill) werewolves, for example, and her accelerated healing. If she was near me, she healed at normal canine speed, and her temperament was similar to that of any huge dog.

However, the spell also involved physiological changes that were too permanent to be nullified: her decelerated aging, her unnatural intelligence, and her armor-like skin. Those parts of the bargest spell were irreparable alterations to her very DNA, which meant magic was no longer actively involved.

I patted the furry parts of her back and told her she was a good dog-monster until she seemed pacified. Then I asked Jesse to head for Chinatown. While he drove, I called Dashiell and repeated the same phrase. He was obviously still upset with me, but we'd set up the protocols for a reason, and he couldn't exactly refuse.

My last call was to Hair of the Dog, the bar owned by the alpha werewolf, Will. It was also the bar where Eli worked, which was why I had put it off until last. I still didn't want to talk to Eli, but Will often left his cell in his desk drawer while he worked. Everyone worth talking to knew to call the bar's landline.

I checked my watch. It was after closing, but Will would still be there. Probably Eli, too. I gritted my teeth and dialed.

Luck was with me—Will answered the phone himself. I gave him the same rehearsed line I'd given the others, got the exact same pause, followed by reluctant agreement. "You know," he said before he hung up, "your boyfriend has been worried about you. He's been texting you every five minutes." There was just the slightest hint of irritation in his voice. Will was an understanding boss, but he had his limits.

"I lost my phone." Not technically true, but learning that my phone had been exploded by a bullet wouldn't exactly reassure Eli.

"Do you want to talk to him?"

Did I? Next to me, Jesse was studiously pretending he couldn't hear what I was saying. This wasn't really the time to get into a fight. "Could you just let him know that I'm fine? I'll try to call him later."

"Fine."

There is a shitty little Ramada in Chinatown that serves as a surprisingly suitable meeting place for the Old World leaders. Security is lax, with zero video cameras, and most of the hotel guests are tourists who don't speak English well enough to find a better place to stay. Best of all, no one in the Old World goes there, stays there, or works there. And there's free coffee in the lobby 24/7.

Jesse handed me a cup as we wandered over to the grouping of chairs in the threadbare lobby. There were two couches and two armchairs, all made primarily of polyester, all grouped around a very large coffee table covered in stained Formica. The lights had been dimmed, and although we were technically in view of the front desk, there was no one actually manning it. If you listened hard, you could hear someone snoring from an adjacent room in the back.

I chose the chair at the head of the seating area, the one that faced the entrance. Jesse sat down to my right, and Shadow curled up over my feet. Before we got out of the car, I had dressed her in the little cape that identified her as a service dog, which got her access to all public spaces. In the US people aren't legally allowed to ask me why I need a service animal, but just in case, I carry a signed affidavit from a neurologist, stating that I need Shadow for a seizure disorder. Dashiell had arranged it for me. It's amazing what you can get away with when you have mind control abilities.

We waited quietly, sipping the stale coffee and watching the door. Kirsten was the first to arrive, giving both of us a tight nod before taking a seat, arms folded over her chest. A slender Swedish blonde in a long dress and denim jacket, Kirsten was looking stormy, and I couldn't blame her. When you traffic in magic, promises are a powerful thing. The murder of a Friend of the Witches, especially by a member of the Old World, was the equivalent of Kirsten breaking a promise.

"Why is Jesse here?" Kirsten asked.

"Because I asked him to help," I said simply. "And because he has a connection with a boundary witch in Wyoming."

"Colorado," Jesse corrected me. I waved a hand, conceding.

Kirsten's eyes widened. "Allison Luther?"

Jesse nodded, but didn't look surprised that Kirsten knew the name. Interesting. "After Jesse talked to her earlier, we've got a theory."

"This better not be some sort of diversion while you break Molly out of my house," Dashiell warned as he entered my radius and strode over to us. I hadn't heard him approach, but then I wouldn't. Will was standing right behind him, looking much more affable, his hands jammed in his pants pockets. "Beatrice has been practicing with her shotgun. I told her to shoot anyone who shows up." I swallowed. Dashiell's wife, Beatrice, was one of the few vampires who seemed to sort of like me, but I had no doubt that she'd shoot me if Dashiell told her it was necessary.

"Dashiell!" Kirsten's voice was more shocked than admonishing, which is probably why she got away with the reprimand. "Scarlett wouldn't do that."

"Wouldn't she?" Dashiell's hooded eyes never left me. "Did she tell you she took Shadow out of the county?"

Tattletale, I thought, but didn't have the nerve to say. "The fastest way to do this is if you let me tell you everything I know from tonight, and then you can yell at me afterward," I told them.

"That sounds fair," Will said, to break the tension.

I walked them through the whole night, starting with the girl showing up at Eli's art fair. I may have glossed over the part where I lied to Eli, and I left the question of whether or not Molly had forced me to drive her to Thousand Oaks open to interpretation, but I didn't leave out any other details.

They all listened without interrupting, even Dashiell, until I got to the part about seeing the news at the hospital. "And that's when I called," I finished.

Will was looking at Dashiell. "You should tell them," he said, his voice calm.

Jesse, Kirsten, and I all turned to the vampire. "I received a text message," he said, sounding a little begrudging. "From Molly. Asking me to come to the house."

"What time?" I asked.

He pulled out his phone and scrolled through his messages. "Five thirty-eight," he said after a moment.

I thought fast. "That was before I arrived at the house," I said slowly. "But Molly didn't have her phone. She'd lost it, she said." I looked back at Dashiell. "Did you come?"

He gave me a tight nod. "But I was delayed. By the time I arrived, the fire department was pulling up. I took a quick look in the windows and saw eight corpses, still burning." He gave an artful shrug. "Then Will called me to say Scarlett wasn't answering her phone. I put two and two together."

Well, that explained how Dashiell had gotten to the storage facility so quickly. But it didn't explain the missing bodies. "I checked every one of those girls' pulses myself," I insisted. "There were twelve, no question."

"We believe you, Scarlett," Will said, and Kirsten nodded. I didn't dare look at Dashiell.

Jesse spoke, keeping his voice soft. "So someone wanted Dashiell to walk in on Molly with eight dead bodies. Why?"

"Because she was supposed to be even more out of it than she was when I got there," I guessed. "Whoever did this wanted you"—I looked at Dashiell—"to arrive at the house and find Molly covered in blood, with eight dead girls. You would have hauled her out of there and called me from the car to come clean up the mess."

Dashiell gave this a grudging nod. It was *exactly* what he would have done. I went on. "No one would have ever guessed the other four girls were there. Molly wasn't supposed to remember that part, just like she wasn't supposed to figure out a way to contact me without her phone. But I was there, and it screwed things up."

"We're getting ahead of ourselves," Will interrupted. His eyes were focused intently on me. "You're saying that Molly *did* kill these girls?"

"Yes. But she was pressed."

I was expecting a big reaction, and they didn't disappoint. Dashiell's eyes bulged with surprise, and Will actually let out sort of a masculine gasp. Only Kirsten seemed to take this in stride, nodding as if it made perfect sense. I turned toward her. "I take it you've seen that before?"

"I've met boundary witches before," she corrected, "including Allison Luther, a few years back. I've never actually seen a vampire get pressed, but I'm aware of the possibility."

I glanced toward Dashiell, raising my eyebrows a little. "I've . . . heard of it too," he admitted. For the first time he looked more pensive than angry. I'd thrown a wrench into his righteous fury. "A very long time ago. But the only boundary witches I've met in my life were too weak to truly affect vampires."

Will was shaking his head. "This is all new to me," he said frankly. "What exactly is a boundary witch?"

I expected Kirsten to answer, but Jesse was the one who spoke. "A witch who specializes in the boundary between life and death," he said. "Death magic. They have a sort of connection to vampires, which allows the stronger witches to actually *press* a vampire."

"A less powerful vampire," Dashiell interjected.

I sipped my coffee, giving them all a minute to absorb it. Finally Dashiell nodded to me, looking sobered. "Go on with your theory," he said. For the first time, I felt like he was really listening.

"Thank you. Here's what I think happened. The boundary witch's press was starting to wear off, or Molly was able to fight it, just a little. She grabbed a kid off the street, Britt, and sent her to get me." This meant that Molly had been keeping tabs on me, which was sort of sweet. "The bad guy must have been close enough to see her do it, but for some reason he didn't stop Britt from leaving. Maybe there were too many people around."

"Britt said she was going to a party, right?" Jesse interjected. "If there were a bunch of college kids in the street when Molly grabbed her . . ."

"Right. Anyway, they couldn't have known what was in the note Molly sent. So instead of taking the girls right then, they made the decision to wait until either Dashiell or I arrived."

"But they didn't hurt you," Kirsten said, a question in her voice.

"No, they didn't," I assured her.

Jesse picked up the story. "My guess is that once Scarlett got there, they figured out who she is—or, more to the point, *what* she is. Is it pretty common knowledge that Scarlett is a null, and she works with you guys?" We all nodded. Anyone in the LA Old World would know about me. Jesse continued, "Maybe they didn't want to fight her just then. My guess is that they didn't have guns with them at the time." Most people in the Old World don't bother with firearms, which Jesse knew.

"But how did they get four girls out of there without you seeing?" Will asked.

"Two possibilities." I ticked them off on my fingers. "If they waited right by the back door for us to leave, they could have snuck them out the back before the fire spread. Or, they might have put the fire out—there was an extinguisher in the kitchen—taken the girls, and restarted the fire. That seems less likely."

"Either way, Scarlett knew how many bodies she'd seen," Jesse said, jumping in again. "So they had to come after her again. They followed her to me, and saw an opportunity to take a shot at Scarlett before she could tell anyone about the number of girls."

"Without Scarlett, Molly looks responsible for all of it," Dashiell said thoughtfully.

"Exactly," Jesse said. "Scar is the only person who can blow the official story."

"Look," I began again. "If I'm right, you have a boundary witch running around LA right now, one who's strong enough to press vampires. But she can't be working alone. Setting aside the fact that she would have to move four adult bodies in a few seconds, I can only think of one reason for her to have stolen those women."

Kirsten paled, and Will went quiet. Dashiell said, "Because they're being turned into vampires."

Chapter 12

It was strange seeing the Old World leaders again, especially in a cheap hotel lobby. Jesse had sort of built them up in his head as the shapers of his destiny, but really, they were just tired-looking people struggling to represent their respective tribes. Even Dashiell didn't look as scary as Jesse remembered, although he supposed it helped that the three of them were all in Scarlett's presence at the moment.

Dashiell's declaration that the missing girls were likely being turned into vampires had silenced the group for a moment. Will and Dashiell had nearly identical thoughtful expressions, as they both worked through the implications. Kirsten just looked unnerved. Scarlett waited patiently, giving them time to absorb it. That surprised Jesse a little, but it was a smart move.

Dashiell finally broke the silence. "So we're talking about a boundary witch and a vampire working together," he said in a hushed voice. "The vampire must have fed those four girls his blood a day beforehand, say by pressing them . . ."

"Then the boundary witch was waiting for Molly when she woke up for the night," Kirsten finished.

Scarlett was nodding. "The mystery vampire probably even helped Molly press the girls to stay still, since I don't think she could have done all twelve at once by herself. My guess is that the bad guys never intended to take all twelve," she added. "They wanted Molly to take the fall for some of it."

"It's kind of slick, if you think about it," Will said mildly.

Jesse was inclined to agree, but Kirsten glared at the alpha werewolf. "Slick? Think about all the families. One way or another, those girls are never coming home."

Will raised his hands, defensive. "I wasn't trying to be glib, Kirsten. But you almost have to admire it, from a strategic perspective. Molly is framed and the girls are turned, all in one move. While we're already distracted by the Trials."

Kirsten just glared at him and turned to Scarlett. "Did they know about Louisa?" she demanded. "That she was a Friend?"

"I honestly don't know. But I wouldn't be surprised if they did. No offense, Kirsten, but killing a Friend of the Witches would make you that much more likely to condemn Molly, and fast."

Kirsten's face clouded over, and Jesse found himself stepping in. "She's right," he said. He looked at the three Old World leaders. "Anyone can see that the quickest way to distract you guys is to threaten one of your own. Or threaten exposure," he added, looking at Dashiell.

"That's not the only threat, I'm afraid," Dashiell said. "If there's a powerful boundary witch running around our city, she can press any of my vampires."

Scarlett was staring at him. "So you believe me?" she said.

He nodded. "I'm still not happy about how you handled this, but yes. I believe you about the girls."

"Then you should let Molly go," she pushed. "It wasn't her fault. She couldn't stop herself."

Dashiell got up and wandered a few feet away, toward the coffee machine. He filled a Styrofoam cup, returned to his seat, and took a tiny sip, making a face. The expression was so incongruous with his usual demeanor that Jesse and Scarlett both stared at him. "Good heavens," he sputtered. "I do not remember coffee tasting like this."

Scarlett looked determined to stay on track. "Molly *is* okay, isn't she?"

"Of course." He gave her an injured look. "I wouldn't kill her without a trial, not even if she had committed these murders with a song in her heart."

"Then you need to let her go," Scarlett insisted. "She didn't do this."

"He can't," Will said abruptly. Everyone turned to look at him. "I'm sorry, Scarlett, but right now, the people who did this think they've won. They're probably holed up somewhere within the city limits, waiting for the girls to turn before they move them." He looked at Dashiell. "Am I right?"

The vampire nodded. "It's difficult to move vampires," he said. "But much harder to move a lot of corpses whose faces are all over the news."

Will turned back to the null. "So we've got a few days before they can flee town. During that time, they need to think that they've won, which means Molly has to stay where she is."

Scarlett looked unconvinced. She couldn't see the big picture while her friend was in danger. "If they know you're on to them, they can find another way to distract you," Jesse said quietly. "Like eating people in the middle of Hollywood Boulevard."

"It's much worse than that, actually," Dashiell said. His voice was as calm as ever, but his face had darkened. "The vampire is dangerous to humans, of course, and to the weaker members of our community. But a boundary witch could make my own vampires do anything, including killing one of us."

That little revelation struck Jesse like a gut punch, but Scarlett wouldn't be deterred. "If you're saying we need to leave Molly where she is to buy time," she said slowly, "I understand that. But it's not like she's joined the witness protection program. You're suggesting we put her on trial for murder."

"Think of the damage these two could do in the city," Dashiell pressed. "If the boundary witch can convince any of your witches she's in the right, or if either of them can manipulate the werewolves . . ."

"I love my pack, but it wouldn't be all that difficult to convince some of them to act against one of the other groups," Will said in a subdued voice. "And several of them hate Molly. If you were to let her go, they would think she was getting away with murder."

"Can't you control them?" Scarlett asked, not unkindly.

Will's expression was pensive and a little sad. "At what cost? You saw what happened the last time they lost faith in me. If I give them orders they don't understand, they'll obey me out of fear. And once I open that particular door, it's very difficult to get it closed again."

"Above all," Dashiell said, in the tone that was kind of scary even as a human, "we have to maintain appearances. It's likely that the vampire and boundary witch are watching us for signs that we're not buying Molly as the perpetrator. It has to appear that we condemn Molly, we don't believe Scarlett, and the Trials are proceeding just as planned."

Jesse's eyes immediately turned to Scarlett, who was sitting up straighter in her chair. "At what cost?" she said, echoing Will's words. Her eyes were narrowed at the vampire. "How far are you gonna let this go?"

"Hang on," Will said. He pointed to Kirsten, Dashiell, and himself. "*We* need to keep up appearances," he said. "But the two of you don't. Scarlett needs to be at the table when the Trials begin, but no one is monitoring her activities until then."

"Or yours," Dashiell said, making eye contact with Jesse. "If you find the people doing this, we can expose them."

Scarlett and Kirsten began talking at the same time, but Jesse held Dashiell's gaze. "You want me to work for you?" he said, barely managing to keep his tone civil. "Because that's worked out so well in the past."

"You're damn right it has," Dashiell countered. "Your work with Scarlett has saved lives, both within the Old World and without. Just because we don't see eye to eye doesn't mean I underestimate your value as an investigator."

Now it was Jesse who stood up and paced away from the group. Despite his resolution to help Molly, he had a hard time with the idea of working for Dashiell and the others in any sort of official capacity. They hadn't betrayed him, exactly, but he'd lost *everything* the last time. It was hard not to feel like Charlie Brown with the football.

Scarlett stood up and came over to him. The others could probably still hear them, but they had the grace to start a quiet conversation amongst themselves, giving Jesse and Scarlett the semblance of privacy.

She touched his arm. "What's wrong?"

Jesse blew out a breath. "This just got real for me, I guess."

She studied his face. "Nothing has changed," she said after a moment. "You're still making a decision to help someone who can't help herself. It's just officially sanctioned." She gestured back toward the group. "Look, the rest of them see Molly as collateral damage—if she lives, fine. If she dies, fine. I could really use another person who cares about saving a life."

"I don't know, Scar."

"Jesse, no one expects you to do this for free. What do you want? Money? I'm sure Dashiell could—"

"I don't need money," he interrupted, holding up a hand. "I've already cashed in on this Old World shit once; I've got no desire to do it again."

She nodded, patient. "Okay. So what do you want?"

What *did* he want? "Scarlett, until a few hours ago I was going for the world record in pajama sulking. I have no idea what I want."

Her eyes probed him. "A job?"

Jesse looked up sharply. Scarlett hurried to add, "Hey, it's just you and me here. You can admit that you absolutely love this shit."

He closed his eyes, feeling like she'd struck him. He *had* loved working Old World cases in the past. They were complicated, exciting, and he'd always played an active role—so much better than doing the dull grunt work so senior detectives could take the credit. He'd been important, and that was intoxicating. Who *didn't* want to be important at their job?

Jesse opened his eyes. "You're right, I loved it," he said. "But I didn't love what it did to me."

"I will not ask you to help me destroy any bodies," she said firmly. "I won't ask you to hurt anyone unless it's to save lives. And I promise that when we find the people who did this, you will get a say in how they are punished."

He gave her a skeptical look. "Can you really promise that?"

Scarlett drew herself up to her full height. "I'm not a naive kid anymore, Jesse. If those are your conditions, let's go back and pitch them. I've got your back." She reached over and squeezed his hand. It wasn't a romantic gesture, but Jesse felt his pulse trip anyway, like his body was just hardwired to react to her.

They went back to the others, who gave no sign that they'd overheard anything. As Scarlett listed Jesse's conditions they all nodded passively, until she got to the last part. "If Jesse helps me find these guys, he deserves the right to have a vote in what happens to them." Before anyone could respond, she added, "Which means there will be five of us. The vote can't be split."

The three leaders all lifted their eyebrows at the same time, which was a little funny, but Jesse was too startled to enjoy it. He'd thought she would ask that he could address the four of them before they did anything; he hadn't expected her to actually push for him to *vote*.

But Kirsten, Will, and Dashiell all looked at each other, and he could practically read their thoughts: even with Jesse getting a vote, it would be the three of them against him and Scarlett. The odds looked good for the Old World.

"You have a deal," Dashiell said, holding out his hand. Jesse took it, surprised. Dashiell had never initiated a handshake before.

"What do you need from us?"

"Access to Molly," Scarlett said promptly. "We need to talk to her."

Dashiell was already shaking his head. "Forget Molly. Finding the boundary witch should be your priority."

Jesse could practically see steam coming from Scarlett's ears, so he jumped in. "Molly obviously wasn't chosen at random. We need to ask her about her enemies. Her history."

"I've never let any prisoners have visitors before," Dashiell said. "And there are too many people at the mansion we might not be able to trust. For all we know, the boundary witch pressed one of my people to report any suspicious activity."

He had a point. "What if we came to see her during the day?" he suggested. "Scarlett can wake her up and we can ask questions then."

The vampire looked thoughtful. "Hold on a moment," he said. He pulled out his cell phone and began scrolling through what looked like a calendar app. After a moment, he looked up and said, "I think I can make that work. At noon, just before shift change, there's an hour where only Abigail and Theodore Hayne will be in the house. If you come then, Hayne can bring you to Molly, and Abigail can make sure the video cameras don't record it."

Most of Dashiell's daytime security people were typical employees—well paid, competent, insured employees, but typical nonetheless. The Haynes were different. They were human, but their family had hundreds of years of service to Dashiell. Theodore Hayne was also Kirsten's ex-husband, and when Jesse had met him years earlier, it had been obvious that he still cared for her. The Haynes were fully invested in keeping the LA Old World intact.

Then a new thought occurred to Jesse. "I know you trust their loyalty, but could the Haynes be pressed?" he asked.

Scarlett shook her head. "Hayne was pressed once, years ago. Since then, Kirsten keeps them both in regular witch bags. They're clean."

Jesse nodded. In the past he had used one of the little charm bags that the witches created to protect humans from being affected by magic. The witch bags that protected against vampires couldn't prevent the human from being drained of blood, but it could protect them from being pressed—or turned into a vampire. "Okay. Noon."

"I need to get back to the mansion," Dashiell said, checking his watch. "I've already been away too long. Oh." He stepped toward Jesse, pulling out his wallet. "You may have to buy supplies or gas," he said, and held out a small plastic rectangle. A credit card.

Surprised, Jesse took the card, a teal-blue Visa. "Anything you need," the vampire intoned. "I'm not planning to ask for receipts."

There was no name printed on the card, just a number. "What if someone asks for my ID?" Jesse asked.

Dashiell gave him a broad smile, like he'd told a very funny joke. "Trust me, it's not going to happen."

"Don't forget," Kirsten reminded Scarlett, "you need to be at the Trials by six."

"I can push Molly's trial to the second night," Dashiell added, "but no further. You need to catch these people before then."

Jesse could see Scarlett clenching her jaw, but she nodded. Dashiell hesitated for a heartbeat, and then added, "Above all, we need to look united. Everyone is watching us to see how the Trials unfold. If we cannot catch these people before Molly's sentencing, Scarlett will still need to sit at the table."

Jesse glanced at Scarlett, who was giving him an incredulous look. Before she could do more than open her mouth, Dashiell raised a hand, his face grave. "Yes. Per your usual responsibilities, you'll be there as we execute her."

Chapter 13

"You've got to be fucking kidding me."

At my tone, Shadow lifted her head and looked suspiciously around the room, trying to figure out who may have wronged me. I reached down with one hand and patted her back. Dashiell just looked at me with an infuriatingly implacable expression. Why was I so surprised? Wasn't this just *classic* Dashiell? In fact, years earlier we'd even been in this same position, only I was the one with my head on the chopping block if I couldn't figure out who'd killed three vampires in La Brea Park. I glanced at Will and Kirsten, but they were avoiding my eyes, which stung all over again. For some naive, stupid reason, I had thought we'd made progress.

Apparently some things about the Old World never change. And it made me feel like a helpless little girl . . . which was my cue to say something smartass enough to get in trouble.

"You—" I began, but Jesse grabbed my elbow and began propelling me toward the doorway.

"Forget it, Scar," he muttered under his breath. "It's Chinatown."

I allowed him to pull me out into the parking lot, with Shadow trotting happily along behind us. Whenever I was in a room with the Old World leaders, Shadow's demeanor was more like a Secret Service agent than anything else. She was always glad to get away from the tension.

As soon as we were through the outer door, I shook free and rounded on Jesse. "Okay, first of all, good movie reference, and second, aren't you the guy who was *just* upset about Old World tactics?" I demanded. "They're going to kill her, Jesse!"

"No, they're not," he said, shooting me a devilish grin. "Because we're going to find these assholes first."

"Jesse—"

"I know," he interrupted. "But you're not going to talk Dashiell out of his plan tonight. The more information we find, the better your case will be if it does come down to an argument. Okay?"

I pushed out a breath of frustration and nodded at him. "Okay, fine. What do we do first?"

"Sleep," he said firmly. "Go home and get a few hours."

I blinked. I *was* already exhausted, but it wasn't like we had time to burn. "Why not start now?"

"Because I think you're right. Molly is the key to understanding this whole thing." He dug into his pocket for a moment and held up a small, shiny object. The safety deposit box key. "Maybe literally."

I groaned at the cheesy pun, but my spirits lifted a little. He could be right, and whatever was in that box could help us. "I thought about that, but are we going to be able to get in?" I asked. "I thought safety deposit boxes required like ID and a blood sample and a picture of yourself in a raincoat juggling avocados."

"Your comprehension of the modern banking system *is* impressive," Jesse said solemnly. "But didn't you once tell me that vampires change identities a lot?"

"Yeah . . ."

"So they must have special rules for vampire clients. Maybe you only need a name or an account number or something."

I tilted my head for a second, considering. "I can text Dashiell and ask him. If he doesn't know personally, maybe he could sneak down and ask Molly."

Jesse nodded. "Cool. What time is sunrise?"

Oh, right. We needed to go back after stupid Frederic had left for the night. "Uh, seven. Well, six fifty-eight." In my line of business, it was important to know. I checked my watch. "But it's almost three thirty already, Jesse. By the time I drive home to Marina del Rey and back to Thousand Oaks . . ."

"Good point." He tilted his head for a second, considering. Then a slow smile spread over his face. "Okay, new plan." He held up the teal credit card Dashiell had given him. "We'll get rooms, grab four hours of sleep, and leave here at seven thirty."

"We'll hit rush hour," I protested, but I was weakening. My arm hurt, and the prospect of getting some sleep was tempting as hell.

"We can take the carpool lanes," Jesse wheedled. "Come on. We're not going to be any good to Molly without at least a little sleep."

I allowed him to pull me back toward the front desk to wake up the concierge. Even though we both knew there were no carpool lanes on the 101.

To the surprise of no one, the hotel still had rooms available. I texted Dashiell—I probably could have caught him in the parking lot, but I figured we needed a little break from each other—and arranged for him and Beatrice to go to Jesse's apartment, get my van, and take it back to my place. Ordinarily Dashiell would have lackeys to do this kind of thing, but we weren't sure who we could trust. I thought he was also trying to prove to Jesse, especially, that he wanted to be cooperative. I suspected the whole "boundary witch running amok in LA" thing had freaked him out a little. I couldn't deny taking a little satisfaction from making *him* jump through hoops for *me* this time.

Dashiell even promised to bring my duffel bag back to the hotel and leave it at the front desk. In addition to supplies for a variety of crime scenes, the bag had a change of clothes and some deodorant in one of the side pockets. I felt vulnerable without the White Whale, but since it could be tracked by Dashiell's security team, it would be better to use Jesse's sedan.

The room was cheap and a little threadbare, but it seemed clean enough. Shadow did her customary security check, and when she was satisfied, I pulled back the bedspread and collapsed on top of the sheets. This was a mistake, because I bumped my stitches. I hissed with pain and squirmed around, trying to find a comfortable position. Eventually I realized that my problem wasn't my achy body so much as my humming brain. I looked at Shadow, who was sitting neatly on the floor next to the bed, watching me. She would wait until it looked like I was drifting off, and then go sleep with her back against the door.

"I should just call him, huh?" I said to the bargest. She tilted her head at me, looking more pensive than confused. She glanced at the bed, then back at me, as if to say *you won't be able to sleep until you do.* Sometimes Shadow's sentience unnerves me a little.

I sighed. "Yeah, you're right." Sometimes you just have to go through with the fight ahead of you.

I dialed Eli's cell phone. "Scarlett?" he said immediately.

I blinked. His caller ID wouldn't have recognized the number. "Hi, sorry. Did I wake you?"

"I was waiting up. Are you okay?"

"Yeah. Well, I got a cut on my arm, but I'm fine." I felt a stab of guilt for not calling him earlier, then remembered my reasons. "You told Will about my job tonight."

A pause. "Yeah, I did."

I made sure my voice was very calm. "Why?"

"Because he's my alpha." There was genuine surprise in his voice. "And because the circumstances were weird, and I was worried about you. Besides, it's not like you warned me not to tell anyone."

Because then you would have known it was a big deal, and been in a really awkward position, and ended up telling him anyway. I didn't say it. There was no point.

There was a long pause, and then Eli said angrily, "Is *that* why you haven't called me? You're punishing me because you think I *tattled* on you?"

"You're supposed to be on my side," I said, sounding stubborn even to myself. "You should have trusted me to handle it."

"And what if you couldn't?" he countered. "Admit it, Scar, you've got a track record of getting in over your head. How many times have you risked your life without a thought to your safety?"

I felt my jaw clench. *Oh look, familiar territory.* "My safety is fine. I can take care of myself."

"With what? A couple of knives?" Real anguish was in his voice now. "Have you ever considered how hard it is for me to watch you dive into these jobs, knowing you're so goddamned vulnerable? I can get hit by a subway train and walk away, Scarlett."

"Maybe if it was going really slow. And you'd need recovery time."

He sighed into the phone. "Stop deflecting. My point is that you're just *out there*, and null or not, you are infinitely breakable. Calling Will was my best way to make sure you were okay. That you didn't need my protection."

"I never asked for your protection," I said softly.

We always ended up back here, at this same old impasse. There was a long moment of silence, both of us aware that we were stuck. I was never going to stop fighting for independence, and Eli was never going to stop wanting to protect me. For a moment I felt a wave of despair. How could we ever make this thing work? We loved each other, but what if we were just wired wrong for a relationship?

"This is my job, Eli," I tried again. "This is part of who I am."

"Cleaning up crime scenes is your job," Eli corrected. "Keeping secrets, charging into dangerous situations, putting yourself in harm's way—that's just shit you do. I thought you finally grew out of this adrenaline junkie bullshit, but here we are again."

"That's not fair," I protested. "I'm not an adrenaline junkie, and I can't control when crises come up in the Old World."

"Maybe not. But you can control when you ask for help. Or when you let your boyfriend know you're okay."

I wanted to smack my head against the plywood-looking night-stand. How had this turned around on me so quickly? "This was a unique situation, Eli. Molly's in trouble."

Another long pause. "Is she okay?"

"No. Not yet, anyway. But I can't tell you anything else on the phone."

He took that in stride. Every Old World faction has been drilled on keeping important matters off telephone conversations. "When will you be home?"

"Not tonight. I'm crashing in a hotel so I can look into something with Jesse in the morning. It didn't make sense to drive all the way back."

"You're . . . staying in a hotel with Jesse Cruz?" He sounded more surprised than outraged, and I couldn't really blame him. Eli had never asked me to stop seeing Jesse, and if we'd been able to make a friendship work, Eli would have dealt with that. But he knew Jesse and I hadn't spoken in years, and that had been a relief to him.

"We have separate rooms, of course. Look, I promise I'll explain everything tomorrow."

"When tomorrow? I have the day shift at the bar."

Right. Like everyone else in the Old World, Eli was taking off work the following night for the Vampire Trials. It was the only time that Hair of the Dog would be staffed entirely by humans. "Find me before the first trial starts," I told him.

He wasn't happy that I couldn't promise to see him before then, but I knew he'd forgive me when he heard about my deadline for helping Molly. We talked for a few more minutes about Eli's shift at the bar and the new chunk of driftwood he'd found for his sculpture work. It was late and we were both exhausted, but I think we needed to reassure ourselves that there was still normalcy between us, and we could get back there again. I drifted off with the phone still pressed to my ear.

Chapter 14

When I dragged myself out of the hotel bed at seven the next morning, there was a mark on my cheek from sleeping on the cell phone. My arm hurt, but when I tried moving it around, it already felt better than the night before. When I lifted the bandage on my chest, the small shrapnel wound had scabbed over. I left the bandage off, which made me feel a lot closer to normal.

Still wearing the clothes that Jesse had brought to the hospital, I took Shadow for a one-mile jog so she could do her business. Outside, the LA morning was cool, gray, and hazy—either very smoggy, very overcast, or some combination of the two. I retrieved my duffel bag from the front desk, took a quick shower, and dressed in the clothes from my bag and the new jacket. Shadow and I made it back down to the lobby by 7:40.

Jesse was already waiting, still in the rumpled clothes from the night before. He'd at least showered and shaved, which looked good on him. He wasn't alone, though; I recognized the slightly taller, slightly paler, not quite so handsome man next to him as his brother, Noah. A reusable Whole Foods bag was planted between their feet. There was some kind of black material peeking out.

"You're late," Jesse said neutrally.

I pointed to Shadow. "If she doesn't run for at least a mile every morning, she paces. For hours."

"You went running in those boots?"

I raised an eyebrow, glancing down at my knee-high leather Fryes. "Cupcake, I could pirouette in these boots." I turned to Noah and held out my hand. "Hey, Noah, good to see you again." Noah returned the handshake, though his expression didn't warm. "What brings you here?"

"Errand boy," Noah said. He glanced at Jesse, half-amused, half-annoyed, and nudged the bag at his feet. "My ugly brother asked me to bring you guys your bulletproof vests. Because I have nothing better to do with my time."

"You're on hiatus," Jesse pointed out. Noah was a stunt double, though I had no idea what show he was working on these days. "You were available."

I blinked, trying not to look as surprised as I felt. I'd forgotten about the bulletproof vest, which Jesse had made me wear on our last case together, or maybe the one before it. It was itchy and uncomfortable, but since I'd already been shot at once, I couldn't exactly say we wouldn't need them.

"Are you really not going to tell me why you want these?" Noah asked him.

"I told you, it's for paintball," Jesse answered. "Scarlett and I are big sissies about getting hit by those pellets."

I tried to make my face look very serious as I nodded, but Noah obviously didn't buy it.

"Uh-huh. Well, I guess I should just be grateful that you're out in the world." He turned to me and pretended to tip an imaginary hat. "That looks heavy," he said, pointing at my own bag. "Can I help you carry it?"

"Thanks, I got it."

"I'll walk you out," Noah said emphatically, and I got the impression that he really wanted to talk to me alone. Shit. I decided to get it over with. I held out my plastic room key to Jesse. "You mind turning these in for us? And maybe asking the concierge if there's a place around here with good donuts?"

Jesse rolled his eyes, but he took the card and handed me his car keys. He trotted toward the front desk, and the rest of us headed outside.

The advantage to knowing we were going to leave so early was that Jesse had been able to park his car in one of those metered parking spots that expire at 8 a.m. It was right in front of the building next door to the hotel, a real estate agency with a little decorative picket fence that had been painted with graffiti. Noah didn't speak as we made our way to the sedan, and I opened the back door so Shadow could jump up.

Noah watched the bargest move, shaking his head a little. "I forgot how big she is. And how . . . visually eccentric."

"She is that," I agreed, setting my duffel bag onto the seat beside her.

"Look, Scarlett," Noah began. Yep. He wanted to lecture me. "I really am grateful that you got Jesse to leave the house. And shave."

I took the reusable shopping bag from him and placed it on the car's floor, in front of my duffel bag. "But?" I prompted.

"But I would appreciate if you didn't fuck him over again," he said evenly.

I blinked. Okay, I'd expected some sort of warning, but not *that*. "Come again?"

He waved a hand. "You know what I mean."

"No, I don't. If you've got something to say, Noah, just spit it out."

"Fine." He checked over his shoulder, but the sidewalk was still empty. Turning back to me, he said in a low voice, "Last time you needed my brother to protect you, he had to pull some very shady moves. I'm not an idiot. I know he quit the force because of that. You led him on, and then when everything fell apart for him you were just gone."

Ouch. Shadow was looking back and forth between us, and I could see her hackles beginning to rise, so I gently closed the car door. I pushed out a breath before I responded, trying to tamp down my anger. It was true that I hadn't been there for Jesse, but that was between the two of us. And I had to be careful here—Noah didn't know about the Old World, and he couldn't find out.

"First," I said, trying to keep my voice relatively low, "you're going to need to decide if you're calling me a whore or a bad friend, because if it's both, I'm going to lose my fucking temper. Second, I don't need him to protect me. That's not what this is about."

Noah looked skeptical. "Then why are you dragging him into your shit again?"

"Because he's smart," I snapped. "And good to the core, and he has a different perspective on things which I find refreshingly helpful. And because I like having him around."

"Okay, whatever," Noah said with a dismissive grunt. "I just don't want you using my brother to hurt people, while you stand back and keep your hands clean. Especially if you're not even gonna fuck him."

I recoiled. That last remark was meant to sting, and it did, but I'd be damned if I was going to take shit from someone who had no concept of my life. I checked the sidewalk out of the corner of my eye. Empty except for a couple of homeless people a block down. "Third picket," I said through clenched teeth.

"What?" Noah asked in confusion.

Quick as I could, I bent down and whipped the knife out of my right boot, flinging it at the graffitied fence without even straightening up. I hit the third picket dead center.

While Noah was gaping at the fence, I snaked out one boot and swept his legs out from under him. He landed heavily, just managing to keep his head from cracking on the sidewalk. While his arms were still flailing, I knelt on his chest and held my second knife to his throat, though not very close. Noah went very still.

"*Fucking* aside," I said, my breath coming hard, "if I need someone hurt, I'll do it myself. And if you speak to me like that again, you are going to find out what that feels like."

Eyes wide, Noah raised his hands and nodded. I stood up, slid the knife back into my right boot sheath, and reached down to Noah. He glared at me for a second, but took my hand and let me pull him to his feet. I had to tilt my head up quite a bit to meet his eyes when he stood, but I held the eye contact. We stood there for a silent moment, glaring at each other.

"Hey, Scar, I think you dropped this," came Jesse's amused voice. In my peripheral vision I could see him standing at the picket fence, tugging my knife free. Without taking my eyes off Noah, I reached out a hand and felt Jesse slap the knife handle into it.

"Everything okay, big brother?" Jesse said cheerfully. He'd obviously seen the whole thing, and was enjoying the hell out of the moment.

"Yeah. Fine." Breaking the eye contact—ha, I won the staring contest—Noah straightened his shirt, brushing sidewalk grit off the back of his pants. "I gotta get going. Good luck with your . . . whatever."

"Same to you," Jesse practically chirped. His grin was as wide as I'd ever seen it.

In the car, Jesse silently entered the storage facility's address into his GPS and pulled into traffic. He was waiting for me to speak first, but I could see his lips struggling to contain a smile.

"I'm sorry," I said eventually. "That was childish."

He gave me a little *eh* shrug. "How much of that did you hear?" I asked.

"Refreshingly helpful?"

I slunk lower in my seat. "Shit."

"Yeah." His voice turned serious. "Look. I figured he wanted to do some sort of 'don't hurt my brother' speech, and we might as well get it out of the way. But he took it too far."

My eyes lifted. "Yeah?"

Jesse nodded. "What happened between us back then . . . it hurt me, but I also know it was a hell of a lot more complicated than you using your feminine wiles to *Postman Always Rings Twice* me. That's just insulting to both of us. Noah was out of line, and he deserved to have his ass handed to him."

"Thanks," I mumbled.

Jesse's face lit up again. "But can we talk for a second about how you just knocked down my enormous brother like he was a cardboard cutout? Have you been taking martial arts lessons or something?"

I settled back in my seat. "Nah. That kind of thing takes years and years to master, and I'm too clumsy to be a quick study. Also, lazy."

"So?" His eyebrows were still raised.

I tried to shrug it off, but it was obvious he was curious as hell. And he'd stuck up for me. He deserved a real answer. "I wanted to be able to protect myself better, and everyone underestimates me anyway, so I decided to cheat," I explained. "Instead of learning a whole martial arts discipline, I learned a few tricks. Throwing a knife isn't that complicated; it just requires a little technique and a lot of practice. While I was doing that, I practiced a handful of aikido throws. Plus how to throw a punch and a couple of kicks." I shrugged. "If I ever went up against someone with serious training, I'd get my ass kicked, but most of the time when someone Old World gets in my radius, they don't know how to handle themselves physically. They're used to using werewolf strength or spells or whatever to defend themselves."

"Who taught you?"

I told him about my lessons with Marko, and how I'd had plenty of time to practice because there had been fewer crime scenes to clean up. "Hayne's been showing me some security stuff, too, like how to look for a bomb under your car or how to cuff somebody." I shrugged. "I'm still shit at lockpicking, though."

"I'm impressed, Scarlett," Jesse said. I wanted to laugh it off, but his face was serious. "You've learned a lot in the past three years."

"In some ways," I said, looking out my window. I was thinking of Eli again. "And in some ways I feel dumber than ever."

Chapter 15

We made a quick stop to fortify with coffee and donuts—Shadow ate six—before we got on the freeway toward Thousand Oaks. As predicted, Jesse hit rush hour traffic, but it was much worse going west to east than in our lane. He managed to keep the car at a nice 45 mph clip. Basically an LA miracle.

We rode in silence for a while. Exhaustion from the night before was seeping back into me after my little adrenaline rush, and I was content to stare out the window at the miles of passing freeway. The smog doesn't usually terrorize LA as much in the winter, but it was overcast in a way that seemed to make everything dingy. Or maybe that was my mood talking.

After half an hour, however, Jesse broke the silence. "How much do you know about Molly's history?" he asked.

"Not much," I confessed. "You remember what it was like when I lived with her. She didn't like to talk about the past or future, just the now. It was like we were characters in a sitcom who only came to life when the TV was on."

"She must have given you some kind of impression," he insisted. "Maybe not details, but something."

"I've been thinking about that. I know she was born in Wales, and she sometimes talked about living on a farm in her human life. I got the impression that her family was poor, with lots of kids."

He nodded. "What about after she was turned?"

"She mentioned living in New York and New Orleans." I frowned. "Come to think of it, her movements did strike me as a little weird. Vampires prefer cities, for the most part, and they do move around a lot, but it's usually pretty . . ." I searched for the right word. "Migratory?"

"What do you mean?"

"Say you're turned into a vampire in Seattle," I explained. "You might move down to Portland first, and after a few years go to San Francisco, then San Jose, Los Angeles, San Diego. If you dislike a certain place you might not stay there for long, but vampires usually move in a straight line. It's more efficient, especially since travel is hard for them. You proceed in a line for decades, and then maybe you make a big jump, like to a new continent. But once you get there, you start the line again."

"That makes sense," he said. "So how did Molly break the pattern?"

"If I'm remembering right, she went from Europe to New York, which is typical, but instead of proceeding in a line, she went to New Orleans, then LA."

"Like she was running from something," Jesse remarked.

"I guess."

"Anything else?"

I searched my memory. "She never talked about the vampire who made her, but she gave me the impression that he was a serious asshole. He must've been, because Molly killed him a couple of decades back. She and Dashiell both verified it."

Jesse's eyes sparked with interest. "Is that common? For vampires to kill their maker?"

"Not at all. From what I've seen, most of them are grateful to their makers, if not outright worshipful. Molly's must have been a bad dude for her to turn on him. But again, he's *definitely* dead."

"Hmm."

By 9:30 a.m. we were pulling into the storage unit. In the harsh light of day, the place didn't look quite as nice as it had the night before. There were plenty of cars in the lot now. Despite the risk, I made the decision to bring Shadow inside as my service dog. This was a vampire hangout, which made it very unlikely that the daytime people knew anything about witches, werewolves, or the bargest. Taking her with us seemed like less of a risk than leaving her in the car to scare people who walked past. If someone called the police, we would get into a whole new kind of trouble.

Inside the lobby, a young Armenian woman stood at the front desk, holding an open book with one hand while she took notes with the other. She wore a pressed white button-down shirt and an engraved name tag that read *Anush*. She didn't so much as look up as we approached. I glanced at the title of the book: *Writing Your First Screenplay*. Oh, Los Angeles, I love you.

By unspoken agreement, I hung back a bit and let Jesse take the lead. He was better at the whole investigation/talking to strangers thing, and it didn't hurt that he was . . . aesthetically pleasing. "Hello," he said to Anush, turning his smile up a few degrees. "We need to get into one of the safety deposit boxes."

"Be with you in just a sec," she said distractedly. At my feet, Shadow let out a loud, almost theatrical yawn. The woman paused and leaned forward to peer over the desk. "Whoa," she breathed. "That is . . ."

"The ugliest dog you've ever seen?" I suggested. I may have been a tad cranky.

"Well . . . yeah." After a quick glance at me, her eyes settled on Jesse—and widened even more. She closed the book and set it down neatly on top of the notes. "What did you say you needed?"

Jesse held up Molly's key. "Access to the safety deposit boxes."

Dropping her pen, the young woman took the key from Jesse's hand, her brow furrowing. "This is from the special section."

"Is there a problem?"

"No, not at all, sir," she said hurriedly, suddenly very interested in pleasing us. "I just don't see these very often during the day. If you give me the code word, I'd be glad to help you out."

Dashiell had texted this while I was sleeping. "Cymry," I said, pronouncing it carefully. I'd Googled the word on Jesse's phone during the drive. It was a Welsh term from the Middle Ages, used to describe the Welsh people. Very Molly.

Anush smiled brightly. "Thank you, miss. Right this way."

She came around the corner and led us down a series of corridors that looked weirdly familiar. Then I remembered I'd seen these doors on the security monitors at the front desk. Duh.

Anush steered clear of Shadow in a polite way, but the bargest didn't notice. Shadow was deeply interested in her new surroundings—her nose worked overtime, and her head turned rapidly back and forth to take everything in. Eventually we wound our way to a small vault door, similar to the kind you'd see in any bank. Anush entered a code into a keypad and turned the enormous handle, revealing a room of safety deposit boxes like the ones you see in every bank heist movie. There was a table in the center of the room, and two chairs. No security camera in here. I went and sat down, partly so we weren't all crowding the small space, and partly because I'm essentially very lazy.

Anush went straight to Molly's box, number 3791. There were two keyholes; she inserted a key in one of them and gestured for Jesse to do the same with the other. After they turned the keys, Anush removed hers but didn't let the door swing open. "Take all the time you need," she said cordially. "The exit door will be locked on the other side, but there's a push bar for when you're ready to leave. Please notify me on your way out, and I'll come back and turn my side of the lock." She backed out of the room smiling and practically bowing, her eyes nervously flicking toward Shadow.

Then we were alone with the box.

Jesse swung open the door and pulled out the drawer, which he set down on the table in front of me. He dropped into the opposite chair, and we both stared down at the contents. The safety deposit box was about the size of the cardboard boxes that knee-high boots come in, and one-quarter of it was filled with neatly wrapped stacks of hundred-dollar bills. Next to them was a carved oak jewelry box, and next to *that* was a packet of papers and supplies. There was a little pile of passports right on top. Jesse picked them up right away and took off the rubber band holding them together. He examined a couple of the passports.

"If these are forgeries, they're the best I've ever seen." He shook his head. "But I don't think they're forgeries."

"Pressing government officials is practically a part-time job when you're a vampire," I said absently. I was spreading the rest of the spy movie stack across the table. There were deeds to land in a few different countries, plus a number of envelopes that held foreign currencies. I found a small stack of Polaroids and began flipping through them. They were probably from the 1970s, judging by the hair and clothes, but they reminded me a lot of the photos at the Scarff Street house: groups of young women standing together smiling. Molly was in all the shots. I didn't recognize anyone else, so I passed them to Jesse.

"Here we go," I said, picking up a small, no-frills address book. You would think someone who's been alive for a hundred and fifty years might have a pretty full contact list, but there were only two or three entries under each letter. "Interesting," I murmured.

Jesse dropped the photos and leaned over the table, craning his head to see what I was reading. "Just first names," he observed. "Vampires?"

"That would be my guess. She probably keeps human phone numbers on her cell like anyone else." I paged through further and recognized the names of a few of the LA vampires, including Frederic. Next to each name there was a dash and a country or state name: "Naomi - Washington State," "Livingston - Croatia," "Morris - South Carolina."

"What happens when there are two vampires with the same name?" Jesse asked.

"A question I pondered for many years. I always figured they'd have a Highlander-style fight to the death, but actually they just identify themselves by their place of birth, like the other entries. See, look." I pointed to the entries for H, where there were actually three different vampires named Henry. They were marked "Henry - Iceland," "Henry - Quebec," and "Henry - Vermont."

Underneath the name, there was always an address, though many of them were P.O. boxes. "Don't vampires move around a lot?" Jesse said. "What are the chances that any of these are still current?"

"The address isn't where the vampire lives; it's how he or she can be tracked down," I explained. "Molly told me once that vampires keep a drop site somewhere, like a P.O. box or an abandoned house that they own. That's how they find each other, when they really want to." I shook my head. "The problem is that it takes time. If your drop site is in Spain and you're currently living in Canada . . ."

"Okay, I can see that. What are the starred names?" He pointed to the entry across from the Henrys: "Georgiana - Pennsylvania," with an address in New York. Sure enough, there was a star next to it.

I frowned. "I don't know. Let's see how many have them."

Jesse produced a small notebook and pen, and we made a list of the starred entries. There were fourteen in all. "They're all women's names," he pointed out. "Her friends?"

"I don't know. In theory all the names in the book are her friends. What makes these fourteen different?"

"Look, some of them have phone numbers."

I checked, and he was right—a few of the starred names had a number penciled in at the bottom. Most of them had been erased several times, like Molly had kept them updated. Interesting.

We spent a few minutes digging through the rest of the box's contents, but didn't find anything else that seemed helpful. The jewelry box was full of expensive pieces, some of which looked very old. I doubted any of it could help us exonerate Molly, so I left them where they were. I also ignored the small velvet bag filled with diamonds, and the envelope that held three locks of braided hair, each the length and thickness of a pencil.

I had brought one of those reusable grocery bags, the kind that can fold up into a tiny pouch, and we packed up the Polaroids and the address book. After a moment of hesitation, I also tossed in one of the passports and three of the stacks of cash.

Jesse noticed me do it, and I saw understanding cross his face. He made a show of reaching down to pet Shadow, pretending he'd seen nothing.

If I couldn't free Molly legally, I was damned well going to have a plan B.

Chapter 16

It was ten thirty in the morning when we left the storage facility, which gave us just enough time to get to Dashiell's Pasadena residence to question Molly at noon. Jesse started in that direction without speaking. I could practically *hear* his brain churning, though, and I knew he was doing his cop thing, analyzing the case for those little loose threads that could lead to a new angle of investigation. His ability to find those threads was exactly why I needed him, so I kept quiet and petted Shadow for a while, scratching the spot under her hairless ear that always gets itchy.

"What about talking to the families of the murdered girls?" Jesse said finally. "Could they tell us anything?"

I thought it over, and shook my head. "I don't see how. That would blow our chance of keeping things quiet, for one thing. Besides, none of those girls knew what Molly really was."

"What about the family who are Friends of the Witches?"

"Even them. I can call Kirsten to be sure, but my guess is they don't know Molly's a vampire. They probably don't know about vampires, period."

He glanced over at me, surprised. "How is that possible? I thought the Friends of the Witches wear those special charms. What do they think they're being protected from?"

"Magic," I said simply. "Bad magic. Families who are active Friends of the Witches know that magic is out there, some of it is dangerous, and the witch bags can help protect them. All of which is true."

"But it doesn't really help us." Jesse sighed. After a few moments of thought, he said, "I think we missed something."

"Where?"

"Our theory is that the two suspects grabbed those four bodies after the fire started yesterday and took them somewhere to hide for a couple of days, before coming after you."

"Right . . ."

"I see why they would want to stop you, especially before you could have a longer talk with Dashiell. But hiding those girls was a two-person job. So how did they know to find you outside my apartment?" he asked.

"Oh." It was a damned good question, and I felt like an idiot for having missed it. After a moment of thought, I said, "Two possibilities. One, the bad guys tracked my van, either with their own tracker or through the GPS system at Dashiell's." I paused for a second, then shook my head. "But Abigail Hayne is in charge of the GPS system. She would die before she betrayed Dashiell, and I mean that literally."

"Okay, what's the other possibility?"

"We've been assuming these guys are from outside LA, and I still think that's true—Kirsten would know if we had a boundary witch in town. But they might be working with someone here. Someone who knew where to find Molly."

"Hmm. Any suspects?"

I shifted uncomfortably in the seat. I could only think of one. "Frederic. When Molly and I got to the storage facility, he seemed a little jumpy. I thought it was just me being a null, but he acted a little bit . . . guilty." I told him about Frederic disappearing and locking the door so I couldn't come back in. "He can't be the vampire bad guy, because he was at the storage facility well before Molly and I got there. But he could be working for them." Another thought occurred to me. "With or without his knowledge, since the boundary witch can press vampires."

"But how would Frederic know where you were going next?" Jesse asked.

I shrugged. "Every vampire in LA knows that you and I have worked together in the past. And it took me well over an hour to drive back into the city from the storage place. More than enough time for them to figure out where you live."

"We should talk to Frederic," Jesse decided. "He's the most likely candidate for vampire mole." A bemused smile crept across his face. "I can't believe I just said that out loud."

"Abigail will know his daytime location," I said. "But you should probably be the one to ask her."

He cut his eyes over to me. "Let me guess: she's the vice president of your fan club?"

"Something like that."

Dashiell owned a Spanish Revival mansion in Old Pasadena, although since his vampire wife, Beatrice, was actually born in Spain, maybe it wasn't a revival? Anyway, it was a stunning place, with long, regal columns, a huge open-air atrium in the center, and a library that came straight out of *Beauty and the Beast*, although Dashiell got really annoyed if you said that out loud. Trust me on this.

Dashiell's property was also well fenced, and private enough that Shadow can roam around the yard off-leash. She's usually happy to do this while I meet with Dashiell, and I think it makes everyone in the house more comfortable too, even the humans. Or maybe especially the humans. A one hundred-fifty-pound dog might be pretty unremarkable to some people, but Shadow's size is only the *first* intimidating thing about her.

"Don't forget to poop on the tiles," I stage-whispered as she trotted off. I love Beatrice dearly, but anyone who imports tiles from Spain just for the driveway is kind of asking for it. Shadow's furry ear flicked backward as if in acknowledgment.

Jesse was watching her go, her giant paws soundless as she loped. "Do you ever just feel really, really grateful that she's on our side?" he said quietly.

"All the time."

Theo Hayne met us at the front door, one hand already extended for a quick greeting. Hayne was an enormous black man with scars on his wrists and probing eyes that were well-trained to spot threats. I wasn't sure I'd ever seen him in anything but a black polo shirt and black pants. He always reminded me of the actor Idris Elba, or maybe Elba reminded me of Hayne.

"We have forty-five minutes before the next shift will start to arrive," he said, walking quickly into the mansion. Jesse and I hurried after him. "Dashiell said you need to be gone by then."

I nodded, and we followed him down a long hallway to the east wing of the mansion, until we reached a large but windowless chamber that didn't seem to match the rest of the building. Most of the mansion was beautifully decorated to match Beatrice's tastes, but this room was as modern and functional as the rest of place was classic and refined. It was packed—with great efficiency—nearly full with computers, monitors, and a bunch of sleek, new-looking equipment that I didn't even recognize. Then again, I'd only been in this part of the building a few times, for meetings with Abigail.

Speak of the devil. As soon as Theo Hayne ushered us through the doorway, Abigail looked up from her massive desk at the back of the room to scowl at me, as though we were tearing her away from crucial, life-threatening work to do our laundry. I should have let Jesse enter the room first, I thought. At least he was easy on the eyes.

A muscular woman of about thirty-five, Abigail looked more like a professional softball player than a computer genius, at least from the waist up. Her thin legs leaned to one side of a wheelchair that was as sleek and modern as the rest of the room. Abigail could stand up and walk for short distances using elbow crutches, but at work she was most comfortable in the chair, and her domain was arranged for it. Hers was the only chair in this part of the room.

Wheeling forward to meet us, Abigail grunted at me and eyed Jesse appraisingly. "Hi, Abigail. This is—" I began, trying to use my manners.

"Abigail Hayne," she said to Jesse, ignoring me. She thrust out her hand, which he stepped forward and shook.

"Jesse Cruz. Good to meet you." He glanced around the room. "Never been in this part of the building."

"This is the nerve center for all our security," she said brusquely. "We try to keep tourists out of here." Her gaze strayed toward me a little pointedly. Hayne was still standing near the door behind us, but I was sure I could *hear* him smiling.

"It's very impressive," Jesse said, his voice full of sincerity. "Really." He gave her a thousand-watt smile.

Abigail regarded him as if she were seeing him for the first time. "Uh, thanks. We can run the whole city from this room. We even keep some vampire bunks in the back in case of emergency." She jerked her head to the back corner, where there were several long platforms set into the wall. Turning the wheelchair, she pointed to two doors at the back corner opposite the bunks. "The door on the left goes to the west-wing basement, which is where Beatrice and Dashiell have their daytime quarters. You don't want to go down there—lots of alarms. And things." *Booby traps?* I wondered, picturing a *Raiders of the Lost Ark*–type situation. Now I kind of wanted to go look. "The door on the right leads to the east-wing basement; that's where we have the cells and some storage." She turned back toward the wall monitors near us and pointed to the four on the bottom left. Three showed small, empty rooms with only a bed and a sink. The fourth chamber was occupied by a tiny figure, curled into a ball on the bed. I recognized the hair, black streaked with blue. Molly. "She's our only guest at the moment."

Seeing Molly in a prison situation left me momentarily speechless, but Jesse filled in the silence. "Is anyone coming down with us?" he asked Abigail a little awkwardly. I could practically see him trying not to look at the wheelchair.

Her brother, who was leaning against the wall, quirked his lips in amusement. "No. We need to stay up here and keep watch, in case any of our afternoon staff shows up early. But we'll both be monitoring from here."

"Is it recording?"

Abigail shook her head and reached down near one leg to tap a large hard drive. "We render our footage once every month, which means the cameras are offline for about an hour, one area at a time. We were due for an update three days from now, but Dashiell has asked me to move it forward." She sniffed, and I realized that to her, Dashiell's precautions would look a lot like mistrust. Crap. Abigail already disliked me, both because I constantly messed with her security—they had to redo all the wards and witch bags every time I stopped by—and because she thought I was a huge liability, a security breach just waiting to happen. It also didn't help that every time I was with Abigail I got nervous and made bad jokes, which she saw as a symptom of my general immaturity/ uselessness. And now I was giving her more reasons to be pissy. "You better get down there," she said in a frosty voice. "You're already late."

Hayne stepped forward. "I have to search you," he said, a little apologetic.

He was extremely thorough, but professional about it. Jesse and I had been expecting this and left our weapons in the car, though I felt jittery without my Taser and my knives. The Polaroids and the address book were in the pockets of my excellent new jacket, but Hayne let me keep them after a quick flip-through. He was searching for weapons, or a way to help Molly escape. He wouldn't have cared if I'd brought Molly porn, so long as there wasn't a metal file hidden inside it.

After checking Jesse, Hayne walked us through the door to the east-wing basement. He didn't speak—he never was a big talker—but at one point he reached over and gave my arm a quick, subtle squeeze without looking at me. I nodded my thanks. Hayne belonged to Dashiell in a lot of ways, but he wasn't unsympathetic to my situation.

I had never actually been in the basement of Dashiell's mansion, and I have to admit that a little part of me had been picturing some sort of medieval dungeon, with torches along the wall, lots of black iron, and, I don't know, maybe hay on the floor? At any rate, I was disappointed. The basement under the east wing was sparse and efficient but clean, with white drywall and low-pile utility carpeting. It looked like the kind of space where suburban moms would send their kids to roughhouse, knowing there wasn't much damage they could do.

I expanded my radius as we walked, hoping to give Molly a few extra seconds to acclimate before we arrived. When we reached the cell door, I sidestepped Hayne, who was fumbling with a set of keys, so I could stand on my tiptoes and look inside the viewing window.

Most vampires are really rattled when they get close to me—Molly herself once described the sensation as waking up from a coma only to realize you'd been beaten half to death. But Molly had lived with me, so she was more accustomed to daytime wake-ups than most vampires. When I peered through the glass she was already sitting up on the cot, her eyes trained on the door, waiting for us. She gave me a weak smile, which I understood perfectly. *Oh, this again.* I worked to swallow the lump in my throat. She looked so small.

Jesse and I crowded inside the tiny room, and Hayne took a step backward. "I have to lock you in," he said, not unkindly. "I'll be back at ten to one, and you need to be ready to move." Nodding briefly at Molly, he turned on his heel. I heard the sound of the heavy-duty bolt grinding over.

Molly looked past me, forcing more effort into her smile. "Hey, Jesse. Long time no see. Thanks for coming."

He reached out a fist, gently bumping it against hers. "Wouldn't miss it."

Molly looked at me. "What did *I* miss?" She was trying to conceal it, but I saw the hope glimmering in her eyes. "I don't suppose you're here to sneak me out."

"Sadly, no. We've got some questions. And some news." I sat down next to her on the bed. Jesse leaned against a wall, trying not to loom over us. "First off, Dashiell believes you were being controlled by someone else," I told her, and began summarizing the recent events. Molly was so relieved to hear about boundary magic—something she'd heard of, but knew little about, much like myself—that silent tears leaked down her cheeks when I explained it. "So I really didn't blood-gorge?" she whispered, her fingers encircling my forearm tight enough to bruise. She was human at the moment, too. "Are you sure?"

I was taken aback. With the exception of the previous night's freakout, I'd never seen Molly so intense about *anything*. "I'm positive you didn't blood-gorge," I told her. "And this boundary magic thing is the only alternative that makes sense, so . . . yeah. I'm sure."

She released my arm, tears of relief pooling into the collar of her dress. It was the same baggy piece I'd hastily grabbed from her apartment building, although someone had taken away the belt.

Then she shook herself, and the solace faded out of her expression, replaced by sorrow. "They're all still dead, though. No matter what happens going forward, they're all dead because of me."

Jesse and I exchanged a look. "Not exactly," I said. I told Molly about the news report we'd seen on the bodies, that only eight of the twelve had been found.

She must have put it together a hell of a lot faster than any of the rest of us, because as soon as I explained the numbers, I could practically see her blood pressure drop. Her pale skin turned the color of snow, and her upper body began to rock a little, like a stiff breeze was about to tip her over. "Molly? Are you okay?"

"Someone's turning them," she whispered. "Oh, God. It's the midnight drain."

Chapter 17

Before I could ask what that meant, one of her hands darted out to touch the wall for support, and the other clapped over her mouth. "I think . . . I'm gonna . . ."

I stood there, stupidly staring, until Jesse grabbed my elbow and steered me to one side, making way for Molly to stumble past us to the small sink in the corner of the room. She leaned forward and began retching.

Whoa. I'd seen vampires react badly in my presence—they aren't used to even very mild shock symptoms, so getting terrible news next to a null was pretty much *two* kicks in the teeth. But in all the years I'd been around the Old World, I had never seen a vampire throw up, Molly included.

She was having a hard time with it, too. There was no food in her stomach, of course, but her system was insisting it needed to purge, so dry heaves wracked her thin frame. I hurried over and scooped her black-and-blue hair out of her face, holding it back as she convulsed and spat bile into the sink. When her body finally relaxed, I turned the sturdy faucet handle so she could rinse her mouth and splash water on her face.

"Are you okay?" came out of my mouth, even though I knew the question was inane and useless. Of course she wasn't okay. "I mean, um, can you breathe?"

Molly nodded, and I let go of her hair so she could straighten up. Keeping a hand on the wall, she tucked herself into the corner next to the sink and slowly let herself slump down to the floor, staring at nothing.

I just stood there for a moment, suddenly very aware of my physical presence. Should I stand there in the middle of the room? Sit on the bed? Go put my arm around Molly? I had no context for this situation, no frame of reference for how to handle it. After a moment, Jesse went to one side of the bed and perched right on the edge, so I did too, shooting him a grateful smile.

"Which four?" Molly asked from the floor. Her voice had taken on a hollow, mechanical tone. It was just how she'd sounded back at the house, when she was still covered in tacky blood. "Wait, let me guess. Hailey, for sure. Taylor, Louisa, and . . . probably Harper."

I hadn't remembered their names, but Jesse had read the online news report. He was nodding. "How did you know?" he asked.

"Because those four are the prettiest."

Jesse and I exchanged another look, but he seemed as confused as I was. "What does that mean?" he asked. "And what's the midnight drain?"

Molly didn't answer him. She just leaned sideways to rest her forehead against the wall. "Molls?" I asked. "We can't help you if you don't talk to us."

She turned, her eyes still wide with shock. "Help *me*?" she echoed.

"Of course." I put a little force into the words. "Listen to me. With a boundary witch running around the city, Dashiell doesn't know who he can trust. Jesse and I need to find whoever's really behind this, or . . ." I forced myself to push on. "Or Dashiell's going to let you take the fall."

That didn't have the effect I'd expected. She just shrugged, looking completely unsurprised. No, not just that, she looked . . . detached. Uncaring. "Dashiell has always cared more about appearances than justice," she said in a wooden voice. "Twelve murdered or missing girls on the news, plus the Trials tonight? Of course he's going to set me up." Her eyes cut back over to me. "The irony is not lost on me, you know," she added. I winced. Molly had evicted me because I kept getting involved in dangerous messes, and now here she was in a mess of her very own. "Not that it matters now."

"Of course it matters!" I protested. "They're going to *kill* you." *And I'm going to have to do it.*

But she didn't answer me. She wasn't even *looking* at me. I glanced over at Jesse, but he looked as puzzled as I felt. I had thought learning that four of the girls might become vampires would . . . well, maybe not cheer her up, but at least help ease some of the pain. Instead, it had prompted Molly to basically go catatonic.

Jesse held up his wrist, showing me his watch. We were running out of time, and so far we'd gotten nothing. I gave him a helpless look. "Molly's gone bye-bye, Jesse," I said under my breath. "What have you got left?"

Jesse touched my hand in support and then stood up, stepping past me so he was looming right over Molly. He squatted down in front of her, like an adult trying to speak to a kid on their own level. "You gave Scarlett the key to your safety deposit box," he reminded her. "You wanted us to help. You wanted to *live*. What's changed?"

Molly just shook her head, like maybe that would make us go away. Her expression was sort of strangled. I couldn't say I was surprised. My former roommate was an expert at creating a blanket of happy energy and wrapping it around herself like a shield. She was always delighted to invite you into her blanket fort, but good luck prying her out of there. It was one of the reasons we'd gotten along so well—neither of us was skilled at emotional depth. Which was fine if you were watching reruns of *Friends*, but not so good when you were keeping secrets that could save your life.

Two minutes that we didn't have ticked by on my watch, and then Molly finally planted her shoulder blades on the wall and inched upward until she was standing with her chin raised, looking past Jesse to me. "You want to help me?" she said with new strength. "Find those girls. Find them before they wake up, and get them to Dashiell. That's all that matters now."

Jesse and I exchanged a look. "Luckily," he said to her, "the best way to find those girls is to figure out who did this to you."

Molly looked at him for a long moment, then nodded. "Okay. What do you need from me?"

Jesse glanced at me, his eyes going to my jacket pocket. I pulled out the photos and the little address book, handing them over. Jesse showed them to her. "Who are these women?"

Molly took the Polaroids from him very gently, as though they might disintegrate. She shuffled slowly through the photos, looking at each one. I was impatient, but Jesse covertly held up his hand where only I could see it.

Finally, Molly handed the pictures back to me, her eyes newly wary. "They're my friends," she said with a shrug. "It was 1973, and the Polaroid SX-70 had just become commercially available. We were messing around with it."

"Then why did you keep the pictures in a safety deposit box for forty-odd years?" Jesse asked.

"They're vampires, aren't they?" I said, before she could answer. "That's why the photos were in the box. They're technically proof that you all exist."

She started to nod, then caught herself. "I forgot how hard it is," she said. "Being around you."

"Being human, you mean," I said dryly. "Why did you keep these? What makes these specific women so special?" Vampires didn't generally hang around in groups.

"We worked together," Molly said, dismissive. "A long time ago."

"Goddammit, Molly!" I yelled, surprising all three of us. "We don't have a lot of time before the afternoon shift shows up and we have to go. You want us to find your friends, the ones who were taken? Answer the fucking questions!"

Molly's careless posture dropped away and her gaze hardened into a glare. She was human in my presence, sure, but no one looking at her in that moment would have mistaken her for a college student. "We were whores, okay?" she snapped, her eyes flashing between Jesse and me. "Actually, that's probably too nice a term. 'Sex slaves' is closer."

Jesse subconsciously shifted backward, the knee-jerk response of a man in the presence of an abused woman. "Oh," I said, my voice echoing with stupidity.

The small room filled with uncomfortable silence. I had no idea what to say. Molly had always given me the impression that she'd been taken and turned into a vampire because of her looks, but I'd sort of thought she'd been abused by a single male vampire. That was horrific in itself, of course, but it had never occurred to me that she'd . . . I couldn't even bear to think about it.

"Your maker," I said softly, as though keeping my voice low might magically make the question not hurt. "The one you killed. He turned you so he could . . . sell you?"

"Twenty years," she said bitterly, as though she'd heard a very different question than the one I'd asked. "That's how long a new vampire's 'apprenticeship' lasts. Every twenty years he took a new stable. Turned all at once. Like a . . . a graduating class."

Molly's eyes flicked subconsciously to the pictures, and I put it together. "They're like your sisters."

She nodded.

A whole new thought occurred to me. "Wait, how many women did he kill trying to fill his stable? I thought . . . vampire magic isn't always infectious." I had always been told that for every five humans who tried to become vampires, only about three would actually turn.

But Molly was shaking her head. "That was Alonzo's gift," she whispered. "Ten out of ten. Always ten out of ten. That's why the council let him go unpunished for so long. Good for our numbers." She handed me the photos. "Keep them safe, okay?" She gave me a pleading expression, wanting me to understand.

And I did. I nodded and tucked the pictures back into my jacket pocket. Molly and her friends had been through hell—twenty years of fear, pain, rape, and misery. I couldn't even fathom it, and now I felt so . . . *young*. Since I'd taken over as LA's resident null, I'd been knocked around a little, and Jesse and I had found ourselves in some bad situations . . . but at the end of the day, I was a privileged middle-class white girl with no mental framework to understand the concept of two *decades* of torment.

I had told Jesse there were no psychotic vampires. I was so tragically naive that it was almost funny.

And yet, this explained so much about the Molly I did know. How she preferred to live on the surface of things. Why she kept to herself so much. The way she hated to talk about history, even though she'd been alive for so much of it. And, I realized suddenly, it also explained why she had moved in with those college girls. It wasn't because they reminded her of me. It was because they reminded her of *them*. Being surrounded by young women gave her comfort.

"I'm sorry, Molly," Jesse said quietly. I had sort of forgotten he was there, but when I looked over he had a calm, resigned expression on his face. Of course, Jesse used to be a cop. He would have interviewed victims of many kinds of abuse. "I know you don't want to talk about this. But someone used a boundary witch to make you kill your roommates, and that same person has them now. What happened to you and your sisters might be happening again."

Chapter 18

And that was when Molly snapped.

"He's *dead*," she shouted, her voice suddenly thunderous in the tiny space. She got up into Jesse's face and shoved him with all her strength, which really only rocked him back a step. He made no move to stop her. "If I know anything in this life or any other, it's that Alonzo is dead, dead, *dead*. I made *sure* of it." Her clenched fingers jerked in a tiny tugging motion.

"I believe you," Jesse said calmly. "I believe you killed him, and you deserve a goddamned parade for it, at the very least. But you said that Alonzo was special, that he had a gift for turning new vampires, right?"

She nodded, still glaring at him. "We call it bloodcraft," she said, her voice cool. "The making of new vampires."

Jesse paused, giving us both a chance to process that. I hadn't known that some vampires could be better at bloodcraft than others, but it made sense. Some witches specialized in certain types of magic, and some werewolves were magically stronger than others. Why wouldn't vampires have varying strengths, too?

"Does that work like human genetics?" Jesse asked. Molly's brow furrowed, but I saw where he was going with this. Witch specialties pass down from generation to generation.

"Would Alonzo's offspring be good at bloodcraft too?" I translated to Molly.

"Yes," she said tightly.

"Then we need to investigate your sisters," Jesse concluded.

Before she could yell at him he rushed to say, "Molly, I've known more than one prostitute who was madly in love with her pimp, even though the guy beat the shit out of her every night. And this Alonzo must have turned hundreds of vampires over the years. If just one of them decided she needed to avenge him, maybe she came after your friends to get back at you."

Molly visibly flinched away from him. As for me, I had to clench my fists to keep from slapping Jesse across the face as hard as I could. In that moment I hated him—not because he was wrong, but because he was a man and he was standing there hurting my hurt friend even more.

"No," Molly said at last. "I don't believe it. Maybe one of them would come after me on her own, but none of Alonzo's villani would turn more women against their will." Jesse looked like he wanted to argue, but she added, "Even if they did, none of my sisters live anywhere near Los Angeles. And I have no way of finding Alonzo's other offspring."

Jesse absorbed that for about ten seconds and then moved on. "Okay, did Alonzo have friends or allies who could have done this?" he asked. "Someone else who would think you deserve to die for killing him?"

Molly burst out laughing. It was not an amused laugh, and it definitely had an edge of hysteria. Jesse glanced my way, but I just shrugged.

"I'm sorry," Molly said once she'd calmed down. "I thought you knew. The answer is *everyone*. Most of the Old World thinks I should die for killing Alonzo. I've been a pariah since the day I took his head. I've had to run—" she cut herself off, shaking her head to say it didn't matter anymore.

And then I got it. This was why she'd moved in an unusual pattern across the US, why she'd laid low even though her tormenter was dead. Because people blamed her for it. "*Seriously?*" I cried, outraged. "Killing the abusive moth—"

"You're both human," Molly interrupted, her voice so quiet that I was forced to shut up or miss her words. It was a kindergarten teacher move, but very effective. "But you have parents, or you did once. Can you imagine murdering them, violently and in cold blood? Even if they hurt you, even if they . . ." she trailed off.

I went still, and I felt Jesse do the same, afraid to break the spell of her words. "And those are just your *parents*," she said abruptly. "There are no magic bonds. Vampire magic evolved for loyalty. We are reborn *needing* to obey our master. We may kill another vampire for war, for territory, but your dominus, the one who sired you?" her voice broke. "You have no idea how hard that is, or how taboo. I was *lucky*"—she gave a bitter chuckle—"they didn't kill me for what I did. If there was still a council, they might have. Dashiell was the only vampire in North America willing to take me in."

I stared at her with my mouth open for a second. No wonder Molly stayed on the fringes of even the small Old World society in LA. And Dashiell was . . . the good guy? I suppose it shouldn't have surprised me—Dashiell was young for a cardinal vampire, and had a lot of ideas that didn't necessarily fit with the old ways.

"Alonzo was a monster, Molly," I said, as gently as I could.

"We're all monsters," she said matter-of-factly. "You know the funniest part? What he did, the way he treated us . . . that wasn't even why I killed him. Not really. But it doesn't matter now."

In the hall outside the door, I could make out heavy, deliberate footsteps. Hayne, letting us know our time was up.

I darted forward and grabbed Molly's hands. She squeezed them, looking surprised. I am not a touchy-feely person, but Molly was. Or at least, I had thought she was. The person in front of me wasn't the bubbly, playful girl with whom I'd lived for so long. She was . . . deadened. No pun intended.

"Give us something to go on here," I begged. "Some way to find whoever did this."

"I wish I could."

"Where would they stay?" Jesse pressed. "What would they need, to keep the girls? Who would they have to bring into their circle of trust?"

She didn't respond to any of the questions, but before she could say, "I don't know," Jesse added, "Who knew you were living by USC?"

Molly paused. I could hear Hayne's key fitting into the door lock. "Actually . . . only Dashiell, Beatrice, and Frederic," she said slowly. "But that doesn't mean they were involved. One of them may have told someone else."

Jesse and I exchanged a look. At least we had our next destination.

Minutes later, with Shadow in tow, Jesse peeled out of Dashiell's driveway so fast that I worried about leaving tire tracks. Not that I cared about Dashiell's pretty tile driveway, but all our efforts to keep the visit a secret would be pretty futile if we left gigantic black marks behind.

"Wow," Jesse said absently.

"Yeah." I pulled out my phone. I hadn't had time to ask Abigail for Frederic's daytime address before Hayne hustled us out of there, so I sent her a text. She wouldn't like helping me, but she'd do it on Dashiell's orders. Or her brother would make her.

"You didn't know?" Jesse said, glancing over at me. "About Alonzo?"

I shook my head. "I figured Molly had been through something, but . . . no."

"So why do you think she killed him?"

"No idea. And aside from Frederic the Likely Dipshit, I can't think of anyone to ask, at least until after sunset," I said. "It would be great if we could get five minutes with Dashiell, but I'm not sure he'll have time, at least not until after tonight's trial. Maybe I could get Beatrice alone—"

My phone beeped. Abigail had texted me an address in Sylmar. I had no idea where that was, but when I told Jesse he made a face and put the address into his GPS.

"What?" I asked. "Bad neighborhood?"

Jesse rolled his eyes. "I hate that phrase. No neighborhood is completely bad. But yeah, crime's been picking up in Sylmar the last couple of years. Drugs and gang violence, mostly."

"Makes sense," I mused. "Vampires tend to congregate at the edge of chaos. Neighborhoods where people go missing or lose time on a regular basis, but not so crime-ridden that police are knocking on doors all the time."

Sylmar was way to the east of Dashiell's Pasadena mansion, almost all the way back to the storage facility. I was getting pretty sick of criss-crossing the county. At least we were traveling in the middle of the day, when we could avoid the worst of the traffic.

Jesse made a little conversation about the traffic—the go-to topic of any Los Angeles small talk—but soon I was barely listening. The closer we got to Sylmar, the more nervous I became about breaking into Frederic's place. I rarely worked at all during the day, and if I did, it was usually to check in with Abigail and Hayne, not deal with the riskier parts of my job. At the very least, I was about to commit breaking and entering, in broad daylight. Much as I complained about him, Dashiell's influence in LA—both vampiric and political—was my safety net, and if I got myself into trouble during the day, I was working without that net. If I got caught, I would have to try talk my way out of it, because spending the rest of the day in jail would mean burning through what little time I had left to help Molly.

I was also worried about Frederic himself. The vampire would lose his strength and speed the instant he entered my radius, but he would still be unpredictable. As a general rule, formidable beings such as vampires do not like to be made vulnerable by a twenty-something who can barely dress herself. Waking them up during the day, with no warning, just emphasized how much power I had over them. Frederic wouldn't be the first vampire to react to it violently.

All too soon, we were cruising past Frederic's condo. Despite what Jesse had said about this part of town, the condo complex seemed nice to me. It was basically one large, two-story square building that some-one had quartered into four units, with driveways facing out on oppo-site sides of the square. Like most LA residences, the emphasis was on maximizing living space rather than creating a yard, so the building was as wide as it could be, framed by a narrow sidewalk running along each side. The sidewalk led to a small side door, although the residents would probably enter and exit through the garage.

Abigail had said that all four units were owned by vampires, so the bedrooms would probably be at the back corner of each unit, where there were no windows. I saw no visible signs of life as we drove by, which wasn't surprising, given the daylight.

"Something's off," Jesse said quietly, making a left to go back around the block.

"Really?" I twisted in my seat, trying to get another glance at the building. "It looked okay to me."

"The side door was cracked open on Frederic's unit," he reported. "If you're a vampire and this is basically your fortress, wouldn't you close and lock the door during the day?"

"Maybe the air conditioning is broken and he wanted the breeze," I offered. "Or maybe his cleaning lady is coming in. Or he just forgot to close it before he died for the day."

"Maybe," Jesse said, but he was obviously unconvinced. "Did you see the shrubs? They're big enough to hide a person. Like maybe a boundary witch."

"Oh. Right." Another common LA landscape choice: the designer had tried to make up for the lack of yard by planting some huge, thick green plants in the narrow space between the sidewalk and the fence delineating the property. There were birds-of-paradise, a flower that's always kind of creeped me out, along with some big, *Jurassic Park*–looking ferns. I hadn't even really noticed the plants, which were all over the place in Los Angeles, but once Jesse pointed them out, it was obvious that the row of foliage was wide enough to hide even a large man.

"Let's do the cautious thing for once, okay?" Jesse suggested. He turned back onto Frederic's street, then parked at the curb, a good ways before the building. Before we got out, Jesse reached into a small safe underneath his seat and pulled out a handgun, securing it in a holster at his hip.

"Guns?" I said, hearing my voice come out plaintive. I *really* didn't like guns. Maybe it was silly, after going up against murderers and psychos, but guns still scared the bejesus out of me, and that wasn't likely to change.

"We know that the people running all this aren't afraid to use them," he explained, loading the weapon. "Frederic might have one with him, or the boundary witch could be here with a gun, or both. You better put on your vest."

I nodded. It took a few minutes, but we both managed to squirm into the Kevlar vests while inside the vehicle. We couldn't really walk around a residential neighborhood in bulletproof vests without drawing attention, so I put the jacket back on over mine, which made it look more or less like a black shirt, at least from a distance. Jesse, on the other hand, had to take his shirt off to put the vest on underneath. As he lifted his shirt over his head I turned away, suddenly very aware of the close quarters, and Jesse's wide expanse of smooth brown skin stretched over muscle. I busied myself with unhooking my knife sheaths from my boots so I could attach them to my waistband.

Hearing our preparations, Shadow stuck her head between the seats and nosed my arm.

"Are we bringing her?" Jesse asked, tugging his T-shirt over the vest. Both he and Shadow watched me closely for the answer.

"If she wants to come." If the boundary witch *was* around, Shadow would be a hell of a weapon. But it felt more respectful to ask rather than assume, and I tried to treat Shadow with the same respect I would give a human. Okay, probably more respect than I would give a human.

I twisted awkwardly in my seat so I could look into her eyes. "We need to talk to someone in that building," I told her, pointing toward Frederic's condo. "But Jesse thinks there might be a bad witch waiting. Do you want to help us look?"

She licked the air, which was an affirmative. Her tail was wagging wildly with anticipation, and there was a look of perfect fulfillment in her eyes that flooded me with guilt. Sometimes I felt kind of bad that I didn't let Shadow kill people more often. "Good girl," I said, and opened the door.

There are some parts of the country where a strange couple and an enormous dog-beast descending on a suburban home in the middle of the day would be considered weird, but in this case LA was playing to our advantage. Movie people always come and go at weird hours.

Still, by unspoken agreement, Jesse and I kept our body language loose and friendly as we approached the condo building with Shadow. Just a couple out walking their dog. You'd have to look close to realize that Shadow didn't have a leash, and Jesse and I had a lot of weapons between us.

Frederic's unit was the one on the left. Jesse slowed down when we hit the driveway, and I realized he was wary of the big ferns. They looked even bigger up close—massive enough to hide the Lakers' starting lineup, let alone one boundary witch.

"Is the witch in there?" Jesse murmured.

Oh, right. Sometimes I got so used to thinking of myself as the opposite of magic that I forgot I could actually detect it. Halting on the sidewalk just in front of the walkway, I closed my eyes, pushing out my radius a little. I got the low-level buzz of Shadow, but there was nothing else, at least not as far as I could reach, which was a ways into the building. I smiled at Jesse. "No witches," I whispered.

His shoulders released a little, and he nodded with relief.

And that was when Shadow snarled and exploded forward into the bushes. A gunshot rang out from that direction, and the garage door began to open next to us. I could hear running footsteps inside the garage.

We'd walked into a trap.

Chapter 19

When he heard the first gunshot Jesse reacted instinctively, shoving Scarlett toward the corner of the building to give them at least a little cover. But the garage door was going up, which presented another avenue of attack. Huddling between the corner of the building and the rising garage door, Jesse peeked around the corner to his right, looking to return fire to whoever was hiding in the foliage. But the gunshots had stopped. The enormous bird-of-paradise fronds were rattling, and he could see Shadow's clubbed-off tail whipping about. He took a step away from the house, trying to get a better look at her target.

Then a bullet whined past him, coming from the garage.

Jesse spun around, but the guy cried out, clutching his shoulder and retreating behind a parked pickup truck. Scarlett had gotten him with one of her throwing knives. Before the man fell back, Jesse caught a quick glimpse of a leather jacket with patches on it and a greasy beard.

"Who the hell is that?" he yelled, but Scarlett just shook her head tightly and said, "Human."

There was a scream from the side of the building, and Jesse returned to his position and checked around the corner. Shadow was backing out of the hedge, the birds-of-paradise near her spattered with blood. One down. She took a few steps toward them, but just then the side door opened and a burly newcomer ran out with an automatic rifle on a strap. Jesse lifted his gun, but hesitated as Shadow raced toward the new threat. He didn't want to hit her by accident, even if she would recover from it. When she was hunting like this, Jesse wasn't positive she could distinguish between friend and foe, at least not for anyone besides Scarlett.

He swore and ducked back around the corner just before the guy opened fire in the general direction of both him and Shadow. Bullets sent up tiny poofs of concrete dust along the sidewalk, and then the bargest let out a loud yelp. Scarlett jerked upright, forgetting about Greasy Beard. Jesse got his shoulder around the corner and leaned out just enough to fire two shots at Burly. Before he even had a chance to see if he'd made contact, Scarlett jerked his arm sideways. "Switch!" she yelled. "Trust me!"

She disappeared around the corner of the house to help Shadow before Jesse even had his footing. He stumbled and brought his gun arm up to cover Greasy Beard in the garage, but a bullet hit his vest first. Pain exploded against his breastbone as Greasy Beard ducked back behind the tailgate of the pickup. Jesse gritted his teeth against the pain and dropped down to his stomach, taking aim at the guy's cowboy boots. He fired, feeling a stab of satisfaction when one brown leather boot seemed to turn into red spray. Greasy Beard fell.

Jesse raced around the truck to check on him. The man was down, screaming with pain. His hands were reaching toward his ankle, but he couldn't bend his body to reach it. Blood striped down the front of his leather jacket, where he'd pulled out Scarlett's knife. Stupid.

"That *cunt*," the guy moaned.

Jesse saw the knife lying on the concrete floor a few feet away, right by the guy's .45. He picked up the gun, engaged the safety, and tucked it into his waistband. "Who are you?" he demanded.

The biker gathered his wits enough to glare at Jesse. "You gonna kill me, spic? Get it over with."

Jesse leaned forward enough to give him a cursory pat down with his free hand. The guy wasn't carrying a wallet, or he'd left it in the truck. Jesse did find a Ka-Bar knife in a leather holster and picked it up along with Scarlett's throwing knife.

"Use your belt as a tourniquet," Jesse directed. He would have liked to tie the guy up, but the gunshots from the side of the house had stopped completely. It made him nervous. He turned to go find Scarlett.

She wasn't on the sidewalk along the house. There was a spreading blood pool coming out of the bushes, and Jesse registered a body lying there, dead. The first shooter. Bloody paw prints led from that corpse to another, the burly guy who had burst out of the side door. He was lying a few feet away from the door, his eyes staring blankly at the sky. His throat had been torn out, and there was what looked like a knife wound in his chest. Jesse had no idea which had killed him. The paw prints led into the condo.

Scarlett and Shadow had gone inside without him.

He made his way through the doorway, checking carefully around the corners before proceeding. He didn't want to call out for Scarlett, not without knowing who else was in the building. The bad guys had obviously realized that Frederic would be their next lead, and they'd laid a trap. Had the boundary witch come along? Or even the vampire in charge of things? Silently, Jesse cursed Scarlett for coming in here without him. She could have at least told him whether there were any supernatural occupants.

The first floor of the condo was empty, so Jesse crept quietly up the carpeted stairs, stopping before he reached the top. He poked his head up and took a quick peek: a short hallway with a metal railing around it, two closed doors, and one wide-open door at the end of the hall. Clothing was draped carelessly over the railing, providing a little bit of cover, but Jesse still felt exposed as he climbed the top steps and started down the hall to the open doorway, weapon raised.

Before he'd even reached the doorframe, he saw Scarlett, standing stock still just inside the room, her hands in the air, glaring furiously at something in the far corner. Jesse quickened his step, coming through the door just enough to see what she was looking at: an angry-looking woman in her early thirties, standing with her back to the wall next to a four-poster bed. She was dressed in a simple long-sleeved tee and black pants, and her reddish hair was pulled into a harsh bun.

Shadow was standing less than two feet in front of the woman, her lips peeled back, a low growl emitting from her deep chest cavity. She was crouched to spring at the woman against the wall, but the woman held a large handgun pointed squarely at Scarlett's center mass. A standoff.

"Hey, Jesse," Scarlett said without looking. "Meet our boundary witch. I haven't gotten her name."

Jesse's gun was already trained on the other woman. "Drop the gun," he said in his most authoritative voice. The woman glanced at him for an instant, but didn't move her gun. "We outnumber you," Jesse pointed out. "Even if you shoot Scarlett, Shadow or I can take you out."

"Ah, but if anyone moves on me, I can still shoot your friend," she said. She had a light accent, Russian or maybe Ukrainian. "I do not think either of you want her to die." Her gun remained firmly pointed at Scarlett. Jesse was impressed—it had to be getting heavy.

"What's your name?" he tried instead. When she didn't answer, he added, "If you don't tell us, Scarlett will make one up for you, and it will probably be mean."

"So mean," Scarlett muttered.

The woman glanced back and forth between them now, looking just a tiny bit confused. "I am Katia," she said. "What is this, this dog-thing that wants to eat me? I am certain I shot it the other night, but it appears fine today."

"She's not a thing, she's a bargest," Scarlett corrected. "Although you're right about her wanting to eat you. She's indestructible. Shooting her just pissed her off."

"Bar-guest," the woman repeated carefully. "I do not know this word."

She was inching sideways very slowly, pretending she was just shifting her weight. She was only about a foot away from the window. "Stop moving," Jesse commanded. The woman froze—and then they heard the screaming wail of police sirens. Someone had heard the shots.

Scarlett glanced at Jesse. "Two minutes, at the most," he said grimly.

Katia bared her teeth. "You two run along. I can wait here for human police." Her smile did not suggest the police would enjoy the encounter.

"Not a chance," Scarlett snarled. "We're taking you with us."

"Ah, you see, that I cannot allow," Katia said, almost regretfully. "We are not finished here, and I am needed."

Jesse risked a glance at Scarlett. He could practically see what she was thinking: they were out of time, and she was wearing the vest. It was a reasonable risk. He opened his mouth to object, but she shouted first.

"Shadow, hold!"

The bargest sprang at Katia, who was already moving sideways toward the window, trying to throw herself against it. She might have made it out, too, except Jesse shot her in the heart.

Chapter 20

It took my brain a second to process what had just happened. Katia had obviously been headed for the window, but she hadn't yet been in the right position to jump or even throw herself against the glass. It almost looked like she'd been sucked out into the California sunshine.

Only then did my ears register the crack of the gun, and I realized that Jesse had just fucking *shot her*. I rushed to the window and looked out. Katia lay sprawled across the same sidewalk that was now covered in bloody footprints, only a few feet away from the dead guy by the side door. Her eyes were wide open, staring, and blood had blossomed on the front of her green shirt.

I pulled my head back in and turned to gape at him. Shadow was looking at him too, with blood on her muzzle and disappointment in her eyes. Jesse shrugged. "Boundary witch," he reminded us.

Oh.

Boundary witches are connected to death magic, and that magic can't or won't let them actually die, at least not easily. I had heard about this in theory, and I knew that Lex, Jesse's friend in Colorado, had died at least once and come back, but I had no idea how it actually worked. I didn't have any time to think about it, either, because Jesse had grabbed my hand and was pulling me toward the door, Shadow right beside us. He didn't let go until we were outside, where he crouched next to Katia's body and checked her pockets with deft hands.

"Looking for a phone?" I guessed. He nodded and rolled her sideways to reach into her back pocket. There was the phone—or what was left of it. The fall from the second-story window had shattered the little piece of plastic. Jesse cursed, dropped the phone, and picked up Katia in his arms, carrying her toward the sedan. We were taking her with us after all.

While he got her into the backseat I kicked at the blood on the sidewalk, trying to cover up the bargest paw prints. An autopsy would reveal that the two dead guys had been mauled by an animal, but there was no reason to give them more details about Shadow's size. They would probably get DNA from her saliva, but Shadow had started life as a dog-wolf hybrid, and I couldn't imagine they'd get any more information than that. As Jesse backed out, I noticed that the garage door was still open, but it was now empty except for a wide smear of blood. The third guy had gotten away, then. And there hadn't been any vampires at all. They had anticipated our next move and set us up.

In another fifteen seconds, Jesse was driving us around a corner while the police cars closed in on the condo. I turned to look over my shoulder. Katia was slumped upright in the backseat, though Jesse had thankfully closed her eyes. The bloodstain on her green blouse seemed huge, but anyone looking in her window would just see the shoulders and head of a sleeping woman, and anyone looking in from the other side of the backseat would only be able to see Shadow. The bargest was hulking next to the boundary witch with her hackles up, growling uncertainly at Katia's body. Shadow still had blood on her muzzle and forelegs, and for a moment my breath caught in my throat, an instinctive fear response that sprung from thousands-year-old reflexes. She was terrifying.

Then she looked at me and whined, her tail thumping against the seat as she sought assurance from her mistress. Right. That was me.

"It's okay, babe," I said, leaning back to pet the top of her head, where there was no blood. "She's dead, but she'll get better. I know it's weird, but it's part of magic, so you don't need to worry." My voice sounded calm, but I realized my fingers were trembling as I petted Shadow's head. That probably wasn't very reassuring, so I sat back in my seat and tried to fasten my seat belt. I kept fumbling it.

Jesse glanced over. "Here." He reached down and snapped the belt for me. "It's just adrenaline. Now that the scary part is over your body has to burn through it. You'll be fine in a minute."

"If you say so," I mumbled. I'd been through intense stuff before—this wasn't even my first gunfight—but it had been three years since I'd dealt with anything more stressful than a bloody nose. I suddenly felt like I couldn't breathe. "Can I take this thing off now?" I said, tugging at the Velcro straps on the vest. Jesse nodded, and I unstrapped the vest and wriggled awkwardly out of it, checking myself. There was a little blood on the vest and on my pants, but I didn't think it was mine. Waterproof or not, I was glad I'd left the pretty, new jacket in the car.

"Can you still feel her in your radius?" Jesse asked, tilting his head toward the backseat.

Oh. I concentrated for a second. Witches in general feel like a very soft buzz in my radius, a constant, not-unpleasant feeling. I hadn't seen Lex in years, but I remembered how she'd felt. Darker: like black noise instead of white noise. Katia had felt the same way when we'd encountered her at Frederic's, so I looked for that again.

I'd gotten a lot of practice tuning out the bargest's "interference," but it still took me a moment to locate Katia's "signal." "Yes," I said to Jesse, "but it's faint."

He nodded. "Better than nothing."

"Those guys," I said as my thoughts shifted abruptly. "They were human. What the hell were they doing helping a vampire and a boundary witch? And what were *they* doing with guns?"

"You said the bad guys probably figured out what you are at Molly's place," he reminded me. "If *you* had to take down a null, what would you use?"

I thought that over for a moment. "Humans with guns," I concluded grimly. I didn't like this one bit. This wasn't how we did things in Los Angeles. We didn't drag in humans, even as hired help, and we didn't fuck around with guns.

Then again, I realized, I'd never lived in any other supernatural community. What if using human goons with Uzis was completely normal everywhere else?

"Even so," I said to Jesse, "who *were* they?"

"I might have an idea about that, but I have to check with some old contacts," Jesse replied. "Meanwhile, we need to call Lex."

"Right now?" Whoops. My voice had come out a little whiny.

"Scarlett, I'm just driving around in circles," he said with great patience. "I need to know more so we can figure out where to take her."

"Right." I shook my head. "Sorry. Of course you should call her. Use my phone; no one has the number yet. No way anyone's tracing it."

Jesse connected my phone to the car's Bluetooth and had me dial the number from his screen so he could watch the road.

Lex answered after one ring. "Luther."

"It's Jesse Cruz. I'm here with Scarlett Bernard."

"Cruz? What's happening?" Wow. At least we didn't have to bother with pleasantries.

"We caught the boundary witch. She said her name was Katia." He described the dead woman in the back of the car, down to the accent. "Do you know her?"

"No, she doesn't sound like anyone I've met thus far." Her voice relaxed a bit. "But I'm glad you've got her. Is she talking?"

"No, not exactly . . . she's dead."

There was a long pause. Couldn't really blame Lex for that one. Then I heard her talking to someone on her end of the line. "Charlie, honey, do you want to play on Daddy's iPad for a minute?" Her tone was bright, which seemed like a foreign language coming from the Lex I'd met. "I *know* I said no, but now I'm saying yes, okay?" There was the sound of a door closing, and then she was back, as businesslike as before. "How?" she demanded.

"I shot her in the heart," Jesse said, sounding a little apologetic. "She gave me no choice."

Well, technically, he could have let her go, but that would have undoubtedly caused more damage in the long run. Plus she probably would have shot me. "I believe you," Lex said. "How long ago was this?"

"Five minutes? We need to know if she'll come back, and when."

"If she's strong enough to press vampires, then yeah, she should come back. But only if you get that bullet out quickly, get her a blood transfusion, and get Scarlett away from her."

"I can do that," I blurted. There was another pause, and I winced. Lex was definitely a member of the We Hate Scarlett club. Charter member. In her defense, I'd sort of cremated her dead sister without asking. "Hi, Lex."

"Hi."

"Sorry. I just meant . . . yeah. I can set up a transfusion and stuff." *Great. Way to sound like a grown-up, Scarlett.* I flushed, and Jesse shot me an amused look.

"Fine."

"When do you think she'll wake up?" Jesse asked Lex, trying to get the conversation back on track.

"It's hard to say. When I died from blood loss, EMTs were trying to revive me right away, and I think that almost . . . sort of *interfered* with the magic. But I can't really remember what happened the time before that." She cleared her throat. "I've seen a couple of boundary witches die since then, but I made sure they wouldn't come back."

Even Jesse's eyes widened a little at her tone. I wanted to scream, *Why are you so scary?* But I managed to keep my mouth shut as he asked, "Best guess?"

"Mmm . . . maybe twelve to twenty-four hours. But that's a guess," she cautioned. "Listen, John gets back from his trip tomorrow, so I'll hand off Charlie and catch a flight tomorrow night or early the next morning."

For a moment, I almost passed out from relief. An adult was coming! She could fix this for me! But then I realized how stupid that was. I couldn't depend on someone else to fix a problem this big, and even if I could, it would look terrible. More important, it was unlikely that Lex would arrive in time to save Molly.

Whoops, she was talking to me again. "Sorry, what?" I said.

"I said, can you clear it with your people? Make sure it's okay for me to enter your territory?"

"Oh." Because boundary witches were so dangerous, Lex would need official permission to run around LA. Under the current circumstances, though, I couldn't see Dashiell or the others objecting to it, especially if Kirsten vouched for her too. Although Kirsten was so busy preparing for the Trials tonight, I wasn't sure I'd even be able to get her on the phone. "Yeah, I'll figure it out."

"Meanwhile," she added, "I've got some resources here. Feel free to call."

That reminded me. "Lex?" I blurted before she could hang up. "Have you ever heard the phrase *midnight drain*? Like as a noun?"

Jesse shot me an approving look. We'd both almost forgotten.

"No," she said slowly, either because she was really thinking about it or because she had to force herself to speak to me. "But I can ask around after sunset."

Jesse thanked her and promised to call back if Katia woke up. When he hung up, he gave me a questioning look. "Where do we take her? Dashiell's in-home jail?"

"No, that's the last place she should be. She could press the vampires to release her."

"Good point. Where, then?"

I sighed. "I really only have one other idea, and it's a terrible one."

Chapter 21

"Wait, you want to bring her *here?*" Eli sounded flabbergasted, which is not a word I use lightly. Next to me, Jesse's mouth twitched in what might have been amusement. I had taken the phone off Bluetooth, but Eli's voice had been loud—not mad, just kind of shocked. I thought maybe he'd resigned himself to sitting this whole crisis out. *Nope, sorry, honey. You get to tag in, too.*

"I'm sorry," I said, meaning it. "But we need Shadow's cell; it's the only secure place with no vampires. Plus, you were a paramedic; you can do the transfusion, right?"

"Well, yeah . . ."

"Great. I already called Hayne; he's sending blood bags."

Eli didn't sound happy, but he understood the concept of "all hands on deck" as well as anyone. "I should probably check in with Will to let him know what's going on," he said warily.

I understood the unspoken question, and for once, I didn't have to worry about making Eli choose. "Please do," I said. "If he has any questions or objections he can call me, but at this point Jesse and I are still operating under our pre-existing instructions."

Eli hung up, and I gave Jesse directions to our place in Marina del Rey.

I love Shadow, but an enormous magical dog-monster does come with some logistical problems, especially in terms of her living situation.

Behaviorally, she acted more or less like an ordinary dog—one who could understand most human speech—but she'd been bred and trained to kill werewolves, and that made her unpredictable. The bargest spell was also a very powerful, very rare form of magic, and it was possible that someone would come after Shadow to try to replicate it. We needed a place with decent security.

Shadow, for her part, seemed happiest and most comfortable when she had plenty of exercise and a little buffer space from strangers, so it had to be a place with few neighbors and a large yard, where we could modify a small room—a walk-in closet, as it turned out—to contain Shadow when I needed to leave her home. At the same time, however, we needed to ensure she stayed well within LA County.

Eli and I were never going to find anything that suited all those needs on our budget, so Dashiell had arranged a house for us. It was actually a small guest cottage on a property that belonged to one of Dashiell's vampire friends, who hadn't lived in the mansion for nearly a decade. Both the mansion and the guest cottage had just been sitting empty that whole time.

Eventually the vampire owner would come back and claim the mansion, and we would probably need to move, but it would be years before I had to worry about that. Meanwhile, we didn't pay rent, but I had to cover the modifications to Shadow's room, any damage she caused, and her extraordinarily expensive "dog food," which was mostly raw buffalo steaks. Most months it amounted to nearly as much as Eli and I had paid for his last apartment.

At any rate, the walk-in-closet-turned-bargest-cell would also hold our new prisoner. And no one would hear if she screamed.

"Whoa, swanky," Jesse said in an awed voice as I gave him the code to the gate.

I rolled my eyes. "Don't get too excited," I told him. "We're not allowed in the big house." He drove the sedan past the mansion and around the back to the small parking area, which was too big to be called a driveway and too small to be an actual parking lot. One of Dashiell's people had kindly delivered my van, as promised. Eli's SUV was parked in his usual spot next to mine. The guest cottage was on the other side.

"Yeah, the big house and the landscaping are really nice," I continued, "but our place is pretty utilitarian. Plus we have to deal with making sure Shadow doesn't eat any of the gardeners."

"That's a full-time job right there," he said in a solemn voice.

Shadow and I went right for the front door while Jesse got Katia out of the backseat, gathering up her flopping limbs. I had to look away, because although she wasn't smelly or rotting or anything, she seemed very, very dead.

The door popped open before I could even put my key in, and suddenly Eli was wrapping me in his arms.

Mmm was the noise that came out of my mouth. I allowed myself a moment to just breathe him in. His hair smelled like saltwater—he must have gone surfing that morning—and when I pulled back he kissed my lips briefly.

"I was worried," he said.

"I know." I stepped back and held my arms out. "But see? Completely fine."

He gave an audible sigh of relief.

"Hi, Eli," Jesse said as he approached, lugging the witch. "Where am I going?"

"Down the hall to the right," I directed.

As Jesse passed us, he gave me a mischievous look and called over his shoulder, "Did Scarlett tell you she got shot?"

"Dick!" I yelled after him.

Eli rounded on me. *"Shot?"*

"It's nothing." I held up a finger and shrugged out of the new jacket so he could see the bandage on my arm. "It was just a tiny graze," I promised. But lifting my arm had caused my shirt to shift in the front, and Eli raised an unhappy eyebrow at the wound there. His hands moved toward my collar to look, but I gently pushed them away. "Just a teeny bit of shrapnel. From my cell phone, not a bomb," I added hurriedly. "I got a clean bill of health at the ER and everything." There was no reason to mention the part where I'd left against doctor's orders.

"You had to go to the ER?" Eli shook his head, hands gripping my shoulders well above the wound. "I don't like this. I'm away from you for less than twenty-four hours, and someone *shoots* you. Here. In LA. What the hell is going on?"

"I will tell you the whole story," I promised. "But we need to take care of the boundary witch first."

His lips turned downward, but the pack's beta werewolf understood priorities. "Fine. I put a bedroll in there, and your buddy Hayne dropped off a couple of bags of O neg and some IV equipment. He left about thirty seconds before you got here."

"Would you please start the IV?" I asked. "I'm supposed to stay away so her boundary magic can bring her back from death. Or whatever."

Eli paused, probably fearing if he let me out of his sight I was gonna ninja-sneak out to get hurt again. "I'm headed straight for the fridge," I told him reassuringly. "I'm starving."

While Eli was getting Katia—or rather, Katia's lifeless body—set up with a transfusion, I sent Kirsten a quick text explaining that we would probably need to allow Allison Luther access to LA for a couple of days. She returned the text immediately, to my surprise, saying that was fine and promising to make sure Dashiell and Will were on board. That surprised me a little, but if Kirsten had met Lex before, she probably trusted her. Lex might be really intense, but she was also sort of reassuring. If she was there to help, things would be better.

That done, I took Shadow out back and used the hose to rinse off the worst of the blood. She hated this process, but I promised her a fresh steak from the fridge, so she bore it with only minimal resentment. Which involved her waiting until I turned off the hose and then shaking her body a foot away from me. "Jerk," I said, wiping a line of water off my face. She opened her mouth in a giant doggy grin.

Afterward we went into the kitchen, where I delivered the promised steak. As Shadow inhaled her meat reward, I washed my hands and began slapping together sandwiches. It was half past two, and Jesse and I hadn't eaten anything since our donut breakfast. We hadn't wanted to hit a drive-thru while we had a bargest and a dead body in the backseat. For some reason.

Jesse found me a moment later and pulled a chair up to the counter, leaning over to watch me. "No mayo on mine," he said.

"I remember." I pointed the butter knife at him. "You were gonna tell me your idea about where those guys came from."

"Where I *suspect* they're from," he corrected, reaching out to snake the first finished sandwich. At my feet, Shadow made a longing noise, so I tossed her some roast beef, which she caught out of the air with a snap that made Jesse's eyes widen.

I grinned. She wasn't even hungry at the moment. "You were saying?" I said.

"Right. The guy in the garage had a tattoo, here"—he touched his breastbone above his heart—"I saw it when his shirt got twisted after he fell. It was sort of a stylized D. It looked like MC ink."

I raised my eyebrows, swallowing a bite of my sandwich. "Master and Commander? Mortal Combat? Mitochloridian Carnage?"

He made a face at me. "What the—no. A motorcycle club tattoo. Biker gang. I just can't remember which one."

I snorted, not bothering to keep the skepticism out of my voice. "You think *bikers* are behind this?"

"No," he said with great patience, "I think whoever's behind this is paying the MC for muscle. And if Shadow hadn't been with us, it probably would have worked out for them."

Well, I couldn't argue with that—Shadow had definitely saved our lives.

I considered his theory while we finished the first sandwiches and started making more. My life is so focused on *supernatural* crime scenes that sometimes I forget there are so many classes of human criminals out there. I didn't know much about bikers, other than what you see on TV shows. And that was just it, I realized—"biker gang" felt like something you saw on television, not actual, flesh-and-blood people you might encounter. Then again, I worked for vampires and werewolves, so who was I to talk about plausibility?

Meanwhile, voluntarily bringing humans into an Old World matter seemed ludicrous to me, but maybe that was exactly why Katia and her vampire buddy had done it. It was a move I hadn't seen coming, and one I had no defense against. I have no special healing skills, and I'm not a soldier like Lex. Even when I use knives and the Taser, I'm pretty much counting on the idea that my opponent isn't used to being human, and will be a little disoriented.

"Okay, so, if the MC really is trying to kill me," I said slowly, "do you think we're safe here?" I gestured around the house.

Unfortunately, Eli chose that moment to walk into the kitchen. "Say what now?" he demanded, looking alarmed. "Did you just say a biker gang wants to *kill* you?"

"See?" Jesse said to me. "*He* knows what MC means." I tossed a slice of bread at him. Jesse ducked, and Shadow pounced on it like a cat.

"To answer your question," Jesse said loftily, "who else knows you live here?"

"Only the other Old World leaders and Abigail," I said, glancing at Eli. He nodded, confirming it. His lips were pressed in a tight line. *Uh-oh.*

"Then I think this place is as safe as any," Jesse finished.

"Scarlett, can we talk?" Eli broke in, giving me a *relationship* look.

"Yeah. Of course." I put down my sandwich. Shadow licked her lips, hoping I was about to make a donation. "Jesse . . ."

He nodded and picked up his paper plate. "I'm going to step out-side and call one of my contacts about the MC. Katia's secure, right?"

"Yeah," Eli said. "She's got the IV going, and there's no handle on the inside of that door."

"Okay, thanks." Jesse gave me a look that said *good luck* and left the room.

Eli turned to me, and I could see him practically shaking with the effort not to run over and grab me. Werewolves rely on touch a lot, and it had become such a habit for Eli that even though he was currently human, he needed to hold me to know I was okay. At the same time, we'd had a few conversations about how I am not a touchy-feely person, and he was trying to respect my space.

It was sweet. I went around the counter and threw my arms around him, hugging him tight. It hurt both of my injuries to raise my arms like that, but he needed to see that I was okay. "I'm fine, really," I told him. "Sit down, and I'll tell you everything."

And I did.

Chapter 22

Okay, I soft-pedaled the part where I got shot, and I conveniently left out throwing a knife to scare Jesse's brother and most of the gunfight at Frederic's. Without outright lying, I may have made it sound like the bikers had been armed with fists and harsh language.

"The cops were coming, so Jesse shot the boundary witch, figuring she might come back from the dead like the one he knows in Colorado," I finished. "And we brought her here because we needed a place to contain her where the bad guys wouldn't find us. Bad *guy*," I corrected myself. "Hopefully there's only one archvillain left. If you don't count the bikers, who are probably just hired muscle."

"Just hired muscle," he repeated, staring at me. For a long moment I couldn't tell if he was mad or just processing. I let him think it through while I finished eating and started putting away sandwich supplies. I got a Diet Coke and a regular Coke out of the fridge, went back to the counter, and set the regular soda in front of Eli.

"We're going to come back to the part where you and Cruz keep putting your life in danger," he said tightly. "But let me see if I'm getting this. A vampire and a boundary witch came to town to frame Molly. You killed and . . . *body-snatched* the witch, the vampire's holed up somewhere making new baby vampires, and Molly's still going on trial tomorrow night because you can't actually prove any of this until the witch wakes up, assuming you can make her talk. Is that right?"

"Wow," I said with genuine admiration. "You should be in charge of all my summarizing from now on. Seriously. Not even kidding."

He opened his mouth to respond, but Jesse came back into the room, still shoving his cell phone in his pocket. "Good news, finally," he declared. "I described the tattoo to my friend at the Santa Clarita Sheriff's Department. She thinks the guys we saw are with the Demon Kings."

I had been taking a sip of my soda at that moment, and while I managed to not spit it out, the carbonation went up my nose, and a few minutes of hacking and coughing followed, while Eli thumped me on the back and I wiped tears from my eyes. The *Demon Kings*? Were they run by an eleven-year-old?

"Scary name," I gasped when I could speak again.

Jesse didn't look amused. Actually, neither did Eli. Tough room. "Jimmy—Jimena Valdez, she's my contact at the Sheriff's Department—said the Kings used to be really bad news. Drugs, weapons, street prostitution. The cops went after them hard, so about twenty years ago, the MC made some changes. Brothels and a little porn instead of street-level hookers, pot instead of heroin, no more guns."

"I swear, that was a cable TV show," Eli said wryly.

Jesse just nodded. "And a lot of the show was based on real MC culture. The Demon Kings aren't the worst of MC culture, but they're still a long way from the Shriners. As evidenced by the assholes we met today."

"But it doesn't sound like they're big into freelance thuggery, and they're sure as hell not Old World," I pointed out. "Why would they be working for a vampire and a boundary witch?"

Jesse shook his head. "That I don't know. But I might be able to find out. Jimmy says Santa Clarita has a confidential informant within the Kings, a low-level guy who the deputies busted for possession with intent. Jimmy called him, and he agreed to meet with me." Jesse's smile looked a little like a shark's. "Or Jimmy convinced him to meet with me. I have to go alone, though."

"No problem," I said, checking the clock. "I need to leave for the first night of the Trials in a little bit anyway."

"I thought they didn't start until six?"

"They don't. Kirsten wards the place to keep out humans, and I have to get inside before she can set the wards, so my nullness doesn't punch a hole through them."

Jesse nodded, then paused. "Where exactly does one assemble the supernatural forces of Los Angeles for a Trials slash party?"

I grinned at him. "You'll like this. Dashiell rented out the Los Angeles Theatre."

"*Seriously?*" Jesse asked, wide-eyed. Until a few years ago, the Los Angeles Theatre was just another one of Los Angeles's abandoned movie palaces. Then it went through a major renovation to apply modern amenities to the original neoclassical style. The grand building was primarily used for movie productions now, but anyone could rent it out for the right (very steep) price.

Jesse's parents and brother all worked in Hollywood, and he'd grown up with one foot in that world. "Now I kind of want to go," he said, looking a little wistful.

"Excuse me," Eli interrupted, and I realized that his face had clouded over. "Have you guys thought about what happens at sunset, when the vampire wakes up and his boundary witch doesn't pick up the phone?"

"Uh . . ." Jesse and I glanced at each other. I didn't want to actually say, "I have no idea," but Eli could pretty much read it on my face. "He's not going to know it was us," I said lamely.

"Of course he will," Eli retorted. "If they recruited human thugs and laid a trap at Frederic's place, they had to suspect you guys were coming. Who else would visit a vampire during daylight hours?"

Jesse and I exchanged a look that pretty clearly communicated *shit, he's right.*

"You think the vampire's going to respond?" Jesse asked me.

I thought it over for a moment. "He—or she—kind of has to," I said. "They're stuck in LA for another two nights while those girls finish turning, and we took away the boundary witch. Katia's a weapon, and we've got it. The vampire's gotta do . . . something. I just don't know what."

"I really wish we knew this vamp's name," Jesse muttered.

"Wish granted," I said solemnly. "From now on, I dub him Count Asshat. If it does turn out to be one of Molly's sisters, we'll change it to Countess."

Jesse held up his hand for a high-five.

Eli glared between us. "This is not a joke," he said, his voice a near-growl. "What if he comes after you? Everyone in town knows exactly where you're going to be tonight."

I shook my head. "True, but it's also where Dashiell, Will, and Kirsten will be. And a hell of a protection ward. Without the boundary witch, this vampire doesn't have a chance against all that."

"What if he has the thugs?" Eli pointed out. "They might not be able to shoot all of us, but they could burn down the theater."

"No," I said, "Kirsten's humans-go-away ward would account for that. Nobody human is going to get on the same block as us, trust me."

Jesse's eyes had lost focus, and I knew he was trying to figure out where Count Asshat could attack, same as me. "What about spouses?" he suggested. "Could the Count go after Kirsten's husband, or Dashiell's wife?"

"Beatrice?" I shook my head. "No. Kirsten's house and Dashiell's mansion have the best security wards in town. Anyway, Beatrice will be at the Theatre organizing the party planning, and Kirsten and Paul split up."

"They did?" Jesse said with his brows raised. It doesn't really matter how big a crisis is: gossip is always interesting. There was plenty more gossip about Kirsten, but Eli broke in before I could continue.

"How much does Frederic know about *you*?" he asked me, looking grave. "Anything he knows, he would tell this other vampire. Could they go after Jack and his family?"

Eli and my brother had actually developed a pretty good friendship, at least as much as a werewolf could be friendly with an unknowing human. He and I had even double-dated with Jack and his new wife, which was so normal it had put a weird taste in my mouth.

"I don't *think* Frederic knows about them," I said, sounding as uncertain as I felt. "But even if he does, Jack and Juliet took the kids to Oahu for their honeymoon, remember? They don't get back until Monday."

We kicked it around for a while longer, but none of us could figure out what Count Asshat was going to do next. He or she could try to get out of town, even with four baby vamps in tow, but boundary witches were valuable, and I doubted they would go without at least attempting to save Katia. It made me very nervous.

But not nearly as nervous as it made Eli. "That settles it," he pronounced when we couldn't come up with anything. "Until this is over, I go where you go."

I reminded myself that he was just being protective because he loved me. Again. "We think this house is safe, but there's still a chance that the Count could figure out where I live," I pointed out. "And come looking for Katia."

Eli saw where I was going with this and started shaking his head violently. "No. *No.* You are not sticking me with babysitting duty while you run around risking your life."

"*Someone* needs to stay here and watch her," I argued. "Jesse has to talk to this MC guy. Kirsten, Dashiell, Will, and I all have to go to the Trials. You're the only other person in the Old World I can fully trust."

I reached across the table to cover his hand with mine, but he jerked away like I'd burned him.

"Absolutely not," Eli insisted. "I'm staying with you."

"I'll be perfectly safe at the Trials, Eli," I argued. "Nobody's gonna be able to touch me around all those people."

Eli shook his head like a dog shaking off water. "Maybe that would be easier to believe," he snapped, "if you weren't coming home *shot*." He pointed at my arm. "These assholes have guns, they're not reliant on magic, and we know nothing about them. They might not be able to enter the theater building, but are you really going to tell me you've got everything under control?"

We'd graduated to yelling voices now, and I realized that Shadow was on her feet, her teeth bared silently in the direction of Eli. She wouldn't normally attack without a command, but if he made a sudden move toward me all bets might be off.

Feeling the tension, Jesse looked at his watch, or pretended to. "I'm going to hit your bathroom," he said. "And then I need to go meet this guy. I'll leave your vest by the van, Scarlett."

Neither Eli or I moved. When Jesse had retreated through the kitchen doorway, I spread my hands on the counter. "What else can I do, Eli?" I asked. "Do you have any better ideas?"

"Stop trying to save Molly," he said immediately, and I realized I'd walked right into that one. *Stupid, stupid Scarlett.* "You're the only person in this whole mess who's trying to get her out of it. If you let it go—"

"Molly dies," I interrupted.

"She did it, didn't she?" he countered. "She admitted she killed those girls. She *should* be punished. And you don't owe her anything. She's barely spoken to you in *years*, over something that was never your fault." For the first time, I realized that Molly keeping her distance from me had actually offended Eli, on my behalf. It might have been really sweet if he wasn't being pigheaded and stupid.

"So because Molly hurt my feelings three years ago, the people who are *actually* responsible for killing eight girls and turning four against their will should just . . . go free?" I said hotly. "No fucking way."

"Have you considered that pushing to save Molly could actually make things *worse*?"

"*What?*"

"Honey." His voice gentled. "Look, at the end of the day, Molly killed a bunch of girls. She goes on trial, she's sentenced to death, that's clean. The system works. But if you wade into this mess and tell everyone that someone's controlling vampires in LA and Dashiell can't stop them, that causes chaos. At the exact time when we can't afford it. And I don't know about Kirsten, but Dashiell and Will know all this."

"They said I could—"

"What? Look for clues?" he said, his tone derisive. "Dashiell has about as much faith in your crime-solving abilities as I have in Scooby-Doo's. He might have moved Molly's trial until tomorrow night, but think about what he *didn't* do. He didn't mobilize his security team to help you, or delay the Trials for a few nights, or even put the word out for vampires to be on their guard against this boundary witch. Because he expects you to fail."

I sat there openmouthed, staring at him. But it wasn't enough to stick the knife in. He had to twist it. "Scarlett," Eli said in a pitying tone, "he sent you on a wild goose chase to keep you calm and well-behaved before the Trials. So you wouldn't kick up a fuss."

I scooted back in my chair abruptly, causing it to squeak on the linoleum. "I need some air," I said through my teeth. "While I do that, how about you call your alpha and see where *he* wants you tonight?"

Without waiting for a response, I stalked out the back door, which I did *not* slam, because I am a motherfucking grownup.

Chapter 23

Jesse was out of the cottage and nearly to his car when he heard Eli's voice behind him. "Hey, Wunderkind! Wait up!"

Jesse rolled his eyes and turned around to see the werewolf jogging— *no, loping,* he thought, that was definitely a man-shaped lope—toward him. Jesse waited next to the car until he caught up.

"I thought you and I had an understanding," Eli practically growled.

Jesse was taken aback. "Is this like a 'stay away from my girl' speech? Because I promise you, the last thing I'm interested in right now—"

Eli batted a hand in front of his face. "That's not what I mean. You're no threat to our relationship." Jesse found himself feeling weirdly insulted. "But I thought you and I were both committed to keeping her safe."

Jesse shrugged. "I want her to be safe, yes. But she's strong, man. She can handle this."

"She *thinks* she can handle this," Eli corrected. "But she's never really been tested, and the people she's up against—the people we're all up against—they don't play fair. They're not going to be impressed by one knife trick, and Scarlett refuses to see that. I thought *you* would know better."

Jesse leaned against his car for a moment, collecting his thoughts before he answered. "Three years ago, after she cured you," he said finally, "and the nova wolf was running amok killing women, you were stuck on the sidelines."

When Eli started to protest, Jesse raised his hands. "I know, you had no choice. I'm not blaming you. But because you were sidelined, you didn't see how she conducted herself during the investigation, or how well she handled herself against physical threats, even when she needed a cane to walk. She did great, and from what I can see, she's only gotten stronger since then."

"You think I don't know she's strong?" Eli demanded. "Who do you think got to be her practice dummy when she was learning aikido throws? You see all those tiny scars on her fingers from the knives? I was the one putting on the Band-Aids. I know she's strong. But I'm pretty sure a bunch of biker thugs are stronger. Plus they have guns, and they're not exactly bound by strong ethics. Scarlett's overconfident."

Eli stepped forward. He'd already been fairly close, like two friends having a conversation, but now he was in Jesse's personal space, trapping Jesse against his car. "And she cares about impressing you," he said through bared teeth. "You're egging her on, making her think she can play detective and walk away unscathed. It's going to get her killed."

Jesse found himself suddenly exhausted. He half-wanted to be mad, but Eli looked so upset and worried that Jesse just pitied the guy. He'd known plenty of cops' spouses, and a lot of them were like this: half-blinded with terror whenever their husband or wife wasn't right in front of them. They were the same spouses who would urge their cop partners to transfer to a safer district, to wear Kevlar all the time, to *be more careful*. What they really meant was *be something else*.

But although Jesse wasn't upset, it was obvious that Eli was spoiling for a fight. His nostrils were flaring, and when Jesse took a quick glance down, he saw the man's hands balled into fists. Werewolf, he reminded himself. Whoops. They had a hard time controlling their emotions, and Scarlett wasn't here to negate the werewolf magic.

Jesse dropped his gaze and took a careful step sideways, sliding away. "I'm not your enemy, man," he said to Eli. "And I'm not going to fight you. That won't keep Scarlett safe."

Eli's body relaxed a little, and he shook his head with a sheepish look. "You're right. I'm out of practice with keeping a lid on . . . things. Sorry."

"No problem," Jesse said, but he took another step for good measure.

Eli blew out a breath, pacing a few feet away and then turning back. "Look," he said, "you're a good guy. I'm just the overprotective boyfriend, but Scarlett trusts you and she cares about what you think. If you tell her to drop all this, she would listen to you."

Jesse laughed out loud, prompting a look of surprise on the werewolf's face. "No, man," he said. "She wouldn't. And even if she did, I'm not going to tell her that. Like it or not, Molly needs her, and so do those missing girls."

Now it was Eli who took a step back, looking surprised. "You've changed," he said after a moment. "Three years ago—"

"A lot of things were different," Jesse cut in. "I was her partner then, and yeah, I wanted something more. I would have done a lot to keep her safe. But now I'm her friend, and she needs someone to believe in her a lot more than she needs my protection."

The anger returned to Eli's expression. "Fine," he said, his voice a half-snarl. "But if something happens to her . . . I'm going to remember this little talk. And we will have a very different conversation then."

Something in his eyes, or maybe his tone, made Jesse's stomach clench. He hadn't spent much time around werewolves without Scarlett, and none at all for years now. He'd forgotten how unnerving it could be. There was something very primal about talking to someone who could literally rip you in half.

Eli spun around and began stalking back toward the house.

Jesse got into the car and locked the door. But he couldn't help himself. He rolled down the window. "You see the irony here, right?" he called.

Eli paused. His shoulders were tensed, his fingers curled like claws. He turned around slowly, scowling.

"Three years ago, she picked you," Jesse went on, not without sympathy, "because I wanted her to be something she wasn't."

Eli actually stumbled back, just a step, as though Jesse had shoved him. Before he could recover, Jesse jerked the gearshift and drove away.

Chapter 24

I had a practice area behind the house, with a big foam target I'd gotten from a sporting goods store and a small bucket of throwing knives. Shadow, who had followed me outside, recognized what we were doing and trotted over to her usual spot, a stone bench that was part of the landscaping. It was close enough for her to keep an eye on me, but far enough away that even when I'd first started out, I didn't accidentally send a knife her way. She leapt gracefully onto the marble, turned around four times, and curled into a surprisingly small ball with her eyes on me.

I saw this out of the corner of my eye as I went to the target and yanked out the knives I'd left last time, tossing them into the bucket with a satisfying *clunk*. These weren't tipped in silver—I only had one of those, though I trained with it regularly—or particularly pretty, but they were great for practice. And for letting off steam. I counted off twenty paces, the bucket clutched in my hand.

Before I turned around, though, I found myself contemplating the little house. I had moved a number of times since coming to LA, but the guest cottage was the first place I'd lived in this city that felt like home. Maybe because I had chosen it, instead of having it foisted on me when I had no time and few options, or maybe because I had personally painted the walls and helped move in the furniture. I had made choices on this house, and I'd been happy here. After nearly three years, it felt more like my own than any place I'd ever been.

And yet I suddenly felt like I was seeing it for the first time. It was strange, realizing how different everything had become in a few short years. Maybe I was just noticing it because Jesse was in my life again, but that didn't make the differences any less valid.

Was Eli right? Had Dashiell and the others sent me on a useless hunt for clues just to keep me busy until the Trials began? Had they already decided to drop the whole thing and let the bad guys get away with framing Molly? I could see Dashiell doing that. And Will would probably go along with it—he wasn't passive, our alpha werewolf, but he was pragmatic when it came to safety.

I didn't want to think that of Kirsten, though. But Molly *had* killed a Friend of the Witches. Did Kirsten want justice badly enough to overlook the nuances?

I whirled around, fast as I could, and threw the first knife. People think knives spin around in the air, but that's a cute party trick, the kind of thing they do at circuses and magic shows. If you want to hurt someone with a throwing knife, I'm a big fan of the quarter-turn method, which lets the blade bury itself further into the target.

The first knife hit the bullseye. And the second. And the third. When the bullseye circle was too crowded for more blades, I went over to the target and began pulling them out again.

This thing with Eli was becoming a problem. I loved him so much, but it felt like we were heading toward some kind of point of no return. He treated me as an equal romantically, but when it came to anything outside of our relationship, he acted like I was a porcelain doll. *Wait*, I thought, my hand frozen on the handle of one of the embedded knives. That wasn't quite right. It was more that he treated me like the Scarlett he had met four years ago, the broken, guilt-stricken girl who blamed herself for her parents' deaths. My head and insides had gotten all twisted up by my psycho "mentor," Olivia, and I'd started experimenting with self-destructive misadventures. My relationship with Eli had started out as one of those misadventures, and now I was beginning to think this was how he still saw me. Someone to be protected. To be saved. He loved me in a way that was uncomplicated, and his love came without strings. He didn't want me to be any more than I already was. He loved me broken.

But what if I wasn't so broken anymore?

On her bench, Shadow lifted her head to watch me closely. I'd been standing there too long without moving. I shot her a reassuring smile and picked up my bucket, taking it back to my starting point.

Eli wanted me to keep my head down, do my job to the letter only, and I couldn't blame him for expecting that, because that's what the old Scarlett would have done. The Scarlett who'd been going through the motions, allowing herself to be herded through choices. I'd never chosen my job, for example—I'd been manipulated into it by Olivia, and then I'd kept doing it after her death because I didn't know what else to do. It wasn't like I'd ever dreamed of mopping up blood or spinning lies to cops.

I hadn't picked the job, but it had crept up on me, bit by bit, and now I—well, if not *loved* it, at least mostly enjoyed it. It was interesting, and challenging, and most important, I felt like the things I'd done had helped some people, even if it was just stopping werewolf bar fights and taking vampires to occasional daytime business meetings. Oh, I wasn't a born do-gooder, like Jesse. I'd never been one of those people who'd come out of the womb wanting to make the world a better place. What I'd wanted was to have a place in the world.

But now that I had that, I found myself oddly grateful that part of my job seemed to involve helping others. Keeping a balance. After what Olivia had done to me, and what several others had tried to do since then, it felt good to right wrongs.

I thought about Molly, and the way she'd looked crumpled on those kitchen tiles, crying and shaking over what she'd been forced to do. And then I remembered what she'd said about Alonzo, and the things he'd done to young women like Molly, for centuries. Someone wanted to do that again. Someone was trying to pick up his mantle.

In my town.

And then I smiled. Maybe Eli was right. Maybe Dashiell and the others *hadn't* actually wanted me to help Molly. But so fucking what?

They weren't stopping me, either.

Chapter 25

Forty-five minutes after he left Scarlett's place, Jesse was sitting down with Jimmy's confidential informant.

Coming up with a meeting place had been a challenge—it had to be somewhere that none of the other Kings would visit, but where a biker wouldn't look so completely discordant that everyone remembered him later. In the end, Jesse suggested the viewing platform at Echo Park, right in front of the pond. At least it was close to his apartment, so he was able to stop at home for a shower and clean clothes.

It was late afternoon, but there were plenty of people walking dogs, jogging, or strolling while they talked on cell phones. There were also several lumpy islands of dirty blankets—homeless people, buried under layers to avoid both stares and the cool wind.

When Jesse reached the viewing platform, the CI was already sitting on the bench, picking at a soupy cup of ice cream he'd brought with him. He was a lean, rat-faced white man with a lackluster goatee who went by the name Rod, though Jesse didn't know if that was his actual name or an MC moniker. Rod seemed jittery, which Jesse sort of expected in a CI, but there was some excitement in his eyes, too. As soon as Jesse sat down, he figured out why.

"Hey, man, *Wunderkind*, is like, my favorite book ever," the guy said right away, keeping his gaze focused straight ahead of them, where a family of ducks was sailing around the pond. "I didn't want to do this meet, you know, but I couldn't resist the chance to have you sign my copy." He pulled a battered hardcover out of the equally battered knapsack at his feet and slid it over to Jesse.

Jesse had to make an effort not to cringe. The book had come out months ago, but the fandom still caught him off guard, especially from this greasy-looking biker who couldn't lace his work boots without missing eyelets. Rod also didn't look like much of a reader, but that was probably unfair.

Jesse left the book on the bench between them, though he flipped it over so his face wasn't showing. "In a minute," he said. "First I'd like to know what happened this afternoon at the condo in Sylmar."

Rod scrunched up his face, his eyes darting to Jesse and then back to the ducks. "I wasn't there, man. I just heard about it later from Carl, okay? He was the only one who made it."

Greasy Beard. "What did you hear?" Jesse asked.

"Some of the guys were asked to do a little freelance muscle for a guy Lee used to know," Rod said. Lee Harrison was the president of the motorcycle club. "He helped Lee get into business back in the day, and figured the prez still owed him one. We were all kind of surprised when Lee agreed, though." Rod gave a little shrug. "Then again, they don't tell me everything. I'm just a grunt."

Jesse made an effort not to let the surprise show on his face. The vampire running this show—Scarlett's Count Asshat—had known Lee Harrison? Or had he just pressed Lee into thinking that? But no, Jesse had a hard time imagining a scenario in which the Count just knocked on Lee's door and magically pressed him. The MC president would be insulated.

"This guy got a name?"

"If he does, they never told me."

"It was definitely a man, though?"

Rod nodded, and Jesse felt a little rush of relief. At least Molly hadn't been betrayed by one of her sisters, on top of everything else. "Which business did he help Lee get into?" Jesse asked. From what Jimmy had told him, the Kings rated pretty low on the crime spectrum these days, but "back in the day" could have been when they were still fairly violent.

"Whores, man," Rod said, keeping his voice low. He stirred idly at the ice cream, now just a pool of liquid with a few slimy gummy bears beached at the bottom. "Before my time."

Jesse felt excitement climb up his spine. This kept coming back to prostitution. "Street girls? Call girls?"

"Nah, like, a cathouse. What's the word?" Rod paused, tilting his head. "Brothel!" he said triumphantly. And a little too loudly. A young white couple with two Yorkshire terriers glanced nervously toward their bench, then hurried along the path. "He was kind of like Lee's silent partner at the time, but Lee got sick of running girls and decided to film them instead. They must have been friendly about it, because Lee said yes when the guy asked for this favor."

"That's a pretty big favor," Jesse remarked. "Was the guy paying Lee?"

Rod shook his head, but then hesitated. "I got the sense—this is just a feeling, you understand—that maybe Lee and this guy are thinking about getting back into business together, here in the Valley. Lee seemed excited, like he does when he's got something in the works."

Jesse felt a chill. Another brothel? No, that might be too big a leap: for all he knew, Count Asshat just wanted to keep paying Lee for muscle. He pushed Rod for more details, but the other man was adamant that he was just speculating. "Anyway," Rod went on, "who knows where that stands now, since it all went FUBAR today. I knew them guys, Ricky and Santos, and they was both good with a gun. They weren't expecting that bitch to have a gunslinger with her."

Jesse saw no reason to mention that he was, in fact, said gunslinger. "What *were* they expecting?"

"Like, a girl in her midtwenties might show up, and they were supposed to scare her. Tie her up and give her to the scary Russian chick. That was it."

"Katia?"

"Yeah." Rod shook his head mournfully. "Lee is pissed, man. If he ever figures out who shot up his guys, there'll be hell to pay."

Jesse thought that over for a moment. "What about the silent partner? Is Lee pissed at him?"

Rod's brow furrowed as if the question had never occurred to him. "You know, now that you mention it," he said slowly, "Lee didn't seem real upset with him. Ordinarily, a guy gets two of the Kings killed, Lee would have his balls on a pool stick. But he didn't want to retaliate."

"Maybe Lee's scared," Jesse suggested, just to see what the other man would do.

Rod shifted uneasily on the bench. "If that's true, man . . . God help whoever goes against *that* guy."

Jesse had a few more questions, but before he could ask, Rod jumped in his seat, and Jesse realized the guy's cell phone was buzzing.

"Gotta get this. Don't talk," Rod said anxiously, answering the phone. "Yeah, it's me." The guy glanced down at his cup. "Just getting some ice cream. What's going on?" He listened for a moment, his eyes darting back and forth to Jesse. "I'm on it."

He hung up the phone and shoved it into his knapsack, along with the book. "You don't want me to sign that?" Jesse asked mildly.

"No time. Boss has a job like, *right now*." Rod stood and slung the knapsack over one shoulder. "Jimmy said this was confidential," he said nervously.

Jesse nodded. "Just getting some background."

"Right. Look, don't call me again, okay? Your face is a little too"— he flapped a hand—"*out there*. If you got another question, go through Jimmy."

Without waiting for Jesse's response, the man turned and hurried away. Jesse counted to twenty and followed him.

Chapter 26

When I went back into the house, Eli was in the kitchen, probably sulking. I already knew why: I'd heard him arguing with Will through the open kitchen window. Will had agreed that Eli needed to stay at the cottage and keep an eye on Katia.

I could have gone in there to talk it out with him, but I just . . . didn't want to. Neither of us were going to change our minds, and I needed to get ready to go. So I bypassed the kitchen, taking a wide berth around Shadow's cell, with the recovering boundary witch, and went into the bedroom to change. Most people seriously dressed up for the Trials, my partners included. Think somewhere between a nice cocktail party and the Oscars. It was, however, generally understood that I might need to get dirty or maybe it was just understood that I didn't much care for dressing up—so I could get away with business casual. I stood in front of the closet for a few minutes, considering, and ended up pulling out a pair of dressy charcoal pants that I could move in and a purple T-shirt. I went outside and grabbed the bulletproof vest from where Jesse had left it leaning against the van door. Back in the bedroom, I put it on over the T-shirt, tightened the Velcro straps, and dug through a drawer until I found the knife belt Eli had bought me for my birthday. He'd gotten it at some kind of science fiction convention where people dressed up in steampunk or whatever, but it was real leather and surprisingly comfortable, as long as I kept it high on my waist so the knives wouldn't dig into my thighs when I sat down. I had brought the bucket of throwing knives inside with me, too, and after I strapped on the belt I fitted eight small throwing knives into the leather slots.

On top of that, I pulled on a long-sleeved black top in a soft jersey material. It was tunic-style and very drapey, designed for women to throw on over yoga clothes while they went out for post-workout smoothies. But it was dressy-ish, washed easily, and covered up the knives and vest. I put on a little makeup so it looked like I'd made an effort and twisted my hair up into a ballerina bun. Then I dug into a box at the top of my closet until I found a thick plastic tub, about the size of a shoebox. These were the things I'd inherited from my mother. I didn't ordinarily wear much jewelry—I had a recurring nightmare where an angry werewolf ripped earrings right out of my lobes—but I picked out a thick, ropelike gold necklace that sat right at the hollow of my throat. It was too short to be much of a liability, unless my attacker was right in my face, and I figured my Taser would dissuade anyone from grabbing at my mother's necklace.

I put my Taser and phone in the discreet pocket on one side of the black top, which was probably designed to hold your keys and wallet on your way to yoga, and checked the mirror. My clothes were a little bulky, and I would overheat easily, considering I was wearing five different layers plus a bra. From the outside, though, I looked okay. I put my two best knives into my boot holsters and started for the van with Shadow following just behind me.

But I halted in the doorway. Any normal dog would probably have bumped into the back of my legs, but Shadow flowed around them in a graceful, snakelike move, lifting her head so she could study my face. I didn't want to leave without saying goodbye to Eli . . . but I also didn't have enough time to get into another fight. Or to spend ten minutes letting him check my vest and my knives to make sure I'd put everything on correctly. "Bye! Love you!" I called over my shoulder, as though I were heading to the drugstore or going for a run. I didn't wait for him to reply.

Outside, I spent a few minutes crawling around underneath the van, checking for listening devices—or, God forbid, explosives. This was one of those times when the security training from Hayne came in handy. But there was nothing there. Either Katia and her pal hadn't thought to track me, or they hadn't been able to find my van to do it. I wiggled out, brushed off my pants and top, and climbed into the van to head downtown.

Before I could even turn the key, however, my eyes caught a bright pink item in the footwell of the passenger seat. My hand froze on the ignition. Molly's backpack. I had completely forgotten about it, and whoever had moved the van for Dashiell hadn't touched it.

I reached down and pulled the pack onto the passenger seat. Every vampire I knew kept a "go-bag" handy, a habit left over from the time when it had been a legitimate possibility that villagers might show up with pitchforks and torches. But I'd never actually looked inside one before. The back compartment held a laptop, and I checked that first, but of course it was password protected. I have many skills, but breaking into a MacBook Air isn't one of them. Abigail might be able to do it, but there wasn't going to be time tonight, and even if I could convince Dashiell's security team to let me talk to Molly, I didn't want to raise too many alarms. We still didn't know who might be working with the bad guys.

I unzipped the backpack's main compartment. The first thing I found was a change of clothes and a pair of shoes. Beneath that, a brick of cash and a passport with Molly's photo and current ID: Molly Arwen Greene. I dropped those on the seat next to the bag and kept digging. There were a few other items that would give Molly's name to the police: her school ID, a lease agreement for her basement apartment, and a few receipts. A cosmetics bag with makeup and a small bottle of hair dye. There were also two small but high-quality pocketknives, probably what she used to cut the people she fed from—vampires could feed with their teeth, but the practice had fallen out of favor decades ago, after the police learned to distinguish between human and animal bites. I unfolded the blades and checked them. I didn't see any blood, but Molly was probably careful enough to clean them, at least to the naked eye.

And that was pretty much it. It was a little disappointing, honestly. I don't know what I had been expecting, but I'd sort of hoped for some kind of smoking gun, maybe a note that said, "Damn you, Molly, you'll get yours!" with the name and address of her archnemesis at the bottom. That would have been handy.

The sky outside my window was beginning to darken. I needed to get on the road if I was going to be close to on time. I was about to pack everything back into the bag, but I reached in and felt around inside first, just in case. My fingers touched something small, cold, and metal, the size of a paper clip. I jerked my fingers back instinctively, but it wasn't sharp, so I reached back in, pinched my fingers around it, and pulled. And kept pulling, until I lifted out a heavy gold chain. At the end was a gold medallion the size of a silver dollar. I turned the bag inside out and found a tiny hole in the lining. Molly had hidden the pendant inside.

I dropped the bag to examine the necklace. It was heavy, and definitely old: the markings on the medallion looked like it might have once been a coin, though they now just looked like a bunch of bumps. I flipped it over. This side had been purposefully worn smooth and shiny, and two dates had been inscribed on it in fancy calligraphy: May 1st, 1905 on top, and below it, May 1st, 1925. Hmm. She'd been turned in 1905, which made 1925 twenty years after she'd been turned. So that was the year her vampire apprenticeship had ended and she'd earned her freedom from Alonzo.

Below the inscribed dates, a third date had been added, but this one had been roughly scratched in by hand, with something like a pin.

March 13th, 1996. I wasn't sure about the significance of that one, but I could take a guess: the day Molly had killed Alonzo.

I weighed the medallion in my hand for a minute, frowning. It reminded me of the dog tags that soldiers wear. Had Alonzo made his prostitutes wear gold necklaces marking their ownership by him? It seemed like the kind of thing a controlling, abusive monster might do. But then why would Molly keep it?

I glanced at my watch, and realized I was going to be late if I didn't get moving. I leaned sideways so I could shove the necklace in my pants pocket, but the medallion was too big—it would leave a lump in my pants that would look funny to a bunch of twitchy, suspicious Old World locals. Shrugging to myself, I put the necklace over my head and tucked it under all of my clothes. The chain was so long that it hung between my breasts, way beyond where anyone would be able to see it just by looking at me. Then I started the van and headed downtown.

Chapter 27

Traffic going downtown on a Friday night wasn't for the faint of heart. While I waited to move the car forward, I called Jesse to check in, but he didn't answer. Probably still meeting with his informant. I left a voice mail explaining that reception was bad inside the theater, but I would call him during the first break, at midnight.

I also checked in with Theo Hayne at 5:30, just to make sure there hadn't been any fresh surprises at the mansion during the rest of the day. He promised me that everything was quiet. Molly had been given a blood bag in her cell, and Dashiell and Beatrice were currently dressing for the Trials. Hayne was going home to catch a few hours of sleep. I knew he was probably exhausted—he'd been working overtime on security for the Trials, including helping Kirsten test her humans-go-away wards. During the Trials was a good time for Hayne to rest, since he couldn't get into the Trials themselves, but he would show up in person to lend a hand afterward, in case Count Asshat decided to make a move at the end of the night.

The sun dipped below the horizon a little after five, taking the golden tones out of the city and painting it in gray concrete twilight. I liked Los Angeles at this time of day. It was less bright and cartoony, less the sunny Hollywoodized LA that everyone sees in the movies. But it wasn't yet nighttime LA, either, which conjured images of either glamorous women in slinky dresses and pin curls, or homeless people sleeping in noxious rags on Skid Row. I always thought LA was its most honest right after the sun fell. This was when you noticed the real people who made the city their home.

Then again, maybe I was just feeling romantic because of my destination. The Los Angeles Theatre was the last of the great downtown movie palaces built on Broadway, back in 1930, when everyone thought LA was going to have a theater district to rival New York's. After World War II, the masses moved out of downtown and into the suburbs, and the Los Angeles Theatre and its brethren stood derelict for years. Some of the palaces were torn down, but a few had been resurrected and renovated in the past thirty years, when LA city planners realized that maybe it wasn't a good idea to turn *all* of the local history into parking structures.

At first, I had thought the idea of hosting the Trials in a building that looked like it had been broken off from Versailles was ludicrous. The Los Angeles Theatre was stunning in its opulence, with a ballroom, a mirror-laden women's lounge, and French Baroque furnishings that would make the phantom of the opera cry with envy. It wasn't exactly what I pictured when I imagined listening to Dashiell hand out death sentences. Even after studying the binders and learning how dry and anticlimactic many of the trials were, a place like the Los Angeles Theatre seemed like a bizarre choice.

It was Kirsten who had pulled me aside and explained Dashiell's reasoning. The whole point of having the Trials now was to appease the members of the Los Angeles Old World who were thirsty for drama, stirring up minor conflicts because they were bored with the peace. By holding the Trials in a theater, Dashiell was giving the people what they wanted: a show.

Moreover, he and the others were hoping that the grandeur of the Theatre would naturally inspire better behavior in the attendees. That might sound naive, but people are conditioned to adjust their behavior in settings like museums, state capitols, and historically significant buildings. Voices are lowered, attire is more formal, everyone is careful of where their elbows and handbags might be bumping. Hopefully this ingrained formality would extend to how the Trials attendees treated one another.

"Plus," Kirsten had added, "it's big enough to hold all of us."

Shadow and I were pulling off the freeway onto 6th Street a little over an hour after we left the cottage. Downtown LA used to be a post-apocalyptic wasteland every night after dark, when all the proletarian worker bees vacated the skyscrapers, leaving empty streets that were well suited to vandalism, assaults, robberies, and worse. A decade and a half of serious effort by the city government had finally begun to resuscitate downtown nightlife, and it showed. The whole area was bustling with food trucks, neon lights, and young Hispanic men waving flashlights at passing cars, trying to direct everyone into *their* parking lots.

I turned the White Whale off 6th and onto Broadway itself, where Hayne had stationed some of his people, guarding sawhorses that blocked off the street. They recognized me immediately—between the van and the bargest, I was not exactly difficult to identify—and waved me through into eerie stillness. Every food truck, trinket kiosk, and newspaper stand on Broadway between 7th and 5th was conspicuously absent tonight. Unlike the street I'd just turned from, there were no pedestrians heading for happy hour at the downtown restaurants. No groups of girls in cheap dresses and wobbly heels, no slouching young men with darting eyes and whistles at the ready. I didn't even see any homeless people. It was like driving into a ghost town.

Dashiell had, of course, arranged all this with the police and local businesses, through his customary blend of mind control and bribery. It actually wasn't as hard as you might think—LA is the one city in the world where you can throw up sawhorses and block off intersections, and if pedestrians complain, you just say the two magic words: "movie shoot." Hayne's people, posing as film studio security, would keep people from entering the street until Kirsten could set up her various protection spells.

I parked in one of the shockingly vacant public lots, and fastened on Shadow's service dog cape. There was an hour to go before the Trials officially began, and I figured there was a good chance that humans would be around delivering food and drinks. I clipped a leash on her collar, purely for appearances, and checked my phone again. Jesse hadn't called. I frowned, not liking it. But Count Asshat would only have been awake for about forty-five minutes, and it would probably take him a little while to realize the boundary witch was missing. How much trouble could Jesse be in?

As if to answer, my phone buzzed in my hand. I managed not to drop it and saw an unfamiliar number with a 303 area code. Where the hell was 303? I answered it with a cautious "Hello?"

"Scarlett, it's Allison Luther. Lex," came a brisk voice. "Cruz isn't answering his phone."

"Oh. He's meeting with someone," I said. To my own ears, I sounded like an eighth grader who's been called on in class and doesn't know the answer. "Can I, um, take a message?"

"That phrase you mentioned," she said. Was her voice always wary, or did I bring out something special in her? "Midnight drain? I asked my boss about it. It's a vampire term. It comes from a poet named Lord Byron."

"What does it mean?"

"If you're talking about two vampires, a midnight drain is taking a very specific and horrible revenge on your enemy," she explained. "Say you have two vampires, John and Jane Doe. If Jane hates John, or feels that he wronged her in a big way, then Jane might find all the living humans that John cares about most in the world. Maybe they're John's current food source, or maybe they're actual human family from when he was alive. Are you following?"

"Yes." And I felt like my heart may have stopped beating, but I didn't say that part out loud.

"So Jane has all of John's favorite living people," Lex went on. "She turns them into new vampires, whom she can control and torment however she wants for the next twenty years. Because new vampires have to obey their makers. So it's not *just* about killing the people that John loves. It's turning them against him through torture and mind control."

"Jesus."

"Yeah," Lex said, and for once, she sounded like a regular human person. "It's basically using vampirism as a curse, in order to enact personal revenge. And in the Old World, it's all technically legal. That's the midnight drain. It's . . . pretty dark stuff."

I almost laughed. Lex was probably the most powerful boundary witch alive; she literally trafficked in death. And she was calling my situation *dark*. Suddenly Molly's reaction to the news about her friends made more sense. Whoever took them wasn't just going to turn them into vampires, or try to use them as prostitutes. They were going to torture those girls simply for knowing Molly, and the whole time, the girls would know exactly why it was happening. And so would Molly.

"Scarlett? Are you there?"

Right. Lex was talking to me. "Sorry, what?"

"I said, any changes with the boundary witch?"

"Still dead." I *needed* Katia to wake up and give us some answers. I just had no idea how I was going to get them.

"I'll be there tomorrow night. If anything changes before then, let me know, okay?"

I said goodbye, and, still reeling, Shadow and I headed into the theater.

Chapter 28

As I'd expected, the lobby was a bustle of activity: human delivery people and caterers, who would be leaving before most of the Old World arrived, plus a number of witches and werewolves who'd been hired to work as bartenders and waitstaff. Before and after the actual proceedings there would be a sort of cocktail party in the downstairs ballroom, run by Dashiell's wife, Beatrice. My only job down there was to circulate at the party, making sure that everyone knew I was around, and capable of removing their powers at any time. Of course, I was also supposed to dissolve any actual altercations before they could escalate into violence.

At eight o'clock, the Trials would begin in the ornate two-thousand-seat auditorium. Afterward, I would need to go back down to the after-party for more peacekeeping. It would be a very long night, requiring a lot of nice manners and diplomacy, two things at which I perpetually sucked. But I was all too aware of how many eyes would be on our corner of the Old World tonight, and on me, especially. I was determined to do a good job even if it meant personally kissing the ass of every single person in the theater until my lips bled.

It's funny; only the previous day, the Vampire Trials had seemed like the most important thing in my personal universe. Now all I wanted was to rush through the next few hours of litigation hand-holding, and then Jesse and I could get back to saving Molly.

And damn the consequences, rang a voice in the back of my mind. It sounded suspiciously like Eli. I told the voice to fuck off.

I wandered around a bit with Shadow, giving a nod of hello as we passed Will, who was addressing a small group of his werewolves. When Shadow had gotten a good look at the whole building, I led her to a small dressing room that had been outfitted to my specifications. Inside was a beanbag chair the size of a Mini Cooper, a buffalo thighbone, several of the world's biggest Kongs, and a tablet that had been rigged by Abigail to play the Nature Channel.

Shadow bounded toward the bone, then stopped, midpounce, and turned to stare at me accusingly. Smart bargest meets obvious bribe.

"We talked about this, remember?" I said, keeping my voice calm and soothing. "You can't be onstage with me during the Trials; it would look bad. But Will, Kirsten, and Dashiell will be right there. I'm not going to be in any danger."

Shadow, who rarely vocalized above a growl, let out an unhappy woof that communicated long-suffering disapproval. Sometimes she reminded me so much of one of the unnaturally prescient dogs in family movies in the eighties and nineties, like Beethoven or Hooch. But then I'd see her absolutely slaughter one of the few squirrels dumb enough to stop by our yard, and I'd remember what I was actually dealing with.

Bringing Shadow anywhere was akin to bringing out the big guns. If I took her into the Trials, it would look like a declaration of aggression, the equivalent of pointing a rifle at the defendant during a court trial. But at the same time I wanted to keep her close in case there *was* trouble, especially werewolf-related trouble. So she couldn't come in, but she needed to stay on site.

Which worked out, since her cell at home was currently occupied.

I crouched down—not very far—and scratched at her ears and sides. She leaned her head forward to rest on my shoulder. "I know," I whispered. "You hate being left behind. But it's just two nights, and you're right here in the same building, see?"

I gave her one last hug and left, feeling guilty. Then again, I also had no doubt that Shadow could break down the ancient door if she really wanted to. I was just hoping she'd choose to destroy the beanbag chair if she needed to punish me. Dashiell had paid for it.

I found Kirsten downstairs in the largest dressing room, tapping thoughtfully on her lower lip as she looked over a pile of spell materials that was spread over the vanity counter. She was dressed in a cream-colored silk blouse, loose but cropped at the waist, covered in itty-bitty sequins. Her satin skirt was an earthy brown, tight at her waist and flaring out at her thighs, and her white-blonde hair was braided around her head, with tiny blue rosebuds embedded in the braid. They were the same blue as her eyes.

I suddenly felt greasy and poor, like I'd wandered into the Oscars in yoga pants. "Wow," I said without thinking. "You look amazing. And very . . . you."

Kirsten glanced up and gave me a frazzled smile. "Thank you." She eyed my outfit, her lips twitching in a "not bad, could be better" kind of look. I fought the urge to look down at what I was wearing. "I like your necklace," she offered. "What's happening with the boundary witch? Any change?"

I'd left Kirsten a voice mail after we captured Katia, but I hadn't known if she'd actually gotten it. I gave her an update about Katia, and Lex's prediction that she'd be dead through the night. As Kirsten listened, her eyes kept flicking back down to the spell materials. It was a big-ass ward, and I knew she was a little nervous about it.

"Where do you want me?" I said when I finished explaining.

She directed me to the downstairs ballroom, where a few early arrivals were already starting to mill around. I didn't know anyone there, so I went over to the refreshment table. Because all of the staff had to be from the Old World, and most of them wanted to see the Trials, we had decided to forgo waitstaff in favor of one long table of hors d'oeuvres and pre-poured beverages, which could be supervised by one or two people trading off. The setup was a lot like a high school dance refreshment table, if your high school had a lot of money, expensive tastes, and access to beer and wine. We had discussed serving blood for the vampires, but it was eventually decided that they could eat before they arrived. Tonight was about keeping the peace, and watching vampires drink blood isn't exactly a peaceful experience.

I nodded at the petite witch behind the table, who was currently making sure the little rows of food were lined up with a precision that would make any OCD sufferer proud. I actually felt kind of bad about grabbing a small container of popcorn, but I did it anyway, because it was the fancy kind dipped in white fudge. And if a fight broke out, I might not get a chance later.

While I was snacking, Kirsten was setting up the wards outside. They involved two complex pieces of magic: first, a go-away-humans spell on the entire block, which would also compel any humans who still lingered to want to leave. Then there was a second, more protective spell that would prevent anyone from entering the building with intent to take a life.

During our planning meetings, I'd asked if she could block anyone who intended to *hurt* someone else, but Kirsten said that was nearly impossible. It was already very difficult and complicated to determine the difference between someone who *wanted* to do something and someone who *intended* to do something. Plenty of the attendees would sort of want to *hurt* one another, and a few of them would maybe even be planning on it, and the difference was particularly slippery. It was much easier to block murderous intent, because that would hopefully be rare.

Of course, magic tended not to work very well against itself, which was why witches couldn't usually spell vampires or werewolves at all. I had mentioned this concern to Kirsten too, but she'd assured us that she'd been experimenting on potential wards for months now. She said she'd figured out a way to blend gravitational magic with witch magic, and she was confident that she'd cracked the problem.

I'd dropped the subject, but inwardly I was still worried, mostly because I couldn't see how Kirsten could have tested her new spell. How many people could she know who truly intended to commit a murder?

At any rate, the bad guy wouldn't be able to send gun-toting humans in here, and hopefully he wouldn't be able to enter either, not if he was planning to kill someone. But just in case, each of the theater doors was being guarded by one vampire and one werewolf in wolf form. These guards had been carefully selected for their temperament, as well as their willingness to miss the main Trials, and they were being paid *very* well for their time.

Kirsten came back inside half an hour later, looking tired but pleased. I wasn't sure how to ask her if she'd been successful without insulting her, so I just showed her a thumbs-up with my eyebrows raised, from across the ballroom. She grinned and nodded. Then she pointed toward the side door. I turned. Two humans in catering uniforms, who'd been unloading crates of beer, suddenly put down their loads, turned, and beelined for the exit at a near trot. I relaxed. So far, so good.

"Scarlett!" cried a familiar, cultured voice behind me. I turned to see Beatrice, Dashiell's wife and the official hostess for the party portion of the Trials. Like everything else in the Old World, this was a calculated decision, like a vampire couple version of good cop/bad cop. Dashiell would be the stern, rule-abiding leader, and his wife would soften the blow by charming and entertaining everyone afterward.

I truly liked Beatrice, who was one of the few vampires I knew who didn't hesitate to be near me. She was still smiling as she hit my radius, and adjusted so quickly that I only noticed a slight tottering on her stiletto heels as she lost her supernatural ability to balance. She kissed me on both cheeks. "I like your dress," I said, making her beam.

"Thank you, my dear," she said, looking down at the tight, white sheath. Beatrice was the only person I knew who *always* dressed like she was at a fancy cocktail party, but for once it was more than appropriate.

We chatted about the party for a few minutes, Beatrice's eyes darting around checking on things the whole time. It was so strange to see her actually nervous. I was accustomed to her natural confidence.

"How's his mood tonight?" I asked, keeping my voice light. Beatrice wasn't the kind of wife who gossiped or complained behind her husband's back, especially considering how much power and influence he had in the city. But she also recognized that Dashiell could be a wee bit abrasive, and there were things that she was allowed to say that he wasn't. Like "Hey, Scarlett, maybe you should avoid Dashiell for a couple of days. He's a bit touchy about you."

That had only happened a few times. Really.

"Actually, he seems pretty positive," she said, her face brightening. "I think he'll be relieved when the Trials end."

Beatrice's eyes suddenly flicked toward me like she was avoiding something, and I instinctively glanced toward where she had been looking a moment earlier. A plump Latina woman in a black dress was glowering at me like she could set me on fire if she squinted hard enough. I expanded my radius a little, until it encompassed her. She was a witch.

And Beatrice had tried not to draw my gaze to her. "Who is that?" I asked. "Why is she giving me that look?"

"Her name is Manuela," Beatrice said in a low voice. "She has a wife, Daphne. And Daphne's daughter Louisa was one of Molly's roommates."

I took a subconscious step backward. Louisa was the Friend of the Witches.

I hadn't given much thought to the connection; I'd been too focused on Molly. But now that I was looking at the stepmother of one of the girls who'd been taken, guilt and sadness twisted my stomach around like it was being wrung out. Louisa was likely to become a vampire, and her parents had no idea.

I stepped closer so we wouldn't be overheard. "Dashiell told you about what's been going on?"

She nodded, reaching over to squeeze my forearm lightly. "I'm sure it will all work out," she said. "If you'll excuse me, I need to check on the refreshments now that the human help is gone."

She was gone before I could respond. I stared at her back for a moment, surprised. Had I just gotten a brush-off from *Beatrice*? That was a first. Why wouldn't she want me to talk about Molly? Was she afraid I'd ask her to intervene with Dashiell?

Or, I told myself, maybe we were just low on wine.

The rest of the first cocktail hour was surprisingly sedate. As the vampires woke for the night and more people arrived, the room began to naturally divide itself into three factions, as everyone stuck to their own kind. At least a few people were mingling around the food table, though. Damn, this really was like a high school dance.

As I watched them interact with each other, I saw a couple of glares being traded between the wolves and the vampires, and a lot of smug smiles, too. There was a certain mood of "just wait till the trial starts; you'll get yours" in the air, and that was just fine with me, because it meant that no one wanted to start anything physical, in case it would affect the outcome of the leaders' decision. I was more concerned about *after* the Trials, when the losers would be upset, and the winners would gloat. And everyone would be drinking.

A very thin, curly haired woman of mixed race wormed through the crowd directly toward me, although it took me a second to recognize her in formalwear. Lizzy was the werewolf pack's sigma, its weakest member, and one of the three newer wolves whom Eli affectionately called "the pups." Tonight she was wearing a slinky, dark green dress that ended at midthigh, along with high heels that would have given me airsickness. Werewolf grace does have its benefits.

"Scarlett! I've been looking for you," she cried, throwing her arms around me. She drew in a long breath through her nose. It usually weirded me out when a werewolf sniffed me like that, but Lizzy was a special case. She had been attacked by the same nova wolf who'd killed Lex's sister, and for nearly two years after that, she'd been out of her mind. I mean that literally.

Will knew a somewhat shady doctor who specialized in the Old World, and when it had become apparent Lizzy wasn't going to recover on her own, he had called Matthias to evaluate her. It was Matthias who'd discovered that the nova wolf attack had induced a sort of magically forced manic depression in the new werewolf, and after a few terrible months of trial and error, he had found a combination of serious drugs that kept Lizzy in balance—although she needed to take them every two hours, thanks to werewolf metabolism. But she was finally stable, and had joined the equivalent of the werewolf freshman class.

Jesse and I were the ones who'd stopped the nova wolf, and afterward Lizzy had sort of imprinted on me, for lack of a better word. She could smell me as much as she needed to.

Finally, Lizzy disentangled, pulling back and tugging at her dress hem. "Have you seen Eli?" she asked, looking anxious.

I felt a stab of guilt. "He's not coming, Lizzy, sorry," I told her. "But Will's here, and all the rest of your pack." She wrapped her arms around herself, looking uncertain. I turned my body to point to the exit. "And by the women's bathroom there's this little room where they used to care for children, with murals on the wall and stuff. We've set that aside as a quiet space for anyone who needs to take a breather."

Lizzy's shoulders finally relaxed, and she gave me a nod. "Thanks, Scarlett."

"No problem."

I had already shifted my weight to move away when she added, "Is it true, about your friend?"

I stopped. "Is what true?"

Lizzy looked embarrassed. "Oh, sorry, I just . . ." She gestured around the room. "Everyone's talking about it, and I thought it was more polite to just ask the source . . . ? Sorry, maybe not."

Following her hand, I looked around the room and realized that, sure enough, half the people here were eyeing me and whispering. I was used to that, to some degree, because having a null in the room was always disruptive in the Old World. But usually they would look away, embarrassed or even a little frightened. Tonight, I was getting *angry* looks, and not just from Manuela the witch.

"What exactly is everyone saying?" I murmured to Lizzy.

"Uh . . ." She twisted her hands together, uncomfortable.

"It's okay," I promised. "You won't get in trouble for telling me."

"Well, the rumor is that your friend, the vampire, killed a whole bunch of college girls, and now you're trying to convince Dashiell to let her go," Lizzy said in a rush. "Everyone's really mad because they think she broke this big rule and now you're going to help her get away with it."

I winced. Not good. "Is it true?" Lizzy added in a soft voice.

"No. Well, some of it. But I'm not trying to help Molly get away with murder. We're just looking into all the possibilities before she goes on trial," I said vaguely. Lizzy nodded, looking uncertain. I wanted to tell her—and everyone else—the whole story, but Dashiell and Will were right. If people found out about the boundary witch, or even the homicidal vampire, in town, it could provoke a serious uprising even now that we had Katia. I prayed that she would wake up in time to testify at Molly's trial. It might be the only way to set things right.

A pleasant but loud chime sounded, and the ballroom went quiet. I checked my watch. Eight o'clock. Showtime.

Chapter 29

Rod hadn't driven his motorcycle to the meeting at Echo Park, probably wanting to remain low profile. Jesse trailed the guy's beat-up sedan
toward the entrance to the 101 freeway, wondering what the hell he was
doing. Rod was probably just going back to Santa Clarita for some kind
of MC meeting, and Jesse was wasting his time. Still, he couldn't go to
the Trials, and he couldn't think of any other way to help Scarlett and
Molly just then, so he kept going. A wild goose chase would be better
than sitting around doing nothing.

But then Rod went south on the 101, the complete wrong direction
from Santa Clarita, and Jesse began to trust his own instincts. Although
he wished he'd thought to bring snacks.

It was a short trip on the freeway—Rod exited after less than a mile,
and Jesse realized with a degree of panic that he was heading for Union
Station. Was the biker fleeing town? Jesse couldn't see why, unless it
was somehow in the call he'd received at their meeting. Had the MC
president figured out that Rod was informing to the police and friends?

But Rod didn't go into the train station; he just cruised around
the parking lot for a bit before stopping behind a Ford SUV. As Jesse
watched, the biker glanced around for pedestrians, squatted down, and
removed the SUV's license plates. He tossed them into the back seat of
the sedan and took off again. Interesting.

They got back on the 101, and keeping Rod's sedan in sight got tricky as hell in the early evening traffic. After more than an hour, the red sedan bumped onto a long stretch of deserted road near Palisades Park, almost all the way to the ocean. Rod turned onto a small dirt road that led into a field of dead grass. Jesse could see several motorcycles and a black SUV already parked along the same turnoff, so he kept driving. Rod may have been too inattentive to notice he was being followed, but his MC buddies might be a little sharper. Jesse pulled over a quarter of a mile down the road and turned around so he could watch the turnoff entrance.

It was fully dark now, but there was just enough light reflected from the LA smog for Jesse to make out the group of men emerging on foot, crossing the street and tramping into the scrubby trees on the other side of the road from the turnoff. Surprised, Jesse got out of the car and jogged after them, wary of being spotted. When he got to the place where they'd left the road, he crouched low and peered into the trees. There was a faint path, possibly just from the men themselves. The group of trees was too small to be called a forest—more like a little oasis of trees in a desert of beach sand and dead grass. Jesse drew his gun and followed the path for three or four minutes before he saw where the men had exited. Just past it was a wide expanse of sand, with no coverage at all. A hundred yards away, there was a wooden cottage facing the ocean. The small back porch held some sort of gear—Jesse couldn't make it out from his hiding place—and a back door. Light was spilling through every window, and Jesse saw at least one shape inside the house, moving at an unconcerned pace.

Jesse couldn't see any of the men at this distance. Everything was alarmingly silent for about four heartbeats, and then all the lights in the house went off at once. Almost immediately, there was the loud pop and the lightning flash of gunfire, followed by indistinct yelling. Jesse started for the house, but the back door banged open with surprising violence. He dropped to the ground and army-crawled back to the cover of the trees.

When he turned back to face the scene, there were six flashlight beams headed his way from the porch. Jesse pulled back further, staying low to the ground. He heard laughter, and the sort of tone that signifies men teasing each other.

"—should have seen the look on Raggers's face!"

"Me! I thought you were gonna piss yourself when the big bastard brought his gun up!"

"How do you think he knew we were there?" wondered a third voice. "We was quiet, yeah?"

The other voices murmured in agreement. Now they were close enough for Jesse to see that four of the six were carrying something enormous between them. Something rectangular—each of them held a corner—and it seemed heavy, judging by their grunts.

"You see some of the shit in that place?" said one of the voices. "Kevlar, shotguns, holsters 'n shit. The fuck does this Negro do?"

"Not much, by the time Lee's buddy gets through with him," said another.

Jesse put it together in an instant. The long black object was a body bag, and it held a large black man who kept weapons in his home.

Hayne.

Their progress through the wooded area was slow, but Jesse still only had a second to think. He couldn't face this many armed men by himself, and he would never be able to make it back to his own car in time to follow them. But he had to try. He whirled around and ran as fast as he could back the way he had come. Despite his best efforts, he made a little bit of noise, but the bikers didn't notice. They had completed their mission, and now they were bragging and laughing, cocky.

Jesse made it about forty yards past the SUV, in the direction of his own car, before the bikers broke from the woods. He dove behind a fat clump of wild rye, ducking down just in time to avoid being hit by the men's powerful flashlights. He was breathing hard—not enough exercise lately—and had to work to control the sound.

When the lights stopped flashing he peered through the fronds of the giant rye, and saw that the body bag being carried across the road to the SUV had started to squirm. Jesse sighed with relief. Hayne was still alive. A couple of the bikers punched the middle of the bag, and Hayne got the message and went still. Jesse ducked his head back down so the headlights wouldn't catch him. There was nothing to do now but wait until the SUV drove off and then sprint for his car.

For the first time since he'd arrive at this location, he tried to think through what was happening. The vampire in charge hadn't attacked the Trials, not without his boundary witch. Instead, he had sent his human muscle to kidnap one of Dashiell's assets. Was he hoping Dashiell would make a trade? Jesse doubted it. The invading vampire had to know that Dashiell would never trade even a loyal human for a valuable commodity like a boundary witch. A null, maybe, but Scarlett was safe at the Theatre; she'd left him a message saying she'd made it. So what would kidnapping Hayne accomplish?

The SUV rolled past his hiding spot. Jesse counted to twenty and broke cover, running toward his car. By the time he reached the sedan, the SUV's taillights had long since disappeared around the corner. There was no way he'd be able to follow them in his car.

Jesse sagged against the driver's door, cursing. He dug out his phone and noticed a voice mail message from Scarlett. She was calling to let him know there was no cell service in the Los Angeles Theatre, which meant he couldn't tell Dashiell or the others about Hayne. Shit. Scarlett had said there would be humans-go-away wards around the whole building, which meant he wouldn't even be able to get close. What a clusterfuck.

He started to open the car door, but stopped with the door about two inches from the frame. Hadn't Scarlett said that Hayne wore those little witch bags that protected him from vampires?

Instead of doubling back, Jesse got into the car and pulled onto Hayne's actual street. He parked so his headlights illuminated the door, which had been kicked in with a heavy boot—there were tread marks next to the doorframe. The light switch didn't work, so Jesse used a small penlight on his keychain.

The house was quite small, and had probably been very neat and sparsely furnished—before the MC guys had trashed it. The bikers hadn't been in there long enough to do serious damage, but they'd done some cursory dumping of drawers and throwing of cushions, probably trying to make it look like a robbery. Just inside the door, Jesse's foot crunched on something, and he moved the light to illuminate the crumpled shape of a plastic baby toy. Jesse frowned. Hayne had a kid? Man, he really was out of touch. But there wasn't much baby paraphernalia, so maybe the kid only lived here part-time. Or maybe it was a niece or nephew who visited often. Whoever it was, at least the kid hadn't been here when the MC showed up.

Jesse stepped through the junk in the living room and moved down a short hallway to the only bedroom. A Pack 'n Play had been overturned and half-collapsed. The bikers had flipped the mattress and box springs off the wood-framed bed. Next to it was a small fireproof safe, the kind you could buy at an office supply store. They'd thrown it down against the stone tiles until the tiles had cracked and the hinges had popped off the safe. Jesse squatted in the mess. No cash—if Hayne had any, the bikers would have taken it as part of their cover. All that remained was a passport for Theodore Hayne, a few official documents—and a gallon-size ziplock bag full of miniature burlap sacks, each about the size of a marshmallow. Jesse grinned. The bikers had left behind the real treasure.

He opened the ziplock and upended it, dumping witch bags all over the floor. As he'd been hoping, Hayne had been prepared for more than just a vampire press: the bags were marked with a simple "V," "W," or "Ww" in black marker. Jesse looped one of each around his neck, just in case. Then he ran for the car.

Chapter 30

I went up the stairs with the rest of the crowd, but broke away when they began filing into the auditorium. A series of small corridors led back to the wings, and through them to the stage itself. The exterior curtain was closed, but the two interior curtains were drawn, creating a large open space. The stage had been set up that afternoon: on one side, three ornate chairs that couldn't *quite* qualify as thrones, and on the other, a long table with three simple straight-backed chairs—the seating for me, the defendant, and the accuser. Lucky me, I'd be sandwiched in the middle of them. Will was already sitting in one of the ornate chairs, and Kirsten was gathering her skirts to sit down in the opposite chair, leaving the middle seat for Dashiell.

I swallowed hard, feeling butterflies in my stomach for the first time. It was all so *big*. I'd been to the theater before, when we were making arrangements, but all of a sudden it felt very, very real. I wished Eli were here. Things were a little rocky between us, but I felt unmoored without him, like a kite without a string. More than anything, I wanted him to be standing with me, squeezing my hand.

I caught Kirsten's eye, and she gave me an encouraging smile and a wave. Right. *Move your feet, Scarlett.* I pushed out a breath and went to my seat at the other table. Just as we'd planned, the distance between me and the other leaders was too great for them to be in my radius.

Dashiell, Will, and Kirsten would retain all their powers during the proceedings.

Dashiell was standing center stage, his back to the curtain. He looked sophisticated and confident in his tuxedo, much more James Bond than concert pianist. As soon as I took my seat, he turned toward us and raised his eyebrows in a simple look: *ready?* The fudge popcorn had solidified to a slimy lump in my stomach, but I forced myself to put on my game face. We all nodded, and Dashiell pointed offstage, cuing whoever was in charge of the curtains. The red fabric began to draw to either side, slowly revealing us. The light onstage was still fairly dim, but a bright spotlight clicked on, pointing right at Dashiell.

"Good evening," he announced. I risked a glance at the crowd, trying to peer past the stage lights. I'd figured we would only need a fraction of the available space, given the Theatre's size. To my surprise, nearly every one of the two thousand seats was filled. Had our intel on the number of people in the Old World been faulty, or had people from outside Los Angeles snuck in to see how we did things? Or was it both? We'd taken so many security precautions, but it hadn't occurred to me to make sure that all the Old World attendees were actually part of the *Los Angeles* Old World.

Then I realized that Manuela, the witch who now hated me, was sitting front row center. Her arms were folded tightly across her chest.

Great. That wouldn't be distracting at *all*.

"Welcome to the Vampire Trials," Dashiell said simply. "As you know, this event is held approximately every three years as a way to solidify the unique arrangement that binds us together in Los Angeles, allowing us to share power." I noticed he didn't say share power *equally*. "As is our custom, we will have five hours of trials, including a break in the middle, followed by several hours of . . . *socializing*." I couldn't see Dashiell's face, but I could hear the humor in his voice. "We will repeat this same schedule tomorrow night."

A murmur went through the crowd, as people shifted in their seats and whispered to their neighbors. Dashiell held up a hand. "I understand that many of you have heard about an incident that took place yesterday evening near the University of Southern California. One of our vampires has been accused of killing a number of young women." He paused, letting that sink in. In the front row, Manuela the witch glared at me with a renewed intensity. I barely suppressed the instinct to slump down in my seat.

When Dashiell spoke again, it was into a void of dead silence. "I can assure you that the vampire in question will be tried for the crimes of blood-gorging and risking exposure. I have scheduled her trial for first thing tomorrow evening."

Another murmur, and maybe I was being paranoid, but this one sounded disappointed. The crowd wanted blood, and they wanted it now.

Dashiell gestured to his left. We had built portable wooden steps and set them at the corners of the stage, on either side of the gaping orchestra pit, so the litigants wouldn't have to leave the auditorium and traipse through the backstage area. "These stairs will be for the defendant," Dashiell announced. He gestured to his right. "And these will be for the accuser. Let us begin." He nodded to a short, stocky vampire standing at the corner of the stage behind a podium with its own microphone. "Lawrence, please read us the first names."

The rest of the onstage lights went up, and Dashiell took his seat between Kirsten and Will. Lawrence, one of Dashiell's most loyal—and most sycophantic—vampires, opened the protective cover of a tablet and tapped at the screen. "Werewolf Travis Hochrest has been accused of theft by Witch Adrienne Pough," he called grandly, as though he were announcing the arriving guests at a ball.

An ample woman in her forties and a skinny werewolf with a bulbous nose both approached their sides of the stage, making their way over to sit in the chairs on either side of me. I hadn't met Adrienne

Pough, but she gave me a prim nod and took her seat, her hands folded on the table in front of her. Travis Hochrest, on the other hand, tried to give me a fist bump. "Scarlett, my man!" he cried. "Long time no see!"

The audience tittered, and I smiled in spite of myself. I'd cleaned up more than one minor mess caused by Travis. I declined the fist bump, which caused him to plop down in the chair with an injured look. A wave of body odor assaulted my nostrils, and I was suddenly very glad not to have enhanced senses.

"Adrienne," Kirsten began, "please tell us what happened between you and Travis." We had agreed in advance that the leader for each party would be the first to address them, and that we would use first names, because most of the vampires only knew each other that way.

The witch beside me looked like she wasn't sure whether to sit or stand. Kirsten gave her an encouraging smile as if to say, "*Either way.*" She stayed seated.

"I used to have a goat," the witch said abruptly. She bit her lip, winced, and started again. "That is, until last year I kept a small goat in my backyard, for milk, mostly. At the Midsummer party, Travis Hochrest said he could smell it on me. He was really . . . interested." A disgusted look crossed her face. "Anyway, I believe he followed me home that night, because the very next morning when I went out to feed Shelly—that was her name—she was . . . she had been killed." Adrienne's voice faltered as she got choked up. "And there were wolf prints in the blood."

"Isn't it possible that a coyote got the goat?" Kirsten asked carefully.

Adrienne shook her head. "No, ma'am. I grew up in Montana, see, and there are wild wolves there. I saw their tracks all the time. I know a wolf print when I see one." She reached into her cardigan pocket and held up a cell phone. "I got pictures of them, too."

Will held up a hand. "That won't be necessary. I have seen Adrienne's photos, and I concur that it was a werewolf." He turned his gaze to Travis. "What do you have to say for yourself?"

"Like, it was a *goat*, you guys!" said Travis, and the audience tittered again. "I'd pay the lady for it, but I don't have any cash right now. I actually, um, owe cash to a couple of the other wolves. We have this poker game and—"

"I think that's enough," Will said, after a glance at the others. "As alpha, I will pay my wolf's debt to Ms. Pough." He sent a kind smile across the stage for her. Then his eyes moved to Travis, and narrowed to something very lupine. I actually kind of felt bad for Travis, even though he was an idiot. "Travis, you and I will work out the details of your debt in private."

I could actually hear Travis swallow next to me. And here I had thought that only happened in cartoons.

And so it went. The next two trials were fairly uneventful, though neither was as open-and-shut as the Case of the Pilfered Goat. One of the vampires was reprimanded for starting a fight at Hair of the Dog—why had the moron decided to hang out in a werewolf bar in the first place?—and two witches were admonished for trying to recreate a strain of an herb that was poisonous to werewolves. Their excuse—that they weren't trying to breed anti-werewolf magic into wolfberry; they just wanted to make it tastier so they could use it in a homemade dessert wine—was so stupid and flimsy it almost had to be true.

We were listening to one of the vampires tell an elaborate story about why he should be allowed to record himself waking up for the night so he could study the footage when I heard a hiss from the wings behind me.

"Scarlett! Scar!"

I jumped in my seat, and the vampire next to me turned to look, too. Dashiell, who was rarely interrupted under any circumstances, much less in the middle of the Vampire Trials, glared at a spot over my shoulder. I turned—and saw Jesse standing fifteen feet behind me, gesturing frantically for me to come over there. Shocked, I shook my head slightly, but that only made him march forward. As he got closer I saw his rumpled, dusty clothes, his torn pants, and the look of desperate determination on his face. I held up a hand—*stop*—and turned around to face Dashiell again. He was still glowering, but he gave me a barely perceptible nod, and I pushed my chair back and stepped offstage, expanding my radius to keep the two people at the litigant table human.

"What the *actual* hell, Jesse?" I whispered, as quietly as I could. Most of the people in the theater had superhuman hearing, and they would undoubtedly be curious about us going off-script. "What are you doing?" Before he could answer, a new thought struck me and I added, "How did you even get in here?"

Understanding the need for quiet, he grabbed my arm and put his mouth near my ear. I was hit with his familiar scent—Armani cologne and oranges. "The bad guys took Hayne," he murmured. "He's alive, for now, but I don't know what they're planning."

I tensed. Without giving it much thought, I whirled around and made my way to the edge of the stage, where I was still out of sight of the audience, who were now whispering amongst themselves. Dashiell, Will, and Kirsten were all staring at me, as was the vampire on trial.

I didn't want to mouth words where the defendant could see me, so I just looked at the Old World leaders, lifted a flat hand and slid it across my throat, the international symbol for *stop it*. Then I mimed tipping my head back for a drink. "Getting a drink" was our code for an emergency meeting, since although I might conceivably get together with either Kirsten or Will to discuss something casual, there was no scenario in any dimension that would involve just the four of us having social cocktails.

Kirsten's eyes widened. Dashiell was glowering at me, and although he wasn't human at the moment, I could easily translate his expression. *This better be worth it, or you're dead.* I just hoped he didn't mean that literally.

Dashiell rose from his chair and turned to address the restless audience. "Ladies and gentlemen," he began, in a tone that left absolutely no room for argument or complaint, "there is a matter which requires my immediate attention. We will take our break early, and resume in ten minutes."

A rustle of dissatisfaction ran through the crowd, but no one dared contradict Dashiell in any direct way. The vampire leader strode across the stage toward me, and Kirsten and Will followed.

Five minutes later, the five of us were congregated in the same sound-proofed dressing room where Kirsten had prepared her spell materials. Dashiell was fixing a laserlike stare on Jesse, as if he might x-ray him and see the truth. "You're saying they took Hayne, who's still alive, but you don't know how to find him. Do I have that right?"

Jesse nodded. He'd already explained stealing the witch bags and his difficult trip through the wards and the guards. The vampire at the front door had recognized Jesse from a previous trip to Dashiell's house—three years isn't much in undead time—but the werewolf had tried to restrain him physically, hence the torn pant leg. Jesse claimed the wolf didn't break skin, but he'd also been smart enough to steal one of the witch bags that protected the wearer from werewolf infection. Of course, now that he was close to me, all his protections had shorted out. I had already decided not to let him out of my sight while we were at the theater.

"The only thing I can't figure out is, why Hayne?" Jesse continued. "In theory, Hayne could let this guy into the mansion, but you and Beatrice are both here, so what could he hope to gain? And it's not like you'd trade Hayne for Katia, right, because he's just a human." Jesse seemed to hear how shitty that sounded, because he winced. "I can't believe I just said that—uh, Kirsten?"

I looked at the head witch. Her lips were pressed in a tight line, but her skin had gone red and fat tears were rolling down her face. She was practically shaking with the effort to keep it together, and I could feel her magic flex involuntarily inside my radius.

Jesse shot me an uncertain look. "Hayne and Kirsten are more or less back together," I muttered under my breath. "They don't live together, but they have a toddler."

"Oh. *Oh*," Jesse looked exactly like I'd elbowed him in the stomach. "I'm so, so sorry, Kirsten. I didn't mean to sound so crass—"

She lifted a hand, cutting off his apology, but she couldn't handle speaking yet.

Will was looking at Dashiell. "Would we?" he asked quietly. "Would we trade this boundary witch to get Theo back?"

"We would undoubtedly *pretend* that we were willing to exchange the hostages, in order to get close to this vampire," Dashiell said without hesitating. "Which is why he won't ask for a trade, especially considering how much we outnumber him."

Jesse blew out a breath, frustrated. "Well, unless he's just trying to kick us in the nuts, I'm right back to having no idea why he took Hayne. Um, Theo," he added, with a glance at Kirsten.

When it hit me, I stupidly clapped a hand over my mouth, because it was so fucking obvious and yet I didn't want to be true. They all turned to look at me.

"Scar?" Jesse asked.

"I know why," I whispered, forcing myself to put my hand down. "They don't want Hayne. They want Molly."

Chapter 31

The four of them erupted into discussion, or questions, or something, but I wasn't listening. My thoughts were racing.

This had always been about Molly, really. Count Asshat had wanted to frame her, turn her friends into vampires, and watch her be killed by her own community, preferably in that order. I'd thrown a wrench in his plans by showing up at Molly's last night. Now, to make sure his original plan succeeded, the Count would make it look like Molly had broken out of Dashiell's mansion and disappeared.

It would be a disaster in so many ways. The whole Old World would think Dashiell had been in on it, because how else could anyone sneak out through his security system? They'd definitely believe I was involved. Faith in the Old World leaders, and the Vampire Trials themselves, would be completely destabilized.

And, of course, Count Asshat would kill Molly.

But only if he could get in. Would Hayne really give up the code to the gate, and show Count Asshat and his thugs how to dismantle Dashiell's wards? I just couldn't see that happening, even if the vampire pressed Hayne. I'd always heard you couldn't press a human to go against their core self, and Hayne's loyalty to Dashiell ran as deep as his blood. Maybe if the bad guys had Kirsten or Ophelia, their daughter, at gunpoint, but Ophelia was on a weeklong trip to Sweden with Kirsten's cousin Runa. The arrangements had been made months ago to make sure Kirsten would have time to concentrate on the Trials. I seriously doubted Count Asshat had found a way to abduct Ophelia from the Swedish witch clan.

"Abigail," I said out loud, and the others stopped talking. Whoops. Thinking with my mouth again; never a good idea. "That's how they'll do it," I said to the others. "Abigail's on duty tonight, right? They'll stand at the gate with a gun to Hayne's head until Abigail lets them in."

Kirsten's already-pale face went a shade whiter. "Will she?" she whispered.

"Yes," Dashiell said shortly. "The security people would only sacrifice their lives for either Beatrice or me. Abigail knows that. She'll trade Molly for her brother."

Suddenly I didn't feel like calling him Count Asshat anymore. "Call Abigail," I said to Dashiell, but he was already touching the screen of his phone.

"No reception," he said, annoyed. At one point, the lack of cell phone service in the theater had seemed like a huge benefit to the Trials—we'd figured it would be an excellent way of keeping the proceedings quiet and orderly. But now I would have given an awful lot of money for us to be doing this anywhere else.

"There's a landline!" Kirsten said, already spinning, her skirts swirling around her, toward one of the makeup stations. I hadn't even noticed the small filing cabinet sitting unobtrusively under the counter. Kirsten yanked open the drawer and pulled out a dial telephone that had probably been designed in the 1990s. There was a long cord attached to it, and a phone jack next to the filing cabinet. "I saw it when I was looking around," Kirsten added, dropping to her knees to plug in the cord. Her usually nimble fingers were trembling. Jesse took a step toward her to help, but she got it plugged in and began to dial. Her back was to us, and I squirmed from the suspense. "What about the Trials?" I asked Dashiell quietly. "Do we cancel tonight?"

He opened his mouth to answer, but Jesse spoke first. "If you do, they will know for sure you're on to them," he said.

"How?" Will asked.

"They got Frederic to join them, by pressing him or just corrupting him," Jesse reminded us. "They could have gotten to any other vampire before we got Katia. They must have a spy here."

I thought of the swollen crowd. There were plenty of Old World people present, and we hadn't exactly made sure every one of them had an LA County address. I didn't think the Count was actually in the building—he would need to communicate with the MC guys who had Hayne, and there was the bad reception working for us again—but Katia might have pressed anyone into service, pun intended, before we'd captured her.

Dashiell's eyes were locked with Jesse's, which would have been really scary if he hadn't been human at the moment. "He's right," Dashiell said, his voice heavy.

"Abby, *slow down!*" came Kirsten's voice from the corner.

The four of us turned to look. Will and Dashiell's faces had taken on the grave stoicism of someone expecting bad news, but I was a female, and therefore didn't need to project emotional fortitude if I didn't feel like it. I rushed over to Kirsten and crouched down. Her eyes met mine, and they were *wild*. I felt her magic push against me again, and although it wasn't actually a physical force, I was almost knocked on my ass from the strength of it. "Is he alive?" Kirsten said into the phone. Her knuckles were white where she held the handset.

I'm not sure who reached for whom, but suddenly she was clutching my hand. Then her face relaxed, just a little. She nodded at me. Hayne was alive. "Did you call an ambulance? Okay . . . okay. I'll be there as soon as I can."

Kirsten dropped my hand and slammed the phone down, turning to face the others as she rose. "We're too late," she told us. Tears were streaming down her cheeks, but her face was impassive, a mask of regal resignation. "They came and exchanged Ted—*Theo*," she corrected herself. Kirsten was the only one who could call him Teddy. "For Molly. It's done."

"He's alive?" Dashiell said quietly.

Kirsten nodded. "Barely. He fought them, probably fearing that you would punish Abigail for her decision."

"We'll talk about that later."

Kirsten's hands fussed at her hair, her skirts. "I need to go. They're taking him to Huntington—"

"You can't," Dashiell said, his voice still low and unnaturally calm. "The Trials must go on. Will," he turned to the werewolf alpha, "would you please go upstairs and announce that we need ten more minutes to handle a technical problem with the wards. Make it sound small and boring, if you can."

Will left, shooting Kirsten a sympathetic look that she didn't see, because she was staring at Dashiell in outrage. They were all human at the moment, but if sparks had started shooting out of her eyes, I wouldn't have been the least bit surprised.

"There is no *fucking* way—" Kirsten began. Whoa. Had I *ever* heard Kirsten drop an f-bomb?

"There's nothing you can do," he told her. "I will have Lawrence make sure that the best medical staff in the city is available to Theodore, but right now there isn't anything you can do that the doctors can't."

She was still glowering at him. "He's human. There are healing spells—"

"For which you have no aptitude," Dashiell interrupted again, but his voice was surprisingly gentle. "There are no thaumaturge witches in Los Angeles, and we both know that the trades spells that deal with healing can be unpredictable. You could wind up doing more harm than good, especially in your emotional state."

Kirsten's mouth shut with an audible snap, and she spun around, stalking a few steps away from Dashiell and muttering to herself. I winced, temporarily surprised into silence. There was a special branch of magic for healing? And *Dashiell* knew all about it? I was used to the vampire playing his cards close to the vest, but I hadn't expected him to know so much about witch spells.

"Scarlett and I can go," Jesse blurted, surprising me again. "If he's conscious, Hayne may have learned something that will help us find these guys." Kirsten turned back around to look at him, but Jesse's eyes were on me, his eyebrows raised slightly. I nodded and stepped toward Kirsten.

"We'll go check on him at the hospital, and Abigail too," I told her, touching her arm. "Is there a number on that phone?"

Kirsten turned to look. "Yes. It's taped to the handset."

"Get one of your witches to sit by it. I'll call as soon as we find out his condition."

Kirsten bit her lip, clearly wavering.

But Dashiell turned toward me. "You are needed for the Trials, too," he told me. "Let Mr. Cruz go alone."

Of course. Of *course* Dashiell was only thinking about damage control. I shook my head. "Can't do it. I'm not sending Jesse out there with a vampire running around. He's my partner." I made it a point not to look at Jesse's face.

Kirsten left the phone and came back toward Dashiell. Then she laid a hand on his forearm. It was a completely innocent gesture, but I felt my eyes bulge. I couldn't remember ever seeing anyone besides Beatrice touch Dashiell in any way. "We can handle this," she told him. "The three of us can control our people enough to keep the peace."

"You *need* us to find Molly," I added firmly. "Everyone in that auditorium thinks you and I are conspiring to let her escape her trial. If this guy tortures her to death, we'll never be able to prove what really happened."

"Besides," Jesse added with a brittle smile, "I bet you can spin this to your advantage. '*We're so confident in our people that we don't even need a security null.*'"

Dashiell looked at each of our faces in turn before finally nodding. "Go." To Kirsten, he added, "You'll need to redo the wards after Scarlett punches a hole in them. It's possible that leaving an opening was part of their plan."

She was already moving toward her spell materials, looking relieved to have something to do. "I can do that."

"Are we taking Shadow?" Jesse asked me. We were already moving down the hall.

I hesitated. Bringing Shadow into the hospital wasn't a good idea, and she was relatively comfortable in her little den . . . but I hadn't forgotten how much she'd helped during the ambush earlier in the day. "Yeah," I said. "I think we may need all the help we can get."

Chapter 32

"Play it again," I said.

Jesse raised his eyebrows. "You sure?"

"Do it."

Jesse and I were in stiff chairs in the ICU waiting room, where he was holding one of the tablets that Abigail had brought to the hospital. Even dinged up and afraid for her job, she was dedicated as hell. She'd pulled up the exterior security camera footage from Dashiell's mansion for us, handed it wordlessly to Jesse, and wheeled away to grab some coffee. Shadow, meanwhile, had been left sulking in the van, where she would probably eat one of the headrests again.

After a quick glance to make sure no one was watching us, Jesse hit Play again, and then touched a command to make the video full screen. The color footage was crisp as hell, but there was no audio. Dashiell's policy, to prevent political issues.

The best footage came from a discreet camera in a tree well behind the wrought iron fence, facing the mansion. Onscreen, a large black SUV pulled up to Dashiell's gate, which was basically decorative—most of the Old World would have no problem getting over or through it. The SUV stopped ten feet shy of the barrier, and all four doors opened at once, plus the back. Four beefy white men wearing balaclavas erupted from the car like a Chinese fire drill. They went straight to the back and did something we couldn't see with a long black shape. Jesse had told me they were unzipping the body bag where they'd kept Hayne. A few of the MC thugs punched at the shape, and then the thugs stepped back and there was Hayne, tottering upright, his thighs leaning against the SUV for balance. He looked like hell already, his lower lip and one eye fat with swelling, and he moved his torso in a gingerly way that even I could recognize as broken ribs.

The MC guys' leader stepped forward and took Hayne's arm roughly. We couldn't see his face because of the balaclava, but he had a slight limp, which I suspected had something to do with Hayne's kidnapping. He certainly looked like he wasn't a fan of Hayne, who said something to Limpy that earned him a new punch in the stomach. It was brutal to watch, especially if you suspected the broken ribs. I'd flinched the first time, but I knew Jesse was concerned about me so I made my face blank.

Limpy made Hayne shuffle over to the camera on the call box. Then the guy pushed the button and pressed the barrel of a fat-looking handgun to Hayne's temple.

We couldn't hear what they were saying, although Abigail had filled us in. Limpy was demanding that Abigail produce Molly and send her out alone, no tricks. They had clearly been warned to stay outside the wards, which had been set by Kirsten earlier in the afternoon, after Jesse and I had left the premises.

A few minutes passed as the MC guys waited for Molly to make her appearance. Hayne seemed to be swaying on his feet, like he was about to pass out from the pain, but since this was the third time we were watching, I knew he was actually preparing to make his move.

I didn't know if he was really trying to win a fight against four armed men, or if he was just trying to force them to kill him. Either way, I watched it unfold again on the screen: Hayne's slow swaying dwindled to a halt, and then Limpy turned his head to yell something at the three men behind him. Hayne, beaten though he was, seemed to suddenly pounce.

Theodore Hayne had spent his entire life training with vampires, and by that, I mean training to *stop* vampires. Moreover, he had always operated under the assumption that he would be outnumbered and overpowered. He kicked at Limpy's good knee, sending the other man crashing to the ground. Limpy's lieutenant ran forward, but Hayne was ready with an elbow that seemed magnetized to the other man's face. It was the wrong angle for us to see the blow, but we could see the splash of bright red blood arcing in the air as the lieutenant's nose shattered. Before he even had his hands all the way up to clutch at it, Hayne kicked him between the legs. The guy dropped next to Limpy, who was still rolling back and forth on the ground, holding one knee. And Hayne did all of that in the time it took me to take a breath.

If they had kept attacking in that stupid way, one at a time with their fists, I had no doubt that Hayne could have taken them down. But after Limpy and his buddy were down, the two remaining men stayed a good ten feet away from their prey, and the one on the left abruptly shot Hayne once in each thigh. I had to work to keep from cringing as the big man crashed to the ground, blood pooling from his lower body.

They stayed that way, with the fallen MC thugs eventually pulling themselves to their feet, until the gate began to open. Then the four thugs raised their guns and pointed them at the space in the wrought iron.

After a few additional seconds, a small woman with bare feet and a dirty dress stepped through the gap and into the light, her black hair hanging loose around her face. Molly. Her arms were raised above her head, and she was moving slowly even for a human, which she most certainly was not. Hayne had told me Molly'd been fed, and her eyes were glittering with life when she glanced at the camera. If I'd never met Molly before this, I would still have known she was a vampire.

There was some shouting back and forth, and it was obvious the MC guys had become unnerved by Hayne and Molly. They were waving guns about, though Molly's responses to them were perfectly calm.

There was a moment when a wide space opened up between the two thugs closest to Molly.

"She could have run," I murmured to Jesse. I felt him nod.

Molly pointed at Hayne, who lay bleeding and unmoving on the ground. The thugs yelled something, but she responded calmly, pointing to Hayne again. Finally, Limpy nodded.

Keeping her hands up, Molly made her way to Hayne. She crouched down and checked his pulse at his neck, then turned to Limpy and said something else. Limpy reluctantly gave his guys an order, and two of them began pulling off their belts.

I took the tablet from Jesse and moved it so close that it was practically bumping my nose. On the screen, Molly tied the belts like tourniquets, using her strength to punch a new hole in the leather to hold them on. And then—this was the part I'd wanted to see—she moved her forearm over Hayne's face.

Her other movements had been efficient and precise, but this seemed oddly clumsy. It almost looked like she was using the sensitive skin at her wrist to check for his breathing. I paused the video, tapped the player to back up a few seconds, and watched it again. And again, until I was sure.

Jesse glanced at me, but I just shook my head and let the video play out. On the screen, Molly reached down and gathered up Hayne, lifting him as if he were nothing. She carried him through the gap in the gates, with all four guns pointed at her. Then she slowly stepped back over to the thugs' side of the fence, and Limpy nodded at the video monitor. The gate began to close.

I don't know if Molly would have run, because that's when the second vampire stepped out of the shadows. Frederic didn't bother with a balaclava—his "cover" had already been blown. He had been hiding in the bushes to one side of the gate, though Abigail still didn't know how he'd gotten there or when. She would need to go back through earlier footage, and there hadn't been time. Molly must have heard him stand up, because she began to turn around—but it was too late. The vampire was already behind her. With a movement too fast for even Dashiell's high-tech cameras, he reached up and brutally snapped her neck sideways. Molly crumpled.

"You're *sure*?" Jesse murmured, for about the fourth time.

"Yes. As bad as it looks, they can survive that. She'll wake up in a few hours needing blood, but she'll be okay. Well, until . . ." I didn't bother finishing the sentence. Jesse and I both knew why Molly had been taken "alive." The vampire behind all this had never wanted Molly to die easily. She would be tortured to death, unless I could find her.

"What will you do now?" came a tired voice from across the room. I actually started in my seat. I hadn't heard Abigail come back in. She'd wheeled to the far corner of the room, where she sat looking drawn and exhausted. I guessed she hadn't really wanted to watch the video again.

Jesse and I exchanged a glance. "I—" I began, but just then we heard an alarm sound down the hall, a screaming *beep-beep-beep* that sent a number of nurses and doctors running toward the noise. Abigail turned her chair to look. "That's Theo's room!" she cried, starting forward.

Jesse and I were already on our feet. Abigail was wheeling herself down the hall, but moving slow. "Can I—" I began.

"Push me, goddammit!"

I pushed. A nurse stopped us in the hall just outside the room, her hands raised in a defensive position.

"That's my brother!" Abigail snapped. "What's happening?"

"Miss, I'm sorry, you need to go back—"

"Like hell," she snarled. "Tell us what's happening right fucking now!"

"The doctors are doing everything they can—"

It went on like that for a while. Security was called, and if Abigail wasn't in a wheelchair I'm pretty sure she would have been bodily lifted and carried out of the building. As it was, she was given the choice of going back to the waiting room or being arrested. For a moment I honestly didn't know which way she was going to go.

We sat at the edge of the waiting room, watching medical personnel run in and out of Hayne's room. None of us spoke, and I had to keep glancing at Abigail's chest to make sure she was even breathing. Her eyes were fixed on the door to the hospital room, as though she could will Hayne to live by sheer force of personality. If anyone could do it, Abigail could.

When the doctor finally came out to talk to her, my heart sank. He had a pretty good poker face, but I knew the signs.

Apparently, so did Abigail, because she started to cry. "No—"

"We did everything we could, Ms. Hayne," the doctor began. "But I'm afraid your brother is gone."

As soon as the doctor retreated, I crouched next to Abigail's wheelchair. She was crying so hard I doubted she could see me through the tears. "Abigail," I said, but she shook her head. "Abby!" I looked up at Jesse, but he had turned away, his eyes rimmed in red. I turned back to Abigail, who had covered her entire face in her two hands. There were people all around us, but it didn't matter. Abigail was an island of grief, and she couldn't hear me.

"He doesn't get eaten by the eels at this time," I said loudly.

Abigail pulled her hands down. Her face was red and swollen with the tears that were still running down her cheeks. "What?"

I lowered my voice, leaning toward Abigail's ear. "Molly. She knew he wasn't going to make it. She fed him vampire blood. You have to get control of the body, right away. Claim religious reasons, whatever."

Abigail hiccupped, staring at me like I'd grown an extra head. "Are you hearing me?" I asked. "Do you get what I'm saying?"

"Teddy's . . . going to be a vampire?"

"No. Well, yes, for now. You gotta step up, Abby. You need to get Hayne's body, by any means necessary. I can't go near it while the vampire magic is working, and Jesse needs to come with me, so this is on you. But—and I cannot emphasize how important this is—do *not* tell anyone in the Old World what really happened. If anybody asks, the hospital believes Hayne died, but you just moved him to a secret location for his own protection. Got it?"

She stared at me. At least her tears had slowed. "Bernard, what the hell are you on about?"

"Please, trust me. I can fix this, but I need you to get your brother's body and hide it somewhere. Can you do that?"

"I . . . I guess . . ."

"Did the bad guys ask for anything besides Molly?" I asked. "Any information on me, or anything else?"

"No . . ."

"Good. I'll call you when we're done here." I stood up and looked at Jesse. "I have an idea. We need to go."

He blanched. "Where?"

I gave him a grim smile. "To wake the dead."

Chapter 33

I could feel Jesse practically vibrating with unasked questions as we half-trotted out to the van, but he managed not to ask any while we were in public. At the van, I tossed him the keys. "You're driving."

"Where are we going?"

"My place."

Shadow hadn't eaten another headrest, but she had shredded her dog bed in protest of being left behind yet again. I was probably supposed to discipline her when this happened, but you try punishing a hundred-fifty-pound dog-monster and see where it gets you. I chose not to comment. This is why I bought dog beds at Costco.

While Jesse drove, I called Matthias, the doctor who had treated Lizzy after she'd been turned into a werewolf. I was kicking myself for not thinking of it earlier, but it had taken a combination of talking to Lizzy and seeing the doctors at the hospital for my tired subconscious to kick into gear and remember that I knew an off-the-books doctor who was used to dealing with magic stuff. Katia was maybe our only chance of finding whoever had taken Molly before he killed her to death. Which isn't redundant when you're talking about vampires. But we didn't have to just wait around for her to wake up; we could actually *do* something about it. Well, maybe.

I wasn't sure if Matthias was an actual MD. He had once treated Eli, but I had been too emotionally overwhelmed that night to ask any questions. Later, I had learned that Matthias came from an old witch family. Like most males, he hadn't inherited the active witch gene, or whatever the phrasing was, so he knew about magic but had no access to it. Matthias had found his niche, though: he had a nice little semi-legal racket treating supernatural creatures like Lizzy, who couldn't go to a regular doctor.

I'd known him for years, but something about the guy forbade questions about his personal life. I didn't know if he'd been to medical school, or if he had a family, or what he did with his time when he wasn't bailing out members of the Old World. What I did know was that he could get results.

One thing about being a slightly shady illegal doctor: you always answer the phone. As soon as he picked up, I explained the problem as quickly as I could. When he asked questions about boundary magic that I couldn't answer, I gave him Lex's phone number. I would probably catch hell for it later—I had a feeling the badass boundary witch would *not* appreciate me handing her cell phone number out to randoms—but I was too wired on adrenaline to care at the moment.

After I hung up with Matthias, I dialed Eli. Matthias lived in Orange County, which meant he might make it to the cottage before Jesse and me. Once again, I launched into an explanation without bothering with pleasantries.

"You mean that guy that gave me the injection . . . that one time?" He sounded disbelieving, like maybe I'd picked tonight to start playing unfunny but elaborate jokes. "You told him where we *live*?"

I sighed. "Yes, and I don't like it either, but this is the very definition of desperate times. We can worry about home security when everyone survives this, Molly included."

There was a long moment of silence, and I thought the call had dropped. And by "call had dropped," I mean "Eli had gotten pissed and hung up." But his worried voice finally said, "Scarlett . . . I love you."

I heard it in his voice. "But?" I prompted.

"But are you sure you know what you're doing?"

"If I don't," I said, my voice coming out harder than I'd intended, "I'm sure you'll tell me."

There wasn't a lot to say after that.

After I hung up with Eli, I took a slow, deep breath, calming myself. Jesse must have figured out what I needed to do next, because he shot me a sympathetic look. I nodded my thanks and dialed the number written on my palm. The phone in the theater.

A witch I didn't know answered the phone. "Get me Kirsten," I said immediately. The witch, who sounded very young, protested that it was almost time for the next break, and could I wait ten minutes? She was probably afraid to interrupt Dashiell, but I didn't have time for hand-holding just then. "I don't care if you have to pull the fire alarm," I said through my teeth. "Get Kirsten now."

Jesse shot me a questioning look. Hayne was, after all, going to be just as dead . . . or, well, undead in ten minutes. "I don't want to risk her calling the hospital herself," I explained, and he nodded.

A few minutes later, the phone was picked up again. I was planning to open with something along the lines of "Stay calm as I tell you this," but the first words out of Kirsten's mouth were, "Is he dead?"

"Err . . . yes. But he'll get better," I added quickly. Before she could even speak, I explained about Molly feeding him her blood.

"A vampire?" Kirsten echoed, sounding crestfallen. In the Old World, different species almost never partnered with each other. It's not like there's some law forbidding interracial romances or anything— nobody actually gives a shit who sleeps with whom. But as it turned out, the various species tended to be sort of physically repulsed by one another. For a werewolf, the thought of sleeping with a vampire would be disgusting, and so on. There was some evolutionary reasoning for this, according to Olivia, but the takeaway was that if Hayne became a vampire, his relationship with Kirsten was effectively over.

"I mean, I'm glad he'll . . ." she said, trying to rally, but her voice trailed off. It was pretty heartbreaking. Kirsten and Hayne had rekindled things a couple of years ago, but they'd been hesitant to fully recommit to each other, even after Ophelia was born—hence the separate houses. Kirsten didn't exactly confide in me, but it was obvious that the two of them were still worried about the same things that had driven them apart the first time. It was equally obvious that they were over-the-moon in love. Now she was afraid they'd missed their chance, forever.

"Kirsten," I said. "Listen to me very carefully, because I'm about to tell you a big fucking secret, okay?"

I heard her breath catch. It sounded a lot like a sob. "I'm listening."

"You remember Ariadne, Dashiell's archnemesis?"

"Yes."

"And remember three years ago, when Eli disappeared for a while and no one could explain it?"

"Yes," she said, a little firmer. Eli's absence had almost created a serious rift between the Old World sects. It wasn't the kind of thing you forgot.

"I . . . well, for lack of a more politically correct term, I cured them," I said. "Both of them. And I can cure Hayne. I mean, probably. I can try."

Jesse, who already knew my secret, said nothing, but he reached over and gave my shoulder a comforting squeeze. He also knew that both times I'd turned someone back into a human, it had almost killed me. But for Hayne, I would try again.

"That's . . . that's not possible," Kirsten insisted. "I've never heard of a null being able to do that."

"Yeah, neither have I," I said wryly. "It's hard on me physically"—I glared at Jesse as he snorted—"and no one in the Old World can know about it." There were so many reasons for this, not the least of which was that half the werewolves would want me to cure them, and most of the vampires would want to kill me.

"But Dashiell and Will know? And they didn't *tell* me?"

Oops. It hadn't been my decision to keep this from Kirsten, but I hadn't exactly fought to inform her, either. In my defense, I'd been practically comatose at the time. "Yes, but you'll have to take that up with them. More importantly, right now everyone has to think Abigail got Hayne out of the hospital and he's hiding out somewhere recuperating." I ran her through what had happened at the hospital. "You can send someone to help her, but it has to be someone you trust completely, because we have to keep this quiet, okay?"

"I've got it," she said. She sounded like she was on surer footing now. Covering shit up was what we *did*. "Don't worry about Teddy; I'll make sure Abby gets him somewhere safe." A pause, and when her voice returned there was a new note of coolness in it. "And I suppose, in return for saving him, you want Molly exonerated."

"Uh . . ." *Stupid, stupid Scarlett.* See, this is why I sucked at everything political. The thought hadn't even crossed my mind.

Jesse shot me a questioning look, but I just shook my head, my thoughts racing. Here it was, the golden opportunity to save my friend. No more running around, no more violence, and I didn't even have to stop Count Asshat if I didn't want to.

All I had to do was leverage the life of a man I liked and respected.

Of course, Hayne *could* survive as a vampire. He would just miss most of his kid's life and lose his relationship with Kirsten. So it wasn't like it was a death sentence if I refused to do it. More like an un-death sentence, pun intended.

Focus, Scarlett. I gave myself the time to take a deep breath and push it out slowly. "Honestly, Kirsten? No. I want Molly safe, but I will do this for Hayne either way," I said into the phone. Silence on the other end. "But you should keep in mind," I added, because what the hell, "that without Molly, Hayne would have bled out in Dashiell's driveway tonight."

"I understand," came her strangled voice. I hung up the phone.

Chapter 34

When we pulled into the driveway of the Marina del Rey residence, I spotted Matthias' vintage Cadillac already in the driveway. The three of us were hurrying inside when Jesse put out an arm, stopping me. Shadow wheeled around and gave him the stink eye. Jesse dropped his hand.

"What?" I asked.

"Maybe you shouldn't go in right away," he pointed out. "If he's trying to use her boundary magic to bring her back . . ."

"Oh. Right." *Null, here.* I could probably go into the house and try to keep Shadow's cell out of my radius, but there wasn't much point in risking it. What if they'd moved her out to the sofa or something? "Can you go in and figure out where we stand?" I asked. Jesse was already moving toward the house, with Shadow at his heels. I guess she wanted to see what all the fuss was about.

A couple of minutes later, Eli came out of the house, trudging toward me with his shoulders slumped. I looked at him in alarm. "Is she dead . . . -er?"

"No," he said, sounding tired. "Matthias did something with his little collection of drugs, and her heart just started beating again. He's going to give her an adrenaline shot to wake her up faster. You shouldn't come in until she's conscious."

I nodded. "Thanks for letting me know."

"We should talk, Scarlett."

I swallowed. For the life of me, I couldn't think of one stupid joke or quip that could deflect the tension. Not even a movie reference. "You're right," I said. "But can it wait until tomorrow? I'm kind of drowning here."

He really looked like he wanted to object, but he shrugged sadly. "Fine. I'm going to the Trials to help Will with the pups."

There was something defeated in his expression that I really didn't like. I stood on tiptoes to kiss him. "I love you," I said.

The corner of his mouth lifted. "I know."

I watched him head for his pickup with a sinking feeling I couldn't quite explain. I was still standing there a few minutes later, when Jesse came looking for me.

"Scarlett?" he said.

"Yeah. What's up?"

"She's awake." He sounded a little awed, like in his heart he hadn't really believed Matthias could do it. Couldn't blame him there.

"Okay," I said, giving myself a little shake. "Yeah. Let's go talk to the big bad witch."

Matthias met us just inside the doorway, carrying an old-fashioned black doctor's bag. Where would you even find something like that? Probably from a vampire, I concluded. "How is she?" I asked him.

Matthias was handsome in a bland-but-excessive way that always reminded me of the actors who play doctors on nighttime soaps. If he were an actor with even a tiny bit of talent, he would be starring on his own *Grey's Anatomy* spinoff for sure. "Alive, but barely," he reported. "The bullet that your werewolf friend took out did not actually pierce her heart, which is good, but it did sever her aorta. I inserted a stent, and by the time I had her closed back up, her heart started beating again." He shook his head a little, smiling. "First time operating on a dead patient. Boundary witches are *interesting*."

Yeah, I didn't love his tone just then. As useful as Matthias could be, he always had just a whiff of "mad scientist" around him, like what he *really* wanted to do was cut up half the Old World and experiment with our parts.

"Riiiight," I said. "Is it okay for me to go near her now?"

"Yes. The stent should keep her alive, but she cannot be jostled or move around. She needs to stay on that cot."

"What if she has to pee?" I asked.

"I put in a catheter," he said, amused. "It will last six to twelve hours, and then the bag needs to be changed. Dashiell should be able to find you a nurse, if you can't do it yourself."

I thanked him as I hustled him toward the door. Matthias told me he'd send his bill to Dashiell, which would probably be entertaining for me later.

Katia looked like hell. The phrase "death warmed over" was accurate on many levels. She was lying on the camp-style cot with every pillow in the house propped under her, and a sheet draped over her nude upper body. She still wore her pants, though blood had dripped into them. Her skin, which had been a healthy tan when we'd first met, was now bone white with just the slightest tint of green. The magic that kept her from dying didn't actually speed her healing, so she wasn't going to be a threat to anyone for quite a while.

The cot filled up almost half the room, and Matthias had pulled in a kitchen chair on top of that. All in all, I was reminded of the cell where we'd visited Molly. Had that really been earlier today? Jesse took the chair, and I leaned on the wall inside the doorway. Katia's sullen, sunken eyes glowered at us.

"We weren't properly introduced before," Jesse said conversationally, "but I'm Jesse, and this is Scarlett. Who are you?"

No response.

"Okay," Jesse said easily. "How about we start with what we already know? Your name is Katia, you're obviously originally from Russia, and you're a boundary witch."

"And she works for Count Asshat," I reminded him.

"Yes, of course, thank you." He turned back to Katia. "You're helping a vampire enslave women and pimp them out for fun and profit."

Katia's eyes narrowed and she opened her mouth, but then snapped it shut. She shook her head with a tight smile. *Nice try.* "You're a witch," I pointed out. "Not a vampire. Why are you serving him?"

Her lips were pressed together in a thin line. "You also helped this same vampire frame a friend of ours," Jesse continued. "Molly. What do you have against her?"

Confusion flashed across her face, so fast I almost missed it. "You do *know* Molly, right?" I asked. "You've met?"

I couldn't be sure, but I didn't see any spark of recognition from Katia, like "Oh yes, Molly, that bitch who ruined my life."

Jesse must have thought the same thing, because he said, "Did she do something to hurt you?"

Maybe it was the soft, sympathetic tone, but Katia actually shook her head slightly. I resisted the urge to fist-pump. We had contact.

"If she didn't do anything to you, why set up Molly?" he persisted. "There are plenty of vampires in Los Angeles."

"She lived with those girls. Good candidates," Katia answered, giving a little shrug. "Your friend was a . . . what's the word? A patsy."

Jesse looked at me, and I could read his thoughts. What if she didn't actually know anything else? If she was just a . . . henchwoman, or whatever, it was possible that Count Asshat really hadn't explained his motives or his plans to her. If that was the case, we were fucked.

And we had just wasted a lot of time reanimating a dead witch for nothing.

Then I caught the hint of gold glinting at her neck, a chain that disappeared under the sheet. Without speaking, I went over and tugged it out. Katia lifted one hand to fend me off, but was too weak to do more than bump her fingers against my wrist.

At the end of the necklace swung a small gold medallion, the size of a silver dollar. I let go and took a step back, triumphant. Then I reached into my own shirt and pulled out the little medallion on a chain. When I drew it out, Katia's eyes widened. I held it up to the pendant dangling near her face. "I found this in Molly's backpack," I said. "You're wearing the same necklace around your neck."

Chapter 35

Katia's brow furrowed, and she reached out a trembling hand for Molly's necklace, glancing suspiciously at us, like the whole thing was a plot so we could smack her wrist. When neither of us made a move, she took it from me and slowly raised it to her face. "That is not possible," she said after examining it for a moment. "I do not know what this is, but there is no way this Molly is one of Oskar's—" Her eyes widened.

"So *that's* his name," Jesse said casually. "Good to know. Why couldn't Molly be one of Oskar's girls?"

Katia just glared at us some more. It was a pretty good glare, and if she were capable of standing or even sitting up by herself, I might have been a little scared of her. "Come on," Jesse urged. "If you really care about this guy, how could it hurt to prove that he *didn't* pimp out our friend?"

"Oskar was turned at around age thirty-five," she said stiffly. "This was in the late 1930s. I have seen an old passport; I know this to be true." She held up Molly's necklace. "Your girl was already free by then. I doubt they even knew each other." She gave us a look of great triumph and tossed the medallion at me. Well, she tried to toss it at me. She was so weak that it went about as far as her own chest.

"Then how come you have the same necklace?" Jesse asked.

She twitched her shoulders in a shrug-like manner. "They are similar, yes. But not the same. Mine was never a coin." She hesitated for just a second, then picked up her own necklace. "It is spelled so it cannot be removed, but you are a disruptor, yes?" She looked at me.

I nodded. I hadn't felt a tiny spell short out when we'd first met Katia, but it was the middle of a gunfight. "No active magic around me," I said.

"Then here, look." She tried to lift it over her head, but I had to help her get it free. When I got it untangled from her hair and sat back she had the oddest look on her face, a combination of fear, vulnerability, and jubilation. I handed it to Jesse, who held up both necklaces, comparing them. Sure enough, Katia's pendant was smooth on both sides, except for a single inscribed date: February 8th, 1997.

"Why does he make you wear these?" Jesse asked. "Just to identify you as his?"

She bristled a little, but answered him. "All the medallions are poured from the same vein of gold. Oskar has a gold coin from it, too. There is a trades witch who can use the connection to find all of us."

So it was a tracking device that the wearer couldn't remove themselves. Smart. I would have shorted out the removal spell, but not the tracker. That kind of like-for-like spell wouldn't require active magic, so being near a null would only negate it until the necklace moved out of my radius.

"Wait," Jesse said. "If that's true, why hasn't Oskar already come for you here?"

Oh. Shit.

But Katia just twitched her shoulders in a tired parody of a shrug. "Most likely, he could not find a trades witch here who could help him. We do not have witch connections in Los Angeles yet, and he keeps his coin on him at all times. When he awoke at sunset and I had not yet returned, he would have needed to fly someone here to find me."

"Or," I said, "he decided to go after Molly instead of trying to rescue you. He abandoned you, Katia."

She gave me an impatient look. "He is not my husband, my boyfriend. To him, I am a useful tool. He will recover me when he is able."

Jesse and I locked eyes. "Talk to you in the hall for a second?" I asked. He nodded, and I stuffed Katia's necklace into the pocket of my top. As long as it was close to me, no witch would be able to use it to find us.

There was nothing in the room that Katia could use as a weapon, but I didn't want to take any chances. "Shadow," I said, and the bargest's eyes snapped to me. "Watch and defend." Her massive hindquarters rose as she padded over to Katia, sitting down with about a foot between her front paws and the witch's cot. Shadow bared her teeth, and Katia instinctively shrunk back on the cot, just a tiny bit. Her eyes were wide. "If I were you," I advised, "I wouldn't move."

We left the cell and went into the kitchen, just a few feet away. I didn't think there was anything Katia could do magically to a bargest, but I expanded my radius, just in case.

Jesse closed the door to the kitchen, and we said at more or less the same time, "We need to move her."

"Jinx," I said smugly. "I prefer my Coke diet."

Jesse opened the fridge, right behind me, and handed me a can before pulling out another for himself. We both needed the caffeine.

"So we move her," Jesse said, "but where? There aren't a whole lot of places where we can hold someone against their will."

True. I considered that for a moment. "Unless it's not against her will."

He raised an eyebrow. "Interesting. Do you have a plan for getting her to defect to Team Scarlett?"

"No," I admitted. "I was really just thinking out loud. But I'm super glad that name is catching on." He held up his can in a toast.

"Anyway," I went on, "she said herself that they're not involved romantically. If she doesn't love him, we've got to be able to offer her a better deal than she's getting from Count Oskar."

"Unless she's just evil," he pointed out. "Maybe she's really into kidnapping and pimping strangers. Lex aside, aren't all boundary witches supposed to be evil?"

I raised an eyebrow. "You mean like how all Mexicans are lazy and all Asians are bad drivers?"

"Hmm. Good point."

"I suppose it's possible that she's full dark side, but then why wouldn't Oskar have told her his reasons for going after Molly?"

"She could be lying about that," he reminded me.

"True . . . but I don't know. I guess Katia just seems more pragmatic. Like working for Oskar is the only survival option she thinks she has. So how about we give her a better one?"

"Hmm." He took a sip of the soda, and said, "What if we offered her a lot of money? Dashiell has plenty, and it doesn't look like Katia's exactly rolling in it. Those clothes *maybe* came from Target, and she looks like she cut her hair herself."

I rolled my eyes. "Okay, Snob McDouchery. If this were a human with human problems, maybe money would fix them. But there's a reason why Katia has stayed as long as she has, and it's obviously not the great pay. He's offered her something she can't find anywhere else. Unless . . ." I trailed off, thinking.

Jesse checked his watch. "If you've got an idea, now's the time," he said. "Every minute we stay here is another minute that Oskar could be getting closer."

"Okay." I went to the fridge and got out a bottle of water, which we keep on hand for guests. I grabbed a beef stick and my own drink, too. Then, hands full, I headed for the kitchen door. "Come on," I said over my shoulder. "Follow my lead, okay?"

We went back into the little cell, where neither Katia nor Shadow seemed to have moved. "Shadow, relax," I said, and tossed her the beef stick. The bargest snatched it out of the air greedily, her tail wagging.

Jesse and Katia both jumped at the sound of her teeth snapping together, which never failed to amuse me. "Good girl."

I held up the Arrowhead water in front of Katia's face so she could see that the seal was unbroken. Then I twisted off the cap and handed it to her, backing away to give her space. She shot me a confused look. "I didn't poison it," I promised her. "And I figure you must be thirsty."

Her face and body language were wary, but she carefully raised her head and shoulders, tilting to the side so she could take a sip of the water. A little bit dripped onto the sheet. "Let me guess," she said when she'd finished. "This is where you do the good cop thing, yes? Water, maybe some food, and you hope I'll spill my guts?"

"Nah. I mean, if you want to spill your guts, that's cool, but I thought we could just chat for a minute. Not about Oskar," I added quickly. "I don't know much about boundary magic, is all."

Her eyes narrowed just a tiny bit. She hadn't expected me to sound so friendly about it. Most people in the Old World hate boundary witches, especially all other types of witches. The way Kirsten tells it, boundary witches were responsible for a decent chunk of the Inquisition. That still didn't make them inherently evil.

"Jesse knows a little more, though," I went on, pointing my soda in his direction. "He's friends with a super powerful boundary witch."

Katia snorted so hard that Shadow's ears pricked up suspiciously. I kept my face absolutely even, and after a moment Katia's expression settled into skepticism. "Sure he is," she said sarcastically, eyeing Jesse. "This *human* is what, a catalog model? And he knows a boundary witch. The rarest of all witch breeds."

"Hey," I protested on Jesse's behalf. "That's not nice. He could definitely go runway."

Jesse shot me a look that said *we don't have time for dicking around, Scarlett*. Okay, that was fair. "Anyway, he knows a null," I said, pointing at myself. "Jesse's pretty connected. Right?" I looked at him.

Jesse, who had probably figured out where I was going with this, nodded. "She lives in Colorado," he said to Katia. "I've known her about . . . mmm . . . four years? Five? Funny thing, though, she hasn't aged a bit."

Katia's jaw clenched, so subtly that I probably would have missed the reaction if I hadn't been watching for it. She was fighting an internal battle, wanting to ask a dozen questions, but also not wanting to give us anything we could use against her. "There have been rumors," she said finally, grudgingly, "of a power rising in Colorado. But you may have heard those same rumors. This means nothing."

It was too late. I'd seen the hope in her eyes, and I knew I was right. Katia was working for Oskar because she didn't have anyone else. No family, no other boundary witches. I could understand that. I had, after all, worked for Olivia for a long time. I put down my soda and stood up. "Let's go for a ride," I said to both of them. To Katia, I added, "and on the way, Jesse's going to make a phone call."

Katia's expression was reluctant, but we didn't give her much of a choice. Jesse picked up one end of the cot and I hefted the other. It was just narrow enough to make it through the doorway. Shadow walked just behind us, growling a little at Katia.

At the van, I opened the back doors and we loaded the cot straight in, urine bag and everything. Katia didn't protest, but her eyes rolled around wildly, watching for one of us to pull out a gun or a machete or something. I had a couple of bungee cords in the back, and I used them to secure the head side of the cot to the back of the driver's seat, so at least she wouldn't be sliding around back there.

Jesse got behind the wheel, and I rode sideways in the passenger seat so I could keep an eye on her, but I didn't really think she would try anything. She was too weak, for one thing, and there was also a hundred and fifty pounds of twitchy bargest drooling about fourteen inches away from her lap.

Before we pulled out of the driveway, Jesse called Lex and explained the situation. I wanted to tell him to make sure Lex knew we hadn't given Katia any private information or anything, because I was deeply afraid of Lex, but I managed to bite my tongue.

The Colorado witch readily agreed to talk to Katia. Jesse passed her the phone—not on Bluetooth or speaker, which I think got him points from our hostage. I told him to head north on PCH, and the van started to move.

For a moment, Katia held the phone like she was expecting it to explode, but after a few seconds, she sort of curled her body toward the window and spoke quickly in a low tone, asking questions. The first few were about boundary magic—making sure Lex was who she said she was. After that, though, there was a lot of listening. I heard Oskar's name and a weird phrase in Latin. And then there was more listening. I was occupied for a few minutes with giving Jesse directions, and when I glanced back again, Katia was crying.

Finally, she reached out—Shadow growled, and Katia moved more slowly—and handed me the phone. "She wants to talk to you," Katia said, her voice shaky. If anything, she looked a little sicker. Had Lex threatened her? I could see why that would scare her. Hell, I'd been there.

I held the phone to my ear. "Lex?"

"I want her," came the boundary witch's brusque voice. For a moment I was preoccupied with relief that she didn't seem mad at me.

"What do you mean, you want her? We're not choosing kickball teams."

"I *mean*," Lex said with fake patience, "I'm getting in the car now, and I'm driving to you. When I leave, I want to bring Katia with me. Oskar has her passport, so she can't fly."

"Oh. Um, that's not my decision to make," I said, glancing at Jesse. "She's done some bad things here, Lex. I can't guarantee she won't need to face punishment for them."

"You're going to have to," Lex insisted, "if you want her to testify in your friend's trial. Which she's willing to do."

I rubbed my eyes with the heel of my hand. Was I willing to let Katia get away with her part in this? She'd helped set up Molly. At the same time, she was probably the only one who could save Molly.

I didn't like it, but I didn't have a lot of choices, not if I wanted to save my friend. "Okay, look," I said to Lex. "Let me get my cardinal vampire to call your cardinal vampire and approve all this, and you've got a deal. Does that sound fair?"

Lex didn't even pause. She'd expected me to say that. "Fair. And Scarlett?"

"Yeah?"

"Keep her safe, get her to me, and you and I are square. In fact, I'll owe you one." And she hung up the phone.

I held it away from my ear so I could stare at it. Seriously? Just like that? I had been pretty sure that somewhere in Lex's gloomy castle, which was where I figured she lived, was a dartboard that had my picture on it. And a lot of bullet holes driven through it.

I turned in my seat to look at Katia. "She seems to really care about your well-being."

Katia's tears had stopped, but she was still sniffling a little. "That is because," she said with a tiny hiccup, "she is my niece."

Chapter 36

See, it was good that Jesse was driving. I would probably have wrenched the steering wheel sideways so I could stare at her. As it was, the van stayed on the road, and Jesse and I both blurted "What?" at the same time. There was no mention of jinxes or Cokes.

Katia was still sniffling, so I grabbed a few fast-food napkins out of the glove compartment and passed them back. Trying to keep my voice level, I said, "Can you please explain that?"

"When I heard about boundary magic being used in the West," she said, "I should have guessed that we were related. There are so few of us left. But I just never thought . . ." She took a moment to clear her throat, swiping at her eyes with the wadded-up napkins. I wanted to go back there and do it myself, so I could get her talking again, but I managed to wait.

Finally she was ready to speak again. "In my family, I was the . . . mmm . . . 'surprise' baby. Change of life baby, it's sometimes called here. I had a sister who was fifteen years older, Valerya. She was like a second mother to me."

Her voice was warm when she said that, but then it hardened. "When I was five and she was almost twenty, she was taken."

"By whom?" Jesse prompted. I could see him fighting the urge to turn around in his seat and look at her.

"There is a group of boundary witches who have dedicated them-selves to the cultivation of boundary magic," Katia said darkly. "This group hunts down the few families who are still strong with boundary magic, and they take the young women. For . . . *breeding purposes*." Her fists clenched, crumpling the napkins. "My parents knew of this group, but they thought we were well hidden in our little village. They were wrong." She paused again, fidgeting. The story was hard for her.

"When they came," she went on, "my mother was too old to bear more children, but they took Valerya. They would have taken me too, most likely, but my father and I were on an overnight visit to my grandparents. When we returned the next morning, my sister was gone, and my mother had been killed trying to save her." Her voice turned bitter. "They beat my brothers badly, but left them alive, in hopes they might grow up and have children with witchblood."

"Until a few minutes ago," she continued, "I did not know what happened to Valerya. I did not think I ever would know. But Lex has informed me that they forced my sister to get pregnant, and she had twin girls. Valerya died in childbirth, and one sister died as an adult. Your friend Lex is the surviving twin."

Jesse and I exchanged a look. We knew the other part of the story. The two of us had stopped the nova werewolf who had killed Lex's sister Samantha—just not soon enough. But I didn't see how telling Katia I had incinerated her niece's body would help at this point.

"How did Lex know you were her aunt?" Jesse asked, quite reasonably.

Katia gave us a tiny smile. "Valerya told her."

When I processed *that*, my mouth was suddenly dry. This is part of why the whole Old World still hates boundary witches. They creep everybody out. "What happened to you?" Jesse asked.

"To make sure this group did not find me later, I was sent to the United States, to be adopted anonymously," she said. She shifted on the cot, clearing her throat. When she spoke again, it was in a rush, like she was getting something out of the way. "The man who was supposed to be my new father was a pedophile. I will not talk about that time. All you need to know is that I ran away when I was thirteen, and Oskar found me a year later. You can probably figure out the rest."

"You worked for him," I said quietly, "in exchange for him keeping you safe."

She nodded. "I am—I was—his daytime contact. I helped him manipulate the girls, it is true. But I helped them as well. By pressing them, I could make them forget any pain. And the men who visit vampire brothels, they like pain." Her voice cracked, and she looked out the window for a few minutes. We were getting close to our destination.

"You think Oskar is a monster, and you are correct," she said softly, not turning to look at me. "But I did make it easier for them to survive. I did not feel like I was working for him. I felt like I was helping *them*."

Jesse and I were silent for another mile. The weight of this woman's story had kind of crushed anything we could have said. Finally, Jesse gathered his thoughts enough to say, "One thing I still don't understand. Oskar does this thing with the necklaces, as a way to take ownership of you. But Molly had a similar necklace, presumably from *her* maker."

It was a very good question, and it doubtless had something to do with how this Oskar was connected with Molly, but Katia shrugged. On a hunch, I asked, "Does the name Alonzo mean anything to you?"

She gave me a look like I might be a little thick. It really did seem like I got that look a lot. "Of course. Alonzo was Oskar's father."

Okay, maybe I did deserve the look. I glanced at Jesse, who must have been thinking pretty much the same thing. "Well, his maker," Katia corrected herself. "He turned Oskar into a vampire so he would have an heir. Oskar calls him Father."

"Of course he does," Jesse said, sounding more tired than anything else. "We've been so focused on Alonzo making new female vampires, we never considered that he might have made a male. An heir."

"Did you ever meet Alonzo?" I asked Katia.

She shook her head. "He died the year before I met Oskar." Her lip curled a little. "But Oskar worshipped him. I think he had to. The bonds between a vampire and his maker are strong."

"We've heard," I muttered.

"So back in the nineties, Molly killed Alonzo," Jesse said, thinking aloud. "Not knowing he also had a son, Oskar. Twenty years later, Oskar tracks down Molly in Los Angeles and kicks off this elaborate revenge scheme."

Katia's eyes widened as she looked up at me, but she didn't speak, just processed the new information. She was probably used to staying quiet.

I wondered how Molly was going to feel when she found out that Alonzo, her worst nightmare, had basically recreated himself. That although Molly had stopped Alonzo, his legacy had lived on, and his "son" had continued selling the young women he kidnapped and turned.

So many women. So many years.

"How could you work for him for so long?" I blurted to Katia. "How could you stand to?"

For a moment I didn't think she was going to answer, but she'd promised Lex to give us any information we wanted. "Do you know," she said slowly, "how a boundary witch activates her powers?"

"No."

"She has to die. And I did. I was stabbed"—she touched her side, though I doubted she was conscious of it—"and buried. Oskar, he dug me up. He saved me from being buried alive, then demanded twenty years of service as repayment." Her face hardened. "It was only many years later that I learned Oskar had ordered my attack in the first place."

And I think that was the moment when *I* joined Team Katia. I no longer cared if she walked away from this scot-free. In fact, I wanted her to.

"When was this?" Jesse asked.

She smiled. "Nineteen years, ten months, and two days ago."

"That's why he came for Molly now," I said, understanding. "He needed you for his revenge."

She nodded. "I did not suspect it then, but you must be right. I thought we were just on another mission to get new girls, and start over in a new city. We did this before. He likes to get new girls every ten years, so there is never a time when he has only new people or only veterans." She sounded disgusted. "This is also probably why he has not yet come to 'rescue' me from you. My time is almost up, and the one thing that you could say for both Oskar and Alonzo, they always keep their promise to release their . . . *employees*." She touched her chest, right where the necklace would have hung if it hadn't been stuffed in my pocket at the moment. "They don't want to anger what little vampire authority remains."

"That's a pretty damned complicated revenge," I pointed out. "He could have just killed Molly."

"The woman who killed his precious Alonzo?" Katia shook her head. "No. That would not be a fitting tribute. Alonzo himself was very into drawn-out, elaborate revenge. Sometimes, I believe, he would set his revenge in motion even before he had been betrayed. And Oskar's greatest wish is to be just like his father."

And this was the guy who now had Molly's friends—four fresh-faced young women who had barely tasted human life before it was taken away from them for darker purposes. Jesse and I exchanged another look. I'm not even sure what it meant, but he inclined his head a little, as if to say *I'm with you.*

"Okay, I'm officially fucking decided," I announced. "One way or another, we are tearing it all down."

Jesse glanced my way, but Katia was nodding. "This is what Lex said you would do. She said you are clumsy and immature, but also as stubborn as she is." There was a smile in her voice. "And you've gone up against bad things before. So I will help you take down Oskar. And you will help me meet my niece."

As she finished those words, we pulled into tonight's safe house of choice—Will's house.

I hadn't had a whole lot of options for where to stash Katia, but the alpha werewolf's place was isolated, it had a security system, and Will had a guest room that was always ready for a werewolf who might need a place to lay low. I figured as long as no one but us and Will knew she was there, she would be safe for the night.

We carried Katia inside, and when we had set down the cot in the living room, I sat down on the couch, near Katia's head, and finally asked the big question. "Where is he, Katia? What else is he planning?"

"I am not sure on either question, though I have a few guesses," she said. Her voice was weakening from exhaustion. "I can tell you what he *was* planning, but not what he will decide to do now that I am no longer helping him." Her expression soured. "He will have moved the girls by now, knowing I have been captured. He does not trust me much."

"Okay, well, what was the plan before?" Jesse said.

"Take the patsy," she said without hesitating. "Sorry, I mean, Molly. Kill her—though now that I know the details, I am sure he will take much time to do this." She shot me an apologetic look. "Sorry, again."

I shrugged. It wasn't like I was surprised. But I was doing everything I could not to think about Molly being tortured. "Then, once she is dead," Katia went on, "I was to sneak into your Trials and begin whispering in ears, sowing seeds of mistrust among the vampires. Dashiell is corrupt, Dashiell let Molly escape to please his pet null—sorry, again," she added to me. "We would let that simmer until the girls woke up, hoping that the rumors would destabilize the community. *Then,* perhaps a few nights after, I would go to some of Dashiell's lieutenants, and if necessary, press them into committing . . . mmm . . ." She searched for a word, and finally settled on "mutiny."

I gaped at her. "You were going to *kill* Dashiell?"

She spread her hands. "Not me, no. I was just supposed to induce some of his loyal followers to turn against him. We would leave it up to them whether they chose to kill him or exile him."

"*Why?*" I burst out.

She looked at me strangely again, like she couldn't believe I was this far behind on the chain of logical events. "Because," she said, "Oskar is planning to take Los Angeles."

Chapter 37

Jesse and I just stared at her.

On the one hand, in that moment, I felt really fucking justified. No one—not Kirsten, not Will, not Dashiell—had taken Molly's frame job seriously. They had all assumed it was just a little isolated revenge plot, and they'd been willing to let Molly die to keep her from spoiling their goddamn Trials. If they had thrown resources into finding Oskar in the beginning, he would never have gotten this far.

On the other hand, I felt like a fool. How had *I* not seen this coming? Jesse's informant had said the man giving the orders was setting up a new business with the MC. And I'd *just* told Jesse about how vampires loved to live on the edge of chaos. What could be more chaotic than a power vacuum? Neither Will nor Kirsten was strong enough to hold the city alone, and the vampires would fight amongst themselves for leadership. Dashiell's stance on peace—that it was okay to share power with witches and werewolves—wasn't as popular as he would like, and there was a great chance that whoever stepped into his role would declare dominance over the others—or war. It might last for years. And while they all fought, Oscar would be making a killing in the sex industry. So to speak.

Before either of us could form words, Katia held up one hand. "Let me clarify," she said. "He does not want to run the city. He knows he does not have enough natural power for that, at least not now. But he wants to take down your structure, to create anarchy. That will allow him to run his new brothel undisturbed."

"He's going to an awful lot of trouble," Jesse pointed out. "Couldn't he just build his brothel somewhere else?"

It was a good point. "I actually asked him that," Katia said wryly. "In a respectful manner, of course. He loves Los Angeles, but more importantly, he has connections here, both in the criminal world and the movie industry. I believe he wants to start a side business in snuff films."

Vampire snuff films. Goosebumps broke out on my arms. Oskar wanted to use his new vampires—Molly's friends—in films where they'd be subjected to human death over and over again.

No. Just a great big no.

"How do we find him?" I said to Jesse, who had dropped down next to me on the couch. He looked as grim as I felt.

"If Katia is sure that Oskar would have moved the girls after we took her"—beside him, she nodded—"I don't really know. Wait." He looked at the boundary witch. "What is Oskar driving?"

"A black Hummer H2," she replied.

"Rental?" he asked, a little hopeful. Even I knew that rental cars had LoJack.

But she shook her head. She seemed to be fading fast, and I wondered how much longer she could talk to us before her body would demand sleep. "It is specially modified to contain a vampire. I drove it here from our current base in Reno."

"Damn."

I turned back to Jesse, who was staring very thoughtfully at the ceiling. To let him keep concentrating, I resisted the urge to dramatically crane my neck and pretend I could see what he was seeing. "The SUV that I saw at Hayne's house—which was the same one they used at Dashiell's—was a Ford, not a Hummer," he said finally. "I can't ask anyone to run the plates, because he swapped them with stolen ones, but . . ." He made a face.

"What?"

"The SUV must belong to the Kings," he concluded. "They would have driven Molly to wherever Oskar is."

I checked Katia. Her eyes had drifted closed. "Can you call that CI?" I asked Jesse.

"No. Jimmy wouldn't give me his direct number."

I grunted, which must have sounded like annoyance, because Jesse added, "She was just protecting him. I'd have done the same thing, if I was on the job and he were my informant. But I can call her and beg her for it."

"Will that work?"

Jesse was starting to look like he was doing some pretty serious long division. "It might," he said at last. "If I can figure out the right story."

Oh. Well, now I could pretty much read his thoughts. I touched his shoulder. "I know you don't like lying to her," I said in a low voice. "She's a cop, like you were. But if we can't find them, Molly dies, and God only knows what Oskar will do next."

He nodded. "I know. In these weird circumstances, lying to Jimmy is the right thing to do. But it still feels shitty." Without another word, he got up and went into the other room to make the call.

I flopped back on Will's couch, which was both comfortable and sturdy enough to withstand werewolf tantrums. A few minutes later, Katia's eyelids began to flutter open. "I fell asleep?" she asked, sounding surprised.

"Yeah. Jesse is making a phone call, trying to find Oskar."

She rubbed her eyes with one hand. "Do you mind if I ask you a question while we wait?" she asked.

I gestured for her to go ahead, figuring it was about Shadow. I always got plenty of questions about Shadow.

But I was wrong this time. "Who *are* you?" she said. "I mean, I know you are a negator; I have heard of these. But you are not just doing this to save your friend, are you? What is your role here? And the pretty guy?" She tilted her head after Jesse. "The human."

The questions surprised me, though they shouldn't have. From Katia's perspective, I was blundering around the Old World with an alarming degree of power and influence, yet I obviously wasn't the one in charge. "I don't have a title, not really," I told her. "But my job is to make sure the Old World stays secret. And Jesse helps me sometimes. You know that we share power in LA, right?" She nodded, though she had the same polite-but-dubious expression I wear when someone says raw vegan diets are delicious. "Well, when someone messes up, and we risk exposure, I come in and clean it up. I would try to stop Oskar just for Molly's sake, but it actually does fall within my job description. At least now that we know he wants to pull apart our whole way of life."

She considered this. "You are like . . . a custodian," she said at last. "Part janitor, part protector."

I grinned at that. "I've been called worse."

We talked a little longer, mostly her asking me questions about Lex and me doing my best to answer them tactfully. I did ask Katia a few things about boundary magic. We didn't have any boundary witches in Los Angeles, though I had cleaned up more than one scene where some trades witches had decided to dick around with death magic. It usually involved at least one dead trades witch.

Katia told me she was okay at pressing weaker vampires—someone like Dashiell would be well beyond her abilities—but she could not, she said, do the big scary move that boundary witches were best known for: sucking the life out of humans and using their life force to do trades magic. "If I had the right supplies, performed the right rituals, I could take the life of chickens or goats," she said gravely. "I have done this a few times, when Oskar demanded it. I do not like to do it, though. It feels . . . too good. I have never done hard drugs, but I imagine it's like that."

I felt her magic flex just a tiny bit within my radius, but I'd been around witches enough to know she wasn't trying to perform an active spell. It was more like she was remembering one, the way your hand automatically rises to your ear when you talk about being on the phone.

When her voice started to drift again, I shut up, letting her get some rest. The woman had been dead only two hours earlier; she deserved some sleep.

After nearly half an hour, Jesse came back into the room. He looked . . . well, nearly as tired as Katia. But it was the bone-deep, my-soul-hurts kind of tired. "We're on," he said. "I know where the girls are."

Chapter 38

When you live in Los Angeles, you eventually acclimate to living along-side and within the film industry. In LA, big movie theater complexes often host way-in-advance screenings, complete with security and celeb-rities. Actors are everywhere, and screenwriters fill every coffee shop and diner in the county. It's perfectly ordinary to have streets or businesses closed for filming, and now and then you'll see cryptic signs with vague code names directing crew members to shoots.

This is our thing, and to residents it becomes part of the landscape, like the skyways that connect buildings in downtown Minneapolis so residents don't have to go outside in subfreezing temperatures, or the gas stations overflowing with Disney merchandise in Orlando. But every now and then, something reminds me that I live in a movie industry town, and it suddenly seems surreal all over again.

Case in point? Forty-five minutes away from where we sat, there was a McDonald's that didn't serve food. Did not, in fact, serve any-thing at all.

"So it looks like a fast-food restaurant, but it exists just for filming?" I said skeptically.

"No, it looks like a *McDonald's*, complete with the big golden arches out front," Jesse corrected. "Everything's just like a regular restau-rant, but it sits empty until the McDonald's corporation needs to film new commercials. It can, however, be rented out to other companies for filming. Which is what Oskar did."

"That is just *so* LA," I said, shaking my head. "And your new CI buddy told you this?"

He nodded. "That's where they drove Molly. Oskar has no reason to suspect we've got an informant within the MC, so he also has no reason not to trust them. I'm guessing he's pressing their leader, Lee, into giving these orders, and the rest of the gang follows them." Jesse seemed troubled. "My guy wasn't actually there, but he called one of his friends and got the location out of him."

Ah. I didn't know how much Jesse had to blackmail or bully the guy to make him do that, but I'd seen enough movies to know that if we went in there with guns—or knives, in my case—blazing, and the rest of the MC figured out how we found them, the CI wouldn't have much of a life expectancy. We needed to do everything we could to prevent that.

"What a weird fucking place to have your hideout," I said.

Jesse shrugged. "I checked a map on my phone. It's a good location for vampires—an office park where most businesses are only open nine to five. I'm guessing the security is pretty good, and if they need to film at night sometimes, there must be pretty high-quality blackout shades."

I checked my watch. It was a little after three in the morning. "If he's as smart as everyone says he is, he's going to kill Molly at dawn," I guessed. "Or kill her *with* the dawn. That's a little less than four hours from now. How many of the MC guys stayed at Mock-Donald's?"

That got a little smile out of him. "Four. Plus Oskar, and God knows who else."

I laid a hand gently on Katia's shoulder. "Katia! Can you wake up for just a minute?"

Her eyes opened again. "Is Lex here?" she croaked.

"Not yet. But there's something we really need to know. Are you with me?"

She didn't exactly sit up, but she shifted a little on the cot. "Yes. What is the question?"

"We know that Frederic was working with you guys. Is there anyone else in the LA Old World who works for Oskar?"

She chewed on her lip. "Yes. There are two other vampires who have been spying for Oskar, and not because I pressed them. They knew Oskar the last time he was in Los Angeles, before I met him. There is a werewolf as well, although I don't know his name."

Jesse and I exchanged a troubled look. "Do you know the vampires' names?" I asked.

Katia shook her head. "I did not need to press them, so Oskar kept their identities secret. As I told you, he never fully trusted me."

"Shit. Will they be with him?"

"No. They are to go to the Trials as they normally would. They were to be part of the later plan to overtake Dashiell."

Well, that was one thing, at least. "Okay, you can go back to sleep," I told her. "We'll give Lex this address and tell her to come straight here."

She nodded and slipped back into unconsciousness.

"So six of them, against only two of us," I said, thinking out loud. "Even if I neutralize the supernaturals, that's six men with probably at least four guns."

"Not to state the obvious," Jesse said, "but we could really use some backup on this."

"Yeah, no shit. But who? Three more traitors isn't as bad as I feared, but it's enough that we can really only trust Dashiell and Will. And Beatrice," I added, "but she's not a fighter."

"Kirsten?"

"Yes, we trust her, but she's a little too messed up tonight to be playing with combat magic."

He winced. "Okay, I can see that."

"And as far as I know, she's the only witch in LA with experience using magic to blow things up. So . . . we're kind of fucked here."

"We could wait for Will and Dashiell," he offered. "Do you think they'd fight?"

"I don't know," I said honestly. "Will, almost certainly. But Dashiell rarely wades into physical confrontation, especially with me around. It's not a cowardice thing; it's more like . . . you wouldn't send the president to the front lines. Too big of a risk."

"On the other hand, Oskar's gunning for his city," Jesse said. "And Dashiell could squash him like a bug."

I pointed to myself. "I'm a mobile *even playing field*, remember? If you want Dashiell to vamp-kill all the humans and overpower Oskar, I'd have to stay home and watch from the cheap seats. Ordinarily that would sound fantastic, but if we send Dashiell in there alone, he could decide a dead Molls is a better political move than a live Molls."

"Yeah." Jesse rubbed his face, looking as overwhelmed as I felt. "What time do the Trials end?"

"They had a thirty-minute break at ten thirty, then another two-and-a-half hour session, and repeat," I explained. "They're done at four, and then it's social time."

Jesse leaned back on the couch. "It's too bad Lex isn't here already," he commented. "It would be pretty frickin' awesome to have her on our team."

"You're not wrong. Let me think for a second."

I leaned back, letting myself be more or less swallowed up by the couch. I was exhausted, but the pain in my arm and my churning brain meant I didn't need to worry about falling asleep.

Guns. Our problems pretty much all came down to guns. Very few people in the LA Old World used them at all, because guns were a hassle. They could malfunction, they needed to be serviced, you had to have special licenses and permits to carry them, and so on. Why mess with all that when you could rip someone's throat out with your hands?

Maybe they were a part of the Old World in a city that wasn't more or less peaceful, but in LA the only real threat to any of us usually came from humans. And even the witches had mild defensive spells that could send a human flying.

For a second I started daydreaming in James Bond levels of ridiculousness: A giant magnet that could suck in firearms, maybe, or bulletproof suits of armor. Maybe a pen that could disable all the firing pins in a given area—

On the floor by my feet, Shadow whined, pawing at my foot. I looked down at her and sighed. "Yeah, you're right."

Jesse raised his eyebrows. I pointed to the bargest. "We're gonna need to bring our secret weapon."

Chapter 39

I had been planning to leave Shadow at Will's house to guard Katia, but there was just no way Jesse and I were going to be able to take down the MC crew without her.

We talked through it, but it was unlikely the MC knew about Shadow. They might have known we brought a dog to the trap at Frederic's house—I couldn't remember if she'd barked, but it was certainly possible—but the only biker who'd survived had been Carl, the guy with the greasy beard and the ventilated cowboy boot. And he'd been inside the garage for the whole fight. There was no way he could have seen Shadow.

Having the bargest along, and a surprise, changed the odds from "we're all gonna die" to "we have a slight chance of living." Especially if Molly was functional enough to fight too. Now we just had to get there before Oskar killed her.

Of course, this also meant leaving Katia without a guard, which I didn't totally love. I believed her when she said she wanted to meet Lex and escape from Oskar, but what if she changed her mind? Lex already knew about Katia and was on her way, so if Katia sent us into a trap, she could still get what she wanted. Actually, it would be a pretty smart way for her to hedge her bets.

On the bright side, she'd recently been dead, so I couldn't see her physically coming after us. I just needed to make sure she couldn't call anyone. Will had a landline at his house, so I went into his bedroom, feeling more than a little uncomfortable. Luckily, Will was so used to the werewolves coming over that the room was always spotless and impersonal, with no signs of creepy sex stuff or dirty underwear. I unplugged the phone to take with me. Then I went into his home office and took that handset, too. While I was in there I grabbed a couple of pieces of paper and a pencil to bring to Jesse. As I took the phones out to the van, Jesse looked up the Mock-Donald's on Google Earth. In the time it would have taken me to figure out how to input an address, he had a rough sketch of the building and its entrances.

"Okay, look," he said, pointing with the pencil eraser. "Green Drive runs along the north and west sides of the building, see? There's one entrance on the north side, two on the west side, and one each on the other two sides." I leaned over him to look at the sketch. The Mock-Donald's was basically a rectangle, with the shorter end at the north side. "I can't be positive, but it looks on this map like the south entrance is the one leading into the kitchen."

"What about the inside?" I asked.

"Hang on a second." He did a little more searching and managed to come up with a website for the production company that owned the building. There was a whole page filled with big glossy photos of the interior.

"Whoa," I said, leaning forward to look at his little phone screen. "Why would they have so many pictures?"

"It's advertising," Jesse said without looking at me. He was adding tables and counters to the sketch. "If they're renting it out to anyone with the cash, they need to be able to show clients what they'll get. Hey, look." He moved his fingers to zoom in on a picture of a staircase. "There's a basement." I leaned over his shoulder to look. Sure enough, there was a downstairs with classrooms, offices, and a lounge area, sort of like a green room.

I sighed. Up until recently, it was incredibly rare for buildings in LA to have a basement at all, but things had been changing, now that basements had better earthquake-proofing. I've even read about people who had basements dug under their existing houses to add space.

"Well, that's where the girls will be," I said. "And where Oskar hides out during the day. But he'll be torturing Molly . . . " I scrolled back through to the photo of a typical fast-food kitchen, with beverage machines, stoves, and fryers forming a sort of rectangle. There was a long, rectangular metal table in the middle of the space. I pointed to it. "Here."

"How do you know?"

I shrugged. "There aren't any good surfaces downstairs for securing someone, for one thing. And I could see Oskar enjoying the theatricality of a big table. Plus . . . you know. There's torture stuff right there."

Jesse took another look at the kitchen equipment and nodded soberly. "I think you're right."

"But that's just Oskar, Molly, and the girls. Where do you think he'll have the human guards?"

"Outside," Jesse decided. "If I were a vampire, and I knew a null was on her way, I'd use the bikers like canaries in a coal mine. When they start shooting, Oskar will know you're coming before he's actually in your radius. That will give him time to grab a weapon or run or whatever."

We were both speculating, but there was enough logic in it for me to bet on us being right. Even if we were betting our lives.

"What do we do if the neighbors call the police?" I asked.

"What neighbors? Look." He went back to Google Earth and zoomed out, pointing to an aerial view of the Mock-Donald's. "There are big parking lots on either side, probably for when they bring in filming equipment. On the other side of the lots there are just office buildings." He checked his watch. "It's almost four in the morning; even the cleaning staff will have gone home."

We spent a little more time with Jesse's sketch, working out a plan for how to handle the MC guards. I was hoping we weren't going to have to kill them. It didn't sound like any of these guys were stellar citizens, but criminals or not, they were just a bunch of dudes following their leader into vampire hell. I had to kind of feel sorry for them.

We could prepare for the humans, but other than torturing Molly I had no idea what Oskar was planning now that we had Katia. So far he had demonstrated an uncomfortably shrewd gift for thinking on his feet: hiring humans with guns to take me out, using Hayne to get Molly from Dashiell's, preparing a second hidey-hole in case something went wrong—like us capturing Katia. It made me nervous. I hadn't been up against a genuinely smart asshole since . . . well, since Olivia.

But we did have two things going for us: first, there was no way he could know that Jesse had an informant within the MC who would be able to point us to the Mock-Donald's and, of course, Shadow. I was hoping the element of surprise would be enough, because I was shit out of other ideas.

When we'd made all the plans we could, I knelt down by Shadow. She had, of course, been listening to everything, but it was impossible to know exactly how much she'd absorbed, so I said, "Shadow, do you remember Molly? The girl we picked up the other night?"

Shadow paused for a moment, then licked the air in front of her face, a yes. "Jesus," Jesse muttered. I glared at him, although I couldn't entirely blame him for being unnerved. Shadow's intelligence was almost as scary as her teeth; I was just so used to it now that I found other dogs boring.

"She's in trouble," I said to the bargest. "Jesse and I are going to go rescue her from some bad guys. They're probably going to try to hurt us. Do you want to help save Molly?"

No hesitation this time: she licked the air and wagged her tail with great enthusiasm. If she could speak English, that would have translated to "Killing people? Where do I sign up?!" A big, glorious doggie grin was spreading across her face, and out of the corner of my eye I could see Jesse scooting back a little.

Oh, boy.

Chapter 40

I didn't know City of Industry that well, but Jesse had been right about the area around the building: it was completely deserted. In fact, the streets were *so* empty that something about it made my thoughts itch. When the GPS said we were about two blocks away from our destination, I finally figured out what felt off: there were no homeless people on the streets. I didn't expect anyone to be panhandling at 4 a.m., but usually you see them all over the city, camped out in doorways and alleys. Around the Mock-Donald's, there was nobody—either because the area was too void of people for them to bother sleeping here, or because they'd been eaten by vampires needing snacks.

I decided not to pursue that line of thought any further.

We had talked about doing a drive-by to scope it out, like we did at Frederic's place, but with no other cars on the street my van would be way too obvious. Instead, we parked on Gale Avenue, almost a full block away, and the three of us crept up Green Drive like we were competing for Most Silent Walker. Shadow won, of course, but Jesse and I held our own. I was glad my boots didn't have heels, or I would have had to tiptoe. It was fairly cool, in the low fifties. Jesse had put on his leather jacket, and I was glad for the drapey top I'd worn over my weapons.

Green Drive was just a little offshoot of Gale, shaped like a big staple, with the Mock-Donald's at the corner. There wasn't much cover—too many big empty parking lots—but we made it to a clump of trees just outside the Mock-Donald's lot without incident. The streetlights were out, just like Jesse had predicted, but it's never fully dark in Los Angeles, where smog reflects all the light of the city back down into it.

Jesse and I paused for a second, looking at the building, checking how it lined up with Jesse's sketch. I could make out the big golden arches and the building's south entrance, which faced the road. Overall, the Mock-Donald's was so eerily perfect that I had a sudden, serious craving for a Quarter Pounder. Not even joking. It shouldn't have surprised me—after all, this was LA, the city that brazenly celebrated the concept of fakery. But it was still jarring to see the familiar golden arches in connection with vampires. Two things that just did *not* go together.

There were lights on inside, but only toward the back of the building, which didn't help us. We could, however, see the beefy guy leaning against the wall a foot from the south door. He was wearing jeans and a flannel shirt, and had an enormous handgun hanging loose from one hand. After a few seconds of letting my eyes adjust to the dimmer light, I saw the walking cast on his leg and recognized the guy: Greasy Beard, the lone survivor from Frederic's condo.

"You ready?" Jesse asked in a low voice.

"Almost." I looked down at the bargest. Shadow had a big, goofy doggy grin, the same look you'd see on a golden retriever on her way to the dog park. I crouched down next to the bargest, scratching the scaly bald area on her neck. "Okay, girl," I said, and her attention whipped to my face. I grabbed Jesse's hand, tugging him down next to me. "Jesse's our friend, and Molly is our friend. You're not going to hurt them, right?"

I don't know if it's physiologically possible for a *regular* dog to roll its eyes, but Shadow gave me a look that said, *Duh, of course not* as clearly as if she'd said it out loud. Why hurt your friends when there were plenty of other people here to hurt? "Good. Just like we talked

about, okay? If you can keep them silent without killing them, do it."
She licked the air near my face. "Go," I whispered.

Without the slightest hesitation, Shadow seemed to slip into the nearest . . . well, the nearest shadow. I knew from experience that watching the bargest at night was like watching a shell game: you sure as hell needed to keep your eyes glued to the target, or you were going to lose track of it instantly. Even so, my eyes couldn't stay with her once she neared the building, so I started watching the MC idiot instead. He was checking something on his cell phone—and then Shadow was on him. She had somehow circled and raced directly toward the guy, face to face, so that by the time he looked up and opened his mouth to scream, she was ripping out his throat with a single jerk. He didn't even have time to lower the cell phone, and we saw the chunk of flesh come loose in the light from the little glowing screen.

Beside me, Jesse started swearing in Spanish, and even I flinched. So much for trying to let them live.

Mission accomplished, the bargest came prancing back to me, as proud as if she'd just taken out a particularly pesky neighborhood squirrel. Tail wagging, she thrust her muzzle into my hand, looking for praise. Wet blood smeared into my palm. I sighed.

"Yes, that was very well done," I told her, "but did you really have to kill him?"

Shadow just pranced in place.

"If it makes you feel any better," Jesse remarked, "the guy called you the c-word earlier."

"Really?"

"Yeah. At Frederic's house."

"Well, okay," I muttered under my breath. "Good girl. Let's move."

We circled the building to the west side. The east side entrance would be closest to where we thought Oskar was keeping Molly, but there were also two doors and two guards there, which increased the likelihood of one of them getting a shot at us. So we went left, and repeated almost the exact same pattern: Jesse and I hung back, Shadow went in and killed the unsuspecting biker, a short, chubby guy who was at least ten years younger than any of the other bikers we'd seen. Then I nodded to Jesse, and he and Shadow trotted toward the south side of the building, while I slipped to the door.

As I moved, I did my best to shrink my radius. This particular trick was actually more difficult than broadening the circle of non-magic around me, but I'd been practicing for months, hoping to make the vampires more comfortable being in a room with me. More than any other Old World creature, vampires hated being near nulls. I hadn't told anyone I'd been working on contracting my radius, because I wasn't that great at it yet. But the longer I could keep my radius small, the longer I could go without Oskar sensing my presence. My record was getting it down to about two feet around me instead of the usual ten to fifteen, but I couldn't hold that for long.

The Mock-Donald's had a lot of windows, so I went in low, moving as quickly as I could. Silently, I pulled a knife with one hand and wrapped the other around the glass door, tugging it slowly. The door was locked, which actually relieved me: an unlocked door would have probably indicated a trap.

I never could learn how to pick locks, which was why I'd stolen a big-ass geode paperweight from Will's home office. I took it out of my pocket, held it carefully so my fingers wouldn't impact, and swung it as hard as I could toward the lower half of the glass doors. Never underestimate the power of hitting something with a big fucking rock.

The door didn't shatter dramatically, like in a movie. The first swing made it crack into a thousand spiderwebs, with a small chunk falling out of the middle. Quickly, I aimed one more shot at the worst of the spiderwebs, and the entire pane of glass collapsed.

Then I expanded my radius.

I felt them right away: two vampires, one much weaker than the other. Only one of them was moving around; that had to be Oskar. He was the weaker of the two, which explained why he'd arranged such an elaborate revenge against Molly: he wouldn't be able to beat her in a straight-up fight.

I could have theoretically stood there and tracked his movements inside my expanded radius, but that would have required so much concentration that he could probably saunter up and kill me with my own rock. Instead, I ran inside.

The counter—fake counter, I reminded myself—was on my left, so I ducked low. The "restaurant seating" portion of the building was dark, with chairs sitting up on tables, but light glowed through the window and door from the "kitchen." I edged along the counter, closer to the door with the light.

"I know you're there, negator," called a man's voice from the kitchen. It had the perfectly flat, accent-free tone of professional actors and vampires. Unfortunately, I didn't think this guy had a SAG card. "As I believe they say in American movies, come out with your hands up."

Anytime now, Jesse, I thought, not responding. He was supposed to be crashing noisily through the back door, distracting Oskar so I could rush in and free Molly.

Then I heard the scream.

If anyone had asked me five minutes ago, I would have said you can't recognize someone's voice based on a scream alone, but the raw, ragged sound that tore out of the kitchen was so distinctly Molly that my heart stopped for a moment. I had to force myself not to run in there. Molly was human right now, which meant she was feeling every bit of the pain Oskar inflicted on her—and she wasn't healing from it. I tried to retract my radius again, to make Oskar think I'd left, but I couldn't focus.

"I'm going to kill her anyway, you know," the same voice called, in a cool, unaffected tone. "So how about I count to three, and if you're not in here, I'll slit her throat and watch her bleed out right this minute."

"Scarlett, get out of here! He's got a gu—" Molly's hoarse voice was silenced, and my guts twisted.

"One!" the man called.

Goddammit, Jesse.

"Two!"

"I'm coming!" I yelled over the counter. I jammed the knife in my right hand into my watch band, pocketed the other one, and stood slowly with my arms up, the knife hidden behind my hand.

There was a man now standing in the lit doorway, holding a handgun that was pointed at my chest. He appeared to be around thirty-five, with dirty blond hair and a lean, athletic build. His features were pleasant enough, but there was crazy in his eyes. He wore a bulletproof vest on the outside of a button-down shirt and jeans. Both were spattered with blood, but I doubted it was his.

He grinned as I slowly stood up, my hands still raised. "Come join the party," he said. "Scarlett, was it? I'm Oskar."

"I'd say it's nice to meet you, but you seem like kind of a dick, so . . ." I shrugged.

"That's no way to talk to your betters," he said without heat. He used the gun to beckon me into the kitchen. "Come in here. Let's get a look at you."

I walked forward, and the guy took a few steps back, making space for me to come into the other room. There were shiny metal appliances everywhere—undoubtedly kept in peak condition for commercial shoots. The only thing in the room that wasn't immaculate was the body tied to the long metal table in the center of the room. Molly. Just as I'd predicted.

Under ordinary circumstances, I might have been pleased about being right. But there was no satisfaction to be found here. She was . . . almost unrecognizable. Over a dozen leather belts were buckled around her body from her neck to her ankles, securing her to the table. I'd expected blood, but not so much that her black hair looked damply glued to the metal. More blood smeared the tattered remains of the dress she'd put on back at her apartment building. It was barely staying on her now, thanks to the long strips that had been cut into it with the carving knife that had been casually discarded on her legs. Most of the cuts from the knife had healed thanks to vampire abilities, but there was a new one, a deep stripe of blood running down her cheek. Both of her eyes had been blackened, which meant he must have hit her just before my arrival. He'd also stuffed a gag in her mouth—a bloody piece of cloth—and her nostrils were flaring as she struggled to breathe around it. Her eyes were wild. She'd lost a lot of blood, which meant that when she was a vampire, she was probably very thirsty.

Oskar let out a low, appreciative whistle. "Not bad, girl," he said, and I realized he'd been ogling me. "God, I love the number of beautiful women in this town. I could rent you out easy. Too bad you're so . . . breakable." His lip curled up. "My clientele prefers their girls a little sturdier."

I made a big show of yawning, because that's what you do to men who traffic in power over women. "Misogynistsayswhat?"

His brow furrowed suspiciously. "What?"

"Exactly." Guess they didn't have that joke in . . . wherever the fuck this guy lived.

Oskar sighed, pressed the gun to the meat of Molly's thigh, and pulled the trigger. She screamed into her gag. "No!" I yelped, starting forward, but Oskar shook his head at me to move back. Tears were running from Molly's eyes.

"Any more funny jokes for me?" Oskar said brightly. I shook my head, mute. "Good. Now, I was just going to kill you, but you know, it's kind of interesting, being around a negator. I can roll with change." He beamed at me like I'd just handed him the keys to a new car. "So. New plan!" he announced.

Then he raised the gun and shot me in the stomach.

Chapter 41

The force shoved me backward, my shoulder blades hitting the wall behind me. I curled into myself, clutching my stomach. The knife I'd hidden in my watchband clattered to the ground, causing Oskar to snort with derision.

"Really? What is that, a fucking pocket knife?" He stomped close enough to kick it away from me, then returned to his spot next to Molly.

"Fuck," I muttered, pressing my hands against my shirt. The bullet had hit the bottom of my own Kevlar vest, and I was pretty sure I had a broken rib or three. I didn't have to fake the look of pain on my face, but I stayed curled up so I could hide the lack of blood.

"Here's what we're going to do," Oskar sang. "While you bleed out, Molly and I are going to experiment with a few methods of torture that only work on humans. A little waterboarding, maybe some light strangulation. Then when *you* die, negator, I'll wheel our girl Molly into the parking lot to wait for the sun." He smiled broadly. "I'm hoping you live until sunrise, because then I can wheel her out *and* I can watch from the windows. How fun is that?"

"You and I have very different definitions of fun," I mumbled. Where in the fuck was Jesse? I was starting to worry.

"That's probably true," Oskar said agreeably. He stepped back to Molly's face. "What do you think, sweetheart? Are you having fun?"

I expected Molly to glare or give him the finger, but she shook her head at him, eyes desperate. I worked my fingers under the hem of my shirt, trying to access the knives belted around my stomach, right above the bullet. "What did she ever do to you?" I asked, to cover any sound. I tugged a knife free.

"You know," Oskar said with pursed lips, "nobody has ever actually asked me that before. Thank you, sincerely." He pointed the gun at me again, this time at my head. "But shut your fucking mouth, bitch. I'm already getting tired of you."

"Wha-t-t-t," I stuttered, my voice weak and frightened. "What if I want to scream?"

He grinned. "Oh, screaming's just fine. I encourage screaming."

"Cool," I said in my normal voice. I took a deep breath and screamed as loud as I could.

It took about seven seconds before the drive-through window behind Oskar shattered under the tremendous force of the bargest sailing through it.

"What the fu—" was all he managed to say before Shadow knocked him to the ground. I saw the flash of her teeth, but Oskar got his gun around and shot her several times in the chest. It wouldn't penetrate her skin, of course, but she did have to fall back to recover. Sensing his opportunity, Oskar wobbled to his feet and started *kicking* my bargest in the stomach.

"Oh *hell* no," I said out loud. The table that held Molly was in my way, so I inched my back up the wall, rising just far enough to send my first knife slamming into Oskar.

Fun fact about throwing knives: if they're sharp and thrown hard, they can puncture Kevlar. I was aiming for his heart, but between his movement and my broken ribs, the knife buried itself in the back of his shoulder. He let out a surprised cry, trying to reach over his shoulder to feel the hilt. He turned toward me and raised the gun at my head, but I had finished standing up by then. I sent the next knife into his chest.

It wasn't a heart shot, unfortunately. I made a mental note to get more practice with moving targets. Oskar howled with pain and stumbled toward the back exit, away from me and my radius. I wanted to follow him—the last thing we needed was for him to heal and come back—but I wasn't going anywhere until I freed Molly. I straightened up gingerly and went to her, yanking out the gag. She spat it out with more than a little blood, making a face at the taste.

"Hey, Molls," I said, pulling another knife from my belt. "This place sucks even for a McDonald's. Let's find Jesse and get the fuck out of here." I tried cutting through the leather, but quickly realized that it would be easier to undo the belts one at a time. I dropped the knife and started doing that.

"Scarlett," she panted, "you need to get out of here."

"No shit. I told you, we gotta find Jesse and—"

"No!" She thunked her head back against the table in frustration. "You're not listening! Remember how I told you Alonzo had a gift for bloodcraft and it passed down his line?" she said all in a rush.

I had gotten the belt on her neck and the one below it loose, and was working on the third one down. "Yeah, I remember. So what?"

"He's got a shitload of guns, the fucker, and because of the bloodcraft—"

I heard movement from the doorway that Oskar had just left. I looked up just in time to see a young woman in bloody clothes charging into the room, followed by more women. Their eyes were glazed with hatred, and they each held a handgun.

"My friends woke up early," Molly finished wearily.

Chapter 42

Jesse and Shadow were circling the building to attack the guard at the south entrance when their luck ran out. There was no one standing next to the door. Instead, the guard was moving away from a nearby tree, zipping his fly. He was big, with a bushy beard that circled his whole head to blend in with his hair. He moved like an athlete, but his stomach was swollen to fat.

He saw Jesse in the same instant Jesse saw him, and both men raised their guns. "Police!" Jesse yelled instinctively. "Put it down!"

Jesse glanced down at Shadow, expecting her to attack, but the bargest swung her whole body sharply sideways, cocking her head to the side. Abruptly, she stalked off into the darkness.

"What the fuck?" Jesse mumbled to himself.

The guy ignored this. He slowly circled forward, studying Jesse. "You're no cop," he said in a gruff voice. "Not anymore, anyway. I seen your book."

Jesse didn't know where Shadow had disappeared to, but he needed to stall until the bargest could take this guy down. "You should walk away," he told the biker. "Lee didn't mean to send you guys here. He was forced."

That made the other man pause. "*I'm* Lee," he growled, and Jesse realized that the poor lighting had disguised the gray in the man's hair.

He was well past fifty. "And you don't know what the fuck you're talking about, son."

Shit. Jesse couldn't undo someone's press, but he could poke holes in it. "Then why would you send men out here on Oskar's orders?" Jesse demanded. "He already got two of your guys killed."

There was the briefest hesitation, and then Lee Harrison said, "Money. A lot of it."

"Have you *seen* any money?"

"Not your concern, boy," he snapped.

"Okay, fine. Did anything seem off about Oskar?" Jesse pushed. "Like maybe he hasn't *aged* since the last time you saw him?"

Lee shook his head like he was trying to clear mental spiderwebs. "I told you," he growled, releasing the safety on his Beretta. "It's not your concern."

"Well, we're kind of at an impasse here," Jesse contended. "Do you really want to stand here pointing guns at each other until someone's backup arrives?"

White teeth flashed dangerously in the light spilling through the window. "I got nowhere else to be, kid. And I got numbers on my side."

"Not anymore," Jesse informed him.

That made the other man frown. Keeping his gun pointed at Jesse, Lee pulled an iPhone out of his pocket. Jesse hoped he would stare at the screen long enough to ruin his night vision, giving Jesse an opportunity to attack, but the old MC president simply pressed down the button and said, "Call Jonesy." He held the phone to his ear, listening, Jesse imagined, to a lot of ringing.

"Short, chubby guy, pretty young?" Jesse asked. Startled, Lee nodded.

"Dead."

"Did you kill him?" Lee's voice simmered with rage, but there was some confusion there, too. He could tell that the situation felt all wrong, but he couldn't put his finger on why, and he didn't want to show weakness. Dammit, Jesse *really* wanted Scarlett to break this guy's press.

"Not exactly," Jesse said. "One of my companions. Do you know what Oskar has hidden in the basement?" he added quickly, before the older man could blame him for the death.

Lee didn't respond, which probably meant he didn't know. "Four girls," Jesse continued. "College kids, from USC. Oskar wants to whore them out, but not exactly in a consenting way, if you get my drift."

The other man's face went stony. "Let me guess," Jesse went on. "Our pal Oskar told you he would set you up with a whole new brothel, somewhere in the valley. Oskar will even provide most of the capital. You run the business by day, he takes over at night. Am I close?"

Lee was silent, but Jesse could see that his gun arm was starting to tremble. "Movies too?" Jesse prodded. "I heard you run a little light porn. He promised you exotic stuff, didn't he?"

Instinctively, the MC president lifted the phone again, probably to call his other backup, but he fumbled it, sending it clattering onto the sidewalk. He stepped away from Jesse with a grunt, eyes flicking downward.

"You're calling down too much heat, Lee," Jesse said in a soft, dangerous voice. "Someone kidnaps a bunch of rich white girls and torches their house? It was all over the news. What do you think's gonna happen when you and Oskar try to whore them out?"

"He told me they were into it," Lee said at last, giving up on the phone for the moment. "They came to *him* after the *accidental* fire. The publicity will die down in a few days—"

Jesse snorted. "You're smarter than that, Lee. Too smart to get into bed with a guy who kidnaps four girls and *kills* eight more. A guy who hasn't gotten any older in twenty years. I don't know what Oskar did for you before, and I don't care. He's bad news, and if you let him drag you into this brothel venture, he'll feed you to the cops the first chance he gets."

For the first time, Lee looked unsure of himself. "I . . . I don't know. Something about this is fucked up, but how do I know *you're* telling me the truth any more than he is?"

"You've seen my book," Jesse said. "You must know people with the cops. You can call them and check—"

A gunshot came from inside the Mock-Donald's, and both Jesse and Lee automatically turned toward the building. A second later, there was a bloodcurdling scream, and then Jesse caught a blur of speed out of the corner of his eye. Too high to be Shadow. Too fast to be Scarlett. "Look out!" he yelled to Lee, but it was too late. A vampire had appeared between them, seizing each man's gun arm. He used the arms to wrench Jesse and the MC president violently toward each other, causing their heads to smack together.

This was why Shadow had disappeared: she'd been hunting the vampire.

Jesse staggered backward, his hand involuntarily releasing the gun. Fireworks of pain bounced around the inside of his skull at the point of impact, and Jesse barely kept his feet. He gathered his wits enough to crouch and feel around for the Glock.

"*Must* you?" the vampire said in exasperation. He kicked the gun away, and then delivered a vicious kick to Jesse's abdomen. Jesse collapsed. "What. The. Fuck," he groaned. "You must be Oskar."

"Hardly," the vampire sniffed. He was Asian, good-looking, appearing to be around thirty. "We haven't officially met," the vampire added. "I'm Frederic."

Chapter 43

The girl in the lead hit my radius and skidded to a stop, looking bewildered. I'd never actually had a just-turned vampire in my radius before, but I imagined it had to be confusing. "Kill her!" roared Oskar's voice from the back. Though she was currently a human again, something in the girl's overloaded brain told her she was supposed to listen to Oskar. She raised her handgun and *shot me again*. Luckily her aim was shitty, and the bullet just grazed my arm. Unluckily, it was pretty much exactly where I'd *already been fucking shot*.

I screeched with pain and dropped low, pulling Molly's table over sideways. Feeling the pain in my ribs, trying to ignore it. The table landed with a crash. Inspired, I pushed it as fast as I could toward the attacking vampires. It was a small room, and the legs of the table hit the lead girl in the ankle, sending her stumbling back into the girl behind her. It must have caused a chain effect, because I heard Oskar shouting obscenities.

"Time to go, Molls," I said, fingers scrabbling at the belts. "Can you wiggle out?" Behind me, Shadow had climbed to her feet and shaken herself vigorously. I'd known intellectually that she would be fine, but I still felt something tight in my chest release. "Shadow!" I yelled. "Can you buy us some time *without* killing those girls?"

Shadow walked—limping only for the first few steps—across the room to the doorway, where the lead girl was just pointing the gun at me again.

"You don't want to shoot me," I said conversationally. "I'm just trying to help your friend Molly. Remember her?"

The girl peered over the side of the table, confirming that yes, the girl strapped to it was familiar. "Molly?" she said tentatively. "I don't understand—"

"I know, Harper," Molly said, as Oskar continued to shout orders from behind the girl. I dropped the belt I was working on and scrambled to grab knives, throwing one at the girl right behind Harper, who still had a gun pointed at me. I hit the upper arm of her gun hand just before it fired. I felt the bullet whiz harmlessly past my face. Shadow stopped worrying at Oskar's legs and turned on the shooter, sinking her teeth into the girl's ankle. She yowled.

Molly had managed to wriggle her lower body out of the remaining belts, which had to hurt like hell with the bullet in her leg. "We gotta go," I yelled over the chaos.

"Not without them!" Molly cried.

"What do you want me to do?"

"Get them out of here!"

There was fresh fire in her voice, and I suddenly understood. She wanted to take Oskar out herself, a sentiment that I could appreciate, even if she wasn't exactly instilling confidence in me. Molly still looked like hell.

But how was I going to convince four armed, completely disoriented college kids to follow me out of this joint? "Tell them to trust me, then!"

"Hailey! Taylor! Louisa! Harper!" Molly roared, in such a commanding tone that all four girls froze. "Forget what this asshole told you. Drop the guns and follow my friend Scarlett to safety. You can trust her!"

The girls were crowded around the bottleneck I'd made with the hallway, and they were obviously about to lose it. Two were already crying, and the other two had trembling lips. Behind them, Oskar was trying to scream a new set of orders. They were currently human, so they had no biological imperative to obey him, but it contributed to the overall chaos.

Molly snatched the gun out of Harper's hand and pointed it at Oskar, which made his mouth click shut as he realized that he was currently human. Suddenly, the whole room was dead silent. Shadow looked at me, whining uncertainly. I was busy looking at the four girls.

They were all pretty, and bedraggled, and nearly naked. Their clothes had been half-burned away, and hung in charred, smelly tatters at their shoulders and waistlines. Each girl had blood near her mouth, which meant Oskar had at least fed them when they woke up. But they'd been through a hell of a lot of trauma, not the least of which was being turned into fucking vampires without warning. If anyone deserved to be wigging out, it was them.

But we just didn't have time.

I stood up, raising my hands to show they were empty. Then I stepped slowly over the table, gently took Harper's hand, and picked up the hand of the next girl in line. I joined them together, and both women tightened their grip. I went down the line, linking the four of them together. Then I went back to Harper and took her free hand. "I'm getting you out of here," I said as gently as I could. "Come on."

They came along with me, docile as lambs. I honestly couldn't believe it. When I looked over my shoulder, the four women were still holding hands in a chain, looking like toddlers on a field trip. As we moved past the downed table, Molly and Oskar stayed exactly where they were, guns pointed at one another. Oskar was breathing hard from the knife wounds, but Molly didn't look so great, either. "Molls, you sure?" I called over my shoulder.

"Get them safe," was her grim reply.

I extended my radius so that Molly and Oskar stayed human until all four women could get through the door. When the last girl in line was a few feet away, I couldn't hold it any longer. I felt the two vampires pop out of my radius. Inside the building, things began to crash.

I picked up the pace. We went down the block to my van, and I opened the back so all four girls could climb up. At my gesture, Shadow hopped up behind them. I climbed in and closed the door partway.

When I turned to face them, the four women were crowded together, shivering. I'd been so busy running around that I hadn't felt the temperature drop. It had to be in the high forties now.

Well, at least that gave me somewhere to start. "There are blankets in that compartment," I said, pointing behind Harper. She turned and began unpacking them. "Okay, guys," I went on, "I don't have a lot of time, so here's the deal. Molly, who is your friend, is actually a vampire. She has been all along, but she's a nice vampire who wouldn't willingly hurt you. Except that blond guy, Oskar"—I pointed a thumb over my shoulder—"forced her to. Did he at least explain that you're vampires now?"

The girl farthest from me, a redhead with smudges of ash on her cheeks and a short, curvy figure, said, "Yeah. He gave us blood to drink. It was . . ." she shivered. "It was good. But I don't want any now." Tears began to roll down her face. "I kind of want a hamburger. And I want my mom."

"That's because I'm close to you," I said, trying to sound kind. *Scarlett is not a good candidate for group therapy leader. Scarlett does not play well with others.* "That's what I do, I'm a null. As soon as I move away from you, you guys are going to be vampires again, and that means you're going to be . . . mmm . . . emotionally connected to Oskar. You're going to want to get out of this van and go help him, but if you do, he's just going to force you to sell yourselves for him. He's a pimp, a murderer, and just an all-around evil guy. Okay?"

Three of the girls nodded. The one who wanted her mom was still sniffling, which I decided to accept as a yes.

I was itching to go look for Jesse, not to mention help Molly, but first I pointed to the bargest. "Shadow here has superpowers. I'm going to leave, and you guys are going to be vampires again, but if you try to get out of this van to help Oskar, Shadow will hurt you. A lot." I made eye contact with each of them. "If she absolutely has to, she will kill you. So just wait here until either Molly or I come for you." I reached for the door handle, but remembered just in time. "Oh, and there's an ex-cop named Jesse here, too. Latino, about six feet tall, insanely good-looking for a mortal. He's with the good guys. You can trust him."

None of them spoke, but I didn't have time to sit there, hold hands, and sing "Kumbaya" until I was sure everyone understood. I looked at Shadow, who licked the air in front of her face. "Good girl," I said, and then I was out of the van and running around the building to find Jesse.

Chapter 44

Jesse had actually thought a lot about what it would be like to fight a vampire. Years ago, Jesse had had a . . . mild disagreement with Dashiell, and the vampire had used just a little bit of his strength to mess with Jesse. After that, he'd thought a lot about what he'd need to do if he ever went up against a vampire for real. And yet here he was, in that exact situation, and his mind went completely blank.

Jesse was still lying on the ground, trying to get his breath back from when Frederic had kicked the air out of his lungs. Seeing that Jesse wasn't going to be an immediate threat, the vampire turned toward Lee Harrison. "Don't look in his eyes, man," Jesse said in a groan. He actually wasn't feeling that bad anymore, but Frederic didn't need to know that. "He can mess with your mind."

The vampire turned his head to glare at Jesse, who avoided his gaze. "Shut up, Mr. Cruz," Frederic barked. "My employer has some questions, but if you open your mouth again I'm going to conveniently forget that he wanted to talk to you."

Jesse went quiet. But Lee must have listened to the warning, because the next thing Jesse heard was a grunt of frustration from the vampire. He changed his grip on Lee, grabbing the old man by the head, but the biker president hauled off and hit him. Jesse winced. It was a damn good hit. Lee had probably broken his hand.

Frederic chuckled. Jesse couldn't see Lee's face, but the biker was cradling his hand, shaking his head in disbelief. *"Look at me,"* Frederic said in a voice so seductive that it probably made heterosexual women drop their pants on the spot.

Jesse began easing his body slowly toward his Glock, which had landed about six feet away on the sidewalk encircling the building. "Open your eyes!" Frederic said impatiently. Lee was putting up a fight. Good.

"All right, fine," Frederic said in a bored, resigned voice. "Have it your way." He grabbed Lee's injured hand and squeezed hard enough to draw a cry of pain from Lee. The distraction caused the old man to forget all about his resolution not to meet Frederic's eyes. "Yessss," Frederic hissed. He was pressing the guy.

Jesse started moving faster.

"You will continue working for Oskar and me," Frederic was saying. "You will not ask questions. You will not interfere with our plans. You will only obey."

Lee nodded his head mechanically, and Jesse actually felt sorry for him. But Frederic would be done any second, so Jesse focused on flopping his body over the gun, wrapping his fingers around the cold steel.

"Good. Now, sit down on the ground until Oskar or I call you," Frederic said, giving Lee a rough pat on the cheek. With that, the vampire turned around to face Jesse, immediately forgetting Lee's existence. Faster than Jesse could even follow, Frederic hurtled through the air and kicked him in the face. Jesse felt his nose give way, and warm blood exploded across his face. A groan escaped his lips.

"Mr. Cruz," Frederic said with a sigh, "I know you're used to hanging out with Dashiell's little whore, but I'm a vampire. Do you really think I can't hear the sound of metal scraping on concrete?"

Fuck it. Jesse rolled onto his back, his shoulders braced against the ground, and raised the gun, putting two bullets in Frederic's chest and one, the money shot, right through Frederic's left eye.

But the vampire didn't drop.

He swayed on his feet for a moment, a look of amusement crossing his face. "Congra'lations," he said. The word was slurred, but his voice was still confident, even pleasant. "You pierced my fron'al lobe. But in jus' a momen' the bulle' will come ou'. And I will scoop ou' your en'rails."

He took a determined step toward Jesse, who raised his gun toward the guy's eyes again—and then had an idea. He stood up, got his shoulder in front of him, and charged the vampire like a billy goat, hitting him in the chest. He angled the blow to push Frederic closer to the building.

"Did you jus' *shove* me?" the vampire said incredulously. "Wha' do you poss'bly hope 'o—"

Jesse pushed him again. And again. Each time, Frederic stumbled back a few feet, looking more surprised and annoyed than actually hurt. The bullet holes on his chest had already nearly closed, and Jesse knew he had only a matter of seconds.

The fourth push did it. Frederic's back hit the side of the building, and something changed on his face. He abruptly crumpled like an empty puppet. Jesse had spent enough time around Scarlett to recognize that look. He grinned. Just as he'd hoped, Scarlett had expanded her radius, and he'd pushed Frederic far enough to force him into it—while the bullet was still in his brain.

Jesse leaned over for a minute, hands on his knees, panting. He was out of shape, and exhausted, and his nose was still bleeding. He could hardly think through the pain in his nose and eyes, which were both already swelling.

A tremendous crash came from inside the building, and Jesse thought, *Scarlett.* He pulled a spare magazine out of his back pocket, reloaded, and ran into the building.

And right into an epic vampire fight.

That's what it looked like, anyway. As Jesse entered the building, Molly and another vampire—this *had* to be Oskar—came flying over what looked like a regular McDonald's counter, hitting and punching each other *in the air*, which Jesse had never seen outside of a martial arts film. He stood there openmouthed for a moment as they crashed into a large round table, upending it. Molly was tangled in chair legs, and Oskar saw his opening. He grabbed a chair and drove one leg through Molly's exposed shoulder. While she was struggling to pull out the chair leg, he picked up another chair, taking the time to angle himself over her heart this time—

And Jesse shot him five times in the chest.

Five rounds from a .45 only made the vampire take two small steps backward and lean a hand on a nearby table, but it was enough for Molly to jerk the table leg out of her shoulder and pull herself to her feet. She sidled to the left, putting herself in between Jesse and Oskar, who was now glaring at him.

"Oskar," she said, her voice pleading, "*stopio, nid oes rhaid i chi wneud hyn.*" Jesse didn't even know what language that was. The other vampire only curled his lip in a snarl.

"Of course I have to," he spat. "You killed him. He set you free, and you betrayed him."

"He betrayed me first. He betrayed both of us," she said, her voice heated.

Oskar straightened up. His wounds were healing quickly, and Jesse didn't understand why she wasn't finishing him off. "Step aside, Molly," he said, raising the .45.

"No, don't," she said, turning sideways so she was holding up a hand to each of them.

Twenty feet behind Oskar, the side door opened. Jesse trained his gun, but it was only Scarlett. He sighed with relief.

"Jesse! You're okay!" she cried, darting forward.

"Stop!" Molly screamed. Scarlett froze, seeing Oskar and his injuries for the first time.

"Molls, what the fuck," she began, but the other woman shook her head.

"I don't want you to make him human yet," she said, tears in her voice. "He'll die."

Scarlett looked from Molly to Jesse, completely flabbergasted. Jesse was pretty sure his own expression reflected hers. "We *want* him to die, remember?" Scarlett reminded her. "He killed your friends. He's trying to take down our whole way of life." Oskar was smirking at her. "He's the *bad guy*."

"He's my fiancé," Molly said with a sob.

Chapter 45

I don't think I'd ever really understood the phrase "knocked me over with a feather" until that moment. When Molly said the word *fiancé*, you probably could have walked up to me and blown on my hair a little, and I'd have collapsed.

"How—" I sputtered, at the same time Jesse said, "What?" in an equally bewildered tone.

Then a phrase popped into my mouth, and I spat it back out. "The midnight drain," I blurted. "He's the midnight drain. This happened to you *twice*?"

Molly nodded, her eyes never leaving Oskar. "We were just kids. Seventeen, and engaged. Alonzo let him live, but later . . . later . . ." she choked on the words, swallowed hard.

"When did you find out?" I asked. I don't know why that was my first question, I really don't. But part of me just couldn't handle the thought that Molly might have lied to us this whole time about not knowing who was after her.

"The moment I saw him tonight," she said in a soft voice. She was giving Oskar a complicated look, sadness mixed with longing and grief. "He looks just like the boy I knew. Before Alonzo twisted him."

There was the slightest tinkling as the bullets from Oskar's chest hit the tile floor. He was almost all the way healed. "Well, dipshit?" I said to him. "You tried to murder the woman you were going to marry?"

His lips curled. "This whore murdered my true father. The one who gifted us with immortality. Who gifted this harlot with—"

"Yo, Kylo Ren," Jesse snapped. His gun was still trained on Oskar's chest. "Say one more horrible thing about Molly, I just fucking dare you. You might heal fast, but I know you still feel pain."

"You don't understand," Molly said in a helpless voice. Her face was twisted with anguish. "All this, everything that's happened, it's my fault."

"How the *fuck* is this clown your fault?" I demanded.

"Alonzo promised me he would leave my family alone if I came willingly," she whispered. She turned toward Oskar. "But I didn't know that Alonzo knew about you."

"Because you never asked," Oskar said, with acid in his voice. "I was right there, the whole time, if you had only looked."

"I thought you would marry someone else," she said. "I thought you would forget all about me. It would be better."

"Forget about you?" He laughed. "I suppose I did, for a little while. But then Alonzo began visiting me. He would knock on my door in the dead of night and tell me things. Some of them were about you, *beloved.*" He spat this last word like most men would use the c-word. Like she was filth. "How you were defiant. Rebellious. Alonzo bestowed the gift of vampirism on you, and you were so ungrateful that it hurt him."

Molly just stared at him with her mouth open, and I couldn't blame her. Katia's words rang in my head. *Sometimes he would set his revenge in motion even before he had been betrayed.* Alonzo had noticed Molly's independence and begun grooming her former fiancé, intending to use him against her.

But Oskar wasn't finished. "I begged him to turn me. I would make you fall in line. Make you obey, as you were always meant to obey me. Alonzo made me wait, though, until I was ready." His voice turned worshipful. "And then I was. He *chose* me to be his heir. His son." There was enormous pride in his voice, and if I hadn't thought the guy was nuts before, this would have tipped the decision.

"You weren't chosen," I said, rolling my eyes. "You were leverage. An insurance policy in case Molly got stabby after her apprenticeship. You're just a brainwashed pawn with daddy issues."

"Better a pawn than a whore," he said nastily, and Jesse shot him in the chest.

"No!" Molly yelped. Jesse gave her an innocent, bewildered look, like maybe the gun had gone off by itself. I approved.

Oskar's hand clutched the wound, but his eyes didn't leave Molly. "I was supposed to protect him from you!" he yelled. "We thought—we both thought—you had moved on. Why did you come back? Why did you kill him!"

"Because he killed them," she said flatly. "I went home, decades later, to see what became of my family. Only as it turned out, they had all died the night Alonzo came for me. My parents, my sisters, my brothers. He had killed them even *before* he promised to leave them alone. He used them to control me, and they were already dead."

For one brief instant, something almost human flicked across Oskar's face. "I did not know about his promise," he said sullenly, and in that moment he reminded me of a teenage boy who's realized he was in the wrong. "I apologize for nothing, but . . . I did not know."

She gave him a tiny nod. I could already see him straightening up, looking less pained. We were running out of time.

"What's the plan, Molly?" I asked. "You don't want him to die, fine. I think it's garbage, but whatever. What are we doing with him instead?"

"We take him to Dashiell," she said, but her voice was uncertain.

"Then Dashiell will just be the one to kill him," I pointed out. "And if you let him go, he *might* leave LA, but he's definitely going to take more women. He's going to keep doing this."

Oskar said nothing. He was eyeing Jesse with a wary look, one hand still clapped over the bullet wound. The guy was crazy, but not entirely stupid.

"I don't know," Molly wailed. "Alonzo fucked with his head, and it's my fault! He wouldn't have done any of it if Oskar hadn't known me."

"Maybe not," I said gently. I gestured toward the vampire, who was still covered in Molly's blood. "But he's broken."

"So were you!"

Touché. That stung a little bit, but she wasn't wrong. After Olivia fucked with my head, I'd been broken, too.

But now that I was seeing this whack job, I realized that I had only been manipulated. Oskar had been full-on reconditioned. Or maybe he'd always had a little seed of misogyny and violence, and Alonzo had simply spotted it and helped it grow. Either way, the guy didn't strike me as redeemable.

I glanced at Jesse, but he just shook his head. He didn't know what to do either. We all stood there, waiting, until the new bullet tinkled to the ground. Then I took a step toward Oskar. Jesse shifted his body so he could keep the gun on the now-human vampire, and Molly wrung her hands, giving me a pleading look.

I walked right up to Oskar until we were almost nose to nose. He smirked at me, but there was a little bit of uncertainty behind his expression. *Good luck hiding behind vampire superpowers now, asshole.* "You got a raw deal," I said briefly, "I get that. But how can you not see that selling the bodies of unwilling women is just plain wrong?"

His smirk faded. He looked at me with incomprehension. "Why?"

I blinked. "Why? Why is it wrong to kidnap, rape, and torture young women? Is that a real question?"

"Women are not thinking creatures," he said, his voice perfectly reasonable, like we were arguing about the cognitive power of, say, kittens. "Alonzo made me see that. They do not know what is best for them. I take them in; I give them a place to live, blood to drink. I make them *immortal*," he went on. "What is a little pain, a little time spent pleasuring the greater sex, in exchange for that?"

I felt a terrible anger building in my chest, and at that moment I couldn't have controlled my radius if I tried. It was expanding by the second. I felt a tiny zip at the new edge of it—the familiar sensation of a vampire's press, fizzing out against my radius—and a terrible idea was born in my head. I just needed to keep Count Asshat talking. "And the eight girls who died?" I said. "What about them?"

"Twelve was too many to control," he said, in the same reasonable tone. "Too many bodies to move to this location. The dead girls were collateral damage." He shrugged in a dismissive way, like when you spill your drink and have to pay for a new one. *What are you gonna do?*

Out of the corner of my eye, I saw movement. It was too far back for Molly or Oskar to notice, although Jesse might have. Louder, I said, "If Dashiell's so powerful, why risk coming to Los Angeles? Was it because of the motorcycle club?"

He gave me a look of condescending approval. "Their leader is a moron who can be easily controlled," he said. "And he has connections in prostitution and pornography. He can watch the business for me during the day, and if the police ever become interested in me, he will make a perfect scapegoat." A sardonic smile. "Besides, this city comes with revenge on my whore of an ex."

Molly flinched. I just stared at the guy, genuinely astonished. The guy was still talking in present tense, as though we were all going to just let him walk out the door and pursue his perverted dreams.

But I needed to keep him on topic. "Three of the MC guys died here tonight," I pointed out. "You got them killed."

Oskar just spread his hands with a smile. "There are always more."

Even though I'd been expecting it, the shot was *loud*. It rang through the small, empty space like a banshee wail, and before the echo died down Oskar had fallen. Molly screamed and dropped with him, kneeling beside him as blood drained from the bullet hole in his forehead. Jesse turned and jerked his gun up, pointing it at the aging, bushy-haired biker, who stood there with a gray face, a big-ass pistol, and no apology in his eyes.

Molly was crying, and when she held up Oskar's body I could see that most of the back of his head was missing. "No!" she sobbed. She looked up at me. "Move away, Scarlett!" she cried. "Maybe the vampire magic—"

I shook my head. "He's gone, Molly."

Molly rose and saw the old biker who'd shot Oskar. She flew at him, but I darted forward and grabbed the back of her dress with the arm that didn't have a bullet graze. The dress came apart in my hand, but not before I'd stepped close enough to wrap my arms around her. She fought me to get at the biker, but even wounded, when we were both human I was stronger than she was. I held on. After a moment, the fight left her. She turned herself around and buried her face in my neck, crying in earnest.

"Could someone please explain," the biker said in a low, dangerous voice, "what in all of fuck is going on here?"

I patted Molly's back, giving Jesse a look that said, *All yours, dude.*

Jesse stepped forward. "You were taken for a ride, that's what happened," he said. He pointed to Oskar's body. "This man gave you mind-control drugs that convinced you to go along with some seriously fucked-up plans."

"What plans?" the guy demanded. "Who is he?"

"He's just some asshole," Jesse said, and truer words were never frickin' spoken. "He made you think that he was a guy you trusted twenty-odd years ago. He got you to send your guys to do some pretty nasty things, Lee."

Lee, for that was apparently his name, shook his head stubbornly. "No. I don't take no drugs. That never happened."

"Then can you explain how you got here?" Jesse's voice was gentle. "Or why you sent your guys to be killed, just on this one man's say-so? You were dosed."

Lee looked uncertain. And then in the distance, I heard the first siren. Apparently, even in City of Industry you can make enough noise to alarm someone.

"Say I believe you," Lee said over the noise. "How the fuck are we going to explain all of this to the cops?"

"I've got an idea about that," Jesse said grimly. "But I'd need you to go along with some things."

Chapter 46

Telling lies to cops is a major part of my occupation. I've done it plenty of times, with and without Dashiell helping the lie along via some creative mind-control. But even I had to admit that the story Jesse cooked up for the police was masterful. Like we should write it on a poster, frame it in gold, and hang it on the wall in Dashiell's mansion kind of masterful.

Here's how it went: Molly, a helpless young college student with a rare sunlight allergy, had had a fling with a biker, an asshole named Carl. According to Lee Harrison, Carl, who was not terrible-looking once you got past the greasy beard, had a couple of very real convictions for rape and assault. Eventually this fictional version of Molly wised up and decided to break it off, but old Carl didn't take the news well. In fact, he showed up at her house, killed her roommates, and burned down the building, all while she was away from home. Molly had run to hide with an old friend, Frederic, but Carl and his biker buddies had found her at his place. Frederic had shot Carl in the foot, and his Rottweiler had killed two of Carl's pals. Carl had beaten the shit out of Frederic and taken him and Molly to the Mock-Donald's in City of Industry, where Carl intended to . . . well, do really bad things to her.

Meanwhile, Molly's old friend Scarlett (me) got wind of Molly's kidnapping and called Molly's ex-boyfriend Oskar, as well as my friend Jesse Cruz, the famous ex-detective. I convinced Jesse not to call the police, and the three of us stormed the Mock-Donald's to rescue Molly. We also brought Frederic's Rottweiler, who helped us "subdue" the bikers. Unfortunately, the evil bikers managed to shoot Frederic and Oskar, killing them both. Lee came to the Mock-Donald's to stop Carl, but arrived too late to save him. We saved Molly, and the (imaginary) Rottweiler ran off. There would likely be searches, and the press would probably have a lot to say about responsible dog ownership. I felt a tiny bit guilty about that, but it was worth it to keep Shadow out of all this.

Under regular circumstances, of course, the police would probably have figured out that this story had a few ridiculous holes. But Dashiell sent his "lawyer," an Arabian vampire named Fahima, to help press the police officers who were questioning us. It also didn't hurt that Molly was so obviously abused and distraught—I'd stayed close enough that she still had the black eyes and the cut on her face, not to mention a lot of blood staining her hair and shredded clothes. And it helped that that Jesse had a solid gold reputation within the department. He wasn't well liked, but he was grudgingly respected, and that counted on our side. Finally, we were told we could go home, as long as we stayed in town.

At 6 a.m., Jesse pulled the van into the driveway at my house, and he, Molly, Shadow, and I dragged ourselves toward the front door. Molly was carrying her go-bag, which still held a change of clothes for her. To my surprise, Eli was not only awake and home, but sitting outside on one of the Adirondack chairs we used when we were playing with Shadow.

"Jesse," I said, "can you get Molly set up in Shadow's cell? The cot's gone, but there's a sleeping bag in the hall closet."

"Yeah, of course."

"Shadow, go with him," I instructed. "Jesse can give you a steak from the fridge."

Shadow's ears perked up, and she practically pranced into the house. At least one of us was unaffected by the night's events. I was gonna have to hose blood off her again, though.

I went and sat down in the chair next to Eli's, tilting my head back. I was so tired that I needed a new classification for tiredness.

"You're okay," Eli said quietly. His voice was heavy with relief, and it was only then I realized that this was why he was waiting up. I hadn't even thought to call him until we were almost back to the cottage, and then I'd figured he'd either be at the Trials or sleeping. "Is it over?"

"For the most part. We'll need to do some more cleanup tomorrow night, but . . . yeah. We got the bad guy." I told him about Molly's friends, who were on their way to a safe house in San Francisco. Fahima had made the arrangements for me. As it turned out, she knew how to access all of Dashiell's business-y stuff. She'd offered Molly a few different cities to choose from, but we'd picked San Francisco because that's where Corry was located. She would be able to check on the girls for us, and give them occasional breaks from vampirism if they needed it. She was even about their age.

"We still need to talk about us," Eli said when I was finished.

"Okay . . ." I said, letting it hang. I could have pled tiredness, or claimed that I'd been through enough for one day, but that wouldn't have been fair. Eli had been patient, setting his personal worries aside until the crisis was over. I owed him this conversation. I gestured for him to start. "You go first."

"Last week, at Jack's wedding, we talked about marriage," he began.

My stomach flopped over, a cold, wet feeling that somehow didn't make an audible sound. "Yes."

"I thought we were heading in that direction. I thought our life together was pretty damned good."

"It *is* good," I insisted. "I really love you."

"I know you do. And I love you. The thing is," he said, and his ice-blue eyes were bottomless in that moment, "until this situation with Molly, I thought we were on the same page about the future, and more than that, about . . . what's really important."

My eyes narrowed. "Are you suggesting Molly's life isn't important?"

He waved one hand. "No, not that, it's just . . . I have this bartending job for Will, and it's fine. I like making the sculptures, and that's fine too. But the things that are really important to me are family—you and the pack. Especially the pups."

I stared at him, not getting it. He sighed. "I know, I'm not explaining this very well. Look, there are people who wake up every morning excited to go to work. They might still complain about their jobs, and they'll take vacations like everyone else, but at the end of the day, their work fulfills them. But that's not me. I'm the other kind of person. I work for a paycheck, and while I don't hate my job, if I lost it tomorrow I'd just go find a new one." He reached across the space between our chairs to take my hand. "What fulfills *me* is being with you, and my place in the pack. I used to think you were a paycheck girl, too, but since this thing with Molly started, I realized . . ." He took a deep breath, pushed it out. "You love your job," he said simply.

I pulled back my hand, hugging my arms to my chest. A few days ago, I would probably have denied this statement. But as much as I hated to admit it . . . I'd had fun, these last two days. Oh, I'd been worried and upset and terrified, but also . . . yeah. I hadn't done any of it *for* the fun, but that wasn't the same as not having any.

"Why is that a bad thing?" I asked. "Don't you *want* me to love my job?"

"Not when it puts you in danger. Not when you constantly feel the need to prove yourself, *risk* yourself."

"But we saved Molly," I said, my voice coming out . . . desperate. I felt like I was on a train that was slowly going off the rails, and I didn't know the magic words to stop it. "The bad guy's dead. It's over."

"Yeah, *this* crisis is over. But there will be another one. Maybe next week, maybe in another three years, but there will be another. And what if we're married by then? What if we have a child?"

An old hurt filled my mouth with bitterness. "I can't—"

"I know, nulls can't get pregnant. There are other options, though. We could make it happen." He reached across the space between us and ran his fingers through a tendril of my hair, which had fallen loose from the ballerina bun. "But either way, the next time something falls apart, you're going to be out there risking your life again, and I'll be stuck here, turning into this person I don't want to be. This possessive, angry person who loves you so much that I feel helpless."

This was a moment when I could have launched into my feminist speech about taking care of myself and not needing him to worry about me. But if I had learned one frickin' thing in this relationship, it was that he couldn't control his need to protect me any more than I could control my need for independence.

Eli got out of his chair and crouched down in front of mine. He reached up and brushed the tears from my cheeks. When had I started crying? "Are you asking me to quit my job?" I whispered.

"I'm asking you," he said gently, "if you think you could even be happy without it. Happy being with me. Being a wife, and maybe a mother, with a job that doesn't require risks."

And this was it. This was the moment where I needed to decide who I was going to be. Hero or housewife?

No, that wasn't fair. It was reductive, and besides, that wasn't really the question. The question was, after all the things I'd done and experienced, could I still be happy in a relatively human life?

Assuming I could walk away from the Old World now without Dashiell and the others penalizing me . . . would I?

Five years ago, I would have left with a song in my heart. But since then, I'd come to realize that being who I was, doing the things I did . . . it helped people. And I liked that.

I reached up to touch Eli's cheeks. He smelled like the ocean and aftershave and laundry soap, all the good clean smells that I now associated with *home*. We had been so *happy*.

And the moment I thought those words, I knew it was over.

"No," I said, pushing my voice past the lump in my throat. "I love you. And I love the person that being with you makes *me*. But I love the other part of me, too. The one who does all the things you're afraid of."

He nodded, and in that instant I knew this was exactly what he'd expected. "You're such a good man," I said, my voice cracking. "This would really be a lot easier for me if you were a dickweed."

He smiled faintly. I didn't want to say the words, but one of us had to, and for once I was determined to be brave. "We're breaking up, aren't we?" I said.

He leaned forward to brush a gentle kiss across my lips. "Yeah. We are," he said.

My heart shattered. I had thought I was already crying, but for a moment there, I lost control completely. Sobbing, snotty nose, can't catch your breath, the whole ugly-cry package. Eli pulled me to my feet and put his arms around me, and I clung to him in that horrible, awkward-desperate way you hug someone for the last time. I felt his tears drop into my hair.

I don't know how long that moment went on. I lost all grip on time. In the back of my mind, though, as grief-stricken as I felt . . . I knew it was the right thing for both of us. People who get into relationships aren't supposed to stop growing; they're supposed to grow *together*. Eli and I hadn't done that. Maybe it was because he was older than me, or maybe it was just our natures, but I had grown in one direction, and he in another. A divide had spread between the two of us, and I could no more bridge it than I could rewire my DNA. And at the end of the day, I didn't *want* to change who I was. I kind of liked her.

When I finally did catch my breath, we managed to stand there and work out a couple of details. I would keep the guest cottage, because I needed it for Shadow. Eli would stay with friends tonight, and call me in a day or two about getting the rest of his stuff.

There was more we would need to discuss, of course, because you can't disassemble three years of living together in five minutes. But I don't think either of us could stand to rummage any deeper into such a new wound.

He kissed me one last time, a quick brush across my lips, and then Eli turned and left.

By the time Jesse came outside to check on me, the tears had slowed to a trickle. I didn't look at him, just sat with my shoulders hunched and my hands clenched into balls so they wouldn't tremble. "Scarlett?" Jesse said cautiously. "Are you okay?"

"We broke up," I whispered, still staring ahead into the dim light from the street, where I'd last seen Eli's taillights. "It's over." I buried my face in my hands. "I'm so tired."

Without a word, Jesse leaned over and took my hands, pulling me to my feet. He hugged me, and kept his arm around me as he walked me back inside. There wasn't anything else to say.

Chapter 47

"Ladies and gentlemen," Dashiell said, in that mysterious vampire way where he sounds grandiose without sounding like he's *trying* to be grandiose, "we will begin tonight's proceedings with the trial you have all been talking about for the last two days." A small, indulgent smile, and Dashiell nodded to Lawrence before resuming his seat between Kirsten and Will. That's one thing you had to say for Dashiell: he didn't draw things out, even with a captive audience.

The vampire toady didn't even need to consult his iPad. "Molly of Wales," he announced in a booming voice. A ripple of whispers rolled through the crowd, "stands accused of risking exposure to the humans," Lawrence finished. From behind Kirsten and Will, Molly stepped out of the wings, looking nervous.

We'd planned this blocking carefully. Molly wasn't brought forth in chains, or held at gunpoint. In fact, the city's most powerful people had allowed her come in at their backs. It was a sign of support.

The whispers in the crowd turned into full-on agitation. Dashiell held up a single hand, and the audience went silent. "This trial will proceed as any other," he said in a firm voice. "Please remain silent."

Molly crossed the stage and sat down next to me at the table. I wanted to squeeze her hand, or at least give her a reassuring smile, but we'd talked beforehand about why that was not a great idea. Even though I wasn't voting, I didn't want to appear to be playing favorites.

"Molly," Dashiell continued, "you have been accused of murdering eight of the human women you were living with, and turning four others without consent from myself, thus risking our exposure to the normal world. What do you say to these charges?"

Molly leaned forward, looking very young and very human. And very nervous. "It's true that I was living with human girls," she said, the mic picking up the quaver in her voice. "But I loved them. We were going to university together, and they were my friends."

"Did you kill them?" Dashiell asked.

"Yes," she said, and another roll of surprise rolled through the audience. "But I was forced."

Gasps. Actual shouts of disbelief. Growling from the werewolves. And then things pretty much just got more dramatic from there.

With prompts from Dashiell, Molly walked the audience through the whole story. When she was done, she stayed right where she was as Kirsten testified about the existence of boundary witches, and Jesse, who was wearing a special witch bag that protected him from Kirsten's wards again, came onstage. Staying well away from me, he explained his involvement and actions in a classic cop tone, like he was filing a verbal report. The audience ate up every word at first, but as the drama faded and explanations wore on, they began to gradually get just a little bit bored. This, too, was according to plan. Drown them in information, in *proof*, until the truth was so obvious that no one would bother denying it.

Just when we started losing the audience's attention, we did the big reveal: Katia came onstage in a wheelchair, with Allison "Lex" Luther pushing her. Maven, who was Lex's cardinal vampire the way Dashiell was ours, had signed off on this whole spectacle as long as Lex didn't identify who or what she was to the LA Old World.

Katia confessed to everything, including pressing Molly the moment she woke up that night. She confirmed Oskar's plans, his reasons for wanting to frame Molly. When she got to the part about helping him steal the bodies of the four new vampires, she teared up a little, but pushed through.

During our pre-Trials meeting, Jesse, Kirsten, Will, Dashiell and I had voted on whether we should let her go to Colorado with Lex. Jesse, Kirsten, and I voted in Katia's favor, and although they'd voted against, Will and Dashiell agreed to honor our majority. Now I saw Lex give Katia's shoulder a quick squeeze, worry etched on her face. I kind of thought the two of them were going to be okay.

After Katia left the stage, I could tell that the mood in the room had shifted. The crowd was getting restless. And, wonder of wonders, they were ready to move on. To them, this whole "Molly Goes Dark Side" saga had had a disappointingly anticlimactic ending, and now everyone was over it and looking ahead to the parties.

It was both aggravating and magnificent.

Manuela wasn't in the front row tonight. That afternoon Jesse and I had gone to her condo to personally explain that her stepdaughter was a new vampire. It was a very difficult conversation, which still hurt to think about. But she hadn't come to glare at me tonight, and I was grateful.

When all the testimonies were finished, Dashiell, Will, and Kirsten made a show of whispering amongst themselves for a moment, pretending they hadn't already decided on Molly's sentence. When they straightened up, the crowd's wandering attention returned to Dashiell, who said in his unintentionally grandiose way, "We agree that it was a mistake for you to move in with human women, and you are therefore partly to blame for what happened to them. However," he added, "we absolve you of responsibility for the murders themselves and the resulting risk of national exposure. Because of the terrible physical abuse you suffered, and because you and your . . . helpers"—in the wings behind him, Jesse winked at us—"were able to neutralize the negative publicity and keep our existence concealed, we're willing to sentence you to time served. Next case, please."

Now, I squeezed her hand.

Epilogue

"Where do you want these?" Jesse asked, bending backward a little so he could see over the top box on his stack.

"Uh . . . living room for now," I said, which was how I had answered the last three times, too. Molly's new bedroom—the cell formerly known as Shadow's—was really too small to support even her few belongings, when you factored in a bed. On the plus side, it was completely sunlight proof, and rent was cheap. Also, her last residence had burned to the ground. It really cuts back on possessions.

"Did you switch out the doorknob yet?" I asked him, putting familiar dishes on the shelf above the sink. This was the stuff from Molly's old house in Hollywood. Handling it again was bittersweet.

"Yeeeees," he drawled. "Molly can now lock us out, and we cannot lock her in. Did *you* order the pizza yet?"

"Nooo," I said back, imitating his tone. "I figured the divorced guy coming out of the months-long depression would know the best place for pizza."

Jesse considered that for a second, and then he gave me a regal bow. "Touché."

"Thank you so much for helping with these, Jesse," Molly said warmly, from behind a stack of boxes that was twice as tall as his. Vampire strength is fun. She set them down well out of my radius and straightened up, tossing her new, short blonde curls out of her face. I hadn't asked about the hair. I figured she'd explain it if she wanted to. "I didn't realize there was so much stuff still in storage."

"Well, we can use the furniture," I said, pausing in my unpacking. Eli had taken the pieces that belonged to him: the kitchen table and chairs, the work desk, a loveseat. Even the soft blankets we had used when we watched movies together.

"You gonna cry again?" Jesse asked, but his voice was gentle. "I can get some tissues if you're gonna cry again."

I looked at the plate in my hand. "Don't throw it at him," Molly advised. "I really like that set."

I put the plate down carefully, picked up an oven mitt, and chucked it at Jesse's head. He ducked it easily. "Go outside and throw the ball for Shadow, please," I instructed. "And let me know if Lex calls you back."

"Yes, Mom."

Jesse had been checking in with the Colorado boundary witch every few days, since she and Katia returned from freeing Oskar's current stable of prostitutes in Reno. Dashiell had been having a lot of conversations with Lex's boss, Maven, both about the liberated vampires and about Katia's rehabilitation and future. I got the occasional "official" update, but Jesse and I liked to keep on top of how Katia was actually *doing*, and talking to Lex was the best route.

Jesse had also been checking cell phone records for Frederic and the others, but we would probably never know who had lined up to help Oskar take down our Old World structure. Both Dashiell and Will had their suspects, and they would take care of them in their own ways. I probably should have been bothered by it, but honestly, I wasn't too concerned. Or rather, I recognized that the problem wasn't mine to fix. Dashiell and Will would need to get their houses in order, and they would let me know if there was any way I could help. That was enough.

After the front door slammed behind Jesse, Molly reached over to touch my shoulder. "Have you heard from him at all?" she asked.

I shook my head. "Will said that after the full moon last week, he's taking a couple weeks off work. Going camping, or something. We're both trying to give each other . . . space."

"And Jesse?" Molly said. "Are you guys . . ." She trailed off. I stared at her, not getting it. "Banging?" she added brightly.

I rolled my eyes. "I can't tell you how much we are not," I told her. "He's raw from his divorce; I just broke up with Eli. You're gonna have to ship someone else, Molls." She pouted. "On the bright side," I added, "we've kind of found a nice friend rhythm. It's working for us."

And it was. Jesse and I had never really done the friendship thing properly. By the time we'd learned to trust each other, back at the beginning of our relationship, he'd had a crush on me. And, okay, I was harboring a little something for him too. And then it just got more complicated from there. But now, years later, we'd finally figured out how to hang out together. It was nice, having someone in my life I knew I could count on, no romantic strings attached.

Molly came up behind me, wrapping an arm around my shoulders in a hug. "That's good."

Well. Someone else.

After the Trials were over, I had invited her over to ask if she wanted to move in with me and Shadow in the little cottage. I could put a crate in my bedroom for Shadow—I'd need to have it specially built, but it was possible—and the second "bedroom" could be Molly's. It was tiny, but she didn't need to put much in there.

I didn't want to rekindle our friendship on a lie, though, so before asking, I had sat her down and told her the truth: I'd known that Lee Harrison was coming into the room, and I'd egged on Oskar to admit how little he cared about the MC so Lee would kill him.

She'd gone silent, staring at me so long that one of my hands automatically twitched toward the knife in my boot. Was she going to come after me? God, I hoped not.

Finally, Molly said in a low, resigned voice, "It's okay, Scarlett. You didn't kill him; you just gave him rope to hang himself. I can't blame you for that."

"Really?" I said, hope lifting my chest.

She nodded. "Now that I have some distance from the situation, I can see what he'd become." She closed her eyes, and I knew memories were flitting around in her head. Old, bittersweet memories. "He wasn't always like that, you know," she said softly. "Back then it was common to view women as possessions, and Oskar wasn't any worse than any other young man his age. He was always arrogant, but he was also kind, once." Her head dropped into her hands, and although I generally suck at feelings, I understood she wanted to talk for a moment about Oskar when he was still good.

"How did you meet?" I asked, the first question that popped in my head.

Her face lifted, and she brushed away tears. She gave me a shaky smile. "I lived out on a farm, but my father and I would go into town each spring to sell our calves. I bumped into Oskar there. He was a shopkeeper's son, but he was very taken with me."

"Did you love him?" I regretted the question the instant it was out, but she didn't seem offended. She just considered it for a long moment.

"I thought I did," she began slowly. "Now I suspect that I was just very young. I ignored his flaws, because he paid attention to me and he was courteous, and I wanted to get off the farm." She shrugged, smiling again. "Oh, I was so happy when he began inviting me into town, escorting me to dances, to the theater. I felt like a princess." The smile dropped off her face. "That was most likely how Alonzo first saw me. Anyway." She straightened up, smoothed down her black pleated skirt.

"I'm so sorry, Molls."

She shook her head. "I still can't believe how much Alonzo twisted him," she whispered. "Maybe if I'd . . ." She gestured helplessly. "I don't know. Said something differently."

"He wasn't going to change. He didn't even want to."

In that moment, I knew she was thinking of those girls: the ones she'd killed, the other ones she'd almost sentenced to a terrible fate. I'd hugged her, and then asked her to move in.

Now, I finished the box of dishes and opened up one that said Blu-rays, rolling my eyes at all the Julia Roberts. Before I could lift out any movies, however, Jesse came back inside, holding up his phone. "That was her," he said, eyes bright with excitement. And maybe a bit of anxiety.

"Lex?"

He shook his head. "Kirsten. It's time."

Oh. Right. I just nodded, butterflies spontaneously moving into my stomach. "You sure you don't want me to come?" Molly said, worry in her voice.

"No. The more people there, the more hyped up everyone's gonna be," I assured her. "Besides, Dashiell flew in Stephanie Noring, that doctor from Minnesota. We got this. Everything's going to be okay for Team Null and Void."

Jesse gave me a good-natured smack on the arm. The good arm, not the one with the bandage.

Kirsten hadn't wanted me to try changing Hayne back to human right away. She had insisted that he take a couple of weeks to actually try being a vampire, which came with its own undeniable perks: no more aging, no more pain from old injuries, no more fear that he would be easily overpowered by one of Dashiell's enemies.

Hayne had taken the two weeks, complaining for every minute of it, and at the end of them, he'd got down on one knee and re-proposed to Kirsten, begging her to let him come back to both her and humanity. Kirsten had laughed and cried a little and called me to set up a time.

I'd gotten the whole story from Abby—she'd given me official permission to call her that—who seemed to have developed a reluctant . . . well, *respect* is too strong of a word for how she felt about me. Let's say

I was growing on her. The handful of conversations we'd had since the night Hayne died had been a magnitude friendlier than all the conversations we'd had before it.

Damn if I wasn't actually acquiring something close to friends.

I went through the open front door. "Shadow!" I yelled. "Time to go!"

The bargest woofed and trotted over from the far edge of the property, where she'd probably found a rabbit to chase. She beat Jesse and me to the van, wagging her tail impatiently until I opened the back for her to jump in. I climbed into the driver's seat.

"You ready for this?" Jesse asked, buckling his seat belt. "Seriously. The last two times . . . didn't go so well."

I gave him an exaggerated wink, faking a confidence I didn't necessarily feel. The truth was, I was terrified. There was a lot riding on tonight. If I could "cure" Hayne, and the consequences weren't too terrible, I was planning to offer the same to the four women Molly and I had rescued. If I could cure them too, I could undo at least a little of the pain Oskar had caused. Louisa and the others could be returned to their families. "That was Old Scarlett," I informed him. "Things are different now."

Jesse turned the radio to his favorite preset and leaned back in the passenger seat. "Can't argue with that."

Acknowledgments

Writing books always seems like such a solitary profession: from the outside, it's just me spending hours hunched over a laptop in a variety of locations. I wrote *Midnight Curse* on a huge variety of couches and kitchen chairs, not to mention while I laid in a hammock on my Hawaiian vacation, from the front seat of my minivan while I waited to pick up my kids, on several airplanes, and of course, sitting on the futon in my office while a hyper chinchilla ran across the keyboard. Always alone.

And yet, for such a reclusive activity, it's surprising how many people were involved in making *Midnight Curse* a book that I'm proud to put my name on. I need to say a special thank-you to the readers who loved Scarlett Bernard and asked me for more, via email and Facebook and Twitter and occasionally even to my face. I might have written this book anyway, because I missed Scarlett so much, but it would never have been published without you guys out there showing me your support and creating demand for another Scarlett novel. I thought of all of you so often when I wrote this book, and I'm so excited that you finally have it in your hands.

Of course, I have a lot more thank-you's to go around. I'd like to thank the book's beta team: my LA expert Tracy Tong, medical expert Jayme Hayne, and Elizabeth Kraft (hi, sister!), whose job is part brainstorming help and part promising me that it's not garbage, usually while

I'm pacing around my house mainlining sugar. I also want to thank fellow author Donna Augustine, who was gracious enough to go through the book as a first-time Old World reader, making sure that *Midnight Curse* would make sense to people who weren't along for the first part of Scarlett's journey.

Of course, I have to thank my publishing team: the dev editor of my dreams, Angela Polidoro, and my acquisitions editor Adrienne Lombardo, who wasn't with me at the beginning of Scarlett's journey, but believed in me and my books enough to let me do a fourth installment. My deep thanks as well to the team that painstakingly goes through this book for errors and typos. Every one of you helps this book be greater than what I started with, and for that I am so grateful.

Along with the people who helped me with *Midnight Curse*, I also owe infinite thanks to all the usual suspects: my understanding husband, who sometimes respects my job even more than I do, and my amazing babysitter, Saint Amanda, who gives me the peace of mind of knowing my kids are safe, happy, and probably having a better time than they would with me. My parents, my extended family (many of whom text me two-sentence reviews of every new book, and, surprise, they're always glowing), my fellow authors who are always willing to listen or grab a drink at conventions. You guys don't just help me with my job, you make my job *fun*. Without all of you, being a writer really would be solitary, and I'm so grateful you all are in my life.

—September 2016

About the Author

Melissa F. Olson was raised in Chippewa Falls, Wisconsin, and studied film and literature at the University of Southern California in Los Angeles. After a brief stint in the Hollywood studio system, Melissa moved to Madison, Wisconsin, where she eventually acquired a master's degree from the University of Wisconsin-Milwaukee, a husband, a mortgage, two kids, and two comically oversize dogs—not at all in that order. Learn more about Melissa, her work, and her dogs at www.MelissaFOlson.com.